Praise for D. B. Reynolds's Vampires In America...

"Captivating and brimming with brilliance, CHRISTIAN is yet another defining addition to the ever-evolving world of Vampires in America created by D. B. Reynolds."

—*KT Book Reviews*

"Did I mention that the sizzling sex factor in this book is reaching the combustible stage? It is a wonder my Kindle didn't burn up."

—*La Deetda Reads on DECEPTION*

"D. B. Reynolds has outdone herself with this exhilarating story; and VINCENT is a worthy addition to Reynolds's always excellent Vampires in America series."

—*Fresh Fiction*

"Terrific writing, strong characters and world building, excellent storylines all help make Vampires in America a must read. ADEN is one of the best so far." A TOP BOOK OF THE YEAR!

—*On Top Down Under Book Reviews*

"In one of the most compelling vampire books I've read in a while, Reynolds blends an excellent mix of paranormal elements, suspense and combustible attraction."

—*RT Book Reviews on LUCAS*

"Remarkably fresh and stunningly beautiful! SOPHIA is as enchanting as she is dangerous!"

—*FreshFiction.com*

"Move over Raphael, there's a new Lord in town."

—*Bitten by Paranormal Romance on JABRIL*

Also by D. B. Reynolds

Vampires In America

Raphael

Jabril

Rajmund

Sophia

Duncan

Lucas

Aden

Vincent

Vampires in America: The Vampire Wars

Deception

Christian

Lucifer

The Cyn and Raphael Novellas

Betrayed

Hunted

Unforgiven

Compelled

The Stone Warriors

The Stone Warriors: Damian

Lucifer

by

D. B. Reynolds

ImaJinn Books

IMAJINN

ImaJinn Books
PO BOX 300921
Memphis, TN 38130
Print ISBN: 978-1-61194-715-1

ImaJinn Books is an Imprint of BelleBooks, Inc.

ImaJinn Books was founded by Linda Kichline.

We at ImaJinn Books enjoy hearing from readers. Visit our websites
ImaJinnBooks.com
BelleBooks.com
BellBridgeBooks.com

10 9 8 7 6 5 4 3 2 1

Cover design: Debra Dixon
Interior design: Hank Smith
Photo/Art credits:
Tunnels © Aniuszka | Dreamstime
Man © As Inc | Shutterstock

:Llok:01:

Acknowledgements

As always, I want to thank Brenda Chin for her encouragement and support, along with her terrific editing skills. Thanks also to Debra Dixon and everyone at BelleBooks for taking such good care of my Vampires, and my Warriors, too.

Thank you to Michelle Muto and Steve McHugh, my longtime critique partners, and to Karen Roma, for being such a thoughtful beta reader.

Special thanks to Joss Whedon for creating Buffy to keep me company while I write. I'm *sure* that's why he wrote it. And to all of the wonderful writers out there who create such beautiful escapes in their stories.

And finally, love and endless gratitude to my big and extended family for all of their love, humor, and support. And love always and forever to my darling husband.

Prologue

Present Day, Montreal, Quebec, Canada

COLIN MURPHY SAGGED against his bonds, the ropes biting into his bare arms, and burning fresh wounds on top of old where they'd cut into his wrists and ankles. And that was the good part. He grimaced at his own twisted sense of humor, but it was the only thing keeping him sane. If he thought about all of the other damage they'd done, all of the other things they'd done . . . .

He shut off his thoughts and reached for the mate bond he shared with Sophia, that shining, indestructible thread that bound them together. It was there, but it had become thin and fragile, and so very distant. It was as if a million minds hung between them, and every one of them was clamoring for attention, blocking his way to her.

It was the blood. His stomach roiled at the memory of how they'd poured the blood down his throat, how they'd forced his body to heal the wounds of their torture night after night. Maybe they'd done it in order to give themselves a fresh canvas for each new, more gruesome session. After all, a kidney could only rupture once; bones could only break into so many pieces . . . unless the body was healed over and over again.

But that was only part of their motivation. In filling him with the blood of another master vampire, in letting that blood heal him time after time, they'd blurred his connection to Sophia, weakening it night by night, until he could barely feel her in the back of his mind.

The door opened. He smelled wet earth and a whiff of rot that spoke to a location well underground. He struggled to open eyes that were nearly swollen shut, the right one so filled with blood that he saw everything through a haze of red. It didn't stop him from recognizing the vampire who stood in front of him.

"Look at you," the traitor taunted, fangs bared in a pleased grin. "And still you won't betray her. Jesus, Colin, if you like vampire pussy that much, I can find you someone who's a hell of a lot easier to live with. I mean, Sophia's a fine piece of ass, but, man, she's got to be totally butch in the sack. Always on top, right?" The traitor snickered at his own pathetic humor.

Colin was barely listening. Hell, he could barely hear. They'd slammed his ears one too many times tonight; the nerves were still numb. He was pretty sure his hearing would return eventually, even without their bloody damn healings. This wasn't his first rodeo, after all. One didn't spend fifteen years as a Navy SEAL without taking some damage.

Of course, he would only heal if they planned on letting him live when this was all over. Which he doubted. The torture had been purely for their entertainment, continuing long after they'd pretended to interrogate him. They didn't really need his Intel. The traitor could provide most of the information they needed, while Colin served his purpose simply by sitting in this room, captive. Or so they thought.

They were fools if they thought his Sophia could be so easily diverted from her responsibilities, from her true purpose. She was his lover and his mate, the love of his life. She'd search for him and never give up, despite their weakened link and his deep underground location. But she was first and foremost a vampire lord—Lord of the Canadian Territories, one of the most powerful vampires in North America and the world. She'd understand better than most that his kidnapping was a ploy to distract her from the defense of her territory, and she wouldn't fall for it.

Sophia would hold her people together, and she'd defeat those who thought to take her territory by force. Then, she'd crush the traitorous bastard standing in front of him into dust. Colin only hoped he'd live long enough to see it. Or, hell, just long enough to see *her* one more time. Even if it was only to kiss her good-bye.

Chapter One

Toronto, Ontario, Canada

SOPHIA STOOD IN the elevator, the cold of the brushed steel wall behind her seeping into the muscles of her back. She should probably move, but found herself strangely unmotivated.

She needed to focus, to put her game face on. Or one of those other sports analogies that men were so fond of, the ones they used to hype themselves up for a challenge. There would be no challenges tonight from any side, but she still needed to play her part. She was a vampire lord. She couldn't afford to appear weak or indecisive, especially not in the midst of what Colin would call a vampire sausage fest. All male and all powerful didn't begin to describe the alpha vampires waiting for her in the downstairs conference room, including the most alpha of them all . . . Raphael.

She sighed inwardly as the elevator slowed to a stop. Her bodyguard, Eleanor, stepped in front of her as the doors slid open to reveal a pair of her own vampires waiting in the corridor just outside. She'd brought the guards with her from Vancouver, because she'd wanted to be certain of their loyalty. Or, at least, more certain than she was of any of the Toronto vampires. They officially owed her the same allegiance as those in Vancouver, but one could excuse her for doubting their loyalty just now.

Eleanor eyed both of the waiting guards carefully before stepping out of the elevator and moving immediately to one side, making room for Sophia to exit into the hallway. Eleanor was the only female vampire on her security detail. She was an incredibly strong one, in terms of pure physicality. That was her gift, rather than vampiric power. She was also fearless, intelligent, and completely loyal. Plus, it was nice to have another female around. No matter what anyone said, women and men simply didn't think the same way. Sometimes, when Sophia was enduring yet another endless meeting, it was everything she could do not to look at Eleanor and roll her eyes, knowing the other female would understand the sentiment perfectly.

Eleanor hadn't been selected as Sophia's bodyguard because of her sex, however. She'd won her position by triumphing over every other candidate in a series of brutal trials organized by Colin specifically for the purpose of filling out Sophia's security detail. He'd been pleased when Eleanor had come out ahead of all the others, seeming to understand, even before Sophia herself, that a female presence would be useful. That was Colin. He was far more perceptive about people than she was.

That thought nearly made her smile, until the most recent images she'd had of him shoved their way to the front of her brain, wiping out everything else, triggering a pang of fear that squeezed her heart.

Before the events of this last month, she'd have sworn that every member of their carefully chosen security detail was loyal. Now, she didn't trust anyone except Eleanor.

And that was why this meeting was necessary.

Eleanor leaned close as they walked down the hallway. "They're all waiting in the conference room, my lady."

Sophia nodded wordlessly. The stakes tonight were too high, the personalities too touchy, and the vampires too damn powerful to contemplate eye rolling or anything else. She steeled herself for what she had to do and stepped into the conference room, pausing in the doorway to study her fellow vampire lords.

Standing on the other side of the room was Rajmund, Lord of the Northeast. He turned from a subdued conversation with his lieutenant as soon as he caught sight of Sophia. She didn't know Raj—as he liked to be called—that well. They'd met, of course, at previous Council meetings. But this wasn't a Council meeting. It was a discreet gathering of certain lords to address a very specific part of a much larger problem. That problem being the damn Europeans who'd somehow decided North America needed a few more vampire lords. They clearly felt it was their duty to fuck up this continent just as badly as they had their own.

Raj was typically less formal than the rest of them, but tonight he greeted her with only a subdued, "Sophia." Because even he understood that this was a particularly solemn get-together.

Next to Raj was Aden. He'd already been seated when she walked in, but he stood to greet her. Like Raj, he was a very big man, both broad and tall. He was also strikingly handsome, with black hair, and the darkest blue eyes she'd ever seen surrounded by thick black lashes.

"Lady Sophia," he said, his voice and formal expression giving away nothing of how he felt about tonight's meeting.

With the formalities observed, Raj and Aden almost immediately leaned into a private conversation, and Sophia stifled a sigh. She didn't want to talk to them anyway. She hadn't called Aden or Raj for help with the current situation—she'd called Raphael. He was the one she knew best, the one who'd been there when her Sire, Lucien, had essentially committed suicide and bequeathed her the territory that he'd ruled for hundreds of years before her. Raphael could easily have killed her in that moment, and seized the territory for himself. Instead, he'd offered her a truce. He was very possibly the most powerful vampire in the world, and the unacknowledged head of the North American alliance. As such, he'd chosen to involve Aden and Raj in tonight's endeavor. And while their presence here indicated their willingness to support her and the alliance, Sophia wanted something more. She wanted Raphael's guarantee.

He didn't come politely to his feet to greet her when she entered the room. He sat calmly at the head of the table as if he belonged there, even though this was *her* territory and, hence, *her* meeting.

Like the others, Raphael had his lieutenant with him. Jared was a darkly handsome vampire of African descent, who was studying her carefully, as if waiting for her to crack into pieces. Sophia would have liked the luxury of falling apart. But it would have been far too easy, and served no purpose. So it wasn't going to happen.

Raphael's mate, Cynthia, was also with him, sitting close enough that they were constantly touching. Her presence was far from typical at a meeting like this, but Sophia wasn't surprised by it. For one thing, she knew that her request for Raphael's presence tonight had caught him literally midair, as he and Cynthia—or Cyn, as they called her—were on their way back to California from somewhere in the Midwest. More importantly, Cyn was one of the most dangerous humans that Sophia had ever met, and Colin had always liked and respected her. Sophia also knew that Cyn returned the sentiment. Cyn had been trying almost non-stop to reach Colin over the last couple of weeks, and Sophia knew that the human woman's concern, and her *persistence*, were a large part of why Raphael had acted as quickly as he did.

Because Colin's disappearance was the reason for this meeting. It was why Rajmund was so uncharacteristically serious, and Aden so thoughtfully polite. Someone had kidnapped her Colin—her mate, the love of her life. While the four vampire lords in this room exchanged polite greetings and whispered confidences, Colin was being torn apart—bones shattered, organs destroyed, screaming in agony.

She didn't have to speculate about these things happening. She *knew* it. Because his captors were providing a running pictorial of his torture, transmitting nightly proof of his treatment at their hands, in the form of photos that not only documented his torture, but left no doubt in her mind that he was being fed some other vampire's healing blood at the end of every session. On the one hand, she was glad that Colin had even that small respite from his torment. On the other . . . it explained why she couldn't locate him, why their mate bond was being strained to the point of breaking, but never beyond that point. The vampires who'd seized Colin had the power to weaken her connection to him—imprisoning him deep underground, using the power of the earth itself to obscure the mate bond, weakening it with their blood. But as long as she lived, as long as they *both* lived, the bond would *never* break. She wouldn't let it.

"Sophia," Raphael said, his deep voice full of unexpected compassion.

Tears stung the back of her eyes, but she didn't let them fall. Colin didn't need a weepy woman, he needed the powerful vampire lord who was his mate.

"Thank you for coming," she told Raphael.

"Of course," he murmured. "Have you heard anything more?"

She shook her head sharply. "Still no ransom demand. Only the . . . photographs, and then tonight, a short video."

Raphael exchanged a quick glance with Cyn. His jaw clenched, and when he looked back at Sophia, there was no trace of compassion, only the cold gaze of a supremely powerful vampire. That suited Sophia just fine. She didn't need his compassion. She needed his insight and his cruelty.

"I know you agree on the need for a coordinated effort," he said. "And I'm sure you'd rather head up the search for your mate, but—"

"You're wrong," she interrupted, even though she wanted to agree with him. With every beat of her heart, her need for Colin grew. She wanted nothing more than to hunt down his captors and paint the walls with their blood, and then to hold him close so that this could never happen again.

She wasn't going to do any of those things. Well, maybe she'd paint a few walls, but only *after* she'd defeated and killed the vampire who was truly responsible for all of this. Not Colin's kidnappers—though they would pay for what they'd done. But it was a European vampire lord who thought he could waltz in and seize her territory. The asshole who thought that because she was a woman, she'd be an easy mark, that he could kidnap her mate, and reduce her to a weeping mess of uselessness.

It infuriated her that her own allies thought the same thing, that Raphael assumed he'd have to *persuade* her to defend her own territory. Sophia glanced over and found Cyn eyeing her curiously, judging her, waiting to see what she'd do. Sophia raised a single brow, and Cyn's eyebrows arched in return, her lips pursed in a mocking smile.

Raphael might not understand, but his mate certainly did. She knew what it was like to be judged on her beauty and femininity, rather than her courage and her brain. Not to mention her willingness to kill to defend what mattered to her, what she believed in. Sophia had heard the stories. She knew what Cyn had done to secure Raphael's release in Hawaii, and what she'd done even before that in Texas.

Cyn might be the only person in this room who understood that, while Sophia *wanted* more than anything to drop everything else and devote herself to finding Colin, she knew that others could pursue the search just as well. While only *she* could protect her people by hunting down and killing the vampire behind this plot.

"Don't misunderstand me," Sophia continued, her gaze raking the room to include all three vampire lords. "I want my mate returned safe and sound, but he is somewhere in the city of Montreal, and if I'm to keep all of my people secure and defend what's mine, I must return to Vancouver. I've asked you here not to defend my territory for me, but to find Colin."

"You say he's in Montreal," Aden said, and Sophia would swear that there was a newfound respect in his gaze. "The mate bond won't narrow it any closer than that?"

Sophia's jaw clenched. It pained her to admit that her enemies had succeeded in weakening her connection to Colin. It shouldn't have been possible, and maybe it wouldn't have been if they'd been bonded longer. If she hadn't wasted—she cut off that train of thought immediately. Now was not the time to rehash ancient history.

"Every night after they—" She had to swallow the bile that rose up at the thought of what they were doing to Colin and why. "—torture him, they're feeding him some other master's blood, so that he will heal, and so they—" She drew a fortifying breath. "—so they can torment him again, night after night."

"Bastards," Cynthia muttered.

Sophia forced herself to continue. She wouldn't let them see the agony grinding at her soul at the thought of Colin and what he was enduring. "I'm certain they're holding him far underground, a sub-basement perhaps. I can sense the weight of the earth surrounding him."

"The underground city?" Rajmund asked, but Sophia shook her head.

"Too civilized. His prison is crude, its walls roughly made. It's damp and cold, with the earth pressing close."

"Do you have people in Montreal?" Aden asked.

She frowned. "Lucien's former lieutenant, Darren Yamanaka, who is Master to Montreal, along with Toronto and Quebec, is my main representative there. Unfortunately, we know for a fact that someone betrayed Colin to his captors, and I don't know who it was yet. That means I don't know whom to trust among my own people. I need someone from outside the territory, someone strong enough to demand respect from my vampires. Someone who I can be assured is actually looking for Colin, not helping his captors torture him."

The truth of this frustrated Sophia. Canada was a large territory, with its people spread out across the continent, but mostly congregated in several larger cities. This meant her vampires were similarly dispersed. Unfortunately, the distance between her headquarters in Vancouver on the west coast, and the other major cities eastward, made it impossible for her alone to keep close tabs on all of her vampires. She had to trust her subordinates to handle some of it for her, and to depend on their loyalty to her personally.

Personal loyalty was the due of every vampire lord, and she'd had no reason to doubt her people before this. Before Colin had disappeared in an instant. He hadn't even had time to blast her a warning, to give her some clue as to the traitor's identity. He was simply gone. It was almost as if his captors had known her routine, had known that on that particular night and at that particular time, she'd be immersed in contract negotiations for the new compound in the city of Vancouver.

It was yet one more sign that she'd been betrayed, that Colin had been deceived by someone he'd trusted enough to allow close to him. It made her reluctant to rely on any of her own people in the search for her missing mate.

Aden's lieutenant, Bastien, leaned over and whispered something in his master's ear. Aden listened thoughtfully, and then nodded. "I have someone," he told her. "With your permission, of course. There is a younger vampire among my guards—young but *powerful*," he clarified, when Sophia would have protested. "He's particularly skilled in matters which require, shall we say, a delicate touch. He's charming as hell and weirdly brilliant. There's no formal education, of course; he's a bastard from Sicily. But he remembers everything, and he sees patterns where no one else does. It all makes him a damn good investigator. He also happens to speak French, or a version of it anyway. Which will come in handy."

Sophia frowned. "A version of it?"

"Cajun French," Aden clarified. "It's not Quebecois, of course. And they might pretend not to understand him, but he'll understand *them*, which will be far more important."

Sophia almost smiled at that. Almost. "How many will come with him?"

Aden shook his head. "He'll bring his own guards, but he works alone."

"Alone. Is that wise in this situation?"

"He's more than powerful enough to defend himself, if necessary. I wouldn't worry on that account."

"And it's better that way," Raphael said, drawing her attention. "It's safe to assume that *most* of your people remain loyal. If we send in an entire team of searchers, especially vampires from another territory, we risk alienating your own loyalists. While a single, expert investigator can be far more discreet."

Sophia turned back to Aden. "And you're sure your vampire won't mind working alone?"

Half of Aden's mouth lifted in a cynical smile. "He'll prefer it that way. Lucifer's a bit of a loner."

"Lucifer," Sophia repeated the unusual name. "That's a potent name for even a vampire to choose. Does he live up to it?"

"It's the name his mother gave him," Aden said. "And, yes, he does."

Chapter Two

LUCIFER PACED BACK and forth, oblivious to the spectacular night-time view visible only a few feet away through the wall of windows. He was alone in the elegant suite, his thoughts two floors below where negotiations among four powerful vampires were about to determine his future. He shook his head at the thought. Too dramatic. His future was bright either way. He'd drawn the personal attention of Lord Aden decades ago, back when Aden had still been the master of Kansas City, and Lucifer had been a gambler, working the riverboats up and down the Missouri and Mississippi rivers.

Lucifer had been without a master for several years before he met Aden, ever since he'd killed his own Sire. The bastard had been a weak master vampire, barely strong enough to turn new vamps to serve him. That weakness had made him insecure and cruel, especially to the female vampires among his children. Lucifer had been forced to wait until he was strong enough, to witness the long list of his Sire's abuses and do nothing…until the moment when he could take it no longer, the moment he'd finally realized he was more powerful than his Sire and didn't have to accept his casual cruelty anymore. Hell-bent on ending the asshole's life, he hadn't given much thought to what would happen next. Until it was over, and suddenly everyone was looking to him as their new master. He'd disabused them of that ridiculous idea right away. He'd finally been free. The last thing he wanted was a nest-load of needy vampires to take care of.

To make his point, he'd moved far away from his dead Sire's home of Houston, traveling to New Orleans where he'd discovered the riverboats and put his natural talents to work. And the rest was history. He had the kind of memory that would get him kicked out of most modern-day casinos, but no one had worried about it back then. Aden had noticed, though, and he'd used Lucifer's skills many times, before he'd finally taken over the Midwest and brought Lucifer into his Chicago household permanently. So, no matter what was decided in that conference room downstairs, Lucifer's future was secure. He was sworn to Aden, and held him in the highest regard.

On the other hand, this situation with Sophia *did* represent a unique opportunity, if only for the challenge. But it would also enhance his reputation and the reach of his power. As vampires counted such things, he was on the young side, but he also had power enough to be a vampire lord and rule his own territory someday. And one never knew where an opening might come up.

This investigation was a chance to impress not only Lord Aden, but the others, too—Rajmund, whose territory neighbored Aden's; Sophia, of course, since it was her territory he'd be working in; and most significantly of all . . . Raphael. It couldn't hurt to leave a favorable impression on the most powerful fucking vampire on the whole damn planet, could it?

Of course, making all of those favorable impressions depended on him performing well, which he would. Confidence had never been his problem. Actually, in this instance, he didn't have a problem. All he needed was the go-ahead from the powers-that-be, and he'd be ready to get started . . . tonight. He'd already studied everything they had on Colin Murphy's kidnapping, including the witness statements, although those were mostly useless since no one admitted to having seen the actual abduction. The only real witnesses were the vampires who'd been part of the plot against Sophia, and, predictably, they were nowhere to be found.

He'd also seen the photos, and, most recently, a video of Colin Murphy, which had been sent to Sophia for the sole purpose of tormenting her. Lucifer wasn't sure he was supposed to have seen those. Actually, he *knew* he wasn't, since he'd acquired them by less than legitimate means. But they were fucking brutal. Those images had to be tearing Sophia apart. Lucifer knew what he'd be feeling if it were someone he loved being tortured like that. His thoughts stuttered to a halt. There was only one woman he'd ever loved that much, and she'd left him long ago.

He very deliberately turned his thoughts back to the matter at hand. This was obviously an inside job, whose major purpose was to distract Sophia. It was the opening bid in the latest attack by the European vampires, who wanted North America for themselves. They looked at enormous expanse of this continent, saw that there were only eight lords to rule it, and decided it should be their new playground. Predictably, the North American lords, including Sophia, were not welcoming them with open arms.

Lucifer realized he'd stopped pacing and had lifted his gaze to stare out the window. The night was clear, the nearly full moon riding high, limning the tall buildings with its liquid silver light. Here and there, he caught movement in nearby windows—humans working late. *Really* late.

He spun around to eye the elaborate clock above the empty fireplace. Nearly one in the morning. They'd been going at it downstairs since eleven o'clock. What the hell was there to talk about? What alternative did they have? He was the best chance Colin Murphy had. Aden already thought so, but he'd have to make Sophia and the others see it.

The door opened behind him, and he looked over just as Aden's lieutenant, Bastien, entered the suite.

"Well?" Lucifer demanded. He and Bastien had been working closely together for a while now, and, as improbable as it seemed, they'd bonded. Maybe it was their shared European backgrounds, or their mutual interest in military history. But, oddly enough, Lucifer considered the French vampire to be his closest friend.

Bastien grinned. "You've got a new job, kid."

Lucifer shook his head at the "kid." It was Bastien's way of emphasizing their age difference. As if Lucifer's seventy-six years of combined human and vampire life made him a babe in the woods. Granted Bastien had a good fifty years on him, but, come on, seventy-six years was a hell of a long time.

"When do I start?" he asked. "And where's Aden?"

"The four lords are meeting privately. They kicked everyone else out. Shouldn't be long, though. The details were worked out before I left the room."

"Details?" Lucifer repeated, suddenly suspicious. "What kind of details?"

Bastien gave a carefully casual shrug, and Lucifer knew he wasn't going to like whatever Aden's lieutenant said next.

"Sophia didn't like the idea of a foreign vampire—meaning you, since you're Aden's—roaming around her territory unsupervised."

"I thought that's what she wanted. That was the whole reason she called this meeting, wasn't it? To get outside help in hunting down her mate?"

"It was. And you called that one, kid. You're the only one of us who thought she'd hustle back to Vancouver to defend her territory instead of leading the search for Murphy."

Lucifer shrugged one shoulder. "You all judged her as a woman, not a vampire lord. She didn't get where she is by being hormonal."

Bastien laughed. "From the mouths of babes. Hell, I think even

Raphael was surprised, but his mate sure wasn't. There was some serious womanly communication going on in that room."

"Womanly communication?"

"It's all done with the eyes," Bastien intoned.

"Yeah?" Lucifer pulled the lid down on his own eye with his middle finger. "Look into my eye, old man, and tell me what you see."

Bastien snorted a laugh. "Such impatience. You're showing your youth."

"Thank God one of us is. Details. Talk."

"Sophia wants you to work with one of her own people. She thinks it'll grant the imprimatur of her authority to your investigation, and people will be more willing to talk to you. It will also make it clear that she's in charge."

Lucifer grimaced. He didn't need a babysitter slowing him down. And he sure as hell didn't need help in getting people to talk to him. It was a gift. He'd had it even as a human. It was the silver tongue that his mother had seen as proof of his evil origins. Once he'd been made a vampire . . . well, let's just say that the vampire symbiote was generous with its gifts. All vampires had some telepathy, but Lucifer's was off the chart. No human could resist his inquiries. Hell, most vampires were even susceptible, especially those lower on the power scale than he was. Which, let's face it, included most vampires.

"Whom is she sending?" Lucifer asked Bastien, dreading the answer. If it was some over-muscled security type, he could make it work for him. All those glowering muscles only made him seem more reasonable by comparison. What he couldn't handle was another vamp who had his own ideas on how to run the investigation. If that happened, he'd have to waste time pretending to go along, while conducting his own parallel investigation on the side. Either that, or simply shut the other vamp down, which might anger Sophia.

"A woman," Bastien said, answering his question. "She's Sophia's closest bodyguard, and the lady seems to trust her completely. She apparently knows Murphy well, too, which could come in handy."

"Is she attractive?" Lucifer asked, thinking this might not be so bad, after all.

"Ah. Good question," Bastien said, grinning. "Unfortunately, I didn't see her. She wasn't in the conference room, and if she was in the hallway, I didn't notice. Not that I was looking. My only thought was bringing the news to you."

"I'm touched," Lucifer said dryly.

"Yeah, about that. Sophia says Murphy's being held in Montreal, and that the female vamp she's sending speaks French."

"I speak French," Lucifer protested. Well, he spoke Cajun French, which was close enough. He could make himself understood just fine.

Bastien made a dismissive noise. "What you speak is not French, *mon ami*. And the Quebecers are very specific in defense of their language."

"I'll get by. When do I meet the mystery lady?"

"That's under discussion. Sophia is returning to Vancouver tonight, and she wants to brief the female before she goes. Also, apparently, she needs time to shift her Vancouver security assignments around, so that she can be sure of having someone she trusts close by, now that the bodyguard will be working with you. And how fucked up is that? She can't even trust her own security people."

"Blame Lucien," came a deep voice that didn't surprise either one of them. Aden was their lord and master. Hell, he was Bastien's Sire, and a damn powerful vampire. When he entered a building—or a hotel suite—they felt it in their bones.

"Lucien?" Lucifer repeated. "What does he have to do with it?" Lucien had been the Canadian Vampire Lord before Sophia took over. The specifics of that transition were blurry. Several versions existed, but they all agreed that Lucien had tapped Sophia as his heir before he died.

Aden tossed his jacket onto a chair, and twisted his neck from side to side. "Fucking meetings are a pain in the neck. Literally. Once a year is bad enough. With these Europeans fucking things up, it's like we're meeting every damn month."

"Why blame Lucien, my lord?" Lucifer asked again, wanting any bit of knowledge that might contribute to his hunt.

Aden shrugged one shoulder. "I never met the guy, but by all accounts, he was well loved by his people. He was also a shitty lord. He was more interested in having a good time than maintaining order, and Sophia's paying the price. She's spent the last year putting out fires, proving herself over and over again. And it doesn't help that she arrived in Vancouver almost literally on the eve of Lucien's death. His people don't know her, and they're not sure they can trust her."

"You think that plays into the current situation?"

"Hell, yes. The Europeans saw a weakness and pounced. And the fact that she's a woman doesn't help either."

Lucifer opened his mouth to protest, but Aden forestalled him.

"I know what you're going to say, and I agree with you. Sophia's as strong as any of us—well, not Raphael, but the rest of us. She just needs more experience actually ruling a territory. Lucien didn't do her any favors by waiting until he was dying to pull her home to Canada."

Lucifer found this all very interesting. Inside information on the lords was hard to come by. But it didn't help his current investigation. He was far more interested in learning more about this female vamp he was going to have on his tail, and whether she was going to make his life, and his hunt, more difficult.

"The woman, my lord?" he reminded Aden. "When will I meet her? I'd hoped to start my hunt tonight. Obviously, that's not going to happen if Murphy's in Montreal. But I can at least get there as soon as possible."

Aden nodded. "The two of you will travel together, leaving later tonight. I had the smaller jet flown in, and it's being prepped right now; it's yours until this is over. We've also made hotel arrangements for you in Montreal. Sophia wanted you to bunk in the Montreal compound, but I refused. I told her you needed to maintain your neutrality during the investigation, but the truth is, I'm not going to trust your safety to a bunch of unknown Canadian vamps. You're strong, Lucifer, but Sophia has no idea who among her people is loyal and who's not, and that includes the compound's daylight guards. No way I'm letting you sleep there. I also told them you always travel with your own guard, which is one more reason for the hotel."

Lucifer arched his brow. "Thank you for that, my lord. I can go directly to the airport—"

"Not quite yet. There's one more meeting, and this time you're invited."

"My lord?"

"Sophia insisted on meeting you first. I think she wants to be certain I'm not sneaking a spy into her territory."

"But she's the one who asked for your help."

"Well, not *my* help specifically. She contacted Raphael, and I think he's the only one she really trusts, to the extent that she trusts any of us. For her, the North American alliance is a marriage of necessity, rather than choice."

Lucifer swallowed a sigh. He knew that Aden respected his skills, and maybe even liked him, but that didn't make him any less Lucifer's lord, and one did not show impatience with one's lord. On the other hand, he was sick to death of all the maneuvering that had gone into what should have been a straightforward assignment. Colin Murphy had been captured. Lucifer was best qualified to find and free him. Therefore, Lucifer should *already* be hunting the streets of Montreal.

Unfortunately, things didn't move that quickly when vampire lords were involved.

"Understood," Lucifer said quietly. "So when do I meet Sophia?"

"Right now. Follow me."

"YOU'LL DEPART LATER tonight for Montreal," Sophia was saying, as she fussed in front of the mirror, displaying an uncharacteristic agitation. She'd been this way ever since Colin had been taken, as if he was her anchor, the stabilizer holding her in place. Eleanor had seen the way Colin looked at Sophia, the way he constantly touched her—small touches, nothing too intimate, at least in public. A hand at the small of her back, a single finger stroking the back of her hand, or, when he thought no one was watching, a gentle graze of his knuckles over her cheek. Their love was the stuff of romance novels, the kind that other women dreamed of. Other women, but not Eleanor. She'd given up on love a long time ago.

As jaded as she might be, however, she could still appreciate the strength to be found in a connection like that, the confidence gained from knowing your lover would always be there for you, no matter what. And then, to have him suddenly yanked away? To know that he was suffering horribly for no reason but that he loved you?

It was no wonder that Lady Sophia had lost her usual cool, unflappable demeanor.

"Are we sure about this vampire of Aden's?" Eleanor asked, more concerned than she wanted to admit. She was willing to do whatever task Sophia required of her, but she wasn't all that thrilled about leaving Sophia's side in the middle of this crisis.

Sophia ran her fingers through her long hair one last time, then turned away from the mirror to face Eleanor. "I trust Raphael," she said quietly. "And this hunter of Aden's, this Lucifer, comes highly recommended by—Eleanor?"

Eleanor couldn't breathe, couldn't move any part of her body. Except for her heart. That was pounding so hard that her ribs were rattling.

"Eleanor?" Sophia repeated, taking a step closer, her face creased in concern.

She blinked, and her throat loosened up enough for the first gasp of air to reach her lungs. "Lucifer?" she repeated. It had to be someone else. A different Lucifer. But how many vampires named Lucifer could there be in the world?

Sophia tilted her head curiously. "You know him?"

Eleanor rubbed a soothing hand over her chest. "Maybe. It might be a different—"

"A different Lucifer?" Sophia chuckled, unwittingly echoing Eleanor's doubts. "I've been a vampire over three hundred years, and I've never met another *person* named Lucifer, much less another vampire. Who is he?"

Who is he? What a great question. Once upon a time he'd been everything to her.

"You loved him," Sophia said softly.

Eleanor wasn't surprised that Sophia could read her heart so easily. Hell, it must have been written on her face. "Yes," she admitted. "A long time ago."

"Did he hurt you? I won't have a brute—"

"No," she said quickly. "Lucifer would never . . . he loved me, and I—"

"And you love him still."

For the first time since she'd sworn her oath to Sophia, Eleanor wished she could hide her thoughts, her emotions. She didn't know how she felt about Lucifer, but she knew it no longer mattered. She was the one who'd left, and Lucifer was as proud as he was beautiful. Her departure would have wounded more than just his heart. And there would have been no shortage of gorgeous women willing to soothe his bruised ego. She was certain he'd have relegated her to the bottom of his long list of lovers by now. Just one among many.

"It doesn't matter what I feel," she told Sophia. "Be assured, my lady, that it won't affect the search for Colin. I won't let you down."

"Of course, you won't," Sophia said, waving away the words. "You never do. You're one of the few people I can truly count on. But, Eleanor . . ." She took another step, bringing her close enough to rest a delicate hand on Eleanor's arm. "Love is too precious to waste. When I walked away from Colin, I was so certain that I knew what was best for him. But I was wrong. Do you understand? I lost so many years with him, years that I can never get back, and now . . ."

"Don't," Eleanor urged Sophia, pressing her hand over her lady's where it still lay on her arm. "Colin is coming back. I'll make sure of it."

Sophia nodded, squeezing their fingers together, before letting go. "Don't make my mistake, Eleanor. That kind of love, the kind that sleeps forever in your heart . . ." She shook her head. "Don't waste it."

Eleanor nodded her agreement, but *her* heart knew the truth. It was too late for her and Lucifer, but she would not let it be too late for Sophia and Colin. She'd work with Lucifer; she'd work with the devil himself, if that's what it took to give Sophia's love story a happy ending. Even if she was never going to get one of her own.

LUCIFER WISHED HE'D had more warning. Dealing with Aden was one thing. He was used to his lord's moods and personality. But meeting Sophia for the first time, and with no time to prepare? That was something else entirely. Of course, he'd been the one complaining about the delays just a few minutes ago, even if it had been only in his thoughts.

He strode down the carpeted hallway next to Aden, aware of the many members of Sophia's security staff eyeballing him as he went past. Mindful of his earlier conversation with Bastien, he couldn't help but wonder how many of these vampires were loyal, though he assumed Sophia had already examined all of her close-in security. Or re-examined them. It was obvious to him, at least, that at least some of the vampires who'd been loyal to her originally had to have been co-opted into this new plot against her.

That would be an important part of his investigation. Finding the initial traitor, the first vampire whom the Europeans had persuaded to their cause.

Some of the vampires in this hallway undoubtedly knew who that traitor was, might even have been recruited by him, whether successful or not.

Lucifer could have reached out and touched their minds right now, if he'd wanted. He had the power. But these were Sophia's vampires, and doing so would have crossed a line that he wasn't ready to breach. Yet. Though it was almost a certainty that he'd have to probe a few minds before this hunt was over.

"Not yet, Lucifer," Aden murmured, as if aware of his thoughts.

Lucifer smiled, because Aden *hadn't* touched his thoughts. It was just that Aden's thoughts paralleled Lucifer's own. There was a reason he'd chosen to swear fealty to Aden. They viewed the world in much the same way.

Although Lucifer was about a thousand times more charming than Aden. Now *there* was a thought that he definitely didn't share.

They approached a set of double doors. The two vampires standing guard stiffened to attention, but they weren't foolish enough to try to block the way.

"Announce us," Aden growled.

The guard on the right touched his ear, activating the ear bud comm device he obviously wore there. He murmured something sub-vocally, and almost immediately opened the right-hand door.

"The lady is expecting you, my lord."

Aden simply grunted and continued on into the suite, while Lucifer gave the guard a conspiratorial wink, which the guard didn't even acknowledge. Some people simply had no sense of the absurd.

"Sophia," Aden was saying as he proceeded past the small vestibule and into a room just like the one where Lucifer had been pacing only a short time ago. The view was the same, too. Same buildings, same lights. Although the moonlight was already shifting. It was a reminder that he needed to get past all of these meetings if he hoped to make it to Montreal tonight.

Lucifer stepped up next to Aden, his gaze taking in his surroundings while he waited to be introduced. This room might have the same view as his, but they were furnished very differently. The colors and furnishings were far more feminine here, and there was a grand piano in the far corner next to the windows. Lucifer wondered if the piano was always there, or if Sophia had specifically requested it for this visit. This *was* her territory, after all.

"And this is Lucifer," Aden said, drawing him out of his thoughts.

Lucifer bowed slightly, acknowledging her position and power, while being exquisitely careful not to let any of his own power leak through his shields. Aden knew how strong he was, but then Aden was sure enough of his own strength to surround himself with powerful, and loyal, vampires. In Lucifer's experience, not every vampire lord was similarly confident. He didn't want Sophia to detect any hint of challenge from him.

Besides, if she knew how powerful he really was, she might not agree to give him the run of her territory. He really wanted this hunt. It would be the biggest challenge yet to his considerable skills, and he was eager to get started.

"My lady," he murmured, as he straightened and met a pair of incredibly dark brown eyes. Sophia was a strikingly beautiful woman, small but voluptuous, with a mane of thick black hair falling down her back. She reminded Lucifer of the women in the village where he'd grown up. She reminded him of his mother, actually, but without the bitterness that had hardened that beauty into something brittle.

SOPHIA NODDED briefly at Aden, but focused most of her attention on Lucifer, this vampire that Eleanor loved. More importantly, he was also the vampire to whom everyone expected her to extend a carte blanche, essentially giving him permission to roam around her territory at will.

She wasn't blind to the contradictions in this situation. She knew she was being inconsistent in asking for help and then anticipating treachery. But what did they expect? She'd been betrayed by her own people, at least some of them. Did they assume she'd offer blind trust? That she'd simply stand back and let the big boys take over? She was so tired of this particular fight, so weary of constantly being judged on her sex, rather than the depth of her power, and her ability to use it. At the same time, she knew her own defensiveness played a big part in her attitude. She expected them to treat her as less, and therefore she looked for it. There was no question that she'd encountered that attitude among male vamps, but not here. Honesty forced her to admit that none of the other North American lords had ever treated her with anything but respect, not even Aden, whose reputation was less than flattering where women were concerned. Although, according to Colin—whose unique position as her mate granted him access to all of the latest gossip via the other mates—Aden had been transformed by the love of a good woman. A woman who didn't put up with any of that sexist bullshit.

But it wasn't Aden who concerned her tonight. It was his boy Lucifer. She was about to trust him with the most important hunt of his life, the most important hunt of *her* life, and she needed to know he could handle it. She also needed to know he could be trusted where Eleanor was concerned. Eleanor was more than a valued guard, she was like a sister, and Sophia loved her. She wouldn't send her off with a brute, no matter how skilled he was.

She studied the vampire in front of her, noting his obvious physical charms. He was nearly as big as Aden, with broad shoulders and a deep chest. A black leather belt with a heavy silver buckle accented his narrow hips, where black jeans clung precariously above long legs and powerful thighs. His hair was as black as hers, and the slight olive tone to his skin told her he probably came from the same part of the world that she did. His eyes, however, were a color she'd never seen before, and she thought she might understand why his mother had named him Lucifer. The people in their part of the world had always been deeply superstitious, especially back a century or two. She didn't know exactly how old

Lucifer was. She could feel the weight of his age, and it wasn't much, not by vampire standards, nowhere near her over three hundred years, but it was enough that his birthplace would have been very different than the world he was living in today.

Those strange eyes made him even more gorgeous, however, and Sophia suddenly understood why Eleanor had always seemed immune to masculine charms. Granted, she'd only known Eleanor for little more than a year, but in that entire time, Sophia wasn't aware of a single man, or woman, that Eleanor had been with. She fed from both men and women equally, but she never seemed to linger with any of them. Now it made sense. Eleanor was still pining for this one, the handsome and admittedly charismatic Lucifer.

But enough worry about Lucifer's physical charms. What about where it counted? What about his power? She couldn't do a deep scan of the vamp; Aden would never stand for it. She probed lightly, and found shields that were surprisingly as strong as her own. She met Lucifer's odd eyes and found him watching her carefully. He knew what she was trying to do, and he was determined to stop her, but without being offensive. There was no question that he had power enough to do it, too—power to stop a vampire lord from penetrating his shields. Which told her all she needed to know about his strength.

So. She needed to make a decision. On the one hand, his power worried her. She hated turning such a strong vampire lose in her territory, especially given his loyalty to Aden. On the other hand, if he was going to succeed in rescuing her Colin, he'd need to be powerful enough to outwit and outfight whoever had betrayed her. He might also need to confront and defeat whoever the traitor had aligned himself with, possibly even one or more of the invading Europeans.

"You'll do," she told Lucifer finally, then addressed Aden. "The plane is fueling. My guard is already there, overseeing preparations." She'd sent Eleanor ahead to the plane, hoping to spare her a public re-union with Lucifer.

"Lucifer will bring your mate back to you, Sophia," Aden said, his manner and voice both demonstrating an unexpected empathy for her situation.

She looked up at him and nodded her thanks. It was the best she could do. If she spoke, she wasn't sure she could hold back the tears. She shifted her attention back to Lucifer. "Thank you," she said, trying to put all of her hopes and gratitude into the two insufficient words.

"It is an honor, my lady," Lucifer said. He gave her a very pretty bow that normally would have made her smile. Now, it just made her hope that Eleanor could survive his charms.

Chapter Three

ELEANOR STARED OUT at the sleek private plane, thankful for the limo's excellent soundproofing that muffled the piercing noise from the jet engines. The aircraft was winding up, getting ready to take her and Lucifer—she had trouble even thinking his name—off on a hunt for Colin Murphy. Just the idea made her uneasy, but Sophia's needs were far more important than Eleanor's tragic love life. The lady's defense of the territory was vital to the life and well-being of thousands of Canadian vampires, but finding Colin was critical to *Sophia's* life and well-being. You couldn't have one without the other.

For Eleanor, it was both a tremendous honor, and a terrifying burden, to be given such an important task.

There were other vampires among Sophia's people who were better hunters with far more experience in such things. But there wasn't a better fighter than Eleanor, and there was a good chance that the hunt would come down to a battle for Colin's life. More than that, however, the lady *trusted* her. And that was the biggest part of it—trust. Sophia trusted Eleanor in a way she did no one else. Ironically, that trust was rooted in the fact that it was Colin who'd seen something in Eleanor that no one else had. She'd been working in the lower ranks, mostly guarding the gate and running perimeter, just as she had for Lucien before his death. She'd never even met Sophia before Colin pulled her out of a crowd during a routine training session, and ordered her to meet him on the mats. She'd been shocked that a human would be ordering vampires around. She'd never heard of such a thing. Of course, she wasn't all that old—not even 49 yet, with her 26 human years still out-numbering her vamp years. And the first few of *those* had been one long, confusing nightmare.

The difference between human and vamp had never seemed to matter to Colin. He'd been superbly confident in his own abilities, something Eleanor had envied back then, but no more. She still admired Colin, but she was no longer lacking in confidence of her own. Colin had pulled her out of obscurity and given her a purpose, the highest purpose any vampire could ask for—defending her lord. Eleanor had run with it. She'd worked her ass off to build on the physical strength of her vampiric gift. She was still petite—the vampire symbiote didn't change that—but it also didn't care about size. She was far stronger than the strongest human, and most vampires, as well.

There *was* one disadvantage that not even vampire strength could overcome, however, and that was the reach of her arms. Most of her opponents, whether on the mats or in a real conflict, were always going to be bigger than she was, with longer arms and greater reach. Colin had actually been the one who'd suggested a weapon to offset that advantage, and Eleanor now prided herself on considerable skill with a bo staff. Of course, one couldn't walk down most city streets carrying a sixty inch steel staff, so she'd found one that collapsed into a twenty-two inch stick, but could be deployed to its full length in seconds. Wielded with the power of her vampire strength and hard-won skill, it was a deadly weapon. The stick offset her short reach, and her skill did the rest.

Colin had believed in her when no one else had. He'd trusted Eleanor with the life of the woman he loved, and she was determined to deserve his trust.

Now it was Colin who needed *her* help, and she'd give her life before she let him or Sophia down. Her biggest concern was Lucifer. Not working with him, she could do whatever was necessary to get along for the duration. Sophia had made it clear that, while Lucifer was leading the hunt, this was still *Sophia's* territory, and Eleanor had the only authority that mattered. If Lucifer stepped one toe out of line, if there was any hint that Colin wasn't his priority, then Eleanor was supposed to call off the hunt. Sophia assured her she had a back-up plan, though Eleanor didn't know what it was, and a tiny voice inside her wondered if such a plan even existed.

More to the point was whether Lucifer would drop the hunt just because Eleanor said so. She didn't know how much power he had; she hadn't been a vampire the last time she'd seen him. But she knew he was domineering and confident, and she suspected he had the power to back it up.

She sighed and wondered, not for the first time, why, out of the hundreds of vampires at Aden's command, she had to be paired up with Lucifer.

A flash of movement hit her peripheral vision, and she turned to see a big, black SUV roll up to the foot of the idling jet. Light flashed on the

Illinois license plate. Apparently, Aden had brought his own vehicles with him, which wasn't all that unusual. Vampire lords were a suspicious lot and tended to drag their security blankets along with them, even when those "blankets" were heavily armored SUVs. Eleanor would have liked to claim it was a testosterone thing, but Sophia did it, too.

Wanting to get their new partnership off to a good start, Eleanor braced herself against the jet noise, and stepped out of the limo to greet . . . Lucifer. Her gut clenched as the SUV's door opened. The first vampire out of the SUV was Aden's lieutenant, Sebastien, a formidable and somber vampire who rarely seemed to smile. He gave her a polite nod as he stepped away from the vehicle, making room for . . .

Eleanor couldn't look away. Even knowing what to expect, Lucifer's appearance hit her like a block of wood to her head. She wanted to run, to duck back into the limo and tell the driver to take her away. To tell Sophia that she couldn't do this job, after all. She just *couldn't*. But that was the coward's way. She'd run away once . . . from Lucifer. She'd promised herself a long time ago that she was finished with running away.

Besides, it was too late. Lucifer had already seen her.

He glanced her way idly at first, caught up in an exchange with Sebastien. But the moment his gaze fell on her, he froze in shock, and lifted one hand toward Sebastien in a bid for silence. Apparently, while she'd known about *him*, he hadn't known about *her*.

She didn't know what to expect. Anger, maybe, at the way she'd left all those years ago. Hurt, betrayal? What she didn't expect was the relief that suffused his handsome face, the sheer joy at seeing her alive and well again. He closed the distance between them in three long strides, arms out, hands reaching for her automatically. Until something made him stop. No, not something. *She* made him stop. The look on her face, the stiff rejection of her body language. Eleanor knew she should pretend to be casual about this, but it was just too much. The shock of seeing him again after all this time, the unexpected swell of emotion that threatened to bring her to tears. Why did she still feel so *much* for him? Deep in her chest, her heart *ached,* but it wasn't pain, it was . . . a reawakening, as from a long slumber. Blood was suddenly rushing out to warm every muscle, flushing her skin, making her feel truly alive for the first time in so long. So *very* long.

"He told me you were dead," Lucifer said quietly, his voice deep and intimate. It was a demonstration of his power that he could make himself heard despite the loud jet noise. "I didn't believe it, but I looked everywhere, and you were gone." He waited, his eyes bright with power as they studied her, and she'd have sworn she could feel the touch of his hands on every inch of her body. "If you'd wanted to leave, I'd have hated it, but I wouldn't have stopped you. But didn't I at least deserve to know you were alive?"

Oh, the pain in his eyes when he said that. A hurt that found an echo in her own heart.

"A single line, a postcard letting me know you were safe and happy."

But maybe I wasn't *happy!* She wanted to say the words, to tell him how miserable she'd been. How much she'd missed him, and how sad she still was sometimes in the darkest hour of the night. But that would reveal too much.

"You look good," she said instead, raising her voice to be heard. She had power of her own. More than most. But not like his. She was completely taken aback to realize that Lucifer's power felt more like Sophia's, that he could well be a vampire lord someday. She studied him with new eyes, with a vampire's knowledge of what he was. What she saw was still . . . her Lucifer. And he did look good. Even better than he had, and he'd always been gorgeous. His eyes would probably be called hazel, but there was so much grass green in them that they defied description. He had a beard now, neat and more of a five o'clock shadow than anything else. His hair was shorter than it had been—no longer worn around his shoulders, but shaped into a classic man's razor cut, close on the sides, but still long on top. He'd always had great hair, thick and silky, and so black that it shone with blue highlights under the moon. He'd been big then, but somehow he seemed bigger now. Maybe it was the air of authority that surrounded him, the confidence fairly reeking from his pores.

She'd have liked to say that it made him less attractive. But that would have been a lie. He'd been handsome back then, but now? Now he was devastating. Which was a good word for what he could do to her heart, if she wasn't careful.

"And you're still beautiful," he murmured. He was visibly pulling back from her, his expressive face shutting down. She mourned its loss, even as she acknowledged it was her fault.

"Are you . . .?" She left the rest of it unsaid, a part of her still hoping Aden's hunter would be someone else. Please God, let it be so.

But Lucifer's mouth curved into a sad smile. "I'm supposed to be meeting Sophia's liaison here. Do you know . . .?" It was his turn to trail the words off in dismay. She saw the realization hit him, and she'd have sworn there was a sharp flash of satisfaction in those strange eyes, before he schooled his features into bland professionalism. "I'm guessing that's you?"

She nodded. "If you'd rather—"

He raised an expressive eyebrow. "Still running away, Elle?"

Bastard. He'd always been amazingly intuitive. Like he could read her mind. Maybe he could, though he'd never admitted it back then.

"Of course not," she said dismissively. "I'm just surprised, that's all. I didn't know you'd become an investigator, or whatever you call yourself."

"A hunter, *cara*," he said coolly, although there was nothing cool about the look in his eyes.

"Lucifer?" Sebastien's deep voice interrupted. "Everything good?"

Lucifer lingered for a heartbeat or two, holding her gaze. And then, without a word, he turned his back on her and walked over to where Aden's lieutenant waited. Sebastien's dark regard rested on her for a long moment, before cutting to Lucifer.

"Problem?" he asked. He made no attempt to carry his words to her, but she read the single word on his lips.

Eleanor didn't know what Lucifer responded, but she saw the two vampires clasp hands and exchange manly hugs, before Sebastien climbed back into the waiting SUV and took off. Leaving her and Lucifer alone.

The next few days, or even weeks, yawned ahead of her, a nightmare of working side by side with the only man she'd ever loved, while pretending that her heart wasn't breaking into tiny pieces all over again.

ELEANOR. FUCK. AS elated as Lucifer was to know that she was alive, her reaction to seeing him, her *unhappy* reaction, had been unexpectedly painful. Anger flashed, hot and sharp. For all the joy he'd experienced in that first moment he'd seen her standing there tonight, he still couldn't believe it. She'd *left* him. And he couldn't figure out why.

He watched as she chose a seat in the back of Aden's private jet, as far away from him as possible. A smile flitted around his lips, and he didn't bother to conceal it. Let her think he was amused by all of this. Better that than to have her know how much it hurt.

She'd been perfect, his fairy tale princess. Hell, the first time he'd seen her, he'd thought she was a figment of his imagination . . .

1993, New Orleans, Louisiana, USA

LUCIFER STROLLED down the crowded street, using just enough power to clear a path through the throngs of humans. Bourbon Street was frequently crowded, but never more so than during the Mardi Gras celebration, when tourists piled into the city with seemingly one goal—to get as drunk as possible. The area was always a fertile hunting ground, and Lucifer never minded a little bourbon with his blood. Or any other alcohol for that matter. Although, he wasn't fond of rum.

He snickered privately at the thought. Blood was blood. And he was hungry tonight. It had been weeks since he'd had a full night to hunt. He'd snuck in a quick bite here and there on the riverboat, but this was the first night he'd had for a leisurely hunt, a chance to select his donor and seduce her the old-fashioned way, rather than relying on the power of his vampire nature.

Spying a particularly raucous group shoving drunkenly down the sidewalk, he chose to step out into the street. He could have shoved them instead, but he was feeling mellow tonight. Let them enjoy their revelry. Human lives were short enough.

He'd gone no more than a few yards down the street, which was nearly as crowded as the sidewalk, when he spied a fellow vampire closing in on his prey. He couldn't see the woman yet, but he could tell from the vampire's behavior, from the intense focus of his gaze, that he had his eye on someone in particular.

More out of idle curiosity than anything else, Lucifer altered his path to intercept the other vampire. He drew closer, and the crowds parted enough that, for the first time, he could see the intended prey. His breath caught in his throat. What was it his grandmother had called it? *Colpo di fulmine.* The thunderbolt. Love at first sight. He had to have this woman, even if it meant stealing her from beneath the other vampire's fangs.

She was perfection. Small and fair, with a lovely face and eyes of such a brilliant blue that they gleamed even in the dimness of a muggy New Orleans night. Long, golden-blond locks curled down her back to rest just above an exquisitely round and tight little ass, while her breasts fit her petite frame perfectly—neither large nor small, but firm and high, with nipples poking against the white cotton of her halter top.

Lucifer frowned, his gaze shooting from her perky breasts to the hunting vampire now standing far too close. Close enough that she was beginning to fall under the sway of his power as he moved in for the kill.

Although "kill" was only a turn-of-phrase these days. Killing was rarely necessary for a vampire's survival in a world where humans lined up at so-called blood houses for the privilege of opening a vein. Some vampires liked the convenience of those houses, but Lucifer preferred hunting the streets.

And thank God he had, or how else would he have found his princess? Because that's what she was—a princess right out of the fairy tales his grandmother had told him when he was a very small boy. His uncles had objected, telling her that such stories were not for men, but for little girls. But his *nonna* had ignored them, and he'd been happy with that, because he'd loved those stories. He liked to think that it was his *nonna's* stories that let him understand women as well as he did. Or, at least better than most. After all, what man could really understand a woman?

But no woman had ever hit him as hard as this one. He had to have her.

He moved through the crowd, using his power freely now to clear a path through the humans, intent on reaching her before the other vampire succeeded in mesmerizing her completely. Utilizing a nearly undetectable thread of power to break the vampire's hold, he stepped up with a broad smile of greeting for the woman.

"Darling," he said cheerfully, closing his fingers lightly on her upper arm and pulling her away from the other vamp. "I'm sorry I'm late."

The vampire growled, fangs flashing, but he quickly backed down at the cold power of Lucifer's gaze. "This one's already mine," he said, sliding an arm around her waist.

The vampire didn't like it. In fact, his jaw was clenched so hard that Lucifer could see white bone through his skin. But he couldn't do anything about it either. He snarled his impotent defiance, then quickly lost himself in the crowd. Lucifer didn't feel all that badly about stealing the vamp's dinner. He'd have no difficulty locating a fresh entrée. Not in this mass of humanity.

Lucifer turned his attention to his own dinner. Though he already knew she was more than that. She held his heart in her hands, though she didn't know it yet.

Tipping her head back with a finger under her chin, he waited until her eyes cleared from the other vamp's spell, and asked, "What's your name, *cara?*"

She gazed up at him, and now that she had a choice, he could see the consideration in her pretty blue eyes, deciding whether to gift him with her attention or not. He could have pushed her one way or the other. It was what he would have done with any other woman, but not this one. He wanted to keep this woman, which meant she had to choose him for herself.

She smiled. "Eleanor Morel."

"Eleanor," he repeated. "And I'm Lucifer."

Her eyes widened. "Is that your real name?"

He nodded. "It's Italian. Somewhat uncommon, but ordinary enough."

"So you're not the child of Satan or anything?" she asked, her eyes sparkling in amusement, which made him want her even more.

"Not according to my *nonna*. Although my mother might disagree."

She laughed, a sound his mind likened to the ringing of delicate bells. And he knew he was well and truly snared.

Present Day, en route to Montreal, Quebec, Canada

"NOTHING TO SAY, Elle?" he asked finally, breaking the uncomfortable silence. Unfortunately for her, the jet wasn't so big that she could avoid him.

She glanced at him and then away, her gaze focused on the files on the table next to her, pretending to study them. He could tell she wasn't actually reading anything. Not unless she was captivated by a single word. Her eyes hadn't moved even the tiniest bit, and there was no comprehension on her expressive face. Her thoughts were far away from whatever was in those files.

"It's going to be a long few fucking days if we can't even talk to each other," he said, taunting her intentionally, trying to force a response. She didn't react, didn't give any indication she'd even heard him.

Lucifer stared a while longer, drinking in the sight of her, dismayed at the effect she still had on him. It was just like the first time he'd seen her, as if all of the intervening years and all of the lies had never happened. Eventually, his wounded heart—and maybe his ego—could take no more. He stood and crossed the aisle, pretending to need his own files from the leather bag he'd brought onboard. He didn't actually need the documents; he had them all but memorized. But it was a good excuse to get up and move, and eventually to take a seat on the same side of the aircraft as Eleanor, one with several seats between them to serve as a barrier that kept him from seeing her every time he looked up.

With nothing else to do, and needing the distraction, he went over what he knew of the case, and contemplated how best to begin his search. Eleanor was a complication, but he wouldn't let her get in the way of his hunt. Nothing got in the way of his hunts. It was part of what made him so effective. Once he was on the trail, he was single-minded, focused and committed. He lived and breathed his quarry, which, in this case, was Colin Murphy. Or the vampires who'd kidnapped him. Either one would do, since one would lead to the other. Colin Murphy took precedence, of course. Retrieving Sophia's mate was critical to the defense of the Canadian Territory, and ultimately North America. They couldn't permit a single European victory, not even the smallest foothold.

He bent his thoughts to what he already knew, which wasn't much. Colin Murphy had been in Toronto, on a fact-finding mission for Sophia, in the aftermath of the European incursions against Raphael in the West and the traitor Anthony in the South. Lucifer had spent a lot of time in New Orleans, but had never met, or even seen, Anthony. He did know that Anthony had abandoned New Orleans after Hurricane Katrina and moved to take over rule of the entire Southern territory, with a base in Houston. Granted, many of Anthony's vampires had perished in the floods, but many had survived, too. And they could have used their master's strength in the days and weeks after that disaster.

Lucifer had looked at Anthony's abandonment, and his own Sire's thoughtless cruelty, and he'd been grateful for whatever fate had put him in Aden's path instead.

He stared out the jet's window, the black sky a canvas for a time in his life that he hadn't thought of in years. But apparently this was his night for memories. It must have been Eleanor. Seeing her alive after all this time had opened the vault door on events that he'd kept tightly hidden away—some because he still second-guessed himself despite the futility and intervening years, and some, like Eleanor, because the memories had been simply too painful.

But it wasn't pain that stopped him from reliving his last days with the weakling who'd been his Sire. It was a sense that somehow he could have done it differently. Lucifer had been raised without a single male role model. His mother's brothers had visited infrequently, and only long enough to voice their disapproval of his existence. His father had never been named—not in his hearing and not on his birth certificate. But his mother had made it clear that *she* thought he was the child of the devil himself—or at the very least, a minor demon—either one of whom had violated her virgin body in her sleep, stealing her innocence and leaving her with a devil child to raise. Lucifer's *nonna* had curled her lip at such fanciful thoughts, saying it was only his mother trying to excuse her whoring ways in bedding a married man.

Lucifer smiled, amused as always by the choice that had left him. He was either the child of the devil, or the child of a whore.

In any event, he'd been raised with love and attention by his *nonna*, who'd instilled her version of a man's code of honor. Foremost had been an obligation to honor and defend the women in his life. His gaze shifted automatically to where Eleanor sat at the back of the plane, staring out the window, no longer even pretending to read. He'd wanted nothing more than to take care of her, to shelter her against everything from the smallest inconvenience to the darkest evil. He'd failed in that, apparently far worse than he'd known, though it had taken him weeks of searching to discover the truth. Or at least what he'd thought was the truth back then. The knowledge hadn't changed anything. Neither had killing the vampire who'd torn her away from him.

1993, New Orleans, Louisiana, USA

LUCIFER WALKED THE streets of New Orleans for the third week in a row, searching for Eleanor. He no longer bothered to go by her apartment. It had been cleaned out. That frightened and puzzled him more than anything else. His first thought, when she'd disappeared, had been that she'd been abducted. She was a beautiful woman, and there was no shortage of men who would simply take what they wanted. But no matter how hard he tried to convince himself of that scenario, it didn't add up. All of her things had been gone from her apartment. Not only her clothes and jewelry, but her personal possessions, the photographs of her family that she'd shared with him, her favorite books, and even the historical journal of her many times great-grandmother who'd been alive during this country's civil war. Those things had no value to anyone but Eleanor.

The inevitable truth was shoving its way into his every thought, suffocating him until he could barely generate the energy to keep moving. Eleanor had left him, and he'd torn her room apart looking for a note, a message scrawled on a mirror, something, anything to explain why. He'd replayed every moment of their time together and found no hint of her unhappiness. Their last night together had been more loving than ever. He'd been ready to move her into his own, much larger, home, and even to trust her with the secret of his daytime sleeping location.

He needed answers. Why was she gone? Where would she go? And, above all, wherever she was, was she safe?

A familiar face caught his attention in the crowd. Derek Pratt. The vampire who'd been hustling Eleanor the night he'd first met her. The vampire who, Lucifer later discovered, had been after Eleanor for some weeks before that night. She'd rebuffed him every time, politely at first, and then with less subtlety. But Pratt had persisted. Until Lucifer had stepped in and, with a single look at the weaker vampire, driven him out of Eleanor's life.

Pratt wasn't looking at Lucifer with fear tonight. No, there was a smug satisfaction as he changed direction and made a point of crossing Lucifer's path, only to stop directly in front of him.

Lucifer spared the lesser vampire a dismissive glance. "Move," he said simply, and waited for his path to clear.

"Looking for someone?" Derek sneered.

Lucifer felt every muscle, every nerve in his body grow still and alert, ready to pounce. "Excuse me?" he asked softly.

"You're wandering around lately like you're lost . . . or like someone else is." Derek laughed. "I thought maybe I could help."

It took every ounce of restraint he possessed to refrain from slamming his fist into the bastard's chest and squeezing his heart until he begged to tell Lucifer whatever he wanted to know. He was going to do it anyway, but not here, not in the middle of Bourbon Street. He struck with his power, a subtle command compelling Derek to follow him into a nearby alley, and at the same time plowed his fist into Derek's gut with every ounce of strength in his vampire-enhanced body.

One woman shrieked a protest when Derek staggered against her, nearly knocking the drink from her hand. But most of the humans were too set on their own partying to notice. They simply gave the two vampires a wide berth and kept going.

Once in the alley and away from human eyes, Lucifer wasted no time with niceties. He was far more powerful than Derek and had no trouble trapping him against the dirty wall, while at the same time gathering shadows to conceal them from the curious.

"Tell me what you know about Eleanor," he ordered, not bothering with persuasion.

Derek tried to gather enough energy to spit at him, but Lucifer hadn't left him enough control to do it properly, so the spittle only dripped down the bastard's chin. He did manage a grin through bloodied teeth, before Lucifer twisted his power around the bastard's heart and stroked the vital organ lightly. Just enough to remind Derek who it was that held his life in his hands.

"She's gone," Derek ground out.

Pain squeezed Lucifer's heart and didn't let go. "Dead?" he asked, trying to sound cool, and knowing he was failing.

The other vampire bared his teeth in something approaching a grin. Lucifer growled and tightened his grip on the creep's heart, eliciting a grunt of real pain.

"She didn't make it," Derek gasped, then looked up as Lucifer's fangs abruptly slid into view. "Not my fault. She was weak. Now, fuck off."

Lucifer's rage became a physical thing, swelling until it threatened to swamp all of his senses, drowning out every sound but the pounding of his heart, dropping a bloody veil over his eyes until he could hardly see the leering asshole in front of him.

"You turned her?" he growled, his voice so guttural that the words were barely distinguishable.

"I told her it was your idea," Pratt said, gurgling a laugh. "She was so sweet, and she cried so prettily. And, fuck, such a tight little—"

Lucifer didn't hear anything else. Slamming his fist into Derek chest, he tore through skin and muscle and shattered ribs, until his fingers actually closed around the bastard's beating heart. And then he squeezed until it was nothing but bloody mush, oozing through his fingers as he yanked it out of the gaping hole in his chest.

Derek's eyes widened in shock in the instant before he died, as if he was honestly surprised at the outcome. As if he'd thought he could taunt Lucifer with what he'd done to Eleanor and walk away. As if Lucifer would ever have let him live after what he'd done.

He stood there, staring down at the greasy pile of dust, barely distinguishable from all of the other dirt in the narrow alley. He tried to feel some satisfaction, a sense of justice, if nothing else. But all he felt was empty. Eleanor was gone. Had she believed Derek when he'd told her that Lucifer wanted her made vampire? Did she know enough about vampire culture to know how unlikely that was? That even if he'd wanted her turned, he'd *never* have left it to any other vampire, much less one as weak and corrupt as Derek. But she didn't know any of those things, and it was his fault. He'd sheltered her all this time, protected her from the raw truth of what it meant to be vampire.

She'd been his princess. His beautiful Eleanor. Now she was dead.

He sank to his haunches against the alley wall, and he wept.

Present Day, en route to Montreal, Quebec, Canada

LUCIFER BLINKED, AS memory faded and he was back on Aden's luxurious jet, speeding to Montreal . . . with Eleanor, who wasn't dead at all. Eleanor, who'd left him. The pain of losing her had faded over time, though it had always been there, lurking beneath the surface of his heart, just waiting for the flash of a pair of blue eyes, or the gleam of golden blond hair to bring it all roaring back, just as raw and fresh as if she'd been gone days instead of years.

He hadn't believed Derek at first. He'd regretted killing the bastard before he could be sure of the truth. He'd searched for her for months afterward, making inquiries through his various connections up and down the rivers, but his efforts had come to nothing, and eventually he'd been forced to accept her death. Because what other explanation made sense? It sure as hell would have taken death to keep *him* away from her back then. And he'd been convinced that nothing but death would have kept her away from him.

Until tonight, when he'd seen her standing there on the tarmac. Every sense he'd possessed had been suddenly swamped by memories of Eleanor—the way she looked, her touch, her scent. Hell, the sweet, sweet taste of her, and not just her blood, but her skin, her mouth, and her delicious cunt, creaming all over his tongue when he'd brought her screaming to orgasm over and over again.

Fuck. And now he was hard as a rock.

He turned his thoughts back to the hunt, intentionally substituting the image of Colin Murphy—bloodied and beaten—in place of Eleanor's pretty, pink lips. Pretty, pink lips. Yeah, *that* wasn't helping.

He pulled out the still photo he'd captured and printed from the latest video, which Sophia had now turned over willingly. It appeared almost identical to previous images sent by Murphy's kidnappers, in that the man was bound exactly the same and was wearing the same clothing, now shredded, but which every witness agreed he'd been wearing the last time anyone had seen him. He also appeared to have been beaten to within an inch of his life. The only changes day to day—and his captors made a point of sending Sophia a new dose of horror every day—were the locations of the cuts and bruises.

But while this latest image was *almost* identical to the others, for the first time there was a marked change. They'd moved the camera somewhat, pulling it back to reveal more of the room. It was a small change, probably not even intentional. Maybe it got bumped, or was in the way of something else. But intentional or not, the change provided a far more detailed view of the room where they were holding Murphy. It wasn't a regular cell. Or at least not a modern one. The walls were rough and raw-looking, like an afterthought rather than a fully finished room. It was as if someone had slapped some plaster on an old, dirt-walled space and called it done. That didn't tell him all that much by itself. Montreal was a relatively old city, after all.

What mattered for Lucifer's hunt, however, was that Montreal had an extensive underground city. The tourist brochures all said it was modern and well-lit, but, as always, Lucifer had done his homework. The underground tunnels were designed to connect the several buildings of the so-called central business district, and were also fully integrated with the metro's more than 40 miles of underground train tracks. And where there were train tracks, there were maintenance tunnels, and all sorts of subterranean passageways where one might hide a prisoner.

"Have you ever been to Montreal?" He spun his seat around—one of the benefits of private jet travel—and called down the aisle to Eleanor.

She jumped, her pretty blue eyes blinking at him in confusion, as though suddenly reminded she wasn't alone. *That* was flattering. "What?" she asked.

Lucifer scowled, not used to being so easily dismissed, especially by a woman. "Montreal," he said sourly. "Have you ever been there?"

"Of course. I've accompanied Sophia there several times. Quite a few vampires live there."

He cocked his head curiously. "How many?"

Eleanor shrugged, as if she didn't know, but Lucifer doubted that was true. *Sophia* sure as hell knew, and Eleanor seemed to be her closest bodyguard. Sophia might not have told her directly, but bodyguards overheard things. And Eleanor was smart as hell. She'd take it all in, and remember it.

"How many, Elle?" he pressed.

She shrugged again. "The greater city of Montreal, the metropolis so to speak, has very nearly four million residents."

"And?"

She narrowed her eyes in irritation. "A few thousand vampires. Maybe three thousand," she clarified at his look of impatience. "What does it matter?"

It was Lucifer's turn to shrug. "Just curious," he said, more to irritate her than anything else. Her big eyes sparked with anger, before she managed to shutter the reaction. He swallowed a smile. "Actually, I'm trying to get a feel for the city. That's a lot of vamps. No way Sophia has even *met* most of them, much less secured a formal oath of loyalty."

"You're right about that," she admitted. "The distances make it difficult. Vancouver's her home city, and we're fairly secure there, but she's had to trust Toronto and Montreal, and even Quebec City, to surrogates."

"Who?"

Eleanor made a face. "For the most part, it was Darren Yamanaka. He was Lucien's lieutenant, and Sophia's main competition for the territory once Lucien was dead."

"Obviously, he lost. How'd he take that?"

"Not well, but she gave him Toronto as a consolation prize, and over the last year, he's taken over Montreal and Quebec City by default. He's a decent administrator, and he seemed to accept his lot after that."

"Seemed," he repeated in sudden understanding. "Has anyone heard from Darren lately?"

Her lips twisted into a grimace. "Not since the kidnapping."

"Wait. I thought Sophia didn't *know* who'd taken Murphy," he said sharply, a little pissed that no one had shared this bit of information with him.

"We don't *know*. It *could* be Darren. Colin certainly would have been in touch with him in the city. It just seems . . . I don't know . . . out of character. Darren's probably still carrying a grudge against Sophia, but he's not bold enough to plan something like this. Maybe he played a part, but there has to be someone else driving him forward."

Lucifer took that in, then asked, "Is Darren Sophia's lieutenant?"

She shrugged. "In a manner of speaking. He has the title, but no power. Sophia's never trusted him. For all practical purposes, Colin's her main advisor *and* her lieutenant."

Well, that was a mistake. Lucifer kept that thought to himself, figuring Eleanor wouldn't welcome any criticism of Sophia. But it wasn't much of a stretch to see how the decision to favor a human, even a mate, would create some serious resentment among a territory's vampires. It was one thing for a lord to treat his mate as a favored advisor; some of them brought real skills to the table, not to mention connections. Hell, Lucas Donlon's mate was a fucking FBI agent. But no human, no matter how smart or intuitive, could understand vampires as well as one of their own.

"Sophia's worked her ass off the last few months," Eleanor said, misinterpreting his lack of response. "She's had all of Canada to worry about, and she didn't even have a place to live. Not a place that Colin would approve of anyway."

"Murphy calls the shots?"

"Of course not. Don't be a pig. But Lucien's old house was a joke. Anyone could walk in the front door. He meant well, but he had shit for security."

"And look what happened to him," Lucifer observed dryly. "Or rather, to the vampires who trusted him," he added, referring to the several vampires who'd died as a result of the old lord's failures.

"That wasn't—" Eleanor started to protest angrily, but bit back whatever she'd planned to say next. Was it because she knew Lucien truly *had been* at fault? Or because she didn't want to engage in a real conversation with Lucifer? "Anyway," she continued, "Colin is a Navy SEAL. He knows—"

"Was," Lucifer corrected, irritated at the familiar way she spoke of the missing human and the affection he could hear in her voice. "*Was* a Navy SEAL."

She tipped her head, acknowledging the correction, but said, "They all think of themselves as SEALs, whether they're currently active or not."

"You've met his colleagues? His team?" he asked with studied casualness.

"Two of his friends visited a while back. I think they helped with the security set-up."

Lucifer studied her silently, looking for what? Some indication that she liked the human warriors? That she'd hooked up with one of them? Maybe more than one? What the hell did he expect to see? And why did he still care?

This was getting him nowhere, and it wasn't his purpose in being there.

"The old city," he said, changing the subject without warning. "Have you been *there*?"

She shook her head. "No. I know what the brochures say, but that's about it. Why? You think that's where they're keeping him?"

He shrugged. "It would be the smart move. All those human minds cluttering the ether, plus machinery, buildings and dirt. It's all helping to mask his presence, even from Sophia. And—"

"And the blood does the rest. That's the key. Don't assume she's any weaker than the rest of the lords, Lucifer. Or that her bond with

Colin is any more vulnerable than theirs would be."

He held up both hands in surrender. "Hey, I never said a word, *bella*." She blushed at his use of the old endearment. "I have no doubt that your Sophia is as tough as they come. Besides, it's obvious that they're healing the poor bastard to keep him alive, and Aden made sure I understood what that would do to the mate bond, especially one that's relatively fresh."

She looked interested at that. "So if they'd been together for a longer time, like ten years or something, the blood wouldn't matter?"

"Not according to Aden, and especially not if the vampire half of the mating was as powerful as Sophia. But that's irrelevant here. It is what it is. Sophia can tell us the city where they're holding him, but little else."

"It's a big city," she commented faintly.

"Yeah, but it's still more than the kidnappers think we know. And we want to keep it that way as long as possible. They won't dare move him. There's too big a chance Sophia would pick up on his presence."

She studied him a moment, and then said, "Okay, I'll go along with that. Sophia and the others must have picked you for a reason. So where do we start looking?"

Lucifer held up the thick file, with its photographs and reports. "Right here."

She wrinkled her nose. Adorable, damn it. "Sounds tedious," she muttered. "And I've already read everything in there."

"So, read it again. Read it backwards, if that's what it takes for a fresh look."

"And what will you be doing?" she demanded.

He smiled. "Exactly the same thing."

She sighed, but opened her own file, and, doing exactly what he'd suggested, went to the last page and started reading.

Lucifer watched her a moment longer, mentally whacking himself for giving her a reason to shut him out. And cursing himself for caring.

THANK GOD THE flight was short. Had it been much longer, Eleanor would have been stumbling down the aisle to be closer to him. Closer to Lucifer. He'd always had that effect on her. Like he was a magnet, and she was one of those refrigerator things . . . She frowned as the analogy fell apart. That made *her* the magnet, and Lucifer . . . the refrigerator? Well, shit, that was just ridiculous. He had her so rattled she couldn't even come up with a decent analogy.

The hell with analogies. She didn't need one to describe Lucifer's effect on her. When they'd been together, she hadn't been able to keep her hands off of him. If they'd been in the same room, they were touching. And he'd wanted her just as much as she'd wanted him.

But not anymore. There'd been that flash of joy when he'd first seen her in Toronto, but nothing since. She could hardly complain, since she'd been the one who'd shut him down cold out there, but still. She was hurting. Being so close, having to pretend it didn't matter. It was a constant ache in her chest.

He'd loved her once. She'd never doubted that. But that was before . . . when she'd still been human.

1993, New Orleans, Louisiana, USA

ELEANOR RESTED HER head against Lucifer's strong shoulder, so happy that she could barely contain herself. She wanted to jump up and dance—not a dignified or graceful dance, either. Just a wild, abandoned gamboling to let the world see the joy filling her heart.

For the first time in her life, she was in love. He was handsome, charming, brilliant, and so strong and protective. And, oh, yes, he loved her, too.

"Are you having a good time, *bella?*" Lucifer's voice was a warm, rumble of sound that made her entire body shiver with desire.

She nodded. "It's all so glamorous. Are all vampire parties like this?"

He squeezed her tightly. "Not all, but the big man's in town for this one."

Eleanor thought that was interesting and wanted to ask who the "big man" was, but just then a vampire couple strolled past, a man and a woman, both gorgeous, the way they all seemed to be, and so wrapped up in each other that it was difficult to tell where one ended and the other began.

"Are those two . . . you know, *together?*"

Lucifer snorted. "Not likely. Nest mates, probably. Those things can get pretty incestuous, but nothing long term. Vamps don't get *together*—" He kissed the top of her head, to soften his teasing. "—for anything more than a casual fuck."

She frowned. "Why not?"

"No blood, Elle. When a vamp mates, he only drinks from his lover. Like you and me."

A rush of satisfaction made her heart swell even further. This beautiful vampire, this magnificent *male*, had chosen her, and only her. She was his lover, but so much more than that. He *needed* her to survive.

"So it doesn't bother you that I'm human, and not one of you?" She'd worried about that. Vampires were so much stronger, more powerful. Why wouldn't he want a woman like that for his lover? "You wouldn't want me to become a vampire like you?"

"No, *bella*. Never." He tugged her hair, turning her face up for a slow, sensuous kiss. "You're perfect for me, just the way you are," he murmured against her lips.

Present day, Montreal, Quebec, Canada

ELEANOR SHOVED the memory away, keeping her head lowered, so he couldn't see the pain that filled her eyes. Her hands were twisted so tightly together that her fingers were bone white against the black fabric of her pants.

With an effort, she concentrated on loosening her fingers one at a time, letting the blood flow, and taking the pain with it. She wouldn't let him see how much it hurt—not only the memory of what they'd once had, but that his only reaction at seeing her again was to be pissed that she hadn't told him she was alive. As if she was somehow responsible for whatever lies that asshole Derek Pratt had obviously told him. As if that was all that mattered. Not that she was alive, but that she'd hadn't told him about it.

The plane hit the runway with a hard bump, jolting her out of her pointless wondering. None of that mattered. They weren't here to reminisce old times. She had a job to do, and so did Lucifer.

Glancing out the window, she saw a pair of SUVs waiting, along with a line of men in identical black suits with black shirts and black ties. It was as close to a uniform as one could get without wearing khaki.

The pilot brought the plane to a smooth stop parallel to their reception committee, and she stood and gathered her things. There was no "full and complete stop" warning on this flight. Vampires didn't worry about such things.

A moment later, one of the pilots appeared to open the hatch and admit the scent of burning jet fuel and overheated engines. And something else. Eleanor frowned and bent over to peer through the round window. Humans. All of those guards were human. Where were the vampires, the representatives of the Montreal nest who should have been there to greet them, or at least to stake their claim against Lucifer's appearance in their city?

"Who are those people?" she asked Lucifer. She jerked to a halt, realizing that she'd gotten much too close to him. Her earlier refrigerator magnet analogy reared its ugly head.

Lucifer bent sideways to glance out the window. "Those are my daylight guards. Aden arranged for them to meet me here."

"But we're staying in the compound. They'll have—"

"We are *not* sleeping in the compound. It's not secure."

"Hold up. This is *Sophia's* territory—"

"And she agreed with Aden's assessment of the security situation. It was decided after you'd already left for the airport. She probably figured I'd tell you. And now I have."

Eleanor flattened her lips against the words that tried to come out. She would *not* criticize her lady in front of Lucifer. But Sophia should have told her about this herself. A telephone call would have done the job. Granted, she'd had a million things on her mind, getting ready to fly back to Vancouver, and not knowing what sort of clusterfuck she'd be facing there. But still . . . she shouldn't have left Eleanor to be blindsided like this.

"Don't worry, *cara*," Lucifer said casually. "We won't be sharing a bed."

She whipped her head around and stared at him. "What?"

He laughed. "I knew that would get your attention. We're going to a hotel," he explained. "A very nice hotel, with a penthouse suite and two bedrooms. It's been modified to accommodate vampire guests. You'll be perfectly safe. And so will I."

Without another word, he picked up his bag, and ducked through the open hatch, leaving Eleanor to eye the empty space where he'd been. Safe? There was nothing safe about this whole adventure. Just being around Lucifer again was . . . upsetting. An insufficient word for how she was feeling. Unbalanced, unsettled, disturbed. Yeah, disturbed, that was it. He *disturbed* her. The jerk. Why'd he have to be so charming, so gorgeous? And so thoughtful, despite what she'd done to him.

Because she was the one who'd let what they'd had together be destroyed. Derek Pratt had definitely played his part in the destruction, but Lucifer hadn't. He'd been the one person with no fault at all.

A sudden wave of sadness for what she'd lost crashed over her, tightening her chest and blurring her eyes with unshed tears. She forced herself to gather her things. Mourning the past was a waste of time, and time was something they all had in short supply. Especially Colin Murphy.

With a glance around the cabin, she made her way down the aisle to the open door, which was already admitting the sounds and smells of the runway. She paused at the top of the stairs. Lucifer was down there, joking and laughing with the guards like they were old buddies. It was a talent of his. If he'd been human, he'd have been a politician, maybe even president. Or hell, maybe one of those preachers with a mega-church and thousands of followers.

Aware of the two vampire pilots waiting more or less patiently behind her, she descended the stairs, stepping aside for them to pass. Dawn wasn't that far away, and they'd want to get to cover. A human pilot, someone they obviously knew, met them on the tarmac. There were handshakes all around, and then the human headed for the stairs, giving her a polite nod as he went by. The human would be prepping the jet, making sure it was ready for wherever they needed to go next.

Meanwhile the vampire pilots had joined the glad-handing around Lucifer. Obviously, they all knew each other. All they needed was some beer, and they could be a fucking TV commercial. A bunch of good ol' boys getting ready for the game. Or some other male bullshit. No wonder Sophia wanted to chuck it all and move back to South America. Just her and Colin in a house in the forest, with sultry nights and fiery music.

Except that the South American lords would never accept Sophia back among them. She wasn't a pretty, little hedonist any more—she was a vampire lord, ruler of the Canadian Territories. For better or worse, that was her reality.

Lucifer's laugh rose over the crowd down below, familiar and wrenching at the same time. His laughter had a joyful quality to it that made her remember better times, and maybe, just a little, wish for something more.

As if he sensed her weakening resistance—because what woman had *ever* been able to resist him—he turned and smiled. "Ready, Elle?" He held out a hand.

She stared at him a moment. No one else had ever called her that. Damn him.

Ignoring his hand, she headed for the nearest SUV. She didn't know if it was the right one, but it was the only one with an open door, and they could damn well make it work. Who gave a fuck which damn vehicle she rode in?

Before she knew what was happening, Lucifer was sliding in behind her, shoving her across the bench seat with the sheer bulk of his body. She glared at him, but he only winked.

"Buckle up, *cara*. We'll have to travel fast if we want to reach the hotel and settle in before sunrise."

"You'd never know it from all the male bonding going on out there," she muttered.

"Sorry?" he asked.

"I asked which hotel we're staying at?"

His eyes crinkled in amusement, as if he knew she was lying. But he didn't call her on it. "It's a boutique hotel in the old city. I didn't catch the name, except to know that it's European. Scandinavian maybe. We've managed to snag the two top floors. You and I have the penthouse, which is the entire top floor, and the most secure. The daylight guards will set up one floor down, with patrols on all the entry points."

Eleanor considered the situation. She'd have felt much better if she could have scoped out the location for herself, and discussed the plans for the daylight guard in detail. But apparently, she'd been left out of that particular discussion, since she was lacking a penis. Almost as soon as she had the thought, she knew it wasn't true. First of all, Lucifer wasn't like that. If she hadn't been hiding in the plane after they'd landed, moping over the past instead of joining the crowd on the tarmac, she'd have been briefed right alongside him. There was also the fact that Aden had made the hotel arrangements, and so it only made sense that Lucifer knew details that she didn't.

"Does the penthouse have a balcony?"

The human in the front passenger seat responded before Lucifer could say anything. "It does. Each bedroom suite has a private balcony. The penthouse is six floors up, and all of the windows have secure shutters that deploy from inside, but we'll also have a man stationed on each balcony, with constant visual contact. That's in addition to the men on the roof, and on the balconies on the floor below, which we control completely."

"Thank you . . ." she said leadingly.

"Cal," he supplied. "Calvin Christensen. I'll be heading up your daylight security for this trip. We'll also maintain a nighttime watch on the hotel suite when you're out. We travel regularly with Lucifer, so we're old hands at this."

"Thank you," she said again. Then she stared out the window like she'd never seen a city before, studiously ignoring Lucifer . . . the weight of his stare, the heat of his big body (which she could feel like a brand despite the several inches separating them,) the scent of his skin, the soft touch of his hand on her hair . . . wait, what?

She jerked her head around and glared at him. He gave her a slow smile. She knew that smile. He was trying to seduce her. To wear her down. And, damn it, it would work. She couldn't fool herself on that front. She still had feelings for him. Still wanted him. All of the years she'd spent running away suddenly seemed pointless. A few hours back in his presence, and it was as if the years had never happened. Nothing had changed. Her heart still warmed when he smiled at her, still fluttered happily while it pumped that warmth into every inch of her body. And that wasn't the only part of her body that reacted to his presence, either. She had vivid memories of sex with Lucifer, his narrow hips spreading her thighs, his heavy body looming over her, making her feel desired, coveted . . . possessed.

All she had to do was take his hand. Reach across those few inches that separated them, and thread her fingers with his. His hands were so much bigger than her own, so much stronger, even now with her vampire strength.

She sighed. She wasn't going to do that. Her feelings might not have changed, but everything else had. What they'd once had was impossible now, and she had to accept that. The best thing would be to get through this investigation, this *hunt*, as quickly as possible. Find Colin and reunite him with Sophia. Then Lucifer could go back to Aden's Midwest, and she'd return to Vancouver with Sophia. This was the reality of their situation, the reason she'd run all those years ago. He didn't need her anymore. And no amount of dreaming could change that.

LUCIFER WAS IN a fine temper by the time they reached their hotel. He strode through the lobby without stopping at the desk. Cal Christensen had already checked in for them before they arrived, so they were able to go straight into the elevator and up to their sixth floor penthouse.

As promised, the hotel was small, only ten rooms on four floors. Vampires tended to prefer private residences, but most major cities had at least one boutique hotel that catered to their kind. And for Montreal, this was it.

They exited the elevator into a wide foyer with a double-doored entry to the penthouse directly in front of them. The doors opened into a substantial living area, with a wet bar to one side and a fireplace on the other. The far wall was floor to ceiling windows with an unobstructed view of the dark sky above the adjacent buildings, all of which were shorter than their hotel. But then Lucifer didn't give a fuck about the view. The temper riding him wasn't interested in starry skies, unless they were the ones under which Eleanor finally admitted she still had feelings for him, which she obviously did.

Hell, what kind of vampire would he be if he couldn't tell when a woman was attracted to him? And he was a damn powerful vampire. She'd been way more than attracted earlier, she'd been aroused. And he'd bet she still loved him, too; that she'd never stopped. Which suited him just fine, because he'd never stopped loving *her*. He'd never doubted back then that she'd loved him, but despite the joy of discovering that she was alive, it came with the knowledge that she'd *chosen* to leave him, to run away in the night without even a word of explanation. There had to be a reason, something truly shattering to have driven her to such an extreme action.

When he'd seen her standing there tonight, alive and well, and as beautiful as ever, all of the love and desire that had made their life together so passionate and exhilarating had come roaring back to life. But along with it came the pain—the hole in his heart that had taken years to stop bleeding, the ache of waking every night and knowing she was truly gone. And the anger. Hell, the rage he'd felt not only with Derek Pratt, but with Eleanor for letting him believe the lie all these years. For not trusting him enough to tell him the truth.

Yeah, he remembered the passion, but more, he remembered the pain. If nothing else, she owed him a damn explanation. Hell, she owed him a fucking apology. If she wanted to ignore the chemistry between them, the attraction that still pulled on them every time they got close, the desire that pulsed between them . . . he'd grant her that freedom, no matter how much it hurt him. But he deserved to know why.

Unfortunately, he wouldn't be getting an apology or even an explanation tonight. Or rather, this morning. The sun was very near the horizon, blazing a trail of heat up his spine in warning. That didn't mean he had to retire meekly to his bed, however. He walked into one of the rooms and threw his satchel onto the bed, then strode back out into the common area, where Eleanor was just thanking one of the guards for wheeling in her suitcase.

Lucifer continued over to the windows, where he examined the control panel for the heavy shutters, which would drop down to secure the room against sunlight. The panel required a code, which he'd be changing before they retired for the day. He never took chances when it came to daylight security, but with Eleanor's safety at risk, he'd be doubly careful.

With a nod of dismissal, he waited until the human was gone before turning his attention to Eleanor. She was staring at him with a mixture of resolve and trepidation, the latter of which pissed him off even further. He'd never touched her in anger, barely cursed in her direction. The fact that she now stood there looking at him as if waiting for him to lay into her only stoked the fire of his temper.

"We need to lay down some ground rules," he snapped without preamble. "We both want this investigation over with as soon as possible. We both have our reasons. So this is how it's going to be. This is *my* hunt. This is what I do, and I'm damn good at it. You're here as Sophia's rep. Fine. I have no problem with that. But we do things my way. We do what I say, when I say it. If you get in my way, you're out. If you or Sophia don't like it, she can talk to Aden.

"The only thing that matters here is finding Colin Murphy and bringing him back alive. And that's what I intend to do. With or without you."

Eleanor hadn't said a word during his entire speech. She'd started out with an intent expression on her lovely face, her big, blue eyes serious and focused, listening to every word. But as he'd gone on, her expression had cooled, even as her eyes had sparked with fire. By the time he'd finished, she was glaring up at him with a narrow gaze that certainly belied the love he was certain she still harbored for him.

She waited until it was clear he had nothing more to say, and then she muttered, "Arrogant ass," spun on her heel, and marched into her half of the penthouse, closing the door with a force just short of slamming it.

Lucifer grinned. "I think she likes me," he commented to no one in particular. But Cal Christensen, who'd come back into the penthouse just in time to witness Eleanor's parting shot, gave him a doubtful look.

"Is that what you think?" he asked.

Lucifer laughed. He and Cal had been paired on several assignments in the last year, and they worked well together. The man was the closest thing Lucifer had to a human friend.

"Trust me," he said now. "She's definitely warming up to me."

Cal snorted his opinion of that as Lucifer headed for his bedroom. "Sweet dreams, boss."

"Vampires don't dream, Cal. I'll see you tonight."

1993, New Orleans, Louisiana, USA

ELEANOR RAN THE brush through her long, blond hair one last time. Lucifer loved her hair, and it had to be perfect for him. Setting her brush down, she picked up her lip gloss and did a final touch-up. It was pink, and strawberry flavored. Lucifer's favorite. Her friends teased her, saying she was losing herself in him. And some did more than tease. But she didn't care. She loved him, and she'd never been happier. And he loved *her*, too. She was sure of it. Not just because he told her so, but because he showed it in a million little ways every single night they were together.

The sound of knuckles hitting the door made her jump in surprise. She'd left the door unlocked, so Lucifer wouldn't have to knock. He didn't like that she did that. He said it wasn't safe. But she could tell that it pleased him, too. Maybe he'd forgotten, or maybe his arms were full. He'd told her last night that he had a surprise for her. Maybe this was it!

She ran for the door, her feet barely touching the ground in her excitement. She finally understood what writers meant when they said that. She really did feel like she was floating on a cloud of happiness.

She opened the door, laughing as she trilled, "Come in, come in—" Her words caught in her throat when she looked up. "You're not Lucifer," she whispered, horrified to realize what she'd just done.

"Gee, thanks," Derek Pratt said, pushing her back as he crossed the threshold she'd just invited him to step over.

"Derek," she said nervously, hoping Lucifer arrived soon. He'd kick Derek's ass for daring to knock on her door, much less invite himself inside. Okay, so she'd been the one to invite him in, but only because she'd thought he was Lucifer, and had been too stupid to check before she issued that invitation. She never would have let Derek enter her apartment, and certainly not when she was alone. He'd been hustling her that first night, the time she'd met Lucifer. Hell, he'd been after her for weeks before that with no success. Though to hear him tell it, she'd finally been ready to give in to his charm offensive, only a heartbeat away from offering him her vein . . . and then Lucifer had intervened and stolen her away.

Talk about delusional.

She'd never liked Derek, had never even *thought* about giving in to his pursuit. What he saw as a charm offensive, she'd considered something tantamount to harassment. He was good-looking enough, if one liked the strung-out rocker look. Tall and slender, bordering on skinny, but muscular and strong, as all vampires were. It wasn't his looks that made her dislike him, though. Even before Lucifer had appeared on the scene, she'd seen the mean side of Derek. Not toward her, not then. But she'd seen the way he dealt with others, the way he coveted, and the way he hated those who aroused that covetousness.

And he coveted her. Especially now that she and Lucifer were together. She didn't think he wanted her as much for herself anymore, but more because Lucifer had her. Derek had never forgiven her for choosing Lucifer, never forgiven Lucifer for intervening. He never would have understood what she and Lucifer had. Lucifer made her feel safe, cherished. Derek didn't even know what those words meant.

And now, standing in her apartment with him, with no one to see what he might do, and sure as hell no one to stop him, she was scared. She was in danger from Derek, and she knew it.

She tried to be polite, to keep him occupied with meaningless conversation, to delay until Lucifer arrived. Where was he? He should have been there already, and he was rarely late. It made her fear the worst, that Derek had done something to him to slow him down or . . . No, she wouldn't think about that. Lucifer was stronger than Derek. That's why he'd been successful in driving Derek off the first night they met. Just another reason for Derek to hate him.

"Why are you here?" she demanded abruptly.

He gave her a smirking grin. "Lucifer sent me actually," he said casually, as he strolled around her small apartment, lifting and touching and moving her things.

She frowned. "Why would he send *you?*"

"You're an insulting little thing, aren't you? You must have a magical pussy for Lucifer to put up with that shit."

She gasped, her eyes going wide at the crude words. "Get out, Derek," she said again.

"I already told you, sugar. Not going to happen."

"Fine. Just tell me why Lucifer sent you and be done with it."

"Not so fast, darlin'. Some things can't be rushed."

"Like what?" she asked sarcastically, absolutely certain he was full of shit.

"Like this." He *moved* in the way vampires could, closing the distance between them in a blur of vampire speed. Grabbing a length of her long hair, he twisted it around his hand and yanked her head to one side. She screamed, pounding on his side, trying uselessly to break away. But it was too late. It had been too late from the moment she'd opened the damn door.

His teeth sank into her neck, his fangs slicing through her skin and into her vein with a painful burn that she'd never felt with Lucifer. She cried out, tears rolling down her cheeks, but Derek only gripped her harder, groaning in pleasure as her blood rolled down his throat, holding her tight against him with one arm so that she could feel the hard jut of his erection against her belly.

She was nearly choking on her sobs, thrashing in his arms like a fish on a hook, weakening more with every passing moment, every draw of his mouth. A renewed heat burned in her veins as the euphoric in Derek's blood hit her, but she was too weak to do much more than shiver, while he sucked ever harder. Her consciousness began to fade, and she realized he was going to kill her. A creeping darkness stole her thoughts, and she drifted weightlessly for a few sluggish heartbeats.

And then there was nothing.

She woke slowly, sitting up with a terrified shout as she remembered the attack. She shuddered, remembering the stench of Derek's breath on her cheek, the shocking pain when he'd sliced into her vein, the acidic burn of his bite in her veins. Reaching up, she touched her neck, almost afraid to discover the ruin he'd left behind. But while her neck was tender and sore, her fingers told her the wound was already healed. She rubbed the smooth skin and came away with flakes of dried blood beneath her nails.

She blinked to awareness. It was dark outside the windows. She sat up. She was . . . so hungry. How much time had passed?

"Welcome to the new world, Eleanor darling. You're mine now."

The truth crashed in on her and she screamed, drowning in a loss greater than any she could have imagined.

Chapter Four

Present Day, Montreal, Quebec, Canada

LUCIFER STEPPED OUT of the shower and grabbed a towel, striding naked into the bedroom of his suite, and not slowing until he reached for the knob and yanked his door open wide enough to see directly into the main sitting room. Head tilted, he stared across the empty space to Eleanor's still-closed door and listened. He could have sworn he heard a scream. But that made no sense. Everything was quiet and calm. He could sense the human guards in the hallway and outside, beyond the shuttered windows. They were alert, their heartbeats steady and even, with no evidence of alarm.

Still uneasy, he stepped back into his suite and closed the door, then walked over and picked up his cell phone, where he stabbed the speed dial for Cal Christensen.

"Lucifer," Cal answered. "You're awake," he said, stating the obvious.

"Were there any disturbances during the day? Anything this evening so far?" he asked, affecting a casual air, as if this was nothing but a routine conversation opener.

"Nothing all day. The noise is picking up some tonight, a lot of traffic and horns. But the hotel's head of security tells me that's normal for a Friday night around here."

Lucifer scowled. He hadn't thought about it being the weekend, but decided it wouldn't make any difference. "Okay, thanks," he said to Cal. "We'll be out in a bit." He disconnected, and with a final glance in the direction of Eleanor's half of the penthouse, walked back into the bathroom and finished drying off from his shower.

EVERYTHING WAS STILL quiet from Eleanor's suite when Lucifer opened his door again and crossed into their shared space. He was restless and unsettled, an unusual experience for him. He tended to be focused, almost single-minded, some would say. Especially when on a hunt. But he'd woken with that sense of missing something, and then there'd been that scream during his shower . . . . No matter what anyone else said, he knew what he'd heard, and he wouldn't be able to let it go until Eleanor poked her pretty head out through that doorway.

He was being foolish, and not very productive. He was the one who'd been lecturing everyone else on the primacy of the hunt above everything else, and here he was, mooning like a day-old calf. And over a woman who'd left him more than twenty years ago.

Determined to complete the task that Aden had set him, which also happened to be the only reason they were in this city, he grabbed the file with pictures and witness statements, and sat at the table in the living room of the penthouse. He needed to go over everything one more time. He'd missed something, something that his subconscious mind had caught, and was trying to warn him about. This was what he was good at. He noticed the tiny details, the slip of a witness's tongue, the seemingly insignificant changes in their statements, the color of the door they'd passed two blocks ago. Combined with his natural charisma, and a vampire-enhanced talent that made people want to please him, it made him a very good hunter.

So he started at the beginning of his evidence, the beginning of what they knew, and went through it piece by piece one more time. Every document was so familiar by now that he could have recited them line by line from memory. But that didn't deter him from reading them again. And when he finished that, he scanned every photograph from edge to edge, noting the tiny details that could make a difference, that could be the one thing he'd missed.

As he sat there, part of his awareness registered noise from behind Eleanor's door, sounds that told him she was awake and alert, moving around, getting ready. She'd be out here soon, and he could ask her about the scream. He frowned. Or maybe not. She probably wouldn't tell him anyway, and they didn't need any more secrets between them.

He was flipping through the photographs, one ear tuned to the sounds Eleanor was making, when something caught his eye. He frowned, staring down at the photograph in front of him. He scrutinized it carefully. Nothing, but . . . the photograph *before* that one. He flipped back two photographs to be safe, and gave them the same careful examination. The first one revealed nothing new, so he moved on to the second photo, the one he'd passed on just before that shock of awareness stabbed his consciousness.

It was a standard interrogation photograph. A young human female sitting at a table, being interviewed by a vampire he didn't recognize. He assumed the vamp was one of Sophia's people, but couldn't narrow it down any more than that.

But that wasn't the thing that was bothering him. He studied the photograph patiently. He never rushed this sort of thing. It didn't work that way. He focused on the woman, since she was the only unique aspect of the photo. The interrogator was the same vampire as the previous interviews, the room was the same room, and no one else was in the photograph.

She was reasonably attractive—early 20s, dark hair cut in a chin length bob, slender shoulders. He glanced at the interview date—just under a week ago, the same Saturday night Colin had been taken. There'd been no delay in discovering his abduction. Several witnesses had come forward almost immediately to report the crime, although most were irritatingly vague on details.

Now that he thought about it, this young woman had provided one of the better accounts of the kidnapping, with details that the others had only hinted at, although even those details had been mostly background, rather than names or faces. He examined the photo more carefully. The woman was dressed casually for a Saturday night, but not every human went out dancing on the weekend. Maybe she'd been meeting friends for a pizza . . . that would fit her clothing choice of a plain white tee and what looked from this angle like ordinary jeans. The T-shirt had a V-neck, and she wore a necklace—a simple chain with a round pendant in an abstract pattern that was saved from being ordinary by the single diamond mounted on the . . .

The proverbial light bulb lit up over his head. It was the pendant. Or not the pendant, but the design. He'd seen that somewhere else. Where, where, where?

It had to be one of the photographs he'd seen. A description wouldn't have itched his brain this much. Another witness wearing the same pendant? No, why would he care about that? But he went through the images just to be sure, running fingers through his thick hair and messing it up as he considered where else he might have seen it.

"Problems?" Eleanor asked quietly.

He spun around, surprised she'd been able to sneak up on him.

"I didn't sneak up on you," she said with amazing acuity. There was no way she could have read his thoughts, but it did indicate a certain intuitiveness on her part. "You looked frustrated."

He regarded her a long moment, trying to decide how much to

share. He wasn't used to having a partner, and wasn't sure he liked it. Not even Eleanor. *Especially* not her.

"A photograph," he said finally with a shrug. "I know I've seen this design somewhere."

"Something connecting witnesses?" she asked, coming over and sitting across from him, placing her own folder on the table, stuffed full of similar bits and pieces of evidence.

Lucifer shook his head. "I can't rule it out, but I don't think so. A link between two witnesses wouldn't have any significance. There were a lot of people on that street, and most of them were with other people. A link between a witness and one of the *kidnappers,* on the other . . ." He paused. No light bulb this time, but the realization was far more profound.

"The kidnapping videos," they both said at the same time. The videos were the only images they had of the kidnappers, so if there was something, it had to be on the video. He grinned at her. "Great minds, *bella.* Want to watch a movie with me?"

She grimaced. "Not those movies."

He tipped his head curiously. "But you *do* want to watch a movie with me," he said, flirting shamelessly. She wanted him. But he'd have to break down the walls she'd erected against the truth of what they'd once meant to each other. What they still could, if only she'd be honest with him. And with herself.

She seemed flustered for a brief moment, but she covered it quickly. "I'll watch whatever it takes to get the job done," she informed him stiffly.

He nodded, trying not to grin. Oh, yeah, he was getting to her. But if she didn't want him to know about it, he wasn't going to force her to deal. That wasn't the way to her heart. So, he simply said, "We can probably throw the video up on the big screen there," he said.

A few keystrokes and a lot of expletives later, he had the video from his laptop playing on the big TV monitor in the penthouse's main room. It wasn't pleasant watching. Colin Murphy's captors were being deliberately cruel, wanting to hurt Sophia as much as they did her mate. Lucifer had to give Murphy credit, though. He was enduring the torture as well as any vampire could have. Even better when you considered the fact that a vampire's pain threshold was much higher, and that any damage the torturers inflicted would heal itself eventually.

"Murphy is a tough son of a bitch," Lucifer observed, trying to keep the admiration out of his voice. He did admire the human's strength and courage, but showing it seemed too much like cheering on his team in a sporting event. And there was nothing sporting about what was happening on that screen.

Eleanor nodded. "Sophia had good reasons for making him her security chief, and not just because she loves him."

Lucifer shifted uneasily. "Yeah. I'm sorry to say this, given the circumstances," he said, lifting his chin to indicate the torture video, "but it was a mistake for Sophia to make him her lieutenant. It—"

"Darren Yamanaka's her lieutenant, not—"

"In name only, Elle. You know it, and so does everyone else. Including Yamanaka himself. I'm not saying—"

"You'd better not be saying what I think you are."

He made an impatient noise. "I'm not blaming anyone," he said clearly. "But as badass as Murphy is, vampires won't accept a human giving them orders. And you can't ignore—Wait. Stop right there," he said, grabbing the remote to move the image frame by frame. "Back up a little," he muttered to himself, slowly putting action to words. "And there. Right there. I noted this earlier. Whoever positioned the camera for this video pulled back a little farther than the previous one. It widens the frame, so you occasionally get glimpses of the off-screen actors. No faces, or anything, just a sense of movement, something the videos before *and* after this one were careful to avoid. We all know there are vampires doing the torturing, but we haven't seen anything of them. Until . . . this."

Eleanor was studying the frozen image, her eyes moving as she scanned every inch of it. She frowned. You mean—" Her frown deepened. "—that hand? What good is that? It's just the back, and not even all of it. Just a couple of knuckles and a finger"

"Not the hand itself, baby. The tattoo. See how it arcs down over his finger, how it ends with a sharpened point like a curved knife or sword."

"Okay," she said slowly. "I still don't know what good that does us. Is it unique, like a logo or something?"

"Unique, but not a logo. Now, look here . . . look at this woman's necklace." He handed her the still photo of the woman he'd locked on earlier. "Look at the pendant she's wearing."

Eleanor studied the two images, going back and forth, her lips pursed enticingly. Lucifer had fond memories of those lips, of that mouth. Kissing, sucking—

"I need to re-interview that woman," he said, dragging his thoughts back to the task at hand.

"I'm not sure they're the same," Eleanor said slowly.

Lucifer ignored her doubts. He was used to that kind of reaction from people around his investigations, and it never stopped him. He knew what he was seeing. It was precisely that kind of catch that made him a better hunter than anyone else.

"*I am*," he said confidently. "But we need to bring *all* of the witnesses back. If she's connected to one of the kidnappers, I don't want to raise her suspicions. You should make the call. These are Sophia's vamps. But have them schedule this woman right away. Tonight, if possible. But not the first interview. Make it later. I want her relaxed, maybe even a little irritated at the inconvenience. A pissed off witness is more likely to make a mistake."

Eleanor shrugged. "It's your investigation. For now anyway," she added, with a dark look. "Besides, it's not like we have a shitload of other leads to follow."

"I'm touched by your confidence in me," Lucifer said absently, his attention on the information sheet that Sophia's security team had provided on each witness. "I want the rest of the witnesses brought in, too, but let Sophia's vampires do that, unless we find something else. Tell them to start bringing people in tonight, but not until they've successfully contacted our pendant girl. I don't want any schedule conflicts. She works retail in the Underground City," he noted, reading the info on the back of the photo. "She probably has irregular hours, but . . . wait. Here's her cell number. Why don't you give her a call? She might respond better to you."

"Because I'm a woman?" she demanded.

"Well, yeah," he said honestly. "What's wrong with that? We need to use every tool at our disposal, and you being female happens to be one of those tools in this instance. Is that a problem?"

"You're the charmer here, not me," she muttered.

"That's true," he said cheerfully. "But my charms work best in person. Which is where I want to be with Miss—" He peered down at the witness info form. "—Fiona Denis. So . . . give her a call for me, okay, bella?"

Her luscious mouth tightened irritably, and he knew it was because he persisted in using endearments, as if they were still lovers. He was doing it intentionally, forcing her to confront her feelings—good or bad—where he was concerned. She'd been trying to keep him at a distance, to put him on a business-only footing, ever since he'd shown up at the airport. But hell if he was going to let her do that. She'd run once rather than confronting whatever bugaboo had crawled up her ass, without even trying to talk to him about it. Not this time. If she wanted to go their separate ways once this hunt was over, to forget he existed, that was fine. But before that happened, she was damn well going to face what they'd had together, what they *still* had together. And she was going to tell him what the fuck had made her run all those years ago.

"What's her number?" she snapped.

He grinned as he read off the phone number, and he was still grinning an hour later when he and Eleanor set out to interview some witnesses, including one Fiona Denis.

ELEANOR WALKED into the small interrogation room and cast a deceptively casual glance at the human woman waiting for them there. Fiona Denis was in her twenties. Blond, with brown eyes, and wearing a V-neck blouse that exposed considerable cleavage along with the necklace that Lucifer was so interested in.

"Speak of the devil," Eleanor thought privately, as Lucifer strolled in several steps behind her. He was a study in masculine perfection, with his black hair and striking eyes, his broad shoulders and narrow hips, every muscle moving in concert with the others. She dragged her attention back to Fiona, and caught the woman eyeing Lucifer with blatant hunger in her gaze.

What the fuck? If Lucifer was right, the human had a lover of her own. There was no cause for her to be eyeing Lucifer like something delicious that she wanted to take a bite of. Lucifer was *hers*.

Her thoughts screeched to a halt. Lucifer *wasn't* hers. Not anymore. And he never would be. That bastard Derek had closed off the possibility forever when he'd decided to make her a vampire. It hadn't been *her* choice, but that didn't change anything. Not when it came to her and Lucifer.

She closed her eyes against the familiar pain, shoving it down where it was less distracting. It never went away, not completely, but at least she could bury it deep enough that she could do what was necessary. And tonight, that meant interviewing a woman who was currently leaning forward, arms bracketing her breasts, all but shoving them into Lucifer's face.

His gaze rested briefly on the offering, before he met the human's eyes and gave her a devastating smile. "Fiona Denis, is it?" he asked, looking down at her file, as if he didn't already know who she was.

"That's right," she responded with a friendly grin of her own. "Can you tell me how long this will take? My boss is a bitch, and I have to get back to work." She was speaking English, but with a heavy Quebecois accent.

"It takes as long as it takes," Eleanor snapped, irritated beyond reason at the nervy bitch. The reason was Lucifer, of course, but she didn't want to acknowledge that. Or why it was so.

"Don't worry about your employer," Lucifer crooned, softening Eleanor's harshness. "We'll take care of all that. She'll understand." He took a seat that put him directly across from Fiona. The seat also happened to put him far too close to Eleanor, his shoulders so broad that her arm was pressed up against his. So warm, so very solid with muscle.

This wouldn't do. She wanted to move, but that would have been too obvious. She didn't want him to know he affected her, but it was everything she could do to prevent her muscles from stiffening at the contact, to pretend it didn't matter. When in reality, it was as if they were two live wires twisting around each other and sparking like crazy.

Eleanor gritted her teeth, and forced her attention back to where it belonged.

Fiona Denis was smiling at Lucifer's reassuring words—a toothy, sunny sort of smile. *Someone* had been spending time with a cosmetic dentist; that was for sure.

While next to her Lucifer seemed to be . . . twitching, as if he was nervous. Eleanor frowned and glanced over at him. Lucifer was *never* nervous. She'd never met a more confident, arrogant son of a bitch. She looked harder. He wasn't twitching, he was laughing, his big body shuddering with the effort to conceal it.

What the hell was so funny? Eleanor had a moment of panic. Was it her? Had he somehow tapped into her thoughts and . . . No, that was impossible. Even for Lucifer. It had been over twenty years since he'd taken her blood; they didn't have that connection anymore. So, maybe it wasn't her at all. Maybe he found Fiona's blatant attempts to seduce him as ridiculous as she did.

"We've gone over your statement, Fiona," he said, speaking her name like a caress. The bastard. "You're remarkably consistent about what you saw."

"I didn't see that much. It wasn't—"

"You must have excellent recall," he said, sounding completely sincere. "I wish every witness was as clear and concise. It makes our job so much easier."

"What *is* your job?" Fiona ventured, speaking in a tiny voice, as if afraid to offend the big, bad vampire.

"Well, one of our own was taken, and we have strict policies about that sort of thing."

"But he's not—" she began to protest, but caught herself. "That is, I heard that it was a man who was kidnapped. A regular man, not a vampire."

"Mmm," Lucifer agreed absently. "But he's also a vampire lord's mate, and that means there's nothing regular about him. Or this kidnapping," he added, perusing her previous statement, as if he hadn't already memorized every word. "Tell me, Fiona—" He glanced up with a quick smile. "You don't mind if I call you Fiona?"

"Of course not," she said, blushing like a fucking virgin. Eleanor snorted quietly. As if.

"Initially, you said you didn't see anything, but then later—" He ran a finger down the page. "—you say you thought you saw the getaway car."

She shook her head. "No, I said I saw a *van* driving away really fast, and I *thought* it might be the getaway vehicle."

"Ah, that makes sense. So you never saw Mr. Murphy's actual abduction, nor do you know who took him?"

She blinked rapidly, as if she needed a moment to process his question, then she nodded, and said, "That's right. I didn't see them kidnap him."

Lucifer tilted his head, as if the human had said something interesting, and Eleanor abruptly knew why. Fiona had carefully answered only the first part of his question. Humans couldn't lie to a vampire, especially not one with any kind of real power. Lucifer had that power and to spare. Eleanor wasn't as strong as he was, but she did have power. More than enough to tell if little Miss Fiona was lying. Hell, she'd had enough power to dump that creep Derek's ass only days after her turning. A real Sire would have had the strength to stop her. But Derek had possessed far more ambition than he had power or brains. Unfortunately, his hatred for Lucifer had been stronger than either of those. She'd never even considered that he might tell Lucifer she was dead.

And there she went again, thinking about what might have been, instead of doing her job, which was to find Colin Murphy. She'd lost the love of *her* life long ago, but she was determined that the same thing wasn't going to happen to Sophia.

"You didn't see the abduction, did you, Fiona?"

She looked relieved at the question. "I'm sorry, but I didn't."

Lucifer raised his head slowly and met the woman's eyes, holding her gaze with the force of his unusual talent. He could probably make a person tell him anything he wanted. Hell, he could probably make them *do* just about anything, too. Eleanor thought about it. Maybe not a vampire lord. They had their own power and talents, which no doubt matched or even, in some cases, exceeded Lucifer's. So he probably couldn't mesmerize *them*.

But he was more than a match for Fiona Denis.

"But you do know who kidnapped him, don't you?" Lucifer asked.

"No," she insisted, while Eleanor did some lie detecting of her own. The woman wasn't lying, not precisely. But she wasn't telling the truth either.

Lucifer tilted his head, giving the human a warm smile that held a touch of complicity, as if they held a secret between just the two of them. "That's a lovely necklace," he said.

Fiona jerked in surprise at the seeming non sequitur. She cradled the pendant protectively, as if afraid they were going to rip it from her throat. "It was gift," she said defensively.

"A very unusual design. I've never seen one like it." The woman started to say something, but sucked in a breath as Lucifer kept talking. "Had *you* ever seen this design before, Fiona?"

The woman's heart was racing so fast and pounding so hard, that Eleanor feared they'd lose her to a heart attack before she could tell them what she knew. Because it didn't take a vampire lord's power to know that Fiona Denis was lying. And it wasn't only about the necklace, either. It was much bigger than that.

"It's a very nice gift," Lucifer said, not waiting for her answer. "Was it from a boyfriend . . . maybe a *lover*?" His voice went deep and chocolaty smooth at the end, and Eleanor found herself responding to the seduction packed into that single word. She could only imagine what it was doing to the human woman. But he wasn't finished yet.

"What's his name, Fiona?" he murmured. "You know you want to tell me."

She was staring at Lucifer, her eyes big and round, and filled with tears, her teeth biting into her lower lip hard enough to draw blood. The scent filled the air of the small room. Eleanor felt Lucifer's attention shift, and looked up to meet his gaze. She saw hunger there. And heat. And it wasn't for the small drop of blood on Fiona's lip either.

A corresponding heat filled her chest. Her lungs expanded with deep, slow breaths. Such a common thing, breathing. And yet it suddenly seemed as if she hadn't breathed fully in so long that she'd forgotten how. Not since . . . oh God, not since she'd been made a vampire and had run away from Lucifer, who was staring at her right now as if he could read every thought in her head, every desire.

Fiona's loud sobbing abruptly shattered the loaded silence between them, dragging Lucifer's attention back to the human woman. Eleanor almost sobbed herself, drooping in exhausted relief, as if she'd just run a few miles instead of simply staring at her former lover for a few minutes. Why had she thought she could do this? She'd been with Lucifer on this hunt for only one night so far, and already she was filled with more emotion than she'd permitted herself in the last twenty years. It was crushing her, forcing her to *feel*. And it wasn't fair. Fate and Derek Pratt had taken him away from her. It wasn't right that she had to sit so close to him, work with him, watch him seduce fucking Fiona Denis and who knew how many other women. And all because of God damned Derek Pratt.

"Get a grip," Eleanor scolded herself. She was better than this. She owed Sophia better than this. The vampire lord needed Eleanor to find her kidnapped *mate* before something even more terrible happened. There was nothing more sacred to a vampire, nothing closer to one's heart, than a mate. And Sophia had trusted *Eleanor* to save Colin, to bring him back home. It was time to do her fucking job.

She forced her attention back to Lucifer's interrogation.

"Who is it?" Lucifer was asking, his knuckles stroking Fiona's cheek gently, before he cupped her fragile jaw in his big hand. "Tell me, Fiona," he commanded softly, but not so softly that Eleanor couldn't hear the force behind the quiet words.

Big fat tears rolled down the woman's cheeks, dripping over Lucifer's fingers. "It's his tattoo," she whispered, and then choked out a single, loud sob.

"The pendant, you mean. It's based on a tattoo," Lucifer said, and Eleanor could hear the satisfaction in his voice. "Where?" he asked, the single word uncompromising in its demand.

"On his hand," Fiona said, crying so hard now, that the words came out on a hiccup of sound.

Lucifer exchanged a triumphant glance with Eleanor, before turning back to his witness. "And what's his name? Your lover," he said quickly, clarifying the vague question. "The one who gave you the necklace."

Fiona had stopped crying, stopped doing anything. She slumped over the table, her head hanging low, her hands clutching her forehead, staring at nothing. "Kevin," she said, her voice hoarse and exhausted. "Kevin Russell."

"Kevin Russell," Lucifer repeated, looking at Eleanor to see if she recognized the name. She shook her head. The name meant nothing to her. "Where's Kevin now, sweetheart?" he asked the woman gently.

She rolled her head on the palms of her hands, seeming too tired to do anything else. "I don't know. I swear. This wasn't his idea."

"What wasn't?" Lucifer asked coyly, but with an edge of cruelty that Eleanor had never seen in him before. It made her stomach tighten painfully, and she wasn't comfortable with his interrogation anymore. He was forcing the woman to betray the person she loved, perhaps to his death, if Lucifer needed him dead in order to get to Colin. And he was doing it casually, as if it meant nothing. Just another piece of the puzzle, another step in the hunt that would end with Lucifer's victory.

"The kidnapping," Fiona said dully. She looked up suddenly, giving Lucifer a pleading look. "They offered him a lot of money, because he worked on the tunnels. You know, like putting in the walls and stuff."

"The tunnels. Is that where they're holding the prisoner?"

She nodded, shuddering with fear. For herself, and her lover. "I think so. But I don't know exactly where, and Kevin hasn't been back since they took him."

"You said they gave him money. Who's 'they'? Give me a name." Lucifer wasn't seducing anymore. There was no kindness, no persuasion. It was a demand for information, and if he liked what she told him, he might let her live. He didn't say the words. He didn't have to. Some part of the human woman's genetic memory, some instinct buried so deeply she didn't even know it was there, understood. Her life was on the line, and Fiona wanted to live.

"Chase Landry, but . . ." She sucked in a tentative breath, as if afraid to say whatever came next. Her eyes widened, and her pupils, already dilated with fear, nearly drowned out her irises completely. "They're vampires," she said quickly. "Kevin and Landry, and probably some others, too."

Lucifer tilted his head curiously. "Well, that makes sense." He glanced at Eleanor once again, asking silently if she knew either of the vamps Fiona had given up. But she shook her head. This was Darren Yamanaka's home ground. He was the one who'd know the names, know the vampires. That was his job. He should have been the one standing here, questioning Fiona, leading the effort to save Colin. His complete absence spoke louder than any accusation about his involvement.

"My lady will know," Eleanor said quietly, then tipped her head in Fiona's direction. She wanted to ask a question. Lucifer nodded.

"Did Kevin ever talk about someone named Darren?"

Fiona shifted her attention to Eleanor, eyeing her up and down, the way some women do. Scoping out the competition, deciding if they can be dismissed as a serious contender. Whatever she found in Eleanor, it made her sit up straighter in her chair, thrusting her breasts out to good advantage, while she ran her fingers under her eyes to remove any mascara that had gathered there. Eleanor could have told her it was way too late, that she was sporting a pair of raccoon eyes that would need a hell of a lot more than a quick swipe of her fingers. But she wasn't feeling particularly charitable toward the woman, so she said nothing at all, simply flashed a hint of fang to let the human know what she was dealing with.

Fiona blinked in surprise, but her survival instinct was in complete on-mode by now, so she nodded eagerly. "Kevin talked about him. Darren Yama-something. Japanese, I think. He's a vampire, too, but way more important than Chase. I think he might even be Chase's boss."

Eleanor sighed. She wasn't exactly surprised that Darren was involved. But it still shocked her that he could have betrayed Sophia so badly. That kind of disloyalty, a violation of every oath he'd made to Sophia as his lord . . . Eleanor simply couldn't imagine it. She looked up and met Lucifer's questioning gaze, nodding to indicate she was finished with the woman.

"Thank you, Fiona," he purred, stroking the woman's cheek in a gentle caress that made Eleanor want to snatch his hand away. "You can go now. And if anyone asks, you told us nothing about the kidnapping, nothing about Kevin or his friends. Because you don't know anything about that, do you, sweetheart?"

Fiona shook her head, an innocent smile on her face. "Kevin told me not to say," she confided sweetly. "So I can't tell you."

"Of course, not. I understand. You can go back to work now. Maybe stop in the restroom to fix your makeup first, all right?"

Her smile widened in relief as she stood up, brushing her hands over her blouse and along the sides of a skirt so tight that Eleanor didn't know how she managed to walk. Fiona gave Lucifer a final flirtatious glance, and then with a little wave of her fingers hurried out the door.

Eleanor waited until the door closed behind her. "Was that wave your idea, too?" she asked sourly.

Lucifer laughed. "Oh, no. That was all Fiona," he said cheerfully, but quickly sobered. "So you don't recognize any of those names?"

"I know Darren Yamanaka, but the others?" She shook her head. "Sophia should know them, though. Maybe not Russell—he seems low on the ladder—but she should recognize Chase Landry if he worked directly with Darren."

"Even if she doesn't know him personally, she sure as hell can still track him down quickly enough. He's a vampire; she's his lord—assuming he's Canadian. She can reach out and touch his heart if she wants."

Eleanor swallowed. She knew that was true. She remembered the night she'd taken her blood oath to Sophia. Her heart had seemed to stop beating for a moment, and she'd been afraid she was about to die. But then she'd felt Sophia's power flowing over and around her, and she'd known she was exactly where she was supposed to be.

"It's late," Lucifer said, gathering up the few files he'd brought with him. "We should get back to the hotel, but first . . ." He studied her from across the room. "Do you need to feed, Elle?"

She found herself blushing, which was stupid. And it was Lucifer's fault. Being around him left her feeling off-balance, not herself. She needed some distance. She needed privacy. Who cared if he was right; she *was* hungry. But the very *last* thing she needed was to go on a blood run with Lucifer Scuderi. Whether it was a club or a dark street corner, the very act of feeding was far too intimate to share with him.

His gaze darkened abruptly. "Stop doing that," he snapped.

Eleanor scowled. First, he had no right to snap at her like that. He wasn't her boss; he was barely an acquaintance. But secondly . . . "Stop doing what?"

"Acting human. It's not necessary. We're *vampires*, we can *be* vampires, and fuck whatever the humans might think."

"I don't know what you're talking about," she said, her own anger rising to meet his.

He studied her silently. "You were doing it last night, too," he said. "The longer you're with me, the more . . ." She watched realization darken his eyes even further. "Is that why you left me?"

She didn't want to answer that question. She'd spent the last twenty-three years avoiding those answers, and she had no intention of letting Lucifer change that now.

"You're right," she said abruptly, and started for the door. "I need to feed. I'll update Sophia, and then I'll see you tomorrow night."

"Eleanor!"

His voice chased her down the hall, but she pretended not to hear, doing what she did best. Running away.

LUCIFER PACED THE main room of the suite he shared with Eleanor, watching the windows, waiting for her to return, feeling the heat of the impending sunrise in his bones. She should be back by now. She was young by vampire standards. She wouldn't be able to remain awake much past the first swell of the rising sun. Perhaps not even that long. It depended on how much vampire power she had packed into her tight little body. He could have checked that easily enough, but he hadn't, because he didn't want to push too hard. Logically, he knew she must be strong, because she was Sophia's bodyguard. It helped that she was a woman, but Sophia would never have agreed to the assignment just because Eleanor was female. If she wasn't up to the task, she wouldn't have the job, no matter how much Sophia liked her personally. In the final analysis, vampires, especially the truly powerful ones, were coldly practical. They made the hard decisions, weighed lives in their hands like so many pennyweights every single night. Power was great, but power brought responsibility with it, the need to do what was necessary, rather than right or convenient. He understood this. Those same instincts flowed in his veins, too. It was what would make him a lord someday, with a territory of his own.

But right now, those instincts were telling him that Eleanor had some power of her own, something she tried to hide when he was around. Hell, it was more than just hiding her power. It was almost as if she was pretending not to be a vampire at all. He was surprised it had taken him this long to recognize what she was doing, but he'd been distracted by the fact that she was here at all, that she was *alive*.

Unfortunately, now that he'd discovered that Derek had lied and Eleanor hadn't died back in New Orleans, he was beginning to suspect why she'd run. And there was nothing he could do to change it. No, not true. There was nothing he could do to change the fact that they were both vampires. But he sure as hell could demand to know why she thought it made a difference.

His head swung toward the double doors as a distant ding announced the elevator's arrival. He heard Cal Christensen, and then he sighed in relief at the sound of Eleanor's voice returning the human guard's greeting. She was back in time; she was safe. But it was too late for the conversation they so needed to have.

Moving quietly and swiftly, he slipped into his bedroom, pushing the door nearly shut just as he heard the hallway door click open. Eleanor's soft footsteps paused for a moment inside the main room, and Lucifer could picture her standing there, her big blue eyes first searching, and then closing in relief to discover he'd already gone to bed. A moment later, she hurried through the living area and into her private half of the penthouse, shutting the heavy doors with a firm click.

Lucifer smiled. She was safe, and that was all that mattered for tonight. But tomorrow was another sunset, and Eleanor was forgetting one thing. He was older and stronger, and he'd be awake much earlier than she would. Which meant that when Eleanor emerged from her bedroom tomorrow night, he'd be waiting. And at long last, there would be nothing but truth between them.

Vancouver, British Columbia, Canada

SOPHIA GLANCED out at the waiting limos as her private jet rolled to a stop on the wet tarmac. It rained a lot in this part of Canada. What had possessed Lucien to establish his territory in such a cold, wet place? He easily could have ruled somewhere in South America. He'd had the power. She missed South America sometimes, with its balmy heat and slow nights. Or maybe she was missing the freedom she'd had when she'd lived there, rather than the place.

She looked away, studying the vampires onboard the aircraft with her instead. She touched each of them in turn, a light touch there and gone, nothing they'd have sensed. But she was driven to test their loyalties these days. It was becoming an obsession. It was becoming a *problem*. She'd had no indication that any of the people closest to her were disloyal, none of her Vancouver staff. Someone had betrayed Colin and set up his abduction, but that had been in Montreal, far from her headquarters and her personal security people or advisors. It was insulting to all of them for her to suspect otherwise.

And yet she couldn't seem to stop herself from doing exactly that.

One of the pilots unlatched and opened the jet's heavy exit door, then pulled it open to admit a wave of cold, wet air. Sophia sighed.

"Welcome home, my lady," someone said.

Sophia looked up at the unexpected greeting. Or rather, not so much the greeting as the person saying it. "Danika," she acknowledged, concealing her surprise. The tall, slender vampire with her white blond hair was well down the ranks of Sophia's security personnel here in

Vancouver. So why was she the one meeting Sophia's plane?

"Where's Tambra?"

Tambra Laws was one of the few Vancouver vampires whom Sophia trusted implicitly. This was largely because Tambra was Sophia's own vampire child. When she'd responded to Lucien's call to return to Vancouver nearly two years ago, she'd had no children of her own and hadn't particularly wanted any. For that matter, becoming a vampire lord hadn't been on her radar either. Then Lucien had died, and left her in charge. But not before fucking up everything. She'd inherited all of his problems and his people, with no popular base of her own. She was sure that most of Lucien's people supported her, if for no other reason than that they depended on her to keep living. But the only way for a vampire lord to be absolutely sure of her people's loyalty was to fill the inner ranks with her own children.

Great. As if Sophia had had nothing else to do over the last year and a half except searching for suitable candidates and creating new vampires. It wasn't something she could do on a whim. She couldn't simply point at humans on the street, and say, "I like the looks of that one. Let's do him."

Her vampire children would be bound to her for life, just as she'd be bound to them. And a vampire's life could be a very long fucking time. She didn't want a bunch of assholes hanging around forever, just because she'd been feeling needy.

She *had* managed to make a few children, but they were scattered across her very large territory. Tambra was one of the few who resided on Sophia and Colin's estate in Vancouver, in the barracks, which were far more elegant than the name implied.

When Sophia had left Eleanor behind in Montreal, she'd fully expected to have Tambra by her side in Vancouver. Keeping her temper in check . . . for now . . . she gazed up at Danika, and waited for an answer.

"Tambra's in Calgary, my lady, dealing with that business over the human trespassers on the Calgary compound."

Sophia knew the case, but she'd thought the hearing was still some weeks away.

Danika saw her frown and intuited its meaning. "The hearing was moved up. We barely had any warning."

Sophia lifted her chin in acknowledgement, finding it curious that Tambra hadn't mentioned anything about this to *her*. They'd spoken on the phone . . . She thought back. Well, they'd only spoken on the phone once while Sophia was in Montreal, and it might have been before the hearing date changed. Or maybe Tambra hadn't considered it worth mentioning, given the overriding fact of Colin's abduction.

"Very well," she said finally. "I want to be kept up to date on the Calgary situation, and I want to speak with Tambra directly when she calls."

"Of course, my lady."

"Do you have a security briefing for me?"

Danika held out an iPad encased in a black leather folio. "Right here, my lady."

Sophia took the device. "Anything of note?" she asked. She'd read the entire briefing before going to sleep this morning, but if there was anything urgent, she needed to know about it. Like the situation in Calgary. She frowned. The more she thought about that, the more it troubled her. Fucking convenient timing to have one of her most trusted aides out of the city during this critical time. It made her want to scan every vampire on the plane all over again.

If only Lucien had stuck around to clean up his own mess, instead of taking the coward's way out and leaving it all to Sophia. And now, just when she'd begun to feel as though she was making progress, this whole European clusterfuck had descended on the continent. Berkhard was the German vampire lord who'd helped Mathilde in her ultimately doomed attempt to murder Raphael, and who now seemed determined to claim a chunk of North America for himself. *Sophia's* chunk to be precise.

She wasn't all that surprised he'd targeted her, however. According to Christian Duvall—the newly anointed Lord of the South who'd recently arrived from Europe and so knew the various lords there— Berkhard didn't credit females with either courage or strength. Forget the fact that he'd been allied with Mathilde. Mathilde had been a few centuries old and, by all accounts, a hard as nails bitch.

But Sophia knew her own reputation. She was powerful as hell, but no one saw that. They saw the beautiful woman who'd spent the last hundred years dancing her way through South America's sultry nights and hot men. And it didn't help that she was Lucien's child, either. Everyone knew that Lucien had selected his children for their beauty. He'd been looking for talented lovers, not skilled fighters.

Sophia wasn't Lucien, and she wasn't one of his all-beauty/no-brains bed partners either. She was one hell of a lot stronger than Berkhard or anyone else credited her with. Normally, she didn't mind being underestimated. It was very useful in a fight, or in a war, which this was shaping up to be. But right now . . . right now, she didn't need this crap. She didn't want to be here in Vancouver getting ready to fight off a European invasion. She wanted to be in Montreal, tearing the city apart until she found Colin.

Instead she was left to worry endlessly, impotently. Knowing that his kidnappers were torturing him, terrified that tonight would be the night they decided to get rid of him. . . . Her fear was a crushing weight, a suffocating blanket of despair. She could barely dress herself every night, much less deal with betrayal and conspiracy in her own court, and that fucker Berkhard trying to take over.

And yet, she *knew* that this—her fear and worry, her distraction—was all part of Berkhard's plan. No doubt he'd invade in force sooner rather than later, but he'd wanted to weaken her first. So he'd taken Colin away from her. And it was working. She opened her eyes every night to overwhelming pain, struggling to draw her next breath, convinced she was sharing Colin's agony through the blood link they shared, and knowing she was helpless to save him. He'd always been there for her, his quiet strength the one constant amidst the chaos of her new life. The one time that he needed *her,* she couldn't deliver. And now she'd lost Eleanor, too. The person she'd come to count on most after Colin.

"If Eleanor calls, interrupt me, whatever I'm doing," she told Danika as she gathered her things.

As much as she missed Eleanor, leaving her to coordinate the search with Aden's hunter vamp had been the right thing to do. First, because Eleanor's loyalty was unquestioned. Not only to Sophia, but to *Colin,* as well. And second, because like Sophia, people tended to underestimate Eleanor. She had that whole blond, Disney princess vibe going, but she was as tough as they came. She wouldn't stop looking until Colin was safe.

She'd find Colin and bring him home. She had to. Because if she didn't . . . well, if she didn't, then Sophia wasn't sure any of the rest of this even mattered.

Chapter Five

Montreal, Quebec, Canada

LUCIFER STOOD AT the big plate glass window. The view from this hotel was very different than the one in Toronto had been. They were much closer to the ground for one, and the street below was far narrower. The building across the way was close enough that he could have seen the smallest detail of the opposite room, if they hadn't had their drapes firmly closed. And on top of that, there was a fire escape that crossed sharply upward on the balcony right outside their suite. It was a very stylish fire escape, very modern and clean, but it cut right across his view, making it necessary to bend down at an angle and peer upward if one wanted to see the moon, much less anything else in the night sky.

Not that Lucifer cared overmuch about the moon. But it would have been something pretty to stare at while he waited for Eleanor to emerge from her daytime rest.

She was already awake. She'd been moving around a bit ago, and then the shower had come on. He'd tortured himself with images of her naked body under the pounding water, more tightly muscled now than she'd been in New Orleans. Between the vampire enhancement of her physique and the obvious work she'd put into staying fit in order to perform her bodyguard duties, his Eleanor was no longer the soft, sweet girl she'd been when he'd met her.

It would have been easier if those changes had made her less attractive to him, if he'd been the kind of man who needed his woman weak and dependent. But that wasn't the case, not anymore. Maybe once upon a time, when he'd been younger and had taken his *nonna's* admonishments to take care of his woman to mean that his woman needed to look to him for *everything*. But no longer.

Maybe it was Eleanor's leaving that had changed him. After she'd gone, he'd chosen women who could take care of themselves, women who never would have been vulnerable to the machinations of a weakling like Derek Pratt.

But now Eleanor was back, and she was strong and capable, a power in her own right, for all that she seemed determined to play human around him. And that was one of the subjects they were going to deal with tonight, before they pursued this investigation any further. From here on out, things were going to get dangerous, and he needed her at full strength. He needed to know that she could and would protect herself, that she could protect Colin Murphy, too, if it came to that.

If not, then she'd only get in the way, and it would be better if she remained in the hotel and waited for his progress reports. Because he had a job to do, and he needed a partner, not a hundred and ten pounds of helpless female.

The door opened behind him. He didn't turn, but he knew when Eleanor crossed into the room. The light soap scent of her skin, the soft fall of her footsteps on the carpeted floor. But more than that, it was the bright spark of her power that registered against his vampire senses, a spark he hadn't felt up to this point, because she'd been masking her true power. And he hadn't noticed, because he'd had no reason to probe beneath the facade she showed to the world. He was powerful enough to have shattered her mask, if he'd wanted. But he wouldn't do that, even now, because it would be a violation of Eleanor's existence.

"How's the view?" she asked quietly.

He still didn't turn. "Terrific. With a bit of contortion, you can even see the moon."

She gave a surprised laugh, clearly not expecting his joking response. Her footsteps drew closer, until she was standing next to him. They remained silent for several minutes, and then she sighed.

"I swear I didn't know that Derek would tell you I'd died. I never suspected he'd go that far." She shook her head. "I've thought about writing you so many times over the years, but I was afraid."

He swung around at that, staring at her. "Afraid of what? When did I ever hurt you?"

"Never," she admitted. "It wasn't that. I wasn't afraid of what you'd *do*. It was . . . I was afraid of what you'd *see* when you looked at me."

He frowned at her in confusion. "What would I see?"

"A vampire," she said simply, as if that explained everything. Or *anything*.

"I don't understand," he said finally. "I know what Derek told you, but I never told him—"

"Forget what Derek said. I never believed you'd ask him to turn me. I knew—" She cut off whatever she'd been about to say. "What happened to him anyway? Everything was so confusing, and then I left. But . . . he's dead, isn't he?"

"Did you think I'd let him live? He told me you were *dead*, and it was his fault." Lucifer heard the arrogance in his voice, and for about two seconds considered softening his words, but just as quickly decided against it. Fuck it. Derek had needed killing, and he was *still* glad he'd been the one to do it.

Eleanor smiled slightly, as if she'd expected his reaction, but there was sadness there, too. "No. I knew you'd be furious when you found out. I would have killed him myself, but I couldn't do it then, and by the time I was strong enough . . . it no longer mattered."

"So, if you didn't stay away because of Derek, that means . . . . I still don't understand, Elle."

She gave him a puzzled look, as if he was missing something obvious. But he had no fucking idea what it might be.

"You just said it, Lucifer. And you'd said it before. You didn't want me to be turned. You didn't want me as a vampire."

He stared at her in sudden comprehension. "You're right," he said slowly. "I *didn't* want you as a vampire. But I didn't want you as a human, either. I just wanted *you*. I loved *you*. I never gave a damn what body you wore, or which blood flowed in your veins."

He was silent for a long moment, aware of Eleanor next to him, her blue eyes boring a hole into the side of his head in wordless demand for his attention. But he had nothing else to say. And maybe he'd already said too much.

"I've got a line on Chase Landry," he said flatly. "I'm leaving in ten minutes, if you want to come along."

He spun on his heel and strode into his private suite, closing the door carefully. He paused for a moment, his eyes closed and his head hanging low, his heart aching. Had he been thinking that Eleanor couldn't hurt him any more than she already had? He'd been wrong. She hadn't trusted the strength of his love. Hadn't believed it would be enough to withstand that damn Derek Pratt, or whatever else life had thrown at them. She hadn't trusted *him*. Hadn't believed in *him*.

He sucked in a breath, and shook loose fingers he hadn't realized he'd fisted. He had a job to do. Maybe Eleanor hadn't believed he loved her enough to stick it out, but Colin Murphy was in a prison somewhere, enduring night after night of torture in silence, refusing to betray Sophia, because he sure as hell believed she loved *him* enough.

Lucifer wasn't going to let him suffer for nothing. He was going to

4

4

track him down and save his life. And then he was going to kill the kidnappers. But not until he'd made them wish they'd never crossed his path.

"SO WHAT'S THE line you have on Chase Landry?"

Lucifer didn't spare a glance for Eleanor where she sat in the passenger seat of the big SUV. The vehicle was far too big for just the two of them, but it was heavily armored, and had bullet-resistant glass. It was the only one Lucifer trusted with his life . . . and Eleanor's. He hadn't loved her forever, just to see her die of a stray gunshot wound.

"Landry's the vampire who lured Fiona's boyfriend into the kidnapping plot. I doubt he's the mastermind behind the wider conspiracy, but it seems likely that he was the vampire responsible for organizing the abduction itself. Kind of a subcontractor, if you'd like. Anyway, when he's not busy kidnapping and torturing Murphy, he has a life outside the tunnels, and that was easy to track down. Believe it or not, our boy's a lawyer, with a vampire-heavy clientele. He specializes in estate planning, which means he mostly helps vampires conceal their assets from greedy government entities, and creates fictitious ownership transfers to conceal their unnaturally long lives."

"How does that help us?"

"Fiona didn't know details, but she thought he lived with someone. I want to talk to whoever that person is."

"Talk," she repeated doubtfully.

Lucifer did glance at her then. "Uh, yeah. That's pretty much why we're here. To find Murphy and bring him out alive. And that means talking to anyone who might give us a clue as to where he is."

"The way you *talked* to Fiona?"

Well, now, she was pissing him off. He didn't need her to sit there and pass judgment on his methods when he was trying to save Colin Murphy's God damned life. Or any other time, either. If she wanted to play human, that was her business. But he was a fucking powerful vampire, and he wasn't going to apologize for it. Hell, he fucking *loved* it.

Eleanor must have noticed his silence and correctly interpreted the reasons for it, because she didn't push on the question of his methods with Fiona, or anyone else. That didn't mean she accepted what he'd done—as if he needed her acceptance—but she changed the subject to avoid confrontation. Which was completely human of her, and only pissed him off more.

"So Landry owns a house?"

"Not exactly."

"HIS GRANDMOTHER?"

Lucifer didn't look at her. He hadn't looked at her much this whole night. "His great-grandmother," he said, absently, scanning the house numbers. "She's still the owner of record, but she died a very long time ago. Landry's more or less lived here ever since."

Eleanor studied the small house as Lucifer slid into a space at the curb. Although "slid" was too kind of a word for what Lucifer did. He was a horrible driver. Horrible. She actually remembered that from all those years ago in New Orleans. If she'd thought for one minute that Lucifer would have gone along with it, she'd have politely insisted on driving this evening. But she'd seen the pain in his eyes when he'd learned why she'd run from him. And ever since then, he'd been like a stranger to her. Cool and polite, very professional, but with none of his usual, teasing banter. And not even a hint of flirting.

It had never occurred to her that Lucifer could still be hurt by her. She'd known when she'd left back then that he'd be wounded, not only by her leaving, but by the way she'd chosen to go, with no word of good-bye. But that was more than twenty years ago, years that he'd spent thinking she was dead. And now, even though she was alive, she was no longer his pretty human princess. She was a vampire. And she'd always known that Lucifer had loved her for her humanity. He'd told her, flat out, that vampire on vampire relationships were rare and even more rarely successful. And he hadn't minced words when it came to the reason for it.

Vampires needed blood to survive. Human blood. And their mates provided that in an act that was seductive and intensely sexual, something that would be missing in a vampire's life if his mate happened to be a vampire, and they both had to feed elsewhere. She'd assumed . . . no, she'd *known* that he wouldn't want her once she was turned. She'd run rather than face his rejection.

But what if she'd been wrong?

The possibility was too awful, the pain too sharp. She couldn't deal with it. Not on top of everything else. She needed time alone to think through it all, and she wasn't going to get that tonight. Maybe not tomorrow either, not until Colin Murphy was found and the current crisis was resolved. Only then could she take some time to resolve her own, personal crisis.

She had a feeling finding Colin was going to be easier.

Lucifer was already walking up the cracked concrete path to the tiny front porch, and she couldn't help admiring the pretty picture he made, with his fine ass in a pair of tight black jeans, his back and shoulders looking all big and strong in a black leather jacket, and above that, his black, black hair. A study in black. Gorgeous.

She shook her head. Yes, he was gorgeous, but he wasn't hers any longer, and she was supposed to be working. She climbed down from the SUV, and hurried up the walk, catching up to Lucifer just as he rang the doorbell for the second time.

"Not much of a house for a powerful vampire," she said, leaning over to check out the window on her side of the porch. She couldn't see much. The window was filthy inside and out. "Is he still living here?"

"Let's find out." Lucifer grabbed hold of the doorknob and twisted. The door swung open, and they stepped quickly inside, which proved this was a vampire residence. Vampires required an invitation to enter a human home. So no matter who else might have lived here once, it was now primarily a vampire's lair, even if it didn't look like one. The neighborhood was older and well-established, the homes modest and mostly better maintained than Landry's. Neighborhoods like this weren't ideal for snooping around. Nosy neighbors watched out for each another, and if they saw two strangers lurking around Landry's place, they might call the police, if for no other reason than the entertainment value of the flashing lights.

Eleanor followed Lucifer down the short hallway. She paused at the foot of the stairs and drew in a deep breath, taking in the slightly musty smell, the dust, the *feel* of the house. "Nobody's been here in a while," she said.

Lucifer was standing several feet away, looking around, studying the tiny living room. "How long, do you think?"

"More than a few days. Weeks, probably."

"Fits the timeline. Murphy was taken…what two weeks ago?"

She nodded. "Tonight's the fifteenth night since he's been gone."

"They'd have needed time to prepare wherever it is they're keeping him, time to plan for the actual abduction. Let's tear this place apart. I want anything that can give us a lead on where he goes, how he spends his time. If you find where he keeps his records—utility bills, that sort of thing—let me know. I'll take that."

Eleanor started up the stairs, fuming inwardly at the implicit dismissal of her skills in Lucifer's parting shot. Like she wouldn't know what was important and what wasn't. Did he think she'd gotten her job because of her looks? But by the time she reached the landing, she'd gotten over it. She doubted he'd meant anything by it. If only because he seemed barely aware she was with him tonight. Not that he thought he was alone. He knew there was another *person* with him, but that person had no particular identity. It wasn't his Elle who was on the job with him. It wasn't even Eleanor. It was just a person sent along to make his job easier.

She sighed, and wondered how they could get past this. *If* they could get past it. Hell, she wasn't even sure she wanted to. It had been easier to believe he was gone, forever out of her reach. To know now that she'd never had to lose him . . . it was almost too much to bear.

A quick scan of the upstairs landing told her there were two bed-rooms and a bathroom. She didn't expect to find much. This was a vampire's house, after all. He sure as hell didn't sleep up here, and most vampires tended to maintain whatever was important to them in the same space where they slept. There were exceptions, naturally. A power-ful vampire lord like Sophia had a huge house, with tons of space, and too many rooms to count. But while Sophia and Colin had many lovely possessions in the daytime parts of their house, the lady's significant files and irreplaceable mementos were in a private office down in the base-ment. Colin had an office upstairs in the sunniest part . . .

What she was seeing finally registered on Eleanor. Landry might not be sleeping up here, but someone else was. The largest bedroom was tidy, with the bed made, the room dusted, and the closet full of neatly pressed clothes that were hung in meticulous order by style and color. On the floor, the shoes were similarly organized on a double shoe shelf beneath the hanging clothes. Huh. The clothes and shoes all belonged to a man. She checked the shirt size, and then bent over to pick up a shoe and do the same. Frowning thoughtfully, she turned and started for the hallway, tossing the shoe back to the floor as an afterthought, and deriv-ing no small amount of pleasure from messing up the compulsive neat-ness of the closet.

She checked out the bathroom next, more to confirm her guess than anything else, and then pushed open the door of the second bed-room. It was completely empty, not even a bed—more evidence that she was on the right track.

Hurrying downstairs, she found Lucifer sitting at a small desk in the kitchen. Every drawer was either standing open or had been dumped onto the floor, while Lucifer sat going through what looked like a bunch of old bills.

Eleanor opened her mouth to announce her discovery upstairs, but he beat her to it.

"Landry has a roommate," he said absently, still flipping through paperwork. "Human, I'd guess."

She wrinkled her nose in irritation. Well, at least she could confirm that much. "Definitely human. He lives and sleeps upstairs."

Lucifer grunted an acknowledgment. "There must be a basement," he said, abruptly throwing the paperwork back to the desk, ignoring the few pieces that slid to the floor. "Let's find it."

THERE WERE ONLY so many places the stairs to a basement could be. Most houses followed a typical architectural pattern, especially tract houses like this one. Every vampire worth his salt knew them all, and that included Lucifer. And probably, he admitted grudgingly, Eleanor, too.

They found the stairs in the first place they looked, behind a short, narrow door beneath the main staircase. He had to duck down to make it through the opening, and then paused to grab the piece of kitchen string that served as a light switch, hanging from a bare overhead bulb. The light barely reached the basement floor, but that didn't bother him. He already knew a vampire lived here, at least part of the time. There was a distinct odor of old blood that told him the vampire was a messy eater. But it wasn't strong enough to be anything more than that. They wouldn't be finding any dead bodies down there, no decayed corpses.

It was on his tongue to tell Eleanor to remain upstairs. Not because he thought there was anything dangerous in the basement, but for the very opposite reason. If there was danger here, it was more likely to walk through the front door, and it would be nice to have a timely warning.

But he didn't feel like explaining himself, or, frankly, like talking to her at all. At least no more than absolutely necessary. So he let her follow him downstairs, and did his best to ignore her, something made more difficult in the close quarters of the basement room, with the fresh soap scent of her skin filling the small space.

He looked around. Unmade bed. Small refrigerator—he opened the door—with two stored bags of blood. He checked the date on the blood. It was nearly three weeks old, almost expired in terms of usefulness for a vampire. Or a human either, for that matter. Red blood cells were red blood cells, no matter who needed them.

"The roommate's a lot neater," Eleanor said from behind him.

Lucifer tilted his head curiously, and then scanned the room one more time, before spinning abruptly and sprinting upstairs. "I need to talk to the neighbors."

Eleanor followed. "Why? What did you find?"

He ignored her and headed for the front door.

"Lucifer!" she shouted. "Stop. Look, I know you're pissed at me—"

He spun back to face her so swiftly that she stumbled back and had to grab the stair bannister.

"Then you know nothing," he said flatly, then turned around and yanked the front door open. Crossing the porch, he jumped down into the scruffy front yard, and paused to examine the houses up and down the street.

"Lucifer," Eleanor persisted.

"Quiet," he snapped. She sucked in an outraged breath, but before she could say anything, he explained. "I'm listening."

Turning his head first one way, and then the next, he studied each house in turn. "Landry doesn't have a roommate," he explained finally, having gotten what he wanted from his perusal of the neighborhood. "He has a lover. Two men were having regular sex in Landry's bed in the basement. As you noted, the room was a mess, and the sheets were far from fresh. And there were no other scents in the house."

Eleanor frowned. "Then he's—"

"Gay, yes." He met her eyes at last. "Is that a problem for you?" he asked coolly.

"Of course, not. I was just—"

"Good. We need to talk to the neighbors. At least one of them will have noticed the comings and goings here. You take the house across the street, two doors down, the one with the older mini-van in the driveway. I'll take the neighbors to either side."

She sighed noisily. "What am I looking for?"

He gave her a slightly disbelieving look. "Anything that will lead us to the identity of the lover. He'll know where Landry is. And if we can't find him, then we need his family, or someone who can contact him."

"You think the neighbors will have that?"

"Probably not directly, and probably not all from the same person. But we should get enough for me to piece it together."

Her lips tightened in irritation. He remembered that expression well. Once upon a time, he'd have gentled the irritation away, kissing her mouth, until her lips opened, once more soft and full and welcoming.

He blinked. But no longer.

"Stay in touch," he growled. "Landry might have a spy in one of these houses."

He waited until Eleanor stormed off toward the house he'd assigned her, probably still pissed at his suggestion that he'd be the one to piece it together. Too bad. He'd spoken only the truth. Eleanor was an intelligent woman, no doubt of that. But there was a reason he was Aden's premier hunter, the same reason he'd been put in charge of this hunt.

Turning in the opposite direction, he put on his most friendly, human face, and approached the neighbor's porch. It was almost a duplicate of the one on Landry's house, except in much better repair. His knock was answered by a man with a lit cigarette in his mouth and a beer in one hand. As he opened the door, he used his beer hand to pull the cigarette from his mouth, holding both in the same hand while he looked Lucifer over.

Speaking French, and making no attempt to disguise his Cajun roots, Lucifer smiled and said, "I'm sorry to bother you. My name's Lewis, I'm Chase's cousin, and—"

"Who?" the man interrupted.

Lucifer put a little push behind his next words. "Chase Landry. Your neighbor."

"You want to talk to my wife," the man said, speaking Quebec French. "Come in."

Lucifer's smile broadened into a grin. That had been too easy. He couldn't compel an invitation, but he could make himself seem *invite-able.* "You're very kind," he murmured and, having been invited, entered the house. It smelled of grease and cooked food, something he couldn't identify. It had been too long since he'd eaten human food.

His host gestured Lucifer into a small sitting room, where a fire burned steadily on a brick hearth, and then took a step down the hallway and called out, "Suzette!"

A plump woman appeared in the kitchen doorway, wiping her hands on a towel. "Who is it?" she asked, speaking the same Quebecois as her husband.

"He's asking about that creature next door. The vampire."

"Chase? What does he want with Chase?"

Lucifer moved to where the woman could see him. He was a little surprised that the couple knew Chase was a vampire, but Suzette seemed like the kind of neighbor who knew everything about everyone. And it certainly didn't seem to have dampened whatever friendship she had with Chase.

"I'm sorry to disturb you," he said, touching her thoughts with his power as easily as he had her husband's. It was second nature to use his talent; it took more effort *not* to use it. "I'm Chase's cousin, Louis. He was expecting me, but there's no one home. Have you seen—?"

"Ah," Suzette exclaimed, coming down the hall with a warm smile. "Louis, of course. Chase mentioned you."

He hadn't, of course, but Lucifer needed information from the woman, and she wasn't going to give out much to a perfect stranger.

"Come, sit," she encouraged, guiding him into the room with a light touch on his arm. "I'm surprised Chase isn't here to greet you. He was so looking forward to your visit."

"Well, I arrived a day early, I'm afraid. We drove, and my girlfriend has a heavy foot," he added, laughing.

The two humans both laughed far harder than the comment deserved. Lucifer had neither the time nor the inclination to fine-tune the manipulation of their thoughts.

"I wonder," he said, "do you know where I might find him? I know he works from home, but is there a bar or—"

"You'll want the *Loon*," Suzette offered right away. "Aubert works there most evenings. It's where they met."

"Of course, I should have thought of that. Is it nearby?"

"Yes, yes, down the block," she gestured. "Turn right and it's just there. Not half a kilometer."

Lucifer bestowed his warmest smile on the couple. "Thank you. We'll be on our way, then."

"Would you like some dinner first?" Suzette said quickly. "We have plenty."

Lucifer eyed the woman, with her generous bosom and broad hips, and her husband's fleshy form. They would indeed have plenty to offer a hungry vampire. But Lucifer preferred not to eat where he hunted. Which made no sense in human terms, but was perfectly logical to him.

"You're very kind, but we've had dinner, and I'm keeping you from yours." He released their minds with a gentle suggestion, and made his way to the door. "Good evening."

The air was cold after Suzette's warm, cooking-scented home, and he zipped his leather jacket while glancing down the block to where Eleanor was making her way back to him.

"Anything?" he asked, remembering to keep his words strictly businesslike.

She shook her head. "They've seen him come and go, and another man, too—the boyfriend I assume—but they don't know anything else. They were reluctant to talk. It's obvious they keep tabs on the neighborhood, but they're afraid of Landry."

"They know he's a vampire?"

"No. Not that I could tell," she amended. "You might have gotten more. But I got the impression he's a bit of a bully."

Lucifer shrugged. "Suzette likes him well enough, and she *does* know he's a vamp."

"Who's Suzette?"

"The neighbor. Let's get in the truck. It's cold out here."

"You still don't like the cold," she commented, with a smile that quickly faded, as if she'd suddenly remembered that they weren't being friendly at the moment.

Lucifer had no comment. He *didn't* like cold. His bones still remembered the heat of his Sicilian home. But once Aden had taken the Midwest and moved to Chicago, he'd been forced to accept frigid weather. Not that it would slow him down any.

"Where are we going?" Eleanor asked, when he'd started the SUV and done a quick U-turn in the direction Suzette had indicated.

"Chase's friend tends bar down the street. I have questions."

He caught the worried glance she sent him. It pissed him off. She was treating him like some sort of rapist who scoured people's brains for fun and didn't care what damage he caused, when the truth was far different. He wasn't a brute, he was a fucking artist. The humans he manipulated never knew he'd been there, and the only time he inflicted actual harm was when he wanted to. He did the same with vampires. In fact, he was the only person he knew who could manipulate a vampire's mind as easily as a human's. It was one of the reasons Aden had brought him on in the first place.

"What's it called?" Eleanor asked, studying each building as they passed.

"The Loon." Lucifer glanced ahead, and saw a spot-lit sign featuring a black and white bird that he guessed was meant to be a loon. "There."

He swung into the parking lot a minute later. It wasn't crowded on this Sunday night, which was just as well. He'd told Suzette he wasn't hungry, but that wasn't true. He hadn't fed since leaving Chicago, and he was feeling the pinch. He wasn't a baby vamp who had to eat every night, but he wasn't one of the old-timers either. His vampiric power was far stronger than most, which let him go longer between feedings, but he still had to eat regularly. Whether Landry's friend was there to-night or not, maybe Lucifer could find a willing female and top off.

That thought had him glancing at Eleanor for some stupid reason, almost as if he felt guilty for thinking about spending some quality time in a dark corner with a succulent woman. Even if he and Eleanor had been more than friends—as if they were friends now, which *so* wasn't the case—he would have had to feed from a human. Vampires could be lovers, and while the euphoric in each other's blood could add to the sexual high, their blood wasn't food. They couldn't feed each other. The image flashed in Lucifer's mind of him and Eleanor sharing a willing human, feeding together, and then fucking their brains out, while still high on the human's blood. His cock was almost instantly hard, uncomfortably hard in his tight jeans.

Fuck. He shoved the SUV's door open, welcoming the rush of cold air that cooled his imagination *and* his cock.

"Who're we looking for?"

Lucifer hadn't noticed Eleanor exiting the vehicle, which wasn't good. He had to get his head in the game.

"His name's Aubert. No last name, but he tends bar, so he should be easy to find."

"Who's doing the talking?"

He gave her a disbelieving look, which thankfully she didn't see. Obviously, *he'd* be taking the lead. Eleanor was strong, but whatever talent her vampire transition had bestowed, it hadn't included anything like his ability for telepathy and manipulation. On the other hand, he'd already seen how difficult she could be when she thought he wasn't taking her seriously.

"I probably should," he suggested, which was about as diplomatic as he could get. "If he's not here, we'll need a phone number or some other way of contacting him, and I doubt they'll give that out lightly."

"Right."

He gave her the benefit of the doubt. She might have been *trying* to keep her disapproval out of that one word. But she didn't succeed. She didn't approve of the way he got into people's heads.

The bar was surprisingly full for a Sunday night, and had the feel of a neighborhood joint. Several people eyed them suspiciously as they wove around the crowded tables and took a pair of open bar stools.

"What can I get you?" a blond bartender asked, speaking the by-now familiar Quebecois as he slapped a pair of coasters down in front of them.

What Lucifer wanted was a beer, but he didn't know any of the Canadian brands. He eyed the whiskeys ranged along a shelf on the back counter. "Tangle Ridge," he said, selecting the only one he recognized. The only decent one anyway. "Double shot, neat. Ice water on the side."

The bartender gave Lucifer a sideways glance of disapproval for his Cajun accent, then looked at Eleanor in silent question. When she'd been human, Elle hadn't been much of a drinker. White wine had been her typical drink. Now that she was a vampire? Lucifer didn't know. Alcohol didn't bother vampires. It tasted good, and left a nice trail of heat going down, but there wasn't even a buzz left behind.

"Nothing for me," Eleanor said in perfect French. "Water and ice would be nice."

The bartender shrugged, filled two glasses with ice, and used his soda gun to top them off with water. He set one glass in front of each of them, then grabbed the whiskey and served up Lucifer's double shot.

Lucifer took a sip, then spun around to survey the crowd. It was a blue-collar bar, and at least two-thirds male. The women were dressed a bit more upscale than the men, but that was par for the course. No one caught his eye, no one gave off a negative vibe. He spun back to the bar, downed his whiskey, and signaled the bartender for another.

Eleanor gave him a disapproving look. What? Like she was afraid he'd get drunk? Or maybe she just knew what he was about to do.

When the bartender brought him his second drink, he dipped quickly into the man's head. He had no idea what Aubert looked like. For all he knew, *this* was Aubert. But, no. The bartender's name was Chris, and he was pissed that Aubert hadn't been to work in several days, leaving him to cover the missing bartender's shifts.

"Aubert around?" Lucifer asked, knowing the answer, but wanting to focus Chris's thoughts on their target.

Chris shook his head sharply. "Bastard hasn't even called."

"You try his cell phone?" Lucifer asked, sliding effortlessly into Chris's head once again.

"Fuck, yeah. It's the only number we have. He mostly shacks up with that boyfriend of his these days. Can't get him at home anymore."

Lucifer grabbed hold of Chris's mind and did a little snooping. Chris didn't know the number by heart, but it was stored in his cell phone, which he now handed over without being asked. Well, without being asked verbally, anyway. Lucifer rewarded him with a big smile, and slid the phone over to Eleanor. "The password's 0420," he told her, stifling a grin. Weed day.

She gave him a hard look, clearly aware that he was digging around the human's head, but that didn't stop her from quickly unlocking the phone and calling up the contacts. From the corner of his eye, Lucifer could see her flipping through the information. He knew the moment she found what she was looking for, and watched as she sent Aubert's contact info to herself.

She passed the phone back to Lucifer, who pushed it toward the edge of the bar closest to Chris. "Thanks for the info," he said politely, then downed his whiskey in a single gulp, and left a big tip before standing away from the bar. "Ready to go, *bella?*" He held out his hand in invitation, partly because he wanted to touch her. He was just that pathetic. But also because he knew it would fluster her. She'd avoided touching him ever since they'd arrived in Montreal, but she wouldn't want to make a scene. Not here, and not now.

He smiled when Elle's hand touched his, when he gripped her fingers and drew her against his side.

"Bastard," she whispered, and he laughed, because he really was a bastard. And she knew it.

"*Touché, bella,*" he murmured, and then risked his life by pulling her even closer as they walked out of the bar.

He expected Eleanor to pull herself away as soon as the door closed behind them, but she didn't. For just a few minutes, the time it took for his heart to go from zero to sixty and his cock to stiffen eagerly, she remained in his embrace, her forehead resting against his shoulder, the length of her body pressed against his. But then she closed her eyes and stepped back, turning away so he couldn't see her face. But he'd seen enough. It had cost her to move away from him. She might not want to admit it, but she still wanted him. So what the fuck was holding her back?

"You have the number?" he asked, his voice rough with emotion, coming out harsher than he'd intended.

Eleanor shot him an embarrassed look. "Yeah. Shall I call him or—"

"Neither one of us is calling him. Give me the number, and I'll have my guys track it. With any luck Landry's keeping his boyfriend close and the cell signal will take us right to him."

"Not if he's in those tunnels. Cell signals down there are for crap, even in the built-out parts of the underground. If they're in some leftover back tunnel, there's no way."

"It's worth a try," he said patiently. "They can't be locking themselves in there with Murphy twenty-four hours a day. If nothing else, the boyfriend needs food, and someone must be going out to send all those torture pics to Sophia."

"Fair enough. Here." She handed over her phone, and Lucifer scrolled to the relevant number. He then used his own cell to call Bastien.

"Lucifer. You have him yet?" Bastien's words were still flavored with his native French, no matter how long he'd been gone from that country.

"Good evening to you, too," Lucifer said dryly. "And, no. Not yet. But we're close. I have a number. Can you track it?"

"*Mais oui.* It's already set up. Everyone is prepared to assist Lady Sophia's quest. I'll send the number to Miguel in DC, and he'll transmit it to Duncan's contacts in the FBI."

So, Lord Duncan was involved, too. His territory included Virginia, which meant the various vampire techs employed at both the FBI and CIA headquarters were his people. Hell, for that matter, NSA headquarters were in Duncan's territory, too. If anyone could track Aubert's phone, *they* sure as hell could. The North American lords really were pulling out all the stops to help Sophia. Maybe this was their way of ensuring she didn't leave the alliance in order to secure Colin's release. Her departure would leave a gap the length of the Canadian/U.S. border. A gap nearly impossible to defend that would touch four separate vampire territories.

"Okay," Lucifer told Bastien. "Get back to me when you can."

"Everything good with you, *mon ami?*"

"Oh, hell, yeah. Remind me to tell you about it sometime."

"Ah, your vaunted charm has failed at last?"

"Hanging up now," Lucifer growled, and then disconnected to the sound of his friend's quiet chuckle. He slipped his cell into the inside pocket of his jacket and faced Eleanor. "We've done all we can for tonight, and besides, I need to feed. I want to be at full strength for tomorrow, just in case this hunt gets ugly. What about you?"

She blushed, and once more Lucifer was both charmed and irritated. Charmed that she could still blush about such a basic bodily function as drinking blood, after all these years as a vampire. And irritated for the same reason. She was hung up on denying everything about her vampire nature . . . for *him*. Because she'd been convinced he wouldn't want her once she'd been turned.

"I fed last night," she murmured, and a sudden sharp blade of jealousy stabbed Lucifer hard as he pictured *his* Elle cuddled up to some human male, feeding, fondling the man's dick . . . *Fuck!*

Eleanor's blue eyes went big and round as she stared up at him, clearly sensing his anger, and just as clearly not understanding why.

"That's good," he said gruffly, then tossed her the keys to the SUV. There was no way in hell he was taking her on a blood hunt with him. No way in fucking hell. "Take the Escalade. I'll find my way back later, after I've fed."

"You don't know Montreal. Maybe I should go with—"

"I know how to find blood in a strange city," he snapped. "This isn't my first hunt, you know."

Her big eyes were shooting sparks at him now. "Fine," she snapped right back at him. "Knock yourself out." She spun away and muttered, "Or maybe I'll get lucky, and someone else will do it for you."

Lucifer stood on the sidewalk, and waited until the SUV turned the far corner, then he called Bastien back. "You get a location on that phone for me yet?" he growled.

"Having that much fun, huh?"

"Just give me a fucking location."

"Sending it now. I don't know Montreal that well, so I can't tell you what it means. But our guy said the phone hasn't moved in the last 48 hours."

Lucifer studied the map Bastien sent him. "That's good. Tell Aden we're getting close."

"*Bon.*"

Bastien hung up as Lucifer hit the disconnect button, his thoughts already on Aubert, and what it meant that his cell phone hadn't moved in the last two days. It could be great news, assuming Aubert was with Landry. Or it could be very bad news . . . for Aubert. Maybe he'd served whatever purpose he'd been intended for, and Landry had disposed of him, as in made him dead. Or it could simply mean Aubert had dropped his phone down the sewer, and the location was a dead end.

His jaw tightened with impatience. More than anything, he wanted this damn hunt to be over with. He wanted to go back to Chicago and pretend he'd never found Eleanor. As if. He stared broodingly down the empty street where she'd driven off earlier. He had a feeling it wasn't going to be that easy to put her out of his head, or his heart, now that she'd reappeared and torn open old wounds. Wounds that had taken years to heal, and then only imperfectly.

He sighed, impatient with himself. He was mooning around like a lovesick teenager. The bar door opened behind him, and two young women emerged, both attractive, both sober enough that he wouldn't be taking advantage. He grinned when they caught him watching, and they gave him happy grins in return. He could detect the light scent of perfume and sweat on their skin, and the longer he watched them, the scent of their increasing arousal. Perfect.

"Ladies," he purred, and pulled them into his embrace.

Vancouver, British Columbia, Canada

SOPHIA HUNG UP the phone, setting the ornate gold and ivory receiver on its matching base. It was ridiculously anachronistic, but it fit the elegant décor of her office, with its 17th century antiques. That wasn't the reason she used it, though. That had been at Colin's insistence. It was a land-line, secured and encrypted, and the one she used for her most critical communications. He'd begun to come around to the idea of a dedicated cell phone, with the improvements in encryption technology. But he hadn't been ready to make the change yet. If anything, he argued that enemies were much more likely to look for cell signals—since everyone used them these days—than to bother with jacking in to a physical line. She found herself smiling at the thought of arguing with him one more time on the subject, until reality crashed in on her fond musings, and she was dragged back to the nightmare of her existence.

Someone knocked on her office door. Both the urgency of the knocking and the stress in the voice calling out her name told her she'd been sitting there staring at nothing for too long.

"Come in," she called, recognizing the mental signature of Danika. Tambra was still hung up in Calgary, with the hearing delayed until Monday evening, in recognition of the vampires' specific requirements. Tambra had called once, but Sophia had been on another conference call and unable to break away.

She couldn't fault Danika, however. The young female had stepped up to fill the void with quiet efficiency. Spinning around before the vamp could push open the door and find her lord staring into space, Sophia forced herself to concentrate on a set of reports that Danika had left with her last night. They were the latest reconnaissance from Vancouver Island where it was beginning to look like Berkhard had set up his camp. If true, it was bold of him to be so blatant about it, though he might have chosen the location specifically because there were so few vampires living there. This was in part because vampires weren't too crazy about islands in general, no matter that Vancouver Island was very large with a significant population that could, in fact, have supported far more than the vampires who lived there. But the vampires of the region preferred the city of Vancouver on the mainland instead, which was where Sophia had her headquarters.

What was troubling, and what had originally generated the suspicion that Berkhard might be moving in there, was that no one had heard from any of the island's vampire contingent in over a week. Moreover, the first scout that Sophia had sent to surveil the situation had never reported back.

It was beginning to look like Sophia would have to check the situation out in person, with the full understanding that if she did discover Berkhard dug in on the island, she'd have to root him out by force. And that, in turn, meant that the final confrontation between her and Berkhard could very well happen in the next few days. She hated the idea of going into battle without Colin by her side. And maybe that made her weak, but no one would question Raphael's preference for having Juro by his side when he went to war. It was only because she was female, and because Colin was her mate not her vampire lieutenant, that she would be judged lacking.

She sighed, and glanced up where Danika was waiting patiently to be acknowledged.

"Was Eleanor's call not good news, my lady?" Danika asked timidly. And that very timidity made Sophia long for Eleanor's presence, or at least Tambra's. Someone who wasn't so afraid of her that they hesitated to ask a simple question.

"Good news?" she repeated, trying not to show her irritation. The girl would probably back her way out of the room in fear for her life, as if Sophia was a wild animal. Returning her nominal attention to the Berkhard recon brief, she said absently, "I suppose. She and Aden's hunter have a lead anyway." Shifting her focus, she indicated a set of photographs that appeared to have been taken using an aerial drone. "Are these the latest images of the Victoria compound?"

"They are," Danika murmured, then circled around to stand next to Sophia. "You can see here, my lady . . ."

Danika continued her narrative, shuffling between recon images and pointing out salient features, but Sophia was no longer listening. She already knew what she had to do with Berkhard, and she was already plotting the best approach in her mind.

But her heart wasn't in it. That aching organ was focused far away, in Montreal.

Chapter Six

ELEANOR WAS SURPRISED to find the living room empty when she emerged from her bedroom the next night. Lucifer was older, and so he woke before she did, and he'd been up and about before her every morning so far.

She'd no sooner had the thought than the door to his half of the suite opened, and there he was. Half-naked. No, not half, completely naked, wearing only a towel.

"Eleanor," he said casually, rubbing a second towel over his wet hair.

Her mouth went dry as she tried to think of something to say, but her brain had completely fuzzed out. Nothing but white noise filled her ears. What little brain power she could summon was focused almost entirely on the towel hanging precariously around his narrow hips, and how easily it could be dislodged, what with him rubbing so diligently at his hair.

"Eleanor?" he said again, dropping his arms to study her, the hair towel held loosely at his side.

She dragged her eyes up, past the washboard abs, the hugely muscled chest and arms, and met his golden-brown gaze. "Lucifer?" she managed to say, hoping it sounded more casual to him than it did to her.

"Everything okay?" he asked, sound vaguely disinterested, as if he didn't really care about the answer.

"Fine," she said, stung by the attitude, even though it was exactly what she'd wanted from him all along. They were colleagues, partners in this investigation. Nothing more. It would have been easy with any other man she'd ever known. But this was Lucifer. She swallowed her sigh, and asked, "Did you get a location on Aubert's cell phone yet?"

"I did. I'll be ready in ten minutes."

"Great," she said, sucking in a breath as he dropped both towels in the open doorway and disappeared into the depths of his suite. He'd never had a proper sense of decency when it came to nudity. Of course, with his body . . . . She tried not to think about how very healthy he looked, how very *well fed,* damn it. He must have found someone last night after she left. Not exactly a shock, since he'd said he was going to. He'd obviously picked up a woman to feed from . . . maybe even from the same bar. The patrons in the bar had seen them together, looking like a couple, but that wouldn't have stopped Lucifer. Even without his vampire powers, he was devastatingly handsome. And too fucking charming for his own good.

She heard her teeth grinding. If they didn't find Colin soon, she wasn't going to have any fangs left. And then she'd starve, and it would be Lucifer's fault. She growled at the ridiculous overdramatizing, but it wasn't far from the truth.

True to his word, Lucifer strolled through the open door of his bedroom just short of ten minutes later. He wore 405 jeans that cupped his package like an offering (the bastard!) A heavy black belt with a silver buckle held the jeans on his narrow hips, and a black long-sleeved T-shirt was tucked in neatly behind it. He was pulling on his leather jacket as he walked, his boots heavy on the hardwood floor. "You ready to go?"

Eleanor's jeans were black, and she wore a turtleneck sweater against the unseasonably cold weather. She wore boots, too, but hers were more elegant, with soft leather and a delicate buckled strap hanging low on the ankle. She nodded.

"Keys?" he asked, holding out his hand in flat demand.

Something snapped inside her. But it was a good thing. It broke his hold on her thoughts, and blew away the fog of her obsession with him. This was Lucifer. She knew him. Biblically. And he was being kind of a prick.

"I'll drive," she said, and headed for the door.

"Whoa." Lucifer grabbed her arm, then dropped it like it burned him when she turned around. "I'm in charge, remember? I'll drive."

She snorted. "You drive like an old lady, and we're in a hurry. I'll drive."

Lucifer eyed her, and she could see the calculation in his eyes. "Fine," he said at last. "Let's go."

LUCIFER ENTERED the coordinates on the SUV's nav system, curious to see what it would turn up. Bastien hadn't given him an address for Aubrey's phone, but a location. He could have checked it last night on his own computer, but by the time he'd fed and gotten his two lovelies tucked away in their beds, both well sated and flushed with satisfaction, it had been nearly sunrise.

"That's not far from here," Eleanor commented watching the map come up. "And it's not in the underground either."

"A home? Maybe a place he lived in before he met Landry, and he didn't want to give it up."

"Maybe. How do we know the phone's with him? Or that he's still there? Maybe he's gone to work by now."

"Bastien will ping me if there is any change, but it hasn't moved in a couple of days as of last night."

Eleanor frowned. "Don't you think that's odd?"

He shrugged. "Hell, yeah. But it's the best lead we have, so we're checking it out. Assuming you plan to leave the garage someday."

Eleanor gave him a narrow-eyed stare, which he pretended not to notice. In reality, there was very little about Elle that he didn't notice. It had always been that way.

"You never complained before," he commented, after they'd gone a few blocks.

She gave him a quick glance, but thankfully returned her attention to the road almost immediately. Elle drove like the proverbial bat out of hell. No wonder she thought his driving was slow. Anyone would be slow compared to her.

"Complained about what?" she asked, without looking at him.

"About my driving," he said, feeling slightly insulted that she was complaining now.

"I didn't want to prick your ego."

He frowned. "And now?"

"Hell, now the damn thing is so big, a little prick won't hurt it."

"*Cara*, there is nothing little about my prick."

She smiled slightly. "Yeah, I remember."

Lucifer barked a surprised laugh, but sobered immediately when the nav console beeped a warning. Leaning in for a closer look, he enlarged the area on the map. "Definitely looks residential," he murmured. He looked up and glanced around. "I don't like this," he said. "There's no one here. No one on the streets."

"It's not the best neighborhood," she told him.

"That's it," he said, pointing to a house on the right hand side of the street. It was in reasonable condition, especially compared to the houses around it. But the paint was still peeling on the trim, and the yard was mostly dirt with a few scraggly bushes hanging on near the concrete front porch.

Eleanor parked two houses down and turned off the engine. "What do you think we should do?" she asked.

Lucifer gave her an amused glance. "I think we should act like fucking vampires, and deal accordingly with whatever, or whoever, is waiting for us inside."

She didn't say anything right away, just narrowed her gaze on the house. "I don't like it. This could be a trap."

He wasn't used to working with a partner, and, for his own part, wasn't getting any vibes off the house or this situation. But he wasn't above listening if someone else's intuition had detected something that he might have missed. "So we go in slow," he said. "But we have to check this out. Or at least I do," he amended.

She flashed him an angry glare. "We're in this together, Luc."

He blinked, and stared. It was the first time she'd used the nickname that she'd anointed him with back in New Orleans. And it was the only nickname he'd ever had. Hearing it now made him long for things that he couldn't have.

He gave himself a mental shake. This was no time for fond memories.

"Let's go," he said abruptly, then opened the door and stepped out onto the bare strip of concrete that passed for a sidewalk. He paused long enough to scan the house. His own power signature was dampened far down from its natural state. Not to hide his presence, but to conceal his strength. No need to frighten the locals before he even got through the front door.

"One vampire, three humans," he murmured when Eleanor stepped up next to him. He did a slight double take at what looked like a martial arts stick of some kind that she had in her right hand, but didn't comment. "All of the humans are active and moving around, so Murphy definitely isn't in there."

"You never thought he was," she countered equally quietly, holding the stick against her right leg and tapping it slightly in a nervous gesture.

"No. But it's always good to check. You don't want to go killing the PC."

"PC?"

"Precious cargo. The rescuee."

She gave him a look of disbelief. "Really?"

He shrugged. "I read it in a book. It was a good book."

She sighed. "Any *useful* notes in that book?"

He smiled to himself. "The lone vampire's near the front door. I'll go in that way. You come in the back, but not until I'm inside. Got it?"

"Yes, sir."

He thought he detected a snarky note to her response, but it didn't matter. He was all business now. He didn't worry about himself. He'd already taken the measure of the vampire inside, and knew he could best him. But Eleanor was an unknown quantity to him. She had power and obviously some skill, given her position with Sophia. But there were humans in that house, too, and humans were unpredictable. Alone, unarmed, they were almost incapable of hurting a vampire. But even an unskilled human could rip a vampire in half with modern weapons.

He speared her with a hard look. "Be careful, Eleanor. Go."

She nodded, and slipped away through the darkness, disappearing into the shadows between the houses before she'd gone twenty feet. Lucifer marked her progress, following the spark that was her life force, tracking her as easily as if she'd been flashing a neon signal. He wasn't her lord. He wasn't anyone's lord. Yet. But he had the power that would make him a vampire lord someday. And Eleanor had his heart. Despite the years and the misunderstandings that separated them, that had never changed.

A dog barked as she rounded into the back yard, quickly silenced. She wouldn't have hurt the animal, so she either knocked it out or simply reminded it of its place in the predatory food chain.

Once she was in position, waiting, he strolled up to the front door and knocked. No need to break down the door; they were expecting him. And, besides, there was always the possibility that this was a human's home, which would mean he couldn't enter without an invitation.

All movement ceased inside the small house. They might have been expecting him, but they hadn't expected him to *knock*. Maybe they'd thought to ambush him when he crashed into the home's natural barriers against vampires.

There were harsh whispers from the humans as they asked for orders, presumably from the vampire, since he couldn't imagine any vampire putting himself at the whim of a human.

"Come in," a male voice called, and it contained enough of an amplified push that he knew it was the vampire.

Lucifer wanted to grin. He loved this shit. He slammed the door open with a hard punch of force, blowing the thing off its hinges, and letting his power flare. The vampire was waiting for him, but his eyes widened in realization when he detected the true depth of Lucifer's strength. The enemy vamp took a step back, as if to retreat, just as a crashing noise announced Eleanor's arrival on scene.

"Too late, asshole," Lucifer growled. He shoved his awareness into the other vampire's brain, and sucked away his consciousness. The vamp fell to the floor in a heap, every ounce of self-will gone. If Lucifer didn't remind him before morning, the vampire wouldn't even retain enough self-awareness to conceal himself from the sun.

The entire confrontation, from the moment Lucifer exploded into the house, until the enemy vamp was limp on the floor, was only a matter of minutes, during which Eleanor had been alone in confronting the three human conspirators. Gunfire rattled from the kitchen, where all three humans had been hanging around a small table. He heard Eleanor curse, and strode toward the sound. A moment later, she cried his name in warning, but it was already too late.

When he stepped into the doorway a human female turned on him with a snarl, an AK-15 in her arms and already lifted in his direction, her finger squeezing the trigger. Lucifer raised his shields, while, at the same time, reaching into the woman's brain and—Shit!

A blur of movement had him staggering back as Eleanor threw herself between him and the gun-wielding human. Lucifer acted without thought, pulling Eleanor into the protection of his shields and killing the woman' in a move more brutal than what he'd intended. But, you know? Fuck her. The human woman didn't matter, only . . .

"Eleanor," he said frantically, pulling her into the circle of his arms, shielding her with his body and his power, even as he made sure the remaining humans were neutralized. "Are you hurt? Are you shot?"

She pushed at his chest, and squirmed free of his arms, until she was standing on her own two feet. Though he noticed that her fingers did grip his leather jacket for a few minutes, and she was breathing heavily, until her heart slowed its headlong race, and settled into a regular rhythm.

"What the fuck, Elle?" he demanded, his relief at her apparent health transferring readily into a raging anger that she'd risked herself to protect *him*. He could take care of himself, damn it.

"I was protecting you," she snapped, shoving away from him completely.

The rage that rolled through Lucifer in that moment was so hot, so boiling, fucking hot, that he was surprised he didn't combust and burn to ash in an instant. But years of discipline took hold of him, and he shoved it aside. Eleanor was fine—though she might not be after he got finished with her later—and he had a job to do.

"Are any of the other humans alive?" he growled.

"One of the men. The other one fired on me as I came through the door, so he's dead. But this one's unconscious. I hit him over the head to get him out of the way." He noticed for the first time that the short stick she'd been carrying was now a full-length bo staff. As she talked, she tapped each end of the staff against the adjacent wall, and, that quickly, it was a short stick again. "He'll wake up before too—"

"He'll wake when I want him to," Lucifer snarled, obviously not doing as good a job of controlling his anger as he'd thought. He checked the enemy vampire who remained safely drifting in unconsciousness, but maybe not for much longer. The vampire wasn't as strong as Lucifer, but he was no lightweight, either. "I'll do the vamp first," he said. "Keep an eye on the human, just to be safe."

"Safe for what?"

"Safe until I can question him," he said impatiently, hoping she wasn't going to go all politically correct again about his interrogation techniques. Not waiting for her response, he knelt next to the vamp, who was lying on the truly filthy carpet, and placed a hand on his head. It wasn't really necessary for him to touch the other vamp in order to rummage through his thoughts, but it seemed natural to do so.

He frowned as he sank into the vamp's brain, searching through the last few days, snagging and discarding bits of information faster than he could absorb. It was a scatter shot search, grabbing everything that might be relevant. He'd examine those bits of data more thoroughly later, and probably discard most of them. It wasn't unlike searching through piles of memos, skimming the titles, keeping some, tossing others, then moving on.

It took a few minutes, but when he returned to the dirty living room, he knew everything this vampire did about the plot to kidnap Colin Murphy. The vamp—whose name was Torres—was of no further value to him, and, in fact, posed a risk if he returned to his masters. So, Lucifer reached out with a fine filament of power and drilled into the vamp's heart, burning the organ to dust in a matter of seconds. He stood and took a fastidious step back to avoid the mess, and then, turning his back on what used to be a vampire, he headed for the kitchen.

He passed Eleanor where she stood in the kitchen doorway, giving him a dagger stare of disapproval, presumably over his killing of the enemy vampire. How the hell she could work so closely with a full-fledged vampire lord like Sophia, and still maintain these delicate human sensibilities, he didn't know. Vampire lords to a man—or woman—were cruel and efficiently ruthless in their dealings with vampires and humans alike.

But he didn't have time to get into a discussion of vampire ethics right now. There was still a human to question, and time was running out. All of the gunfire would have attracted attention, and he had no doubt that the authorities were already on their way. He had minutes at best to question the human, gather Eleanor, and get out of the neighborhood before the police arrived on scene.

The lone human survivor of the initial skirmish didn't pose any risk, not the way the vampire, Torres, had, and he was a lot more fragile. So, Lucifer slid carefully into the man's brain and brought him back to consciousness, even repairing the tiny blood vessels that were bleeding as a result of Eleanor's love tap with her bo staff. He didn't do it because he gave a fuck about the man's well-being, but because he wanted the guy able to answer questions intelligently.

Keeping him semi-conscious to minimize resistance, he slipped into the man's brain telepathically. Rather than dig around the way he had with Torres, he simply "thought" questions at him. Torres would have fought tooth and nail against divulging any shred of information, whereas this human was already thoroughly primed to cooperate.

Lucifer pursued a broad line of questioning first, asking for anything he knew about Colin Murphy's disappearance. The man's name was Jack Anderson and as it turned out, he knew quite a lot. To begin with, the dead man, the one who'd fired on Elle, was Chase Landry's lover, Aubert. That explained the cell phone's persistent pinging in this location.

Lucifer nodded to himself at the discovery. It made sense that Landry—or whoever was running him—would require at least some human assistance. And who better to trust than his live-in lover? Jack and the now dead Aubert had initially been part of the initial daylight guard contingent. They'd been replaced after only a few days, and had never actually *seen* Murphy, because the prisoner's cell remained closed and locked the entire time.

They'd been picked up in the city, and driven to an entrance to the underground, where they were eventually hustled into an unused and unfinished side tunnel. And all while blindfolded, unfortunately. Jack only knew that it wasn't one of the regular tunnels because he'd worked in the mines for a while when he was younger, and he recognized the wet earth and stone *smell* of a freshly-cut tunnel, as well as the gritty feel of an unfinished floor. For all of that, however, the area where he assumed Murphy was being held was in reasonably finished shape. The walls were crude, but the doors were heavy, and had secure locks.

Lucifer lifted his head as the distant sound of sirens intruded into the mental conversation he was having with the human guard. Time was running out, and he still had to wipe this man's mind before leaving with Eleanor.

Taking a precious few seconds to sweep the human's memory for every face he'd seen in the tunnels, he then wiped all knowledge of the last twenty-four hours, wanting to be certain that there were no remaining recollections of Eleanor or himself. Let Chase Landry and his cohort deal with the human authorities. There would be nothing and no one left to tie Lucifer or Eleanor to the scene.

When he was finished, he dropped the man into a deep, unconscious state, slid carefully out of his mind, and, finally, stepped back and took a quick cell phone image. It wouldn't hurt to run an identity search on him, and maybe discover where he worked, and whom he hung around with.

Lucifer didn't waste any time after that. Grabbing Eleanor's arm, he pulled her from the house, keeping her close as he blanketed the two of them with a "no-see-me" suggestion for any minds in the vicinity, and went directly to their SUV. Eleanor yanked her arm away at the last minute to go around to the driver's side, and Lucifer was glad she had those extra steps to travel, because he was sure she'd have left him behind if he'd been a few seconds too slow.

He almost grinned at that thought, but he was still too angry with her for trying to defend him at the cost of her own life. And she was just as furious with him, although he couldn't have said why. He'd done nothing wrong. He was a vampire and proud of it, and he was under no obligation to pretend to be less than he was, or something other than *what* he was, just because she persisted in clinging to human sensibilities—sensibilities that might work for humans, but could get a vampire killed.

The cold silence between them lasted all the way back to the hotel, while they turned the vehicle over to one of Cal's guards, while they crossed the lobby to the elevator, and during the ride up to the penthouse floor, with the small box fairly vibrating with their combined anger.

Lucifer nodded politely to Cal, when the human met them in the narrow vestibule outside the penthouse doors, and he held the door open for Eleanor, despite her outraged glare. As if common courtesy was now a crime.

Once inside, he closed the door, then crossed to the big windows, checking to make sure they were closed and locked, before securing the shutters and pulling the drapes against the thinning darkness.

When he turned from that task, Eleanor was watching him with a new wariness, as if she'd finally realized how truly, *dangerously* angry he was.

Lucifer took his time, intentionally doing a thorough scan of the room, to be certain he hadn't missed any danger that might have snuck in during the night. And then he stalked toward Eleanor with all the deadly intent of the alpha predator he was. His attention was focused and unwavering, catching every furtive movement that signaled her intent to escape, every spark of defiance in her big, blue eyes.

She glanced over at the closed door to her bedroom and began to back away in that direction, as if that flimsy barrier could stop him.

"Lucifer," she said slowly, warning him off. But he was too far gone for that.

He strode right into her personal space and grabbed her upper arms, careful to temper his strength despite his anger. Her vampire physiology could handle far more than a little rough handling, and would sustain little or no damage, but that didn't matter. This was Eleanor. He could never intentionally hurt her.

"Don't you *ever* risk your life to defend mine," he snarled.

Eleanor stared at him. She'd known he was angry, but clearly hadn't understood why. It didn't take her long to recover, though, as surprise was quickly eclipsed by outrage.

"Are you kidding me?" she snarled right back at him. "Hello! This is what I *do*. You get that, right? You might be the vampire version of Sherlock Holmes, but I'm a fucking *bodyguard*, you ass! I'll risk whatever I need to—"

"The hell you will. You're not *my* bodyguard. You're too important to waste your—"

"Important? I'm nobody, a security grunt. You're way more—"

"You're important to *me*, damn it. I lost you once, and I won't do it again. I can't."

His growled words shocked both of them into stillness, inches apart, staring at each other, their chests heaving with angry, uneven breaths.

When they finally moved, it was as one, pouncing on each other, attacking with teeth and nails, shredding clothing, nipping hungrily at every newly bared inch of skin. Moving his grip to her waist, Lucifer lifted her off her feet and slammed her against the wall, holding her there with the press of his upper body, as he ripped off the rest of her clothes . . . until there was nothing left, nothing beneath his fingers, nothing under his lips, except smooth, delicious skin. *Eleanor.* Christ. It had been so long since he'd touched her, so long since he'd first *loved* her, and yet nothing had changed. His senses remembered every tiny detail.

Her skin was still creamy pale and silky soft, her neck an elegant column as he licked his way down to the full, round globes of her breasts, with their petal pink areolas and large nipples. She moaned when he rasped his tongue over the swollen tips, crying out when he bit down gently, not breaking the skin, not yet. He'd waited twenty-three years to taste her again. He was going to make it last, lingering over every single lick and suck, and then he was going to fuck her until she screamed his name just the way she used to.

"Lucifer," she moaned. It wasn't the scream he'd be hearing later, but the soft, hungry sound had his dick stiffening, crushed against the zipper of his jeans, as he recalled every moan, every cry she'd ever uttered, as clearly as if he'd just left her in his bed a few hours ago.

The realization crushed him.

He stopped, and cupped her face in his hands, studying every perfect detail. "Eleanor," he whispered, trying to convince himself that this was real. He'd had this dream so many times; he half-expected to wake up and find her gone.

Her beautiful blue eyes opened, filled with crystal tears. "Lucifer?"

"I love you, *bella,*" he murmured against her mouth as he kissed her. He took his time about it, savoring the brush of her soft lips, the stroke of her tongue against his as they tangled in a slow, sensuous dance. A tear slid down her cheek to mingle with their kiss, and Lucifer licked it up, relishing the satiny, salty flavor as he followed it to her elegant jaw and down even farther. Running his tongue along the smooth line of her neck, he sucked gently, scenting the rush of her vampire blood beneath the skin, feverishly hot and spiced with euphoric.

He lifted his head with a growl, his eyes clearing as he gazed at her, worshiping her body with his eyes and hands, stroking the firm muscles of her smooth arms, a vampire's muscles. Stronger now than when he'd last made love to her, but more beautiful than ever. He leaned back just enough to drag his hungry gaze up and down her body, lingering at the sight of her pale pussy with its bare dusting of curly blond hair. She was perfection.

"Put your legs around me," he growled, and pressed her up against the wall once more, freeing a hand to rip open his own jeans, reaching in and fisting his cock as she obeyed, lifting her slender legs, vampire strong, to band around his hips, holding him tightly, as if fearing he'd try to escape.

Never.

Studying her with eyes narrowed beneath half-lowered lids, he pumped his cock with deliberate slowness, up and down, seeing the desire in her gaze that matched his own.

"Lucifer," she whispered, betraying a thread of anxiety that he'd leave her empty and longing, aching. His heart soared and his cock swelled at the soft pleading in her voice, the *need*. For him.

Guiding his cock to the heated opening of her sex, he teased her, rubbing the tip in the satiny cream between her swollen pussy lips, feeling the sticky wetness of her thighs that gave proof of her arousal. Eleanor's head rolled back against the wall, and her eyes closed as she repeated his name over and over again.

Lucifer held back, reveling in the feeling of having Eleanor in his arms once again, wet and begging for his cock. He remembered everything about her, had dreamed of this moment so many times. From the earliest days of her leaving, when he'd been certain she'd return, to the desperate realization that she was gone forever. He'd never stopped longing for her, had still dreamed that someday he would find her.

And now that the moment had come, he didn't want it to end. He wanted to remember every second of this night, to burn into his memory the elegant curve of her cheek and brow, the delicate flush of her pale skin, and the golden silk of her hair as it fell over her creamy shoulders. It was all so familiar, and yet, it was if he was learning her for the first time.

His cock jerked hungrily. Lucifer might want to stare at her for hours, but his dick had other plans.

"Look at me," he ordered.

Her eyes flashed open. He hesitated a fraction of a second, and then pushed deep into her body, riding her slick arousal into the hot, tight glove of her cunt. So tight. If she hadn't been so thoroughly aroused, he'd have been hard pressed to squeeze his way into her pussy.

He'd no sooner had the thought, and wondered at the reasons for her tightness, than they both froze, staring at each other, shock and desire warring in their identical gazes.

"Lucifer," she murmured, as fresh tears filled her eyes.

"Baby," he whispered, his chest aching with emotion, with fucking relief that he'd found her, that she was safe, and she was his. No matter what else came of this hunt, he was *never* letting Eleanor go.

Gripping the firm round globes of her ass, he held her in place and fucked her, pounding in and out of her slick pussy, driven by the agony and frustration of all those years of wondering where she was, and why she'd gone. He fucked her mindlessly, determined to imprint on her body, to brand her soul, so that she'd never leave him again.

ELEANOR'S HEART was racing, thudding against her rib cage like a trapped animal, as Lucifer fucked her so much harder than he ever had before. He'd always been a wonderful lover, so caring, so skilled. And almost too gentle. But he wasn't being gentle tonight. He was ferocious and greedy, an animal claiming his mate, pounding his big cock in and out of her body, until she could feel the heat of its passage along the delicate tissues of her trembling sheath.

She wrapped her arms around him, holding him close, needing the skin to skin contact of her breasts against his massive chest, her nipples scraping the scattering of soft, dark hair spread over his pectorals. But more than the contact, she needed to hide the hot tears flooding from her eyes to soak into the skin of his neck. It wasn't pain. Or rather it was, but not from the brutal slam of his delicious cock. It was the realization of everything she'd missed, everything she'd thrown away. This moment and a thousand like it, with Lucifer's gorgeous eyes filled with such joy, such relief at having found her.

She couldn't remember anymore why she'd ever run.

The suppressed emotions finally spilled out of her in a choked sob. Her lips opened against his neck, sucking up the salty sweat, the slight taste of blood. It made her hunger for him. She wanted every part of him to be hers. She bit into his skin, burying her tears in the heady taste of his blood . . . vampire lord's blood, powerful and intoxicating. He might not be a lord yet, but he would be someday. Blood didn't lie. And she drank it in like the sweetest nectar.

Lucifer growled, and his cock seemed to swell inside of her as his blood flowed from her bite, dripping down her chin. His fingers speared through her hair, and he squeezed, gripping so tightly that her scalp burned, the pain mingling with the seduction of his blood. Her pussy convulsed, grasping his cock so tightly that he could no longer move.

They groaned in the same moment, hers muffled where her lips were still molded to his skin, his a deep vibration of warm air against her ear.

"Eleanor," he murmured, like a prayer, and then he started moving again, forcing his way through the greedy clutches of her pussy, scraping every tiny nerve and muscle as he thrust in and out.

Glorious sensation spread from her pussy to her clit, throbbing, pounding in time with her heart. Each pulsing beat was a fresh wave of erotic pleasure, until she thought she'd shatter with the sheer, overwhelming passion of it. But Lucifer held her together. Lucifer with his strong arms and powerful blood, with the love that seared her soul with every glance from his golden eyes.

"Come, Eleanor," he snarled. Uncompromising, a demand. His gaze was hard and deadly as he stared down at her. But it wasn't the demand that sent a spark of desire shooting from her clit to the tips of her breasts. It was the vulnerability that hid behind the cruelty in his eyes.

Eleanor screamed as her body surrendered to the need in Lucifer's gaze, drowning in the ecstasy that swept over her in waves, each swell deeper than the last, lighting up her nerves and bowing her back, as Lucifer's fingers dug into her ass, holding her open to his carnal assault until, with a guttural roar, his cock bucked and he filled her with a rush of heat.

LUCIFER DRIFTED, sliding his cock lazily in and out of Eleanor's creamy pussy, smiling at her occasional gasp when her body jolted, as if firing the final sparks of her climax. She clung to him, her arms loose around his neck, her breath hot on the still throbbing wound where she'd bitten deeply enough to drink his blood. He rubbed a soothing hand down her back. His blood was potent, and not something he shared lightly. In fact, he'd never shared blood before with any other vampire.

But now, Eleanor was his. He'd claimed her with his blood, and his cock.

And as for the rest, for Eleanor's half of the claiming? He didn't need to drink any of her blood to be hers. He was already. She'd claimed his heart a long time ago.

Moving his hands to a more secure grip on her sweet ass, he straightened, pulling her away from the wall. Eleanor murmured a soft protest, and he shifted to carry her in his arms, heading for his bedroom.

She was in his bed now. Back where she belonged. And where she was going to stay.

Chapter Seven

ELEANOR WOKE ALL at once, the way she always did since becoming Vampire. And as always, she lay perfectly still, taking in her surroundings, running down a checklist of sound and smell . . . She froze for a long moment, and then sighed in almost reluctant pleasure.

Lucifer.

She could never forget this. The intense heat of his body, the masculine scent. The sheer size of him that had always made her feel so delicate. So safe.

She was a vampire now, strong and capable. A highly trained bodyguard who could take down a man or woman three times her size, whether vampire or human. She wasn't a potential lord like Lucifer, but she had power, and she knew how to channel it into her fists and feet, wielding her bo staff with deadly skill. She had far more power than her petite frame might indicate, and she certainly didn't need anyone to take care of her anymore.

But that didn't make her feel any less cherished when Lucifer wrapped his big arms around her and pulled her against his chest, surrounding her with his powerful body. Because it wasn't his physical size or his vampiric power, it was love. Lucifer had always loved her. She'd never doubted that.

Until she hadn't been human anymore.

The treacherous thought made her stiffen in his arms, made her remember all the reasons she'd run. Reasons that still held true.

"Talk to me, Eleanor."

"About what?" she said cautiously, but she already knew. He'd felt her stiffen, how could he not? He wasn't asking her for conversation, he wanted *the talk*.

"Eleanor," he chided. "Tell me what you're thinking. Tell me why you hate it when I manipulate humans into spilling their guts, or even when I killed that vampire bastard, Torres." His arms banded abruptly tighter, preventing her from escaping . . . again. "God damn it, Eleanor, tell me why you ran away."

"I told you. I didn't think you'd want me after—"

"Why?" The single word was filled with such grief that she felt guilty. Because the truth was that she'd known within days of running that she'd made a mistake. She'd told herself that she couldn't go back, that Derek Pratt, the bastard who'd changed her, would claim his rights as her Sire. But it was a lie. She simply hadn't wanted to see the look in Lucifer's eyes, the disappointment that she was no longer human, or even worse, that as a vampire she wasn't strong enough to be useful.

She'd learned the lie of that eventually, too. Once she'd pledged her loyalty to Lucien, the old Canadian vampire lord, and then to Sophia as his successor. She'd been shown the true nature and depth of her power. But by then, it was too late. Her path was set, and so was Lucifer's. And they were thousands of miles and years of history apart.

Eleanor buried her face in the warm crook of his neck, her arms around him, squeezing tightly, as if she could make up for the pain she'd caused him if she just held on long enough.

"I'm sorry," she said against his skin. "I was just so confused."

He sighed, his body slumping against her in surrender. She felt even guiltier than before, but more than that, she felt humbled by the abiding nature of his love. That after all these years, and all the pain she'd caused him, he loved her exactly the same.

"Tell me what happened. Tell me what he did to you." There was reluctance in his voice, but it was tempered by determination, by the need to *know*.

"He didn't rape me, Lucifer," she assured him softly. "It wasn't that."

He laughed sharply. "Oh, I know that, *cara*. I scrubbed that fucker's brain to shreds before I let him die."

She winced.

"That," he snapped. "That right there. Tell me what the hell happened that makes you reject me mind-fucking even that asshole Derek Pratt. If anyone deserved—"

"It's not him," she interrupted, and felt him stiffen against her.

"Someone else? Tell me who, and I'll—"

"No. Jesus, Lucifer, you can't hunt down and kill every vampire I've encountered in the last two decades."

"Try me," he snarled, and she breathed a soft laugh.

"The problem is me," she explained. "I mean, yeah, it started with what Pratt did to me, but I didn't understand back then."

"Understand what? That you had the right to *consent* to whatever the hell he wanted from you?"

"But that's just it. I *did* consent. But it wasn't because I wanted to. He invaded my thoughts, took over my will. He made me *want* what he was offering, made me want *him*."

"Tell me," he demanded. And so, she let her mind drift back to that awful night.

1993 New Orleans, Louisiana, USA

ELEANOR HAD NO idea where she was. It was dark, and vaguely musty smelling. Like the place needed a good scrubbing. She lay perfectly still, terrified, struggling to remember. Where was she? How had she gotten here? And then her memory slowly returned, and she wished it hadn't—Derek crushing her against his body, his hands everywhere, squeezing her breasts, her ass, even—she shuddered to remember— even shoving his fingers into her pussy, while she writhed in his arms.

She sat up, choking on the horror of what Derek had done, of what she'd become. And with it came the knowledge of where she must be. This was Derek's place, and he'd brought her here. She did a cringing survey of her body, dreading what she might find. She was naked, which was bad. But other than sore breasts, and some minor tenderness between her thighs, there was nothing. He might have intended to rape her, but something had delayed him. Maybe he'd feared Lucifer would show up at her place, which should have been true. Where was Lucifer?

A door opened across the room, casting a pale rectangle of light on the dark room. Eleanor raised a hand to shade her eyes against a light that seemed far too bright for what it was.

"Welcome to the new world, Eleanor darling. You're mine now."

She twisted around at the sound of Derek's voice. What the hell was he . . .? Horror dawned as she felt the pull of his mastery over her. It made her want to drop to her knees and beg him to use her . . . again.

Oh my God, had she done that? Had she begged Derek to fuck her? What would Lucifer think? Would he understand?

"Get up. I've got places to be, and you're going with me."

She hated his voice, his smell, everything about him.

"I'm not going anywhere with you," she snarled. She forced herself to stand, ignoring the aches and pains, the soreness, the embarrassment of her nakedness. She might have made the stupidest mistake of her life, but she was still herself. And there was no way in hell she was letting Derek Pratt tell her what to do. "When Lucifer finds out what you did—"

He laughed, the noise harsh against ears that were so much more sensitive than they'd been only a few hours ago. Like her eyes. Would it always be like this? Should it be? Was there something wrong with her?

Derek grabbed her upper arms without warning. She tried to twist away, but he was too strong. Way too strong.

"You think he'll want you like this?" he mocked. "What good are you to him? You're a vampire now, no longer his perfectly fuckable princess. Hell, you're not even good for food anymore."

She told herself that Derek was lying, trying to hurt her even more than he already had. Or maybe it was Lucifer he was trying to hurt. Doubt teased the edges of her mind. But if that was true, if Derek had made her a vampire in order to wound Lucifer, then maybe he was telling the truth, taunting her with a new reality that she—and Lucifer— were helpless to change. Derek was an asshole, but he was also a vampire. He understood a vampire's needs and preferences far better than she did.

She thought back to the many nights she'd spent with Lucifer, and all the things they'd talked about. He'd told her about his life, about what it meant to be a vampire, and how it had changed everything for him. About how much he loved her humanity, how he fed from her during sex, and the erotic heights they'd soared together because of it.

And she realized how all of that would change now.

Her chest ached from too much anger, too much loss, and all of it fighting to get out, while she struggled to keep it contained. She wanted to scream her pain to the world. She wanted to *kill* fucking Derek Pratt, to stomp on his dying face until he was . . .

Eleanor blinked in surprise at her own thoughts. Was this what it meant to be a vampire? These bloody, violent thoughts? She grabbed her head as if she could squeeze the images out, like juice from an orange. Her fingers tightened, yanking her hair until the sharp pain brought her back to earth.

Across the room, Derek chuckled, amused by her agony, by the hell that he'd made her life. She eyed him darkly, dredging up the satisfying image of him bloody beneath her boot.

As if he'd heard her thoughts, or maybe he'd simply read them on her face, he sobered. "Forget it, bitch. I'm your Sire now, and you can't do a fucking thing to me."

Eleanor tipped her head, eyeing him appraisingly. She could feel the bond tying them together. He was right about that much. But the tie was fragile, and weak, just like Derek. She weighed their relative power without even knowing what she was doing, and found him lacking, and yet . . . . Something inside of her, some new perception she'd never possessed before tonight, told her she couldn't kill Derek.

But if she stayed, he'd use her. And she'd let him.

She cursed. She had to run, to get as far away from Derek as possible before his hold on her grew any stronger. But even more, she had to leave town before *Lucifer* found her. Before she had to face him with what she'd become, to see the horror, the rejection in his eyes. She couldn't survive that. She wouldn't want to.

Ignoring Derek's increasingly strident demands, she gathered the pieces of her clothing that were scattered on the floor, then got dressed and shoved her way past him. She would have laughed at the shock on his face when she slammed him against the wall, but there was nothing funny about what was happening tonight. Her life was being ripped to shreds, minute by minute. She just had to hold on to the few fragments left long enough to get out of town, to go . . . she didn't know where but somewhere had to be better than here.

But first . . . oh God, the horrors just kept coming, because *first*, she had to eat.

Present day, Montreal, Quebec, Canada

"JESUS, ELLE," LUCIFER breathed. "Why the fuck would you believe anything Pratt told you? When did I ever—"

"I know," she said, putting a hand over his mouth to stop him. "But I wasn't thinking straight. You have to understand that, right? I was so confused by all the new sensations and feelings, and there was no one to explain anything. Derek only cared about sticking it to you. He wasn't going to teach me anything. And I was so terrified, Luc."

"Baby, baby," he murmured, hugging her tightly as if he could make it all go away. "I'm sorry."

"It wasn't your fault. *None* of this was your fault. It was that asshole who started it, and then . . . I just panicked."

He rubbed his jaw against her hair in silent comfort.

"It took me a week to stop running, another week to realize what I'd done. I knew you'd never have enlisted Derek to do *anything* much less make me a vampire. And if you'd somehow lost your mind, and *had* asked him, you'd never have left me to go through it alone." She slid her arms around his rib cage, stroking up over his back to his shoulders, holding him against her. "But it was *done*. I couldn't change that. And knowing how blind I'd been, knowing you'd never have gone along with it, only convinced me even more that you wouldn't want me this way." She shrugged. "I couldn't face that. I was learning to cope with all the other shit, the hunger, the increased strength, enhanced senses . . . all of the new urges that wanted to dictate how I lived, what I thought. But the one thing I knew I could never survive was discovering you didn't love me anymore.

"So I just kept on running, until Lucien found me. It was pure chance that our paths crossed. Or at least as much pure chance as anything that happens to vampires. He was powerful and kind, and willing to teach a young, stupid vampire how to live without making a mess of it."

"Did he fuck you?" Lucifer growled, and his fingers dug into her hips.

"Lucifer," she chided. "What difference—"

"Come on, Elle. Everyone knows that Lucien picked his vampires for their fuckability. And you're a beautiful—"

"So you've been celibate all these years? No lovers for the great Lucifer?"

He narrowed his eyes at her in irritation. "It's not the—"

"If you tell me it's not the same for men and women, I will geld you where you lie."

He laughed in genuine amusement, obviously not too terrified by the potential loss of his favorite body part. "You wouldn't do that," he murmured, sliding a hand down to cup her ass, holding her in place as he rubbed that very *firm* body part against her belly.

"I might regret it," she admitted.

He smiled. "How'd you end up on Sophia's security detail?"

"Under Lucien—and don't *even* go there—I was part of his security team, but that didn't mean much under his rule. I think everyone knew how lax Lucien's security was. It got him killed in the end, and—"

"It got a lot of other vamps killed, too," he interjected harshly.

"I know," she admitted, though it pained her. Lucien had been good to *her,* but he hadn't been a good lord for his territory. "Anyway, when Sophia became the new lord, Colin took over her security. She didn't have any staff of her own, and not even a single child. Colin was looking for a female bodyguard for Sophia, and he held a sort of tryout."

"And Murphy picked you."

"He didn't *pick* me. I won the damn tryout by a mile. I'd been training for two decades by then. It started as a reaction to Derek. I was afraid he'd come for me—"

"He was long dead by the time you met Lucien. You should have felt—"

"I did feel something, but I didn't know what it was. I was still running scared back then, and when the Sire/child connection between us was severed, I just chalked the feeling up to one more vampire sensation that I didn't understand, and kept preparing myself to be ready when Derek came after me.

"Anyway, after that, the security job came naturally. Vampires all have talents, and that was mine."

"Some of us have more than one," he murmured, turning her in his arms to run a caressing hand over her body.

"You didn't get *that* talent from being a vampire."

He grinned. "True. But it has given me a very long time to improve my technique."

She sighed. Lucifer's hand was a warm caress, rubbing up and down her back. It was so fucking soothing that she checked her awareness, wanting to be sure it was just physical, that he wasn't manipulating her. But she'd no sooner had the thought than she recoiled. It was that kind of thinking that had made her run. Lucifer deserved better. He'd deserved it then, and he still did now.

"After what Derek did, I couldn't stand knowing that my mind wasn't my own anymore," she said quietly.

"You should have come to me—"

"You were a vampire," she said simply. "Just like Derek—"

"The fuck I was!"

"I know, I know," she murmured, kissing his neck in apology. "But I didn't know then; I didn't know *anything*. And by the time I learned enough to know better, I figured you'd have already moved on. You were so beautiful. There were always women—"

"Was? So, I'm not beautiful anymore?" he grumbled.

She slapped his amazing chest. "Stop that. You know exactly how good looking you are."

He made a self-deprecating moue with his lips, and she nearly laughed. But there were still things that needed to be said.

"It left a mark," she told him soberly. "Even once I discovered that not all vampires were like Derek. That, in fact, vampire law forbids changing a human without consent. Even after that, the idea of one of us slipping into another's mind and learning their secrets, of making them tell you things they wouldn't want you to know, secrets they haven't even told their lovers...it makes me sick. Physically sick."

"I make you sick?"

"No, no, no," she said quickly. "Never. But it was difficult to get past that. It still is."

"I don't understand," he said, pulling back enough to see her face. "You've been Sophia's close-in bodyguard for how long? A year at least, right?"

"Just over that, yeah."

"You can't tell me that she hasn't interrogated anyone during that time, that there've been no enemy vamps coming at her, or challenges from her own people."

"Of course not, but—"

"But what, Elle?" he asked, seeming genuinely puzzled. "Sophia uses kind persuasion instead? Or is it that someone else does her dirty work for her? Murphy's not doing it, but maybe she has an interrogator, some truly medieval vamp—"

"No!" she shouted. "No," she repeated more calmly. "Most of the vampires who've challenged her weren't anywhere near strong enough to defeat her. She was a complete unknown to the Canadian vamp community, and I think they confused her playgirl reputation with weakness."

"God knows why," Lucifer said dryly. "She wasn't any different than Lucien, and they followed him willingly enough."

"You don't really need me to explain that, do you? Vampires are a total boys club, and Sophia doesn't have a penis."

"Well, that's a relief. She's a stunning woman, and . . . and I think I'm finished with that thought," he said, grinning down at her.

"Uh huh. Anyway, her two biggest challengers came before I was brought on board. That was Darren Yamanaka, and, oddly enough, a vampire named Thierry Lavoie who was Master of Montreal when Sophia took over. She killed Lavoie."

"She *should* have killed Yamanaka. We wouldn't be here right now if she had." He frowned a moment, then said, "But then you and I wouldn't be in this bed together, so I'm not complaining."

"Of course, if she had killed Darren, then Colin wouldn't be enduring horrific torture every night either, but it's good you have your priorities straight."

He shrugged, and Eleanor had to remind herself that Lucifer didn't know Colin Murphy the way she did. He wasn't personally invested in Colin's well-being, other than as a general principle. It was cowardly to torture a vampire's human mate in order to get what you wanted. And besides, in this case, the vampires holding Colin were colluding with the

European invaders, which involved every vampire lord in North America, including Lucifer's Aden.

"So, you're telling me you've never seen Sophia dig into a vampire's brain? That hardly seems likely, given—"

"No, of course, I have, but it's not the vampires that bother me. It's the humans. Sophia has almost nothing to do with humans, other than her own daytime staff, and Colin oversees all of the daytime people, from gardeners to security guards. He shields her from most of that."

"Another mistake, but beside the point."

She scowled. She was getting a clear picture that Lucifer didn't think much of Sophia's way of running her territory, and it was pissing her off.

"Look, all I'm saying is that when you started digging into those humans' brains—"

"I don't 'dig,' Elle. It's much more subtle than that."

"Whatever. It brought back bad memories, okay? That's all I'm saying."

He studied her for a long moment, then nodded. "Okay. I can understand that. But *you* have to understand that sometimes it's necessary. Those humans had helped kidnap your friend Murphy, and they had information that I needed to find and rescue him. I could have used physical force. I could have tortured it out of them the way Murphy's captors are doing him. But *because* of Murphy, I don't have time for that. Besides, the humans I brain fuck never even know I was there. I'm just that good. And, frankly, I'm getting a little tired of being compared to that asshole Derek Pratt. I'm a fucking genius—a Mozart compared to Pratt's one-year old pounding on a toy piano. You're a vampire, Elle. You *know* what I am."

"I do," she said, rubbing his chest soothingly. "And I know *you*, Luc. You're a good man."

"Well, don't tell anyone that. I have a rep to maintain."

"Your secret's safe with me," she said, laughing, but then she sighed. For a little while, this had been like old times. Back when they'd had nothing to do but love each other, they'd spend plenty of nights lying in bed like this, talking, making love, and then talking some more. Unfortunately . . .

"We have to get up, you know," Lucifer said, echoing her thoughts.

"I know. What's on the agenda for tonight?"

"Well, first," he murmured, rolling her under him and slipping his knee between her legs, "I'm going to make love to you."

Eleanor's breath caught in her throat as his thigh pressed against her pussy. Such a careful touch, and such unbearable tension. His cock was hard against her thigh, firm and enticing, ready for action. And yet, he was making no move to spread her legs and slide that hard length inside her. Damn him.

He seemed determined to drive her insane first, licking and kissing every inch of her, starting with her face—her eyes, her cheeks, a soft caress over her lips. And then her neck, lingering over the pulse point of her carotid, his tongue pressed against her skin as if to feel the throbbing of her blood as it passed through the artery. Her heart nearly stopped when he closed his teeth over the soft spot of her neck, bringing back all those times he'd done the same when she'd been human, a knife's edge of memory, so clear and so sharp. Warm, dark nights with Lucifer, making her feel beautiful, loved, cherished. And then the incredible passion of his bite, the hot rush of raw desire singeing every nerve, every muscle.

Lucifer's deep growl brought her back to the present, to the feel of his fangs closing over the soft ridge of her clavicle. "Do you think I can't make you scream without the bite euphoric, Elle?" he demanded, guessing her thoughts with startling accuracy.

Her eyes flashed open to see his glaring down at her, power gleaming in a golden light that limned his face and made him seem unreal, a beautiful temptation sent to lure her into hell. He held her gaze long enough for her to see the wicked gleam in their depths, and then his dark head bent over her breasts, and her heart nearly forgot how to beat.

Lucifer's mouth closed over a nipple, sucking hard enough to sting, letting his fangs graze over the delicate skin of her breast, before moving to the other breast and doing the same. He lifted his head and blew gently on the wet tips, watching her reaction, smiling at the hunger she couldn't keep from her face, and then he abandoned her aching breasts to move downward. His mouth was a delicate torment as he kissed his way past her stomach, nibbling at her belly while he pushed her thighs open and she realized where he was going. She wanted to protest, to tell him she couldn't stand it, that it had been too long, that no one had made her feel so damn *much* in all the years they'd been separated. But the words wouldn't come. Because she *wanted* it, wanted him, more than her next breath. She'd missed him. All this time, she'd thought she was fine, that her past was just that. But she'd been a fool.

The brush of a finger over her clit brought her back to the moment, this exquisite, tantalizing moment with the most beautiful man between her thighs, his breath hot against her wet pussy. He spread her swollen lips with his thumbs, his eyes still glowing with power as he studied her bare sex.

"Such a pretty pussy," he murmured, almost as if to himself. "So pink, so delicate . . ." His tongue speared out, and he licked the length of her slit, from her opening to her clit, his tongue swirling around that sensitive nub without touching it, and back again. "So tasty, *bella*. So wet and creamy."

Eleanor groaned, embarrassed, but so unbearably aroused as he licked yet again, lapping up the cream of her arousal. She threw her head back, fighting the urge to thrust her pussy into his face, to beg him to lick harder, lick more. Her arms were over her head, her hands gripping the wooden slats of the headboard until she thought they'd crack. She didn't know how to handle this overload of sensation. She wanted to scream, she *needed* to come. Why wouldn't he let her come?

His tongue rasped over her clit without warning, and she jerked in surprise. Her pussy clenched greedily, looking for something to fill it. She groaned, a plea in her throat, ready to beg him for release. But this was Lucifer. He knew what she needed, and he held nothing back.

His tongue stabbed into her pussy, hard and thrusting like a cock, while his thumb toyed with her clit, circling, brushing, promising but never giving her relief. She did beg then, gasping his name. And he rewarded her, sucking her clit into his mouth, biting down with just his lips, pinching the hardened nub, so engorged with her blood, so exquisitely sensitive. The climax slammed into her, hard and ferocious. For all her begging, she was completely unprepared for the strength of it. Her back bowed, lifting from the bed until there was nothing holding her to earth except Lucifer's mouth between her legs, his strong hands on her hips. She leaned forward, bent nearly in half as she gripped his short hair and hugged his head between her breasts, even as he continued to suck her clit. Her orgasm rolled on and on, shuddering through her body until she was sobbing for a different kind of relief. She couldn't take this, couldn't deal with the overload.

Finally, his head lifted and he gathered her close, making soothing noises, holding her, giving her strength as she trembled in the aftermath, as lingering sparks of orgasm set off firestorms in her muscles.

He kissed her, and she tasted herself on his lips. "Delicious, isn't it?" he murmured, sensual and unrepentant.

Despite the flush of embarrassment staining her cheeks, she smiled. She'd never met anyone like Lucifer. Not before meeting him, and not in the many years after. Or maybe she'd just never let anyone else get that close. She'd fed from many men since leaving him, and she'd fed from women, too. It didn't matter to her. They were food, and nothing more.

She hadn't had a lover, hadn't let anyone get close. Because Lucifer had always been there in her heart.

She was abruptly aware of his cock, a solid, throbbing presence between her thighs, nestled between her trembling pussy lips like a delicious promise. And her body knew what it wanted. Her sheath was pulsing, tightening and releasing, as if sensing the heaven that was so close.

"Do you want it, baby?" he murmured, flexing his hips, sliding his hard length through her wetness.

She nodded against his chest, her throat too dry to speak.

He pulled back to study her, and something softer passed over his face, changing his expression. Something solemn and gentle. "Have I told you I love you, *bella?*"

Tears filled her eyes. She nodded, her chest tight with emotion. "I love you, too."

"That's good, baby." He rolled her to her back, tucking her beneath him, as he settled between her thighs and slid his cock deep inside her. She was so wet that it went in easily, her inner muscles stretching eagerly to accommodate his thickness, her body so ready for him that it was almost embarrassing. He'd always been able to do this to her, make her hunger for things she hadn't even known she wanted. And what she wanted more than anything was Lucifer.

She flexed her hips against him, tightening her inner muscles and squeezing his cock. His pupils flared in appreciation a moment before he reversed their positions, rolling her on top of him with ease, his cock still firmly seated inside her.

"Play with those beautiful breasts, baby. I want to watch."

Eleanor felt a rush of sensual power, and did as he asked, squeezing her breasts together, and pinching her nipples into puffy, pink pearls of flesh.

"So pretty," he murmured, his eyes riveted. "My pretty, pink princess."

"Not any longer," she said, suddenly meeting his eyes.

"Still," he insisted. "You're still Eleanor. And, baby—" He flexed upward to take one nipple into his mouth, sucking until it was flushed bright pink with blood. "—you're still pink." He bit the nipple playfully, then switched to her other breast, sucking while he continued to the pinch the other, until they were both red and engorged with blood. And then he bit one of the swollen tips, lapping up the blood while the euphoric in his bite zipped into her blood stream, zinging along her nerves.

It wasn't the same as if she'd been human, but Lucifer was one powerful, fucking vampire, and his bite had power still.

And so did hers. As he drank her blood, his cock hardened even more, swelling until she worried for him, wondering if it might *hurt*. But then he was grinning, her blood on his lips, his big hands gripping her hips, holding her still as he began thrusting up into her, totally in control for all her superior position. He slammed into her fast and hard, going deeper with every thrust, changing the angle to go deeper still until she felt the first warm rush of his release. He groaned, his fingers digging in her flesh, as she fell forward, her breasts crushed against the flat planes of his chest, her pussy squeezing, grasping his cock as it bucked deep inside her a moment before her climax hit, and then she could only hold on as her entire world collapsed down to this one room, this one bed, and Lucifer in her arms.

They clung to each other in the aftermath, both of them trembling, muscles shivering beneath their skin. She kissed the smooth skin of his shoulder, tasting the salty, blood-flavored sweat coating his skin, and she sighed in contentment. They had to get up soon, but they could take a few more minutes, a little more time—

Lucifer slapped her ass smartly. "Time to shower, *bella*. The world awaits."

So much for a few more minutes, she thought sourly. But he was right. Because it wasn't the world that was waiting for them, it was Colin Murphy.

Chapter Eight

Vancouver, British Columbia, Canada

SOPHIA PUSHED BACK from her desk, and threw her iPad down, hearing it skid across the desk and fall to the floor as she paced over to the window. There was nothing to see tonight. A heavy cloud cover had moved in, making the night as dark as her mood.

She sensed Danika outside the office door, hesitating a moment before knocking lightly. The vampire seemed to be everywhere underfoot lately, sticking her nose into every aspect of Sophia's business. An argument could be made that she was doing her best to serve her lady, trying to compensate for Colin's abduction, and then Eleanor's absence, not to mention Tambra's supposed preoccupation with that business in Calgary—a preoccupation, coincidentally that had prevented her from even calling Sophia to check in. And that was the problem right there. There were too many coincidences for Sophia's peace of mind. All three of her most trusted advisors were gone, leaving Danika to step into the void. And although she'd probed Danika's mind and found no deceit, she'd been left uneasy with what she did find. The female vampire's natural shields had been a touch too strong, her resistance to the probe a touch too resilient. Sophia had pushed anyway, far enough to be confident that there was no deception intended. She could have gone further, could have torn the female vampire's mind apart to discover what had inspired those tough shields, but that would almost certainly have caused permanent destruction, and Sophia was reluctant to go that far without some evidence of wrongdoing.

And the evidence wasn't there. So far Danika had been nothing but helpful. But maybe that was the most suspicious thing of all. Danika wasn't her child; she hadn't even been with Sophia for very long, so why the sudden devotion?

Or maybe Sophia was simply seeing conspiracy everywhere she looked.

"Come in," she snapped, impatient and resigned in equal measure.

And that made her pause, made her examine her feelings. Because as irritating as Danika could be, she didn't usually engender such intense emotion.

Danika had no sooner opened the door, than Sophia was rocked by a wave of rage . . . and then pain. She reached out blindly, her hand hitting the desk as she fought to parse the emotions rolling over her in waves.

"Calgary," Sophia rasped, as she dug down for the strength that made her a vampire lord, and sent it storming back along the path to her beleaguered vampires.

"My lady?" Danika questioned.

"Be ready to leave in ten minutes," she said, already striding for the door to the private quarters she shared with Colin. "I want the chopper waiting on the pad by the time I get there."

"But the weather—" the female vamp started to object, before Sophia spun on her with a snarl.

"I don't give a fuck about the weather. That chopper is on the pad in ten minutes, or the pilot can find himself a new profession. Assuming he lives that long," she added in a mutter. The pilot was a damn vampire. If he couldn't fly in a little bad weather, he wasn't of any use to her.

Sophia didn't wait to hear what Danika had to say. She strode out of the office and into the small vestibule outside her private quarters. Leaving the female vamp behind, she entered the complex door code which changed automatically every sixth day. Memorizing the new numbers was a pain in the ass, but Colin had insisted, and when it came to security, she always listened to what he had to say.

The thought would have made her smile if circumstances hadn't been so dire. Colin would have said that security was the *only* issue on which she never argued with him. But the situation *was* dire, and there was no time or energy for anything else. The Calgary compound was under attack, and vampires were dying. The very desperation she'd felt from so many minds at once told her how bad it was, but it told her more than that. The attack had come from within the compound. There was no other way it could have hit so fast and so hard, with no warning.

There was more treachery among the ranks of her vampires, and it rankled. She'd tried to avoid what Colin called "the nuclear option," tried to avoid ripping through her every one of her vampires' minds until she'd weeded out every single traitor. But it seemed her compassion had been misplaced. And now innocent vampires were paying the price.

Eight minutes later, she'd changed into the kind of simple clothing that wouldn't get in the way of what she was about to do. Her first order of business was to repel the invaders, which meant bloody, up-close fighting. But the bloodshed wouldn't end there. Vampires were going to die tonight, and they might be the lucky ones.

Calgary, Alberta, Canada

SOPHIA LEANED OVER the pilot's shoulder, surveying the battle scene below. It was blatantly obvious that the attack had come from within. The massive gates to the compound were still closed, while the battle raged in the courtyard, and flames licked from the windows.

She wasn't a soldier, she didn't have the warrior's heart that Colin did. She didn't spend hours in the gym building strength, or shooting weapons. But that didn't mean she couldn't fight, and right now there was only one answer to the fury burning inside her heart. And that was the blood of her enemies soaking into the ground at her feet. She tapped the pilot's shoulder.

"Get me low enough to drop, but don't endanger the chopper," she said over her headset. She waited only long enough to see his nod of acknowledgment, before moving to the open door of the helicopter. She'd brought fighters with her, and they waited now, standing patiently at her back while she stood in the opening, eyeing the scene below, deciding on her strategy as they dropped closer.

The chopper evened out, and the pilot's voice sounded in her ear. "This is it, my lady."

Sophia nodded, and spoke over the headset, saying, "Find a safe spot to set down and wait for my call back."

"Yes, my lady."

She held up a hand for her fighters, five fingers counting down. When she had only one finger left, she picked her spot down below, and stepped into the open air.

The chopper's wash buffeted her briefly, but then she was falling straight and true, right into the center of the courtyard, where the fighting was most fierce. Several of her vampires stood in a semi-circle around the open front doors of the building, making a last stand against their attackers.

Sophia dropped in front of her people, and immediately spun to face the invaders. A quick survey told her who the most powerful attacker was, a massive vampire who seemed to be directing the others, and backing them up when they fell.

Tightening her shields close to her skin, she formed a blazing sword of power and waded into the fray, cutting down unsuspecting vampires left and right. They'd been too taken up in their own battles, and hadn't noticed the hovering helicopter until it began raining warriors upon them. Sophia laughed at the shock on their faces as she cut them down, felt the rush of an unfamiliar bloodlust heating her veins. The battle was shifting all around as her fresh warriors joined the fight, but she had eyes only for the big prize, the massive vampire who was now striding toward her, his eyes gleaming red with power.

He was twice her size and three times her weight, but none of that mattered as her own power blazed forth in an amber gleam that lit up the courtyard with its strength. Her giant opponent hesitated briefly, no more than a stutter step, before his jaw tightened and he charged forward the last few feet, clearly hoping to use his physical size to overcome her overwhelming power advantage.

But Sophia hadn't been born yesterday. She wasn't going to stand there like a post waiting to be run over. She waited until he was seconds away from crashing into her, and then she moved. She took a single step sideways and raised her blade of pure energy, letting its wickedly sharp edge slice into his gut and out through his back as he bulled right by her.

He roared as he went down to his knees, her blade severing his spine and taking his legs right out from under him. Screaming in pain, he still forced his body to remain upright, swinging his much heavier blade in her direction. She lifted her shining sword to block.

High carbon steel met vampire magic, and the steel melted.

Her opponent shouted his defiance, but the sound was tinged with despair as his useless blade fell from his hand. "My master will bathe in your blood," he growled.

Sophia bared her teeth in a vicious grin, her fangs gleaming. "I'll tell him you said so," she said, meeting his tortured gaze. "Or you can tell him yourself after I kill him." And then she swung her glowing blade back, and with a mighty push, shoved it into his chest, skewering his heart with a surge of power that burned the organ to ashes in a matter of seconds. The light in the vampire's eyes went dark, and he crashed to the ground, falling to dust as he hit the cobbled stones of the courtyard.

Sophia straightened immediately, and spun a full circle, seeking her next opponent. But the battle was over. Most of the enemy vamps, shocked by their leader's death, had been cut down where they stood, but a few had fallen to their knees in surrender, and now waited to see if Sophia had any mercy to bestow upon them.

Sophia's people gathered at her back, their strength a solid wall that grew stronger with every minute, as they drew from her power, the power of a vampire lord defending her territory. A familiar presence stepped up to stand next to her. Sophia glanced over at Tambra. She was bloodied, as they all were, from battle, but her clothes were ragged and filthy, and she appeared gaunt with hunger.

"Tambra," Sophia said quietly, placing a light hand on her aide's shoulder. It was just enough to provide her vampire with a much-needed boost of energy, and she saw the female's eyes close in relief.

"Thank you, my lady," Tambra whispered.

Sophia tightened her hand briefly, then turned to face the rest of her vamps. "Let's get these fires out, and—" She noted the enemy vamps who knelt huddled together on the ground. "Gather the trash," she said sharply. "But keep it handy. I want answers."

Her vampires moved immediately, some running back into the house to deal with the flames, while others rounded up the defeated vampires and hustled them in the direction of a stone outbuilding that had probably been a barracks once upon a time. The Calgary compound was an old, human construction, but it had been repurposed by vampires more than a hundred years ago, largely because of its sturdy construction and expansive underground facilities. Those facilities had been sub-stantially upgraded over the years, and recently renovated. In fact, those renovations had been the reason for Tambra's visit, which had turned out to be a stroke of luck, putting her in a position to help with the defense until Sophia arrived.

"What can you tell me about all of this?" Sophia asked, and then, noticing the effort it was taking for the female vamp to remain upright, guided her over to the short wall surrounding a dry fountain on one side of the courtyard. "Sit," she ordered.

Tambra breathed out a sigh of relief and sat, slumped over in appar-ent exhaustion. "Forgive me, my lady."

Sophia waved away her protests, and sat next to her. "Tell me what happened. Let's start with the brute I sliced and diced."

Tambra nodded. "Virgil."

Sophia gave her a doubtful look. "Virgil?"

The female vamp smiled weakly. "It doesn't fit, I know, but he's loyal . . . or rather he *was* loyal to Berkhard. He came with him from Germany. Most of those others—" She indicated the sorry group of vamps now being shuffled into the former barracks. "—they're locals who fell for Berkhard's lies."

"Was Berkhard himself here?" The possibility conflicted with all of the Intel she had on his whereabouts, which concerned her.

Fortunately, Tambra shook her head. "No, Virgil was his apostle, so to speak, spreading the gospel of Berkhard."

"And what's that?" Sophia asked, wanting to know what could persuade vampires, *her* vampires, to betray their sworn lord.

"He's portraying himself as an enlightened lord, a modern ruler who only wants Vancouver. He says the rest of them are free to establish their own small territories, as long as they swear fealty to him. He's comparing it to the feudal systems of old Europe. They rule their territories, and as long as they pay an annual tithe to him, they're on their own."

"That makes no sense," Sophia said, puzzled. "Most of them, hell, nine out of ten of them, won't be able to exist on their own. They'll ending up begging Berkhard to take them back under his protection."

"And the terms will be far worse," Tambra agreed. "I've done some research on him, contacted some friends in Germany. And Berkhard's not an enlightened despot, he's just a despot. But there's a lot of residual resentment around here over Lucien."

"Lucien?" Sophia repeated in surprise. "You mean, the way he died?" She'd witnessed his death, but had nothing to do with it. He'd essentially committed suicide.

"The way he lived, my lady. He didn't demand much of his vampires, but he didn't give them much either. I think some of them were prepared to suffer a tyrannical lord, rather than none at all."

Sophia cursed. What the hell did she have to do to prove she wasn't Lucien born again? Maybe they needed this war, maybe they needed to see their own blood running in the gutters before they'd recognize that she was the one who kept their hearts beating and their lungs sucking air. It was her strength that gave them the courage to face every new night. Although, maybe this lot wasn't so courageous after all.

She looked around the wrecked courtyard, and beyond, at the charred walls of the estate house, where blackened drapes hung in shreds from the windows.

"Someone must have let him into the compound tonight. Do you know who it was?

Tambra nodded. "Efren Lacroix."

"The security chief? Is he still alive?"

She lifted her chin in the direction of the prisoners. "He's over there."

"And what about Ahmed?" Sophia asked, referring to the leader of the Calgary compound.

"Dead," Tambra said wearily. "He tried to stop Efren, and he killed him."

Grief stabbed Sophia, sharp and bitter. She hadn't known Ahmed well, but he'd been a good leader, a good man, who'd served Lucien loyally for centuries. He'd deserved far better than betrayal from within.

"All right," she said, making a decision. "There's no point in dragging this out." She stifled a sigh as she stood and faced the outbuilding where the rebellious vampires awaited her judgment. Most would never see morning. Their deaths would be at her hand, and on her soul. It was the lot of a vampire lord. She gave them life, but she also delivered death. "This won't take long," she said, glancing over at Tambra, who'd stood alongside her. "You can stay and organize the recovery, or come home with me."

Tambra looked around. "I think I'll stay if it's all right, my lady."

Sophia nodded, respecting her decision. "They can certainly use your talents, but I want you to stay in touch. Call me personally with anything you need, or if any problems arise. I have to get back to Vancouver tonight. Berkhard is still out there, still plotting. This was a feint, a test run meant to gauge our strength and response. I have a lot of work to do to be ready when he knocks on my door.

IT WAS NEARLY dawn by the time Sophia closed and secured the doors of her bedroom, safe in the vault she'd had constructed by Raphael's own builder. They'd had to start from scratch. None of Lucien's residences had been suitable as a headquarters, and none had anything close to the security of this sleeping vault.

As she'd done every morning since his capture, she stared at Colin's half of the bed, his absence a physical ache in her heart that never went away. Some mornings she thought she'd finally die from the pain, that she'd never wake up again. And every night when she opened her eyes, the ache was there, waiting for her.

She took off her make-up and washed her face, finding relief in the numbness of routine. Pulling a long, silk nightgown over her head, she glanced over to verify that her cell phone was on the charger and noticed that a new message had come in from Eleanor.

Her spirits lifted, but only slightly. If Colin had been freed, she'd have known it without the need for a phone call. But hoping for good news, at least, she lifted the cell phone and listened to Eleanor's message.

"My lady," she began formally. Eleanor was always so proper. "I know it's not enough yet, but we *are* making progress. We know where Colin is being held, and we know who has him. Lucifer is confident that it won't be much longer. And, my lady, just in case, let me be blunt … don't trust Darren Yamanaka. He's in the thick of this. Sleep well, and I'll call again tomorrow."

Sophia stopped the voicemail recording, but didn't delete it. She'd want to listen to it again later, when she woke for the night. Her mind would be fresher, her senses less dulled by blood and smoke.

But there was one thing she already knew for certain. Eleanor was in love. She could hear the joy, the deep contentment in her voice, the happiness in every syllable when Eleanor said Lucifer's name. The younger vampire had reunited with her long lost lover, and Sophia couldn't help wondering at the twist of fate which had given Eleanor back her love, at the same time that Sophia's beloved Colin was in such jeopardy. But she'd learned long ago that fate was cruel, and those you loved most in the world could be gone in an instant.

Chapter Nine

Montreal, Quebec, Canada

"WHAT'S ON THE schedule for tonight? Did you get something from that vampire, Torres? A lead of some kind?"

Lucifer heard the frustration in Eleanor's voice, but he didn't have any answers for her yet. And asking him the same question over and over wasn't going to get the answer any sooner. Partner or not, he wasn't about to change the way he worked, and he definitely wasn't going to leap to conclusions before the evidence was solid. So she'd have to wait.

"Lucifer."

She said just his name, but he had to smile at all of the feelings she packed into that one word.

"Don't you laugh at me."

He was stretched out on the couch, where, until a few moments ago, free-floating images had been flashing quickly behind closed eye-lids, as his unconscious mind made connections his conscious mind would never have seen. Unfortunately, Eleanor was a powerful distraction. Apart from her persistent questions, her presence alone made him think of hot nights and silky skin, rather than the job at hand. He wanted to take her somewhere far away from kidnapped mates and traitorous vampires, somewhere they could make love for hours, emerging from bed only long enough to feed, before diving into each other all over again.

But with every minute that passed without a clear investigative path to follow, Colin Murphy's suffering increased. Lucifer had a duty to his lord, Aden, and an obligation to Sophia, to complete this hunt. But more than any duty or obligation, he was aware that Colin Murphy was waiting for him.

"*Pace, bella,*" he murmured as he sat up and opened his eyes to see her glaring down at him. Laughing, he pulled her onto his lap, holding her tightly despite her outraged attempts to break free.

"Don't make me hurt you," she growled.

He laughed even harder, which complicated his efforts to hold onto her. "Stop," he managed to say, and received an elbow in his gut, before barely managing to save his balls from her well-placed fist. "Fuck, Elle. That's not cool." He wasn't laughing any longer. Not when his balls were at stake.

She shoved him back against the couch and jumped to her feet. "Talk to me, you arrogant Italian bastard. We're supposed to be partners in this thing."

"I'm not the only one who loses if you take out my balls, you know." He was genuinely offended that she'd make that play. He could understand if he was an actual threat to her, but they were lovers for fuck's sake. Exactly. For *fuck's* sake, she should have left his balls out of it.

"Aw, you want me to kiss it and make it better?"

Normally he'd have accepted that offer, but there was a gleam in her eye that told him it might not be a good move at this point. He was about to tell her what she could kiss instead, but his cell phone rang at that moment. He picked it up and saw the call he'd been waiting for.

"Impeccable timing," he said to the caller.

"Your little vampire giving you trouble?" Bastien inquired.

"You have no idea. What'd you find out?"

"Twins, just as you suspected."

"Damn, I'm good. What's the brother do?"

"He works at McGill University. Archeology Department."

"Well, that explains a hell of a lot. Thanks, Bastien. You'll brief Aden?"

"Already done."

"I'll call you when we have him."

With that confident promise, Lucifer disconnected and addressed Eleanor. "Do you want to hear what I've figured out? Despite your incessant nagging, I might add."

Her gasp of outrage almost had him laughing again, but his balls wouldn't let him. "Look, sit wherever you want, but just listen first, okay? Save your questions until you've heard the whole thing."

She rolled her eyes, but gave him a muttered, "Fine," as she settled on the chair sitting at a right angle to the couch.

Lucifer took a moment to get his thoughts organized. He considered jumping right to the suspicion which had motivated him to send Bastien a certain photograph this morning, but he knew Eleanor. She'd never settle for the big finish. She'd want to know every detail—where he'd picked up the pieces of information, how he'd put it together. So he started at the beginning.

"Okay," he began, leaning forward on the couch, elbows on his spread thighs, hands clasped loosely between his knees. "We know they're in the tunnels, and we know from the human who survived last night's trap—"

"What's his name?"

Lucifer gave her a flat stare. "I'm sure I said no questions."

"And I'm sure you're not the boss of me. What's his name?"

"Who?"

"The human. The one you scanned at the house last night."

Lucifer sighed. The man's name didn't really matter, but since he, or at least his twin, was about to play an important role, he told her. "Jack Anderson. May I—"

"You tend to depersonalize humans. It's a mistake that all of you older vamps make."

"I'll bear that that in mind. May I finish?"

She waved a hand in agreement.

He gave her a dark look, but continued. Time was short, and they had a lot to get done tonight.

"As I was saying . . . We know from *Jack's* interrogation last night that they're in an undeveloped section of the Underground that's not accessible to the public. That also fits with Fiona's tattooed boyfriend, whom they wanted because he'd worked in tunnel construction.

"But one question kept coming back to me. How did they find a suitable tunnel? There are nearly 20 miles of tunnels, which is what . . . around thirty-two kilometers, with well over 100 access points. How did they know that the area they're using even existed? Moreover, it's perfectly suited to their needs. Maybe the walls needed some finishing, but it's good enough to provide a lockable cell, and, while maybe it's remote—which is a good thing from their point of view—it's still accessible."

"Why accessible? It's not like they're taking Murphy in and out all the time, not that we know, anyway. So why do they need easy access?"

"You're right about that. I bet they haven't moved Murphy since they sent that first video. All of the images have the same background. But at the same time, there's no way in hell that Darren Yamanaka, or even Chase Landry, is spending all day, every day, and every night in that tunnel. Which means they're coming and going, and they can't be taking the public tunnels night after night, blurring every human they pass. There are too many people, and eventually someone would notice the sudden rash of memory lapses."

"Okay, but I'm not following you. How does this lead us to Colin?"

"*Someone* had to help them locate that tunnel. But who? No one stood out, not in Torres's mind, and not in Jack's. And *that* was the anomaly. There were too many memories of Jack Anderson, not only in his own mind, but in Torres's, too. Far more than any other actor, which didn't fit. Jack was a grunt, not a main player."

Eleanor had been watching him with growing impatience, but now she stilled, with a thoughtful look on her face. "A twin. That's what you said to Bastien on the phone."

"Exactly. Jack Anderson has an identical twin brother who's a lecturer at McGill, in the *Archaeology* Department, Elle. Who better to know about the tunnels underneath the university? Either they're actually hiding in some unused part of the McGill tunnels, or there's an unknown connection between McGill and the Underground, and they're using that."

"When did you figure all of this out?"

Lucifer shrugged. "Last night, this morning. My brain works on stuff during the day sometimes. I can't turn it off."

"And the picture you sent to Bastien?"

"I snapped it last night with my cell phone and sent it to Bastien as soon as I woke up this morning. As you pointed out, I'm older than you are. I wake up sooner."

"Huh." Eleanor stood and walked over to him, shoving him back and sliding onto his lap. "I don't remember you being this smart. It's kind of sexy."

"I was always sexy."

"Does this mean we're going to McGill tonight?" she asked, arching her neck to give him access.

"In a round-about way." He licked up one side of her neck, and over her jaw, to her mouth. "I'm hoping to catch Andy—that's the twin's name, Andy Anderson. Too cute, right?" He licked the seam of her lips.

"By a mile," she gasped. "Where are we going to catch him?"

Lucifer took advantage, slipping his tongue into her mouth and kissing her, their tongues twisting in a teasing dance. "He still lives with their mom. We're going to her house."

"Now?" she asked breathlessly.

"Not until I hear you moan my name," he said, and slipped his hand down her unzipped pants, his fingers exploring her warm, wet opening. "My princess has a creamy pussy." He slipped one, and then two fingers deep inside her, and began pumping. Adding a third finger, he fucked her with his fingers, stretching her with every thrust.

"Luc," she moaned, her legs straining to spread wider against the confinement of her tight jeans, her fingers digging into his shoulders as she arched to give him greater access to her hungry sex.

Lucifer bent over and closed his mouth over her breast, sucking on the nipple he could see pushing against her T-shirt, beneath the confines of her bra. He sucked harder until her T-shirt and bra were wet enough to show the outline of her rose-colored areola, and the hard nub of her nipple.

Eleanor was panting, each breath ending with a small, desperate cry, as his fingers fucked and his mouth sucked her delectable flesh. He waited until the greedy walls of her inner sex began to clench against his fingers, and then his thumb stroked roughly over her clit, even as he bit down hard on her swollen nipple.

Eleanor exploded into orgasm. Her pussy clamped down on his fingers, a warm, wet clasp of soft flesh that gripped ever tighter, her entire body writhing in time to the sensuous pulse of her climax. And she screamed.

Lucifer fought to hold on to her, his delicate princess who fucked like a wanton woman. He stroked his hands soothingly over her trembling body, holding her tight against his chest. His Eleanor, whom he'd thought lost forever, was safe in his arms, sated and warm.

"You bastard," she muttered, even as she curled more deeply into his embrace.

"You didn't like that, *bella?*" he asked innocently.

She punched his arm, but there was little strength and no anger to it. "I owe you one."

He chuckled lightly. "I'll be happy to collect." He stood, taking her with him and setting her on her feet, grinning at her disheveled state. "But later. Right now, we have work to do."

Eleanor nodded, and drew a shaky breath as she zipped and buttoned her jeans. She examined her T-shirt, with its wet circles outlining her still-hard nipples, then shrugged and pulled on a fleece hoodie, zipping it all the way up the front nearly to her chin.

Lucifer watched her intently, finding himself growing hard at the idea of the wet T-shirt beneath her hoodie. The T-shirt wasn't the only thing wet, either. He raised his fingers to his mouth and licked them deliberately, seeing her eyes jump to follow the slow movement of his tongue.

"Lucifer," she whispered.

"Ready to go, *bella?*" he asked.

She nodded jerkily. "How come I'm all flustered, and none of this bothers you?"

He yanked her against him in a sudden movement, one hand flat against her lower back, pressing her against the hard ridge of his erection. "I'm bothered," he growled. "We're both going to enjoy this later."

She threw her head back and looked up to meet his eyes, her own big and blue and shining with emotion. "Promise?"

He grinned. "Oh, yeah."

She flattened her lips and nodded sharply. "Okay, let's go chat with Mom."

ANDY ANDERSON and his mom lived in a modest home about ten miles from McGill University. It was a thirty minute drive in good traffic, which it was at this time of night. The house looked as if had benefited from some recent improvements, which only added to Eleanor's suspicions about Andy and his brother Jack. It was one thing for Andy to do a favor for his twin's vampire friends, but it made much more sense to her that he'd have done it for money. Especially since, unless he was blind, he had to have known that his new vampire associates were up to no good. It'd be hard to miss the locked room and the round-the-clock guards, even if all he did was provide regular access to the tunnels beneath the university.

Lucifer was already standing on the strip of concrete walkway that led up to the small front porch, when Eleanor climbed down from the big SUV and came around to stand next to him.

"New paint," he said, sniffing to indicate he'd smelled the same thing she did. "And a new car in the driveway."

She'd seen a car parked in the back, near the detached garage, but hadn't noticed it was new. "Aiding and abetting pays well, apparently."

He lifted his chin in acknowledgement, then stared at the house, his eyes losing focus as he scanned for life forms. "No vampires," he told her. Not a surprise there. "Four humans. I can't tell what they are—male or female—humans all feel the same to me."

"Tastes like chicken," she commented.

He turned to her with a half grin. "Exactly. Let's ring the doorbell." He led the way up the walk, taking the four stairs in a single, graceful leap. Eleanor could have done the same, but it didn't look nearly as graceful when she did it. More like a bunny hop. So she settled for taking them one at a time, but using her vampire speed, so that when Lucifer pressed the button on the doorbell, she was standing next to him.

Footsteps approached from inside the house. Light, short steps that told her the human was probably female. The porch light went on a moment before the door opened, and a pleasant-looking older woman stood there, her gray hair a curly pixie cut around her head.

"Can I help you?" she asked, standing well back from the screen door, far enough that she could slam the wooden front door if necessary. But since her visitors were vampires, she was actually quite safe.

"Mrs. Anderson?" Lucifer asked, using his most persuasive voice. "We're friends of Andy, from the University. I wonder if he's home?"

"Andy? Oh, of course. You must be the ones he's been talking about. Jack's friends?" Of course, she'd love Jack and Andy's new friends. After all, they'd paid for the upgrades on her house.

"Yes, exactly," Lucifer agreed happily, as if he was just *so* pleased that she'd made the connection. "I saw Jack yesterday (well, *that* was true enough) and I thought we were meeting here tonight, but maybe—"

"Oh, no, I'm sure you've got the right of it. I don't know about Jack, but Andy called. He's running a little late, and he'll be here any minute." She glanced over her shoulder. "I've got my bridge club tonight, but—"

"That's all right," Eleanor said, speaking up for the first time, doing her best to look small and non-threatening. Which wasn't much of a stretch. It didn't matter that she could throw a grown man around like an empty trash can. Her small size, coupled with her long, blond hair, and a face that would forever be that of a twenty-something human, did the job very nicely. "We'll just wait in the car."

"No, no, that's not necessary," she said, opening the door. "It's cold out there. You come on in, and sit in the living room where it's warm. We're all back in the den, but you probably don't want to listen to our gossip and such."

"That's very kind," Lucifer murmured, crossing the threshold before the woman could change her mind. Eleanor followed, with a final glance at the neighborhood and the street. Most of the houses had lights on, but there wasn't much traffic, and no one was around. There'd be no witnesses.

"Forgive my manners," the woman said. "I'm Muriel Anderson, Andy and Jack's mother." She gave them an expectant look.

"Luc and Ellen Scuderi," Lucifer said promptly, and Eleanor had to refrain from rolling her eyes. Apparently they were married now. "Andy's been such a great help with our research on the Underground."

Muriel's eyes lit up. "He's always been so fascinated by the tunnels in this city. Ever since his father took him to McGill. He was a professor there, you know. His father, that is. Andy, too, now. But when he was little—" She stopped herself with a dismissive wave. "But you don't want to hear about all that. You make yourselves comfortable. Would you like a cup of tea while you wait?"

"Not for me. Ellen?" Lucifer asked, his eyes twinkling with mischief, as he took her hand, threading their fingers together.

"No, thank you, Muriel. We're having dinner after this, and I don't want to spoil my appetite," Eleanor said sweetly. She had to cover a wince when Lucifer's fingers nearly crushed her hand.

"If you're sure," Muriel said slowly. Her voice trailed off at the end, and her eyes took on a glaze that told Eleanor Lucifer was messing with her mind.

"I love bridge, Muriel," he said smoothly. "Why don't you introduce me to the others?"

Muriel nodded agreeably and started toward the back of the house. Lucifer lingered long enough to meet Eleanor's worried gaze. "I'm not hurting her. But I want her and the other women out of the line of fire, if it comes to that. They'll be perfectly safe."

Eleanor nodded, feeling somewhat bad that he felt the need to explain to her. But at the same time, she was pleased that he'd bothered. "I know," she said, putting all of her trust into those two words.

She walked over and sat in one of the chairs next to the fireplace, appreciating the warmth. Vampire or not, she felt the cold. It might not kill her—her vampire-enhanced metabolism could regenerate almost anything short of an actual amputation—but the cold still got into her bones. She'd been born and raised in the warmth and humidity of the Louisiana swamps. Apparently the body never forgot its roots.

"All set," Lucifer said, gliding into the room to sit across from her. "Now we wait for Andy."

"Think he'll have company?"

Lucifer shrugged. "His brother, maybe. But I don't expect any vamps to be with him. Not that it matters. We'll handle whatever happens."

He'd said "we." A rush of warmth filled Eleanor at his confidence, not only in his own abilities, but in hers, too. "What do we do with the twins once we have what we need from Andy?"

"I wiped Jack's memory when we sprang their trap at the house last night. If he's with Andy tonight, he'll need a little extra. But either way, once I'm finished with them, they'll both forget they ever heard of vampires and secret tunnels."

"Will we go after Murphy tonight?"

Lucifer seemed to think about it, but then shook his head. "I hate to wait, but we need to get a sense of the layout and timing. There's just the two of us, so any way you look at it, we'll be outnumbered down in those tunnels. I'm hoping to avoid Yamanaka and Landry during the rescue. That's where the timing comes in. Once we have Murphy safely ensconced back at the hotel, we can go after both of them, assuming they don't come after us first. It might be better if they do, actually. It'll save us the trouble of finding them."

"What about Colin? Will he be safe at the hotel? I don't want them coming after him while we're off dealing with the others."

"Don't worry about Murphy. He's a warrior. Give him a little blood to bring him back to fighting form, a few hundred rounds of ammo, and he'll take care of anyone who walks through the door. He'll have Cal and his team here with him, too."

Eleanor drew a deep breath, and nodded thoughtfully. "You're right. Colin's solid."

"But not as beautiful as me," Lucifer commented.

She laughed. "No one's as beautiful as you are."

"That's what I thought." His head came up, and his eyes sharpened. "Andy's home."

LUCIFER DIDN'T BOTHER to get up when Andy Anderson came through the front door. He stopped dead in the arched opening to the living room, and stared.

"Who the hell—" he began, and then Lucifer flashed some fang, and recognition flooded Andy's face. "How'd you get in here?" he asked, with a worried glance toward the back of the house and its bridge players.

"Muriel invited us in. She and her friends are perfectly fine, by the way. You should worry more about yourself. And your brother."

"I told you people—"

"But we're not the same people. Have a seat. Let's talk."

His reluctance was obvious, but he'd had enough experience with vampires recently to know that resistance was futile. Lucifer chuckled inwardly at the words that had bubbled into his brain, but they were certainly accurate.

Andy set his briefcase down, shrugged off his jacket, and hung it on a wooden hall tree in the entryway. Coming into the living room, he perched nervously on the edge of an armless tapestry chair, the farthest one from where Lucifer and Eleanor sat near the fireplace.

"What do you want?"

Lucifer smoothed a hand over the fine slacks he'd worn that night, wanting to make a good impression on the twins' mother. He could manipulate minds when necessary, but it was much easier not to. "I want the same thing the others did," he said plainly.

"What others? I don't know what—"

Lucifer stopped him with a single look. "Don't play games with me. You won't win. We both know you sold information to some vampires. A sale most likely set up by your brother Jack. So don't bullshit me. I want what you gave them."

"It's not a blueprint or anything. I have to show you, just like I did them."

Lucifer studied the human, trying to figure out if the man was playing them or not. "Eleanor."

She looked at him, a question in her eyes.

"I need to know if Andy here is being honest with us."

"What? Why would I lie?" Andy blustered, but Lucifer didn't care about the human. His attention was only for Eleanor, and if she'd let him do what was necessary to ensure their safety. He needed to scan Andy's brain. It would be gentle, but there was question that it would violate the human's mind.

Eleanor's gaze on him softened. "Do whatever you have to," she said quietly. "I trust you."

Her simple declaration meant more to him than all of the accolades he'd received from Lord Aden or any of the others over the past few years. He wanted to grab her, and kiss her, and never let go.

"Later," he promised, and he knew from her smile that she understood. "But right now . . . Andy," he said returning his attention to the human. "I need the truth."

With a single thought, he froze the human in place, sliding smoothly into his mind with the ease of long experience. It helped that Andy was one of those humans with no natural shields whatsoever. It horrified Lucifer to think about going through life so unguarded, but the human probably wasn't even aware of it.

"Tell me about the vampires," he told Andy. "What did they want? And what did you give them?"

"Jack told them about me, about my hobby with the tunnels," he said, seeming unaware of Lucifer's manipulation. "They wanted somewhere underground, a place no one knew about. Or rather, no one, but me. It had to have at least two rooms, or, you know, dead ends that could be made into rooms. But that turned out not to be necessary. There's an old storage tunnel down there. I think they used it to store supplies and equipment during the original construction."

"And that's where you took them?"

Andy nodded. "Jack introduced us, and I showed them the way."

"So this is from the McGill University tunnels, not the Underground."

"Strictly speaking, yes. The tunnels connect through the Metro, if you know where to look."

"And you know, of course," Lucifer said dryly.

"Sure. No one knows those tunnels better than I do."

"Why'd you help them? What'd they give you?"

"My brother's pretty high up—"

"You're brother's a tool, Andy. If you learn nothing else, know that. He's a disposable hired gun, a human who's only still alive because I spared his life. Remember that."

Andy stared. "I talked to him today. He didn't say anything about that."

"Because he doesn't remember, and neither will you. You didn't answer my question. What'd they give you for your information?"

"Money," the human admitted. "Enough to fix up my mother's house, with sufficient left over to make sure she can stay here for the rest of her life without worrying."

Lucifer had trouble believing Yamanaka would leave Andy alive with all of this information in his head, but maybe they weren't finished with him yet. He'd have bet good money that when all was said and done, when Sophia was dead and Murphy along with her, and Berkhard or whoever sat on the territorial throne . . . one of the first deaths would be Andy's. The information in his head was too valuable to risk having an enemy vampire discover it—an enemy like Lucifer.

"All right, let's go."

"Go?" Andy said, surprised. "Go where?"

Lucifer stood, and Eleanor with him. "You're going to show us what you showed the others. And then I'm going to save your life, Andy. You and Muriel, both."

"What about Jack?"

"I can't make any promises about Jack. I kept him alive once, but—" He shook his head. "No promises," he repeated.

Andy was understandably distressed about that, but Lucifer's compulsion dulled his emotional responses so that they didn't interfere, at least for now. Once the compulsion was lifted . . . well, Lucifer wouldn't be here, and didn't really care what happened then. The human twins had made a choice to work with some very bad people, and sometimes there was a price to pay.

Chapter Ten

LUCIFER WAS SURPRISED at the extent of the tunnels beneath the university. Supposedly, they'd been built to give students a safer, warmer transit between buildings during Montreal's harsh winters. He'd never heard of a similar tunnel system beneath any of the U.S. universities located in colder climates. It was a good idea, but it was certainly an invitation to abuse. And who better to take advantage of this open invitation than vampires?

He followed Andy Anderson along an unlit and barely finished tunnel that they'd accessed via a maintenance closet. It hadn't been a real closet, just a room with a few metal shelves filled with cleaning supplies, whose main purpose was to conceal a second door at the back of the room. That door had been protected by a keypad lock, for which Andy had just happened to have the code.

"You didn't discover *that* by accident," Lucifer had commented quietly, while Andy tapped in the 16-digit code.

"I have a friend who freelances computer work. Some of her most lucrative jobs are borderline criminal."

"Sounds like a match made in heaven, now that you've crossed that same line."

"All I did—"

"Save it for the judge, bud."

They'd gone about thirty yards down the hall when Andy slowed, but kept walking. "There's a dead-end up there," he said, whispering for the first time since they'd descended into the tunnels. He gestured with his flashlight into the stygian darkness. The flash was the only light they had down here, and it wasn't that strong. But it was more than enough for Lucifer and Eleanor. If anything, it was too much, and they had to be careful not to temporarily blind themselves by getting too close to it.

Lucifer looked ahead, where Andy had indicated, and could barely make out a wall of rock and dirt, even rougher than the walls to either side of them. Whoever had dug these secret tunnels had done so in a hurry, and with an eye toward secrecy. He was sure Andy had some history on that, too, but he didn't care enough to ask. All he cared about was finding Colin Murphy, and getting him out of here. Once that was finished, it wouldn't be Lucifer's problem, because he'd be back in Chicago.

He scowled as the ramifications of that thought penetrated his brain. He'd been so fixated on finishing the job and getting back home. But that had been before he'd reunited with Eleanor. Now that he had her, he wasn't ever letting her go, but what did that mean for their future? They were sworn to two different North American vampire lords.

He was still mulling over that when they reached the dead end.

Andy flashed his light to the right, and walked for a short distance before making another sharp turn to the left, and that's where he stopped, careful to keep his light down low. "That's it down there," he whispered.

Lucifer was tempted to do a quick mental scan down the tunnel to determine who, if anyone, was there. But he and Eleanor were both shielding like crazy to hide their presence in the tunnels, and if he did a scan and Yamanaka or someone equally powerful happened to be around, it could give them away. And he was reluctant to invite a fight without knowing whom, and how many, they'd be facing.

Instead, he settled for a careful scan of Andy's thoughts, looking for any evidence of deceit. But Andy was an open book. If Lucifer had to guess, he'd say this was the first time Andy had ever done anything even remotely illegal. He'd bet that wasn't true of his twin brother, Jack, though. You didn't end up as a human guard for a criminal vampire enterprise by obeying the rules.

"*What's* down there?" Lucifer asked quietly. He couldn't see anything.

Andy gave him a surprised look. "The door to the place where they're staying."

"You mean where they're holding our man prisoner," Lucifer said bluntly, forcing the human to confront what he was involved with.

"I don't know anything about—"

"Yeah, yeah. You're completely innocent. What exactly is between here and there?"

"We should go back to the closet to talk," Andy said sullenly. Apparently he didn't like being reminded of his complicity in the kidnap and torture of another human being. "Sound carries down here."

That made sense to Lucifer, and, frankly, he didn't need the human anymore, so they trooped back the way they'd come, and then huddled in the closet to talk.

Once the door was closed, Andy handed him a piece of paper with the 16-digit door code. Lucifer didn't need it; he'd memorized the code when the human had punched it in earlier. But he glanced at the numbers on the paper, just to make sure they were the same as he'd memorized. They were, so he simply folded the paper and slipped it into his pocket.

"All right, so what's down that hall?"

"I've drawn a diagram for you." Andy handed over another, larger, piece of paper.

"Why don't you text or e-mail that to—" He broke off when Andy shook his head.

"None of this is on any computer. It's not safe."

The man had a point. Oddly enough, if you really wanted to keep something secret these days, you wrote it down on paper and hid it really well. Better yet, you memorized it, and then burned the paper. Although, granted, not everyone had Lucifer's nearly perfect recall for everything he read. Or at least those things he wanted to remember.

"All right," he said, then bent his head to study the diagram. "So there's actually *two* doors after that last turn?" he asked, wanting to be sure he was reading the diagram correctly.

Andy nodded. "They're about ten meters—um, thirty-three feet—apart. The doors are wood, thick and heavy, but no locks. I don't know about the guards, though. I was only down here once, during construction. It was before they brought . . ." His words faded out as he realized he'd been about to admit that he'd known about Murphy's capture and imprisonment. "I didn't know what they were going to do," he muttered.

Lucifer wanted to ask if he'd tried to find out, or if it would have made a difference. But it sure as hell didn't matter now, and so he ignored it. "Did you see any guards at all?"

"No one was on the first door, but there were two guards when we opened the second door, plus two more, farther inside. But like I said, that was before they . . . did what they did. There wasn't anyone locked up in there yet, plus it was daytime, so—"

"So there might be more guards at night when the vamps are awake," Lucifer said, finishing his thought. "Did Jack say anything about the big bosses coming to visit? Darren Yamanaka and maybe one other vampire?"

Andy pursed his lips, looking like he'd just bitten off something bitter. The man obviously knew more than he wanted to admit, but he had no secrets from Lucifer. Not anymore.

"Jack said the big bosses, like Yamanaka, only come by once or twice a week, mostly to—" His jaw clenched and he drew a calming breath. "—to ask questions. The rest of the time, it's just the prisoner—I don't know his name—and his guards. That's Jack and his buddies during the day, and vampires at night."

Lucifer took a moment to absorb all of this, and to pat himself on the back for getting it right. "What's the layout inside?" he asked finally.

"It's semi-finished, like the tunnels, but it has two more rooms, with doors *and* locks, this time. One has a window and a sliding bolt, but the other one has a digital lock, just like the one here. I don't know what the code is for that one. I was never close enough to scan it."

"Did you wonder what they were doing all of this for?" Eleanor demanded.

Andy flushed with embarrassment, or maybe it was guilt.

Lucifer didn't know which. And he didn't care either. "What about the lock on the windowed door?" he asked, no longer interested in Andy's rationalizations for getting involved in a criminal activity.

"It's a fairly heavy sliding bolt, with an eye latch for a padlock. But they hadn't added one yet, when I was there."

Lucifer looked over and met Eleanor's even stare. "That's probably changed by now," he told her. "But it shouldn't be a problem as long as the doors are wood."

"They're definitely wood," Andy chimed in. "They're thick, though. You can't expect to kick them in or—"

"*You* can't," Lucifer corrected. "But Eleanor here has a mean side kick. She's tougher than she looks."

Eleanor looked at the human and nodded solemnly. Lucifer wanted to grin, but that would have ruined the moment, so he made a mental note to kiss her later. Because she was so damn adorable. Not that he'd tell *her* that. Not if he valued his balls.

"Okay, let's get out of here," he said, gesturing for Eleanor to proceed through the crowded closet and back to the legitimate part of the McGill tunnels.

The human gave him a startled look—as if he'd expected Lucifer to kill him and bury his body in the tunnel—but he shuffled after Eleanor quickly enough, and soon all three of them were back in the well-lit tunnels that everyone knew about.

"You should go home and forget about all this," he told Andy as they started for the exit back up to street level. His tone was conversational, but as he spoke, he was pushing a new set of facts into the man's very receptive brain. The closet was just a closet, the 16-digit code a meaningless number.

By the time they were out of the tunnels, and Andy was hurrying down the street toward his car, the biggest problem he had was a strong breeze that was stirring the lush foliage along the sidewalk, and carrying with it the scent of an unseasonal thunderstorm.

Eleanor stood next to Lucifer, watching the man walk away. "That's it?" she asked, sounding surprised.

"What'd you think I was going to do, Elle? Kill him and Muriel both?"

"Of course, not," she replied quickly, but he could hear the hesitation beneath her words.

He tried not to be insulted, or, even worse, wounded by her doubt. "Let's go," he said almost tiredly.

She gripped his forearm, half apology and half reassurance. "Are we going back in there tonight?"

Lucifer turned to study the exit. He nodded. "I need to get close enough for a quick scan first. It'd be good to know—" He stopped abruptly, then grabbed Eleanor and pulled her into the shadowed doorway of the closest building, wrapping them both in his toughest shields. "Someone's coming from inside," he sub-vocalized, right up against her ear. "Someone powerful."

She turned to look at him, her big eyes wide, her pulse racing with adrenaline. "Who?" she mouthed silently.

Lucifer shook his head, and concentrated on answering that question without giving away their presence. Whoever was coming had power, but he apparently didn't suspect anyone was around, because he wasn't bothering to conceal his strength or his presence.

Moving slowly, Lucifer turned Eleanor in his arms, so that they both could see the approaching vampire as soon as he became visible. Lucifer's gaze was riveted on the man-shaped form just detectable through the glass windows of the building's door. The shape grew larger until the door pushed open . . . and Darren Yamanaka was briefly illuminated by the weak light above the exit. The door closed, and he continued down the walk, heading their way.

Darren Yamanaka. And all alone. If Lucifer hadn't had Eleanor to protect, if he'd been on his own, he'd have—Shit, what was he thinking? Eleanor didn't need him to protect her. She had plenty of power of her own, and was more than capable of defending herself. Hell, with Yamanaka broadcasting his power like that, Lucifer could already tell that he had a good chance against the other vampire. Add in Eleanor fighting by his side, and it was no contest.

Lucifer placed a hand along Eleanor's jaw, and gently turned her to face him. Meeting her gaze, he "knocked" carefully on her thoughts, asking for entry. Vampire hearing was too acute to risk Yamanaka overhearing. He might look like he wasn't paying attention, but Lucifer didn't believe it. This was the master of three cities, including Montreal. He was undoubtedly an asshole, but he hadn't gotten this far by being careless.

Lucifer hadn't needed to "knock" for Eleanor's permission. He was a powerful enough telepath to have broken through whatever shields she had in place. But this was *his* Eleanor. He wanted her trust, and that meant treating her with the respect she deserved.

Eleanor met his gaze directly, and nodded.

"Hey, baby," he said playfully, coating the simple greeting in layers of affection.

She smiled and rolled her eyes.

"I'm going to challenge Yamanaka," he 'pathed, going from playful to deadly serious in an instant. *"He's wide open and alone. This might be our best chance."*

"What if he has guards?" she asked.

Lucifer considered it, but shook his head. *"It's late, and he's sneaking around out here all by himself. I'm betting no one will look for him before tomorrow night, and maybe not even then, if I'm careful. According to Andy, most nights it's just Colin Murphy alone with his guards. If we take Yamanaka tonight, we can go in and get Murphy first thing tomorrow night, and not have to worry about him showing up to stop us. And by the time anyone misses him, we'll already have Murphy under our protection."*

It was Eleanor's turn to think it over, which she did briefly, and then gave him a single sharp nod. *"How?"*

Lucifer paused, then pulled Eleanor even closer, as it became clear that Yamanaka was going to walk right past them. Lucifer locked his power down, not wanting Yamanaka to sense anything, adding an extra layer of shadow to their concealment. Together, they watched Darren stroll past no more than fifteen feet away from them.

"Let's follow," Eleanor suggested. *"The streets get darker down that way, more trees, fewer lights, and no people this late at night."*

Lucifer nodded and loosened his hold on her. *"I'll take the lead,"* he told her plainly. This was going to be a serious challenge. There was no room for egos or delicate feelings. Eleanor had considerable power, but Lucifer had one hell of a lot more, and he was the one who'd be issuing the challenge to Yamanaka.

Eleanor nodded her understanding, but then touched his arm to get his attention. Once she had it, she placed her hand above her heart, then pressed that same hand to *his* heart, and slowly curled her fingers into a fist, as her expression turned fierce.

Lucifer nodded. He understood. Eleanor was offering her strength to him in the coming battle. Offering *herself* as a reservoir of power for him to draw on, if necessary. His eyes closed on the barrage of emotions that tightened his chest in that moment. Love for his Eleanor—a love that had survived more than twenty years of believing her dead. Admiration for her courage, gratitude for her generosity. And simple fucking relief that she was alive and standing there next to him.

"Let's do this," he said.

They moved swiftly out of the shadows, trailing Yamanaka down the tree-covered street. The other vampire seemed unconcerned about his surroundings. He didn't glance around even once, and was actually whistling in a breathy, tuneless way. He seemed quite cheerful, in fact, which made Lucifer wonder what he'd been up to with Murphy, and if Sophia was going to receive another gruesome video from tonight's work.

Not that it would matter. By the time Lucifer was finished, Yamanaka would be no more, and Sophia would be receiving an entirely different kind of message from Montreal.

Yamanaka slowed, as he approached a black Mercedes and stepped off the curb. Certain now that the city master was all alone, Lucifer touched Eleanor's arm in warning, and then dropped the concealing shadows that surrounded them, and stepped into a patch of moonlight between the trees.

"Darren Yamanaka," Lucifer said quietly.

Yamanaka spun, plainly shocked and surprised. He searched Lucifer's face, as if trying to place him. They'd never met, but Lucifer was certain the vampire had spies inside Sophia's camp at least, and maybe even Aden's, though that was less likely. Aden hadn't brought that many people with him to Canada, and no one who hadn't been in Toronto would know about Lucifer.

"I don't know you," Yamanaka said finally. His gaze shifted suddenly to look over Lucifer's shoulder, and it was everything Lucifer could do not to turn around to be sure that Eleanor was safe. But it could just as easily have been a feint on Yamanaka's part, an attempt to distract Lucifer long enough for him to launch a surprise attack. Besides, Eleanor could take care of herself.

Yamanaka's attention swung back to Lucifer. "My name is Lucifer Scuderi," he supplied. His mouth lifted in a half smile, as he waited for the other vampire's response, his power held carefully in check.

"What the fuck do I care who you are?" Darren demanded.

Lucifer's smile turned into a grin. "You should know the name of the vampire who took you down."

Yamanaka stiffened to attention, his expression intent and probing as he studied Lucifer anew, becoming smug at what he found there. "Turn around and go home, boy. You have ten seconds, and I'll let you live."

Lucifer loosened the tight hold he'd maintained on his power, freeing it completely for the first time in longer than he could remember. He wanted to laugh with the joy of it, as if he'd been wrapped in a straitjacket for years, decades even, and now he could breathe again.

"I'd make you the same offer," he crooned. "But you need to die."

Lucifer was strong, but so was Yamanaka, with age and experience on his side. He struck first, a powerful blast of concentrated energy designed to knock Lucifer off his feet. The attack assumed Lucifer was untried and unskilled. But you know what they said about assumptions.

Lucifer smirked as Darren's blast of energy warped around him, briefly adding to his own shields before dissipating completely. He might not have fought that many challenges, but Bastien was his best friend, and a masterful fighter. He'd drilled Lucifer to exhaustion, insisting he had to be ready for whatever the war might bring him.

And that was why Lucifer's smirk didn't linger. Bastien had taught him many things, the most important of which was never to count your enemy out until he was dead and dusted. He gathered his own magic for a counterattack, not wasting energy on a blunt force strike like Yamanaka's, but rather narrowing it into a spear tip of concentrated power that he sent flying directly at his enemy's heart.

Yamanaka saw it coming and shifted his shields at the last minute, but not fast enough. The spear penetrated to stab deep into his chest, but he'd managed at the last moment to deflect enough of its force to prevent it from doing any more than barely touching his heart. It shocked him though, both physically and mentally, and he seemed to recognize his danger for the first time that night.

But it didn't kill him, and Lucifer cursed his failure. Now was not the time for recriminations, however. He changed up his strategy, hardening his shields as he strode closer to his enemy, studying Yamanaka's energy pattern, looking for weakness. He needed a way in, a way to utilize his most powerful weapon—his telepathy. Every vampire lord had a unique weapon that was his alone. It was part of what marked them as different, as capable of ruling a territory and binding its vampires to his life force. Lucifer's ability to wield his telepathy as a weapon against other vampires in the midst of battle gave him a tremendous advantage, not only against weaker, shopkeeper vampires, but powerful masters like Darren Yamanaka, and maybe, someday, the territorial lord who would fall to Lucifer's challenge.

But tonight it was Yamanaka who was bringing all of his considerable power to bear, and drawing on the power of his city to fortify his strength against Lucifer. He wasn't a vampire lord, and the power he could pull from Montreal's vamps wasn't even close to what Sophia would have been able to draw, but it was enough to make Lucifer stand up and notice. Enough to let him know that he had to win this fight sooner, not later.

Redoubling his efforts, Lucifer launched another bolt of energy at Yamanaka's chest, changing trajectory at the last minute to dig the weapon into his gut instead. The vampire groaned in pain, but launched a blistering counterattack with a snarled oath, pounding Lucifer's shields with razor-sharp stars, like Japanese *shuriken,* but formed of pure energy. They chipped away at Lucifer's protection, their numbers and persistence a distraction, demanding his attention and energy to shore up the damage they were doing to his shields, while at the same time, he was trying to concentrate on his next attack.

Lucifer howled his anger, and Yamanaka bared his teeth in a victorious grin, mistaking the howl for frustration and surrender. He took two quick steps closer to Lucifer, arm outstretched as if intending to reach through Lucifer's shields and crush his heart. But it wasn't surrender that Lucifer was howling, it was impatience. Enough with the bullshit parrying back and forth, with the weapons crafted of energy instead of steel. Narrowing his focus down to the one thing he did best, he pierced Yamanaka's shields with a finely crafted needle of energy, and created a pinhole of an opening, just enough to forge a connection with his enemy's awareness.

Yamanaka stumbled suddenly, his eyes wide with surprise. Lucifer could feel the vampire's shock at the intrusion, something no powerful vampire would ever expect. Lucifer met his stunned gaze with a victorious grin of his own as he drove through Yamanaka's resistance and forced him to lower his shields. Not completely, Yamanaka was too powerful for that, but enough to create a vulnerability, a weak spot that Lucifer could exploit, as he reshaped a part of his energy into the same spear tip of power that he'd attacked with earlier. But this time it succeeded, driving all the way into Yamanaka's chest, and knocking him backward with the sheer force of it, slamming his body against the trunk of his Mercedes, and setting the alarm off in an obnoxious blare of sound.

Yamanaka stared at Lucifer in confusion in the final moments of his life, disbelief written plainly on his face. This should have been his moment of triumph, the completion of his plan to be rid of Sophia, and to rule a territory of his own. He wasn't supposed to die, to find his death at the hands of an unknown, an unexpected . . . nobody.

And then he was gone, dust scattering in the cold breeze as the car's alarm continued its rhythmic pleas for help.

Lucifer staggered when Yamanaka's life finally fled. He was still telepathically linked to the other vampire at the moment of his death, and he found himself fighting for his own life as his awareness tried to follow Yamanaka down that final path. It was Eleanor who pulled him back, who intuited what was happening and reached out with her own solid strength to anchor him to his living body, to the earth beneath his feet, and, more than anything else—the tie that bound him more closely to life than any other—to Eleanor herself.

Lucifer went to his knees, Eleanor's arms strong around him, her energy a warm blanket of comfort.

"Stay with me, Luc," she murmured. "Take what you need."

He realized with a start that she was completely unshielded, her mind wide open and vulnerable. It terrified him, even as it touched something deep inside that she would leave herself so exposed in her efforts to give him what he needed.

Driven by the need to protect her, he twisted around and pulled her into his arms, covering her with his own shields, which he'd never lost completely and was now rapidly rebuilding.

"Eleanor," he murmured, cuddling her close, finding as much comfort in her love for him, as he did in the knowledge that she was safe.

"Are you okay?" she asked, pulling away so she could see his face and look into his eyes. "Did he hurt you?"

Lucifer grinned. "You know, he did hurt me. I think you need to kiss me all over and make it better."

Eleanor *tsked* playfully, but then wrapped her arms around his neck and hugged him. "I was so scared," she murmured against the skin of his neck. "When you yelled like that . . ."

"That was anger, *bella*, at my own ineptitude. Bastien taught me better than that."

"Oh. Well, we can't let *Bastien* down," she muttered.

He laughed, then gripped her long hair and tugged her head back so he could give her a slow, luxurious kiss. "It wasn't Bastien I was fighting for, baby. And, it sure as hell won't be Bastien I celebrate with." He kissed her again, a loud, smacking kiss. "I'm starving. You up for a blood club?"

She cocked her head and gave him a curious smile. "A blood club? Like . . . each of us finding a partner to feed from?"

"Oh, hell, no," he growled. "No one partners you but me. We'll find a willing human to *share*, and then we'll go home and fuck ourselves to exhaustion."

"Oh, my. What woman could resist such a romantic proposal?"

"You want romance, baby? How's this? I'm going to take you home and kiss every inch of your luscious body." His hands echoed his words, sliding down her back and over her ass, squeezing gently, before cruising around to her belly, and stroking upward to cup her breasts, gently squeezing the full globes with his fingers. "And then," he continued as his thumbs strummed her nipples into eager awareness, "I'm going to spread your lovely thighs, and kiss that perfect, pink pussy until it creams all over my tongue, and *then,* I'm going to make love to you until the sun comes up." He licked her cheek, and then the crease of her lips, opening her mouth to his kiss. "Is that romantic enough?"

Eleanor's heart was pounding against his chest, her cheeks flushed, and her pupils wide with arousal. She stared at him, and then swallowed loudly enough to be heard. "Sounds good," she breathed, nodding weakly.

"Only good?"

"Great," she amended, her heart still triple-timing. "When do we leave?"

"Right now. The air around here is a little dusty for my taste," he added, with a wink.

Eleanor groaned. "You were doing so well." She stood and offered him a hand, pulling him up with a strength that still surprised him. "Let's go. I want the full, promised ravishment, and that takes time."

Lucifer laughed and looped an arm over her shoulders. "One ravishment coming up. But first, dinner."

"Hmm. No," Eleanor said somberly. "*First* I must phone my lady."

Vancouver, British Columbia, Canada

SOPHIA STEPPED BACK, swiping her forehead with one arm to get rid of the sweat. She was in the gym, sparring with Fausto, who was one of her regulars. All of her sparring partners were skilled in multiple martial disciplines, and all-around self-defense. But each of them had a particular talent or two that forced her to change up her fighting skills, depending on which of them she sparred with on any given night. Fausto, for example, was a highly skilled swordsman, which one might think was an unnecessary talent in this modern age. Except that, in Sophia's case, her opponents were very likely to be hundreds of years old, meaning they were often more comfortable with a blade than a gun.

Sophia herself was from a time when the sword was a man's first choice of weapon, but as a female she hadn't been expected to defend herself at all. And until she'd become Lord of the Canadian Territories, her life as a vampire hadn't involved much in the way of self-defense either, beyond that which she could accomplish with raw power alone.

It was Colin, naturally, who'd insisted she become a fighter. A warrior queen, he'd called her. And, fortunately, the vampire symbiote had agreed with him. No one knew how it worked, but everyone agreed that the symbiote made vampires more aggressive and more violent than they'd ever been as humans. And those few who were gifted with the power to become vampire lords were the most aggressive of all. Added to a vampire's superb physical abilities, that aggression made her a deadly combatant . . . when she finally put her mind to it and stuck to the killer training regimen that Colin designed for her—"killer" being more than just a euphemism, in this case.

She was grateful for that regimen now, because her people were under attack, and she was prepared, both mentally and physically, for whatever her enemies threw at her. But also because right now, the speed and violence of the sparring floor forced her to think about something other than the latest nightmare scenario her brain had conjured up for Colin's torture.

Perhaps sensing her distraction, Fausto produced a knife from somewhere. She'd never figured out where he carried all of them, but she was ready for it regardless. He'd drilled this into her until it was pure muscle memory that had her reaching out with her power to cripple his blade hand, even as she attacked him physically, moving faster than even most vampires could follow, catching the blade as it flew from his fingers, then twisting around to yank his head back and place the blade at his throat.

"*Give,*" he rasped, his Adam's apple sliding beneath the sharp edge of the knife. He slapped the mat at the same time, making his surrender clear. Sophia wouldn't have harmed him, not intentionally, but they hadn't always gotten along, so he probably figured it couldn't hurt to be sure. He'd been born in the same era, the same part of Spain, as Sophia, and she still carried a great deal of anger and resentment against the men of her past. It had taken her some time to get over it and see Fausto for himself and for the skills he could bring.

She released him in a single, smooth move, lifting the knife and standing up and away before he could react. That was another lesson she'd learned from Fausto. That she should never put all her faith in an enemy's surrender. Always be prepared for the double-cross, for treachery.

"Excellent disarm, my lady," he said now, coming gracefully to his feet.

She nodded, but kept her distance . . . and his blade.

He grinned, and took up a defensive position of his own, ready to continue sparring. But even as Sophia rocked on her feet, preparing to move, she was struck by a blow she couldn't have anticipated.

Death. In that first second, she thought her own heart would stop. Until the truth hit her—it was Darren Yamanaka who'd died. He was sworn to her, and that made him hers, but, despite the physical blow of his demise, she was having difficulty finding any grief in his death. She quickly stepped back, out of range, one hand up in an unnecessary signal to Fausto, who'd seen her reaction and known something terrible had happened, something that demanded his vampire lord's attention. And that was all he needed to know. She wanted to keep this death very close to her vest for now.

Almost from the beginning, she'd suspected Darren had been the one who betrayed her, and kidnapped Colin, but in the absence of clear proof, she'd cautiously, and grudgingly, given him the benefit of the doubt. And now he was dead, but his death alone didn't give her any answers. Had he died at the hands of her enemies or her allies? A moment's reflection told her it was probably the latter, mostly because Eleanor had warned her not to trust him. And Eleanor was still alive. She wanted to call her and demand to know what was happening. But she held back. If there was a battle going on, Eleanor didn't need the distraction, and Sophia trusted her to call as soon as she could.

So, she waited. Not patiently, but she waited. Eleanor had a unique ringtone, so there could be no question of who was calling. But Sophia obsessively checked to be sure the ringer was on, that it was loud enough for her to hear while she showered and dressed, and then she tucked the phone in her pocket as she stood staring out the big picture window in her office, all the while telling herself there were a million and one things she should be doing instead.

When the call finally came, she snatched it up mid-ring.

"My lady," Eleanor said, sounding breathless.

"You killed him?" Sophia asked. There was no reason to say who "him" was. They both knew.

"Not I, my lady. It was Lucifer. But there was no question of his guilt in Colin's kidnapping."

"The fool," Sophia murmured, but privately her thoughts were less prosaic. *Lucifer.* Sophia wasn't thrilled that it was Aden's big hunter who'd killed her enemy. Lucifer was too clever and far too powerful for her peace of mind. Powerful enough to make a play for her territory. Not today, maybe, but give him a few more decades to expand his skill and experience, and he might very well be looking for a territory of his own.

And now, he'd killed Darren Yamanaka, which effectively gave him the three Canadian cities that Darren had ruled. Not formally, since the cities were in her territory, and he'd need her blessing to take them, and to get that, he'd have to swear fealty to *her.* But if he decided to fight her for it, to demand the cities as his due . . . . It would be one more battle she'd have to fight in a war that was already full of pitfalls and betrayal.

"Can your Lucifer be trusted?" Sophia asked bluntly. She knew that Eleanor loved the handsome brute, but Sophia was confident that the female wouldn't be so swayed by his pretty face that she'd betray her sworn lord.

"Absolutely," Eleanor assured her. "We weren't hunting Darren; it just happened. We were subtly reconnoitering the tunnels where we believe Colin is being held, when Darren suddenly exited the location. He was completely alone, and so Lucifer seized the opportunity to eliminate a powerful enemy with no witnesses. And Lucifer doesn't think Darren's power was enough to cause an identifiable ripple. People will know someone died, but not who. Which means his allies won't know he's gone before—"

"*I* knew," Sophia interjected sourly, but then forced herself to admit, "But he's right. Unless Darren had children that I don't know about, no one but me—and you—will know exactly who it was that died. But you said you thought Colin was there. Did you see . . ." Sophia couldn't ask the question, couldn't bear to know what Eleanor might have discovered.

"We didn't see him, my lady," Eleanor said gently. "We didn't get that far into the tunnels before Darren emerged. But we have reason to believe that's where he's being held. We tracked down and questioned the human who guided Darren and the others to an unfinished and abandoned section of tunnel. The twin brother of this human works for one of the vampires who—But that's not important. What *is* important is what he saw when he was there, including a prison cell and at least one sleep chamber for vampires. Lucifer and I are confident that's where we'll find Colin."

"Excellent. I can have the jet prepped and be there—"

"Forgive me, my lady," Eleanor interrupted. "But you can't tell *anyone* what I've just told you. And you cannot come here. Too many people will suspect the reason for your trip. If Darren's allies get the smallest hint that we know Colin's location, they could move him, and we'd have to start all over again. Lucifer and I will go in first thing tomorrow night. From what we've discovered, visits by Darren and the others are sporadic. Most nights, there are only a few guards on hand. And since Darren was just there tonight, the odds favor us for a rescue tomorrow night."

"Tomorrow," Sophia whispered. "Why not tonight?" she asked suddenly, suspicion about Lucifer's loyalties blooming once again.

"Lucifer challenged and defeated Darren Yamanaka less than an hour ago, Sophia," Eleanor said gently. "Obviously, he won, but he was also injured. He needs blood. We both do if we're to be at full strength for tomorrow night's operation. We hope we'll only be facing guards, but we have to be prepared for anyone."

"Of course. Forgive me."

"Oh, no, my lady. There is nothing to forgive. I try to think what I'd do in your shoes, if Lucifer were the one being tortured, and I cannot even imagine it. You're strong, and so much braver than I could be."

Sophia understood that Eleanor wasn't referring to vampiric power. It went without saying that she was stronger than all but a few vampires on the whole fucking planet when it came to *that*. For all the good it did her in this situation. But Eleanor was referring to something else, to her decision to leave Montreal and return to Vancouver to defend her territory and her people, leaving Colin's rescue to someone else. What Eleanor didn't understand, however, was that it wasn't really a choice. Being a territorial lord was a heavy burden, one that forced your hand in so many ways, unless you were a monster who didn't care how many of your people died to serve your personal ambitions.

She wasn't brave. She was bound by her people, and trapped in a way she might not have accepted if she'd known the cost.

"I will call you the moment we know something, my lady. The moment he's safe."

"Keep yourself safe, too, Eleanor. And I suppose I must thank that handsome devil you're so fond of for eliminating the traitor."

"I'll convey your gratitude," Eleanor said with a hint of laughter, but then grew serious once again. "There are more traitors than him. We haven't identified them all yet, but you must be careful."

"Yes." A delicate chime sounded, as a new message popped up on her cell phone. "Until tomorrow, then," she said, and disconnected without any further good-byes. She was a modern woman, but had been born in a country and culture that was filled with superstitions, and bidding someone "good-bye" was like daring the gods to interpret the words for themselves.

Besides, there was nothing good about what she was about to do. Eleanor and Lucifer were hunting for traitors in the eastern half of her territory, but she'd begun her own hunt here in Vancouver. She'd been too soft-hearted, too much like her Sire, who'd thought only of the pleasures of life. What had happened to Lucien would never have happened to Raphael, or any of the others. And she couldn't help thinking she was as culpable in Colin's torment as Lucien had been in his own. She'd been too benevolent in the way she ruled, and others had seen it as weak.

No longer. She was questioning everyone. No one was safe. And if it took pain to get the truth, then that's what she'd do.

She glanced down at the clothes she'd chosen for the night. All black. Perfect. It wouldn't show the blood.

Montreal, Quebec, Canada

"YOUR SOPHIA DOESN'T trust me," Lucifer commented, and Eleanor thought he sounded more amused by it than worried.

"*Lady* Sophia doesn't know you like I do."

"And thank God for that. I mean, she's a beautiful woman, don't get me wrong, but—"

"You should stop talking now."

Lucifer laughed. "You know I love only you, *bella*."

"Uh huh. That's the place, up there on the right. Purple awning."

He ignored the blare of horns as he swung to the right-hand curb, coming to a stop in front of Montreal's busiest blood club. One of the valets opened her door, and Eleanor climbed down from the SUV, noting the long line of humans waiting for admission. It seemed unusually busy for a Tuesday night, but then, she wasn't in Montreal all that often, so maybe this was normal. She knew about this particular club because she'd been here once before, during a visit to the city with Sophia. Ironically, her guide on that visit had been Darren Yamanaka. His duties as master of the city had included oversight of the various blood houses and clubs in Montreal and its suburbs. He'd assured her at the time that this particular club was the most exclusive of them all, the one that attracted a better class of humans, which meant they had money and/or prestige. They were the city's elite, or at least, the elite's off-spring. As with any exclusive venue, vampire-controlled clubs were very selective about whom they admitted. And just as human chefs insisted that their food *look* good as well as taste good, so, too, did vampires. Doormen surveyed everyone who sought entrance, and admitted only those who looked acceptable.

Eleanor and Lucifer cruised past the pair of vampires guarding the door. She didn't know whether that was because they recognized *her* as one of Sophia's people, or if it was the palpable nimbus of power still surrounding Lucifer in the aftermath of his fight with Yamanaka. Probably Lucifer.

But while he was in a power overload after killing the other vamp, Lucifer's insistence that he needed to feed made her think the power surge was taking a toll rather than boosting his energy.

"You okay, Luc?" She stood on her tiptoes to make sure he could hear her in the crowded club, and even then he had to bend down to catch what she was saying. Eleanor was 5 feet 2 inches on a good day. Add in the heels she always wore in one form or another, and she was anywhere from 3 to 5 inches taller. But Lucifer was well over 6 feet, and all of that was muscle. She had skills and strength, and deserved her position as Sophia's primary bodyguard, but around Lucifer, she would always feel delicate and petite. She could have resented that. She'd worked damn hard to fight her way up the ranks of Sophia's security contingent. But Lucifer didn't make resentment possible. When she'd been human, he'd always treated her like a rare piece of fine porcelain, something breakable and precious. And he'd protected her accordingly, always making her feel treasured and safe. She'd expected that to be a problem in their new relationship. He still had more power than she did, and she'd been prepared to have to fight him for recognition of her strengths and abilities. But not Lucifer. He hadn't once treated her as anything less than he was, or tried to shove her to the back of a fight. Well, except for when she'd tried to stop a bullet meant for him by using her body as a shield. He might not think twice about letting her kick some vampire ass, but there was no way in hell he'd ever stand by and let her bleed for him. He was still Lucifer, after all. And he protected the women he loved. The *woman* he loved.

After all these years, Lucifer still loved her just the way he always had. Eleanor wanted to hoard that knowledge, to tuck it into a safe spot in her heart and never let it go. Decades would pass, people would live and die, but she would always have that piece of Lucifer that no one else could touch.

"You with me, Elle?"

Lucifer's voice drew her out of her romantic daydreams—were they still daydreams if she was only awake at night? Did a vampire's reality turn the words on their heads?

"Elle?"

She looked up at him with a big smile. "I'm with you. What's the plan?"

Lucifer took her hand and pulled her across the room. The blood bar was set up like an old-time supper club, with period décor that included large booths with velvet upholstered benches and matching curtains that could be closed for privacy. Eleanor eyed those curtains and wondered if that was all the privacy they'd get. Would Lucifer expect her to join him in one of those booths? The two of them feeding off some human, watching him thrash in the throes of sexual ecstasy, with nothing but a bit of velvet fabric between them and an entire bar full of people?

"Relax," Lucifer murmured, and led her to one of the bigger booths where six vampires sat, watching them approach with varying degrees of curiosity and hostility. But a single look from Lucifer had them hustling to vacate the booth, murmuring words of respect as they passed him by on their way back to the dance floor.

Once they were gone, he waved Eleanor onto the padded seat with a grand gesture that made her laugh.

"Nice trick," she said, gliding her hand over his flat belly as she sat down. She scooted her way around the table, with its lone, electric candle, and into the back curve of the booth. Lucifer followed, sliding around until he was right next to her, his arm along the top of the seat behind her shoulders. "What do we do next?" she asked, suddenly nervous all over again. She'd never hunted with another vampire before, and wasn't sure how this was going to work. Feeding from a human was intensely sexual. Whatever evolutionary leap had been responsible for the creation of vampires had also made sure they could survive. And that meant making humans *want* to give blood. Granted, as recently as a hundred years ago, vampires had literally hunted humans on the streets and sunk fang without permission. But even so, once the biting commenced, the human donor *did* experience tremendous sexual pleasure. Assuming the vampire didn't drain them dry. A century ago, that was more common than not.

But not anymore. Now, humans lined up to open a vein precisely *because* of that sexual high. And that was Eleanor's problem. She didn't know how she felt about sharing Lucifer with another woman, especially one who could provide him with the sustenance he needed to live. Actually, she *did* know how she felt; she didn't like it. It was a scenario that fed right into the insecurities that had sent her running away from him in the first place—her fear that since she couldn't feed him anymore, he wouldn't want her.

Unfortunately, the only alternative was a male donor, which had its own problems. She'd been feeding from male humans ever since becoming a vampire, but she'd never fucked a single one of them. She'd occasionally gone as far as stroking the man off, if he'd been particularly charming, or if she simply liked him better than most. But usually, she'd let the euphoric do its thing without her participation, once the biting was over with.

"You're overthinking this," Lucifer commented, his voice like a brush of black velvet against her ear.

She shivered. "All right, so tell me how this goes. How do we get someone to join us?"

He chuckled softly. "Come on, Elle. Have you *ever* had a problem attracting a donor?"

She blushed, in spite of herself. "No," she muttered, swallowing the word.

"What was that?" He leaned down as if he hadn't heard her, but the laughter in his voice told her the truth.

"Fine," she snapped. "Like *you* haven't been fighting off hordes of willing women."

"Fighting them off?"

She elbowed his rock hard gut. "Stop teasing. How do we . . . choose?"

"You mean, do we want a man or a woman," he said, intuiting her real question.

"Yes."

"You choose."

"Me? Why me?" she asked in alarm.

"Because I sense you're more uncomfortable with this than I am."

"So you should do it then."

"No, I want *you* to be comfortable. So you choose."

She made an exasperated noise, but knew he wasn't going to budge on this. "All right," she agreed, and then had a sudden thought. "Have you, um . . ." She had trouble getting the question out. "Done it with men before?"

"If by 'done it' you mean sexual contact, then, yes, in a heavy petting sort of way—lots of touching, but no anal penetration by either one of us. I'm assuming your experience is exclusively male?"

"Why would you assume that?" she bluffed.

He dropped his arm over her shoulders and hugged her close, touching his lips to the side of her head. "It's okay, baby."

"What's okay?" she demanded, knowing she was only putting off the inevitable, and covering her nervousness with aggression. "I don't need your blessing for things that happened in the last twenty-three years."

Lucifer stiffened, and then grew very still. "If you're not ready for this, Eleanor, there's blood at the hotel."

Her blush was so hot this time that it flooded from her face to her neck and chest, leaving small drops of perspiration to pool between her breasts. He thought she hadn't even fed from the vein yet, that she still needed the bagged blood stored back at the hotel. That was even more humiliating than her lack of sexual experience. Only the newest newbie vampires drank blood exclusively from a bag.

"That's not—" Her lips flattened together, and she exhaled through her nose in frustration. *"Just come out with it, Eleanor,"* she scolded herself. But she couldn't. She couldn't admit to him that she hadn't had a single lover since being made vampire, that there'd been no one but him since the day they'd met. He'd been her first lover, her only lover. And he still was.

"Okay, look," she said finally. "I've never had sex with a woman, and I'm not all that comfortable with fucking strange men, either. So . . . I don't. I bite them, and that's it. I let the euphoric do its thing. No sex."

He stroked a soothing hand over her hair, and down to her shoulder, which he squeezed gently. "That's good, because—fair warning—if you ever touch another man's dick, I'll kill him."

Eleanor blinked at the flat statement, then said slowly, "Then how—"

He didn't let her finish. "Here's how it's going to work. We'll pick a guy we both like, we'll take him somewhere suitable—a private room, if this club has them."

"It does."

"Good. We'll feed from him together, giving him twice the rush, and then we'll kick him out the door, and take out our sexual frustrations on each other."

"Kick him out the door?"

He shrugged. "We get him another room or, hell, one of those booths will do. Close the curtains and let him sleep it off."

"No, I meant . . . *him?*"

"Or her. Whichever you like."

Eleanor steeled herself mentally. If she and Lucifer were going to stay together—and if she had anything to say about it, they definitely were—then she had to do this. Besides, she trusted Lucifer implicitly. She drew a breath for courage. "Okay, a guy then. Who looks good and tasty?" She put her elbows on the table, and leaned forward to better survey the packed dance floor.

Lucifer laughed. "That's my delicate princess. You pick."

He was right about one thing, she thought as she studied the crowd. They didn't exactly have to beg for volunteers. A virtual parade of human flesh almost immediately began gliding past their booth—men, women, and pairings of every possible combination thereof. Some of the humans simply walked slowly past, making eye contact, while others trailed their fingers suggestively over the table or themselves, and still others strode right up to the booth and stood there expectantly, almost demanding the right to be their dinner. It was a strange experience.

"You're temptation itself," Lucifer commented, for her ears only.

She leaned back, resting a possessive hand on his muscled thigh. "It's a good thing I'm here, then. You'd starve without me, you poor thing," she added dryly.

His chest shook in a laugh, just as a waiter approached their table.

The twenty-something male was of average height, lean and very fit, with a smoothly muscled chest and well-defined arms revealed by a tight, black T-shirt. He smiled and leaned closer, not stopping until the table's edge was pressed against his thighs. "Can I get you anything?" he asked. His smile had spread to his eyes, a wicked gleam that caught the stray flash of light from the artificial candle.

Lucifer grinned back at the man, but he didn't say anything, leaving the choice up to her.

"When do you get off work?" she asked.

The waiter's smile widened. "An hour ago, my lady." His studied first her, and then Lucifer, with equal appreciation. "Which one?"

Lucifer speared his fingers into her hair, and tugged her head back, giving her a long, hungry kiss, with lots of tongue.

She was breathing hard when he finished, so caught up in the kiss that she barely heard Lucifer's drawling response to the young man.

"Both."

The waiter gasped loudly, and seemed literally breathless for a moment, as if he was so excited that his lungs had seized up. Eleanor wondered if they'd gone too far, or picked the wrong human. But then the young man bent forward, both hands flat on the table, his expression full of lust as his gaze traveled between them, back and forth, as if he couldn't decide which one he wanted to fuck first. He nodded decisively.

Hmm. Maybe he needed to know the ground rules before things got out of hand. "Okay, first, you need to—"

"Come with us," Lucifer interrupted. "What do you think, *bella*?"

Eleanor turned so she could see his expression, wanting to be sure she understood the question. "You mean—"

"What's your name?" Lucifer asked the young man.

"Josh Nelson, my lord."

She blinked as she stared up at Josh, abruptly aware of the line she was about to cross. Did she want to do this? It wasn't exactly a sexual ménage, but . . . She frowned. On the other hand, did she want the alternative? Lucifer feeding from strange women *without* her? Oh, hell, no.

"You like this one?" Lucifer whispered against her ear.

"Yes," she said clearly. "Let's go."

Lucifer chuckled softly, then slid out of the booth and offered a hand to help her stand. Like she needed it or something. But she took it anyway, because such courtesies were simply a part of who Lucifer was. And maybe because she *was* feeling a little wobbly with nerves.

"Tell me, Josh, does this club have private rooms?" Lucifer asked.

"Yes, my lord," Josh said eagerly. "I've one already reserved."

"Well, aren't you efficient," he said, sliding an arm around Eleanor's waist. "Lead the way."

FOR THE FIRST time Eleanor wished alcohol worked on vampires. A nice double shot of something strong would have come in handy right about now. She couldn't remember ever being this nervous, certainly not since she'd been made a vampire. Not even when she'd been standing on the gym mats with all of the other contenders, getting ready to prove that she deserved to be Sophia's bodyguard.

"Relax, baby," Lucifer murmured, as he closed the door to one of the private rooms along the back hallway of the bar. "Nothing gets done here unless you want it." He reached out and dialed the lighting down to a dim, *romantic* glow.

"I'm fine," she insisted, even though she knew Lucifer would hear the lie. This was ridiculous. What was the worst that could happen? For fuck's sake, it wasn't like Josh could take advantage of her in any way, shape, or form. She'd wipe the floor with him in a heartbeat. That realization, coupled with Lucifer's warm hand at the small of her back, finally calmed her down. This was an adventure, a little fun. Something she'd had precious little of in her day-to-day life lately. She took her responsibilities to Sophia very seriously.

She drew in a deep breath. "Okay, I'm good."

"You're beautiful, my lady," Josh purred, as he kicked off his boots and crawled onto the king-sized bed that dominated the small room. "You both are," he added. He gave Lucifer a suggestive glance, and then lay back on the pile of pillows in the middle of the bed. *He* certainly wasn't nervous.

"Make yourself comfortable," Lucifer said dryly. "You've done this before?"

"With two of you?" Josh clarified. "Only once before, and they were nowhere near as lovely as the two of you. How do you want me?"

The question was pragmatic enough, but Eleanor could see by his eager expression that he was hoping the answer would involve nudity. Sadly for Josh, it didn't. Not tonight anyway. Maybe years from now, after she and Lucifer had done this a few hundred times, and . . . . Eleanor's thoughts came to a screeching halt. Years from now? Where had *that* come from? Oh, hell, she knew the answer to that one. She loved Lucifer just as much as she ever had. They'd been planning a lifetime together back then, and here she was doing it again. Except that everything had changed. Not just the fact that they were both vampires, but also that they served different lords. She was bound to Sophia and couldn't imagine leaving her. Lucifer was sworn to Aden for now, but he'd be a lord himself someday, and who knew where that would take him? Hell, there was talk among the Council members of sending a few of the more powerful North American vampires over to Europe, taking the war to them instead of waiting for their next attack here. Lucifer would be the perfect candidate for that.

So what future could they really have together? She turned a stricken gaze on Lucifer, tears burning the backs of her eyes as she drank in every familiar thing about him—his sudden smile and easy laugh, the deep rumble of his voice as he spoke to Josh, his unusual eyes, burning a burnished gold now as his power rose along with his hunger, his big heart . . . and the way he loved her.

Those unusual eyes shifted to Eleanor, and darkened in concern. "Eleanor?" He stepped closer and brushed away a tear with the back of his fingers. "Baby, what's wrong?"

She shook her head. "Nothing. Just happy," she told him, honest in at least the second part of her response.

His too-perceptive gaze searched her face, and she knew she hadn't fooled him. But she also saw his decision to table that discussion for later, when there wasn't a human listening in. A human who, she saw from the corner of her eye, had just pulled his T-shirt over his head, baring his chest and the strong column of his throat. She could hear the racing thump of his heart, and knew his pulse was pounding the same beat.

"Hungry?" Lucifer murmured. He wrapped his fingers in hers and backed up, pulling her toward the bed.

Eleanor nodded. "Do we—" She looked up at him. "—take turns?"

He smiled that shark's grin of his. "If you wish. There are no rules here."

She matched his grin. "Then, you first. I want to watch."

"Kinky," he said, with a leering wink. "My kind of girl."

Lucifer dropped his leather jacket to the floor, leaving his broad chest and thickly muscled shoulders defined beneath a T-shirt, his long legs encased in a pair of jeans that hung low on his narrow hips, and bared his flat belly. He was pure, sinful grace as he slid onto the bed next to Josh, his eyes fixed on Eleanor as he scraped his long fingers through the human's hair and jerked his head back, straining his neck taut and outlining the duel contours of both swollen jugular veins.

Josh's heart, which was already racing, sped up to a pace that was almost alarming, his bare chest working as he panted rapidly. Eleanor might have worried for the man, but Lucifer wasn't at all concerned. He was still eyeing her with that lazy, sensual expression that invited her to come play.

Her own heart was thumping, her mouth watering. She could *taste* the blood rushing through the human's plump vein, could smell the sexual arousal evidenced by the erection straining behind the zipper of his black jeans.

Without conscious thought, she found herself moving toward the bed, taking the opposite side as she stretched out next to Josh, so that the human was now bracketed by the two vampires. He moaned, and his eyes rolled in her direction, unable to move his head with Lucifer's fingers still gripping his hair tightly.

"My lady," he managed to whisper, just as Lucifer shifted his grip, yanking the human's head away from her and exposing the tight expanse of his neck, his big jugular like a blue rope beneath the skin.

Eleanor glanced up and found Lucifer watching her, his eyes nothing but slits of old gold through lush, black lashes. She licked her lips, and his gaze followed the movement of her tongue. Her breasts were tight and aching, her sex pulsing in time with her heart. Lucifer smiled slowly, the kind of smile that could lead good men, and women, straight to hell, singing his praises while they burned. And she was about to burn with them.

Lowering her head, she forced herself to go slowly, despite the hunger that had her fangs sliding out of her gums, dripping with saliva. She inhaled deeply, savoring the rich bouquet of Josh's blood, the luscious scent of healthy young human. A low growl filled the air, and she realized it was coming from her. Her eyes shot up to meet Lucifer's, his gaze never wavering as he ran his tongue up the length of Josh's neck on the other side, indulging in a slow, savoring tasting of the human, as his tongue primed the man's vein. His fangs were on full display, sharp and white, gleaming in the low light. But he didn't bite. He was waiting for her.

Eleanor licked her lips again, before placing one hand on Josh's firm chest, her fingers smoothing over his pectorals, finding the trail of dark hair and following it down over his stomach and belly to where it disappeared into—

A deep, threatening growl had her lifting wide eyes to meet Lucifer's narrowed gaze once more, but it was filled with warning this time. "Remember what I said, *bella,*" he muttered. "You touch his dick, and he dies."

Josh made a strangled noise, quickly cut off as Lucifer scraped his fangs over the human's neck, drawing a thin line of blood, and changing the man's protest into a groan of pleasure.

Eleanor grinned wickedly, loving the power she had in this moment. Not only over Josh, but Lucifer, too. He was full of threat and alpha male posturing, but, in the final analysis, he'd never hurt her. Blowing him a kiss, she transferred her hand to Josh's jaw, dipping her fingers between his lips as she bent her head to his neck, and struck. Fast and deadly, her fangs sank into his flesh, his warm skin parting like silk, the delicate vein puncturing with a rush of thick, delicious blood. It filled her mouth in an instant, coating her teeth and tongue. She swallowed, and it was the sweetest honey as it slid down her throat. She moaned, in hunger and pleasure both, and sucked again, deeper this time, taking a long, slow draught of the man's blood.

She caught the flash of Lucifer's fangs, felt Josh jerk in surprise, and then the scent of fresh blood filled the room as Lucifer began to feed. The human convulsed beneath her hands, and she didn't need to touch his dick to know it was straining to break free of the tight denim. He was grappling with his zipper, trying to release what must have been a painful erection, when Lucifer reached down and tore the man's pants open. His cock sprang out of his pants, full and thick, and dripping cum. Eleanor matched gazes with Lucifer again, both their fangs still buried in Josh's neck, his blood dripping down their chins. Lucifer's eyes were full of warning for her, but then he reached down and grabbed one of the human's thrashing hands, guided it to his rigid cock, and closed his fingers over Josh's, gripping the thick shaft and squeezing.

Josh moaned loudly, and Lucifer began pumping his dick, his hand over Josh's, fingers gripping hard as they stroked up and down, lubricated by the cum dripping from the engorged tip. Josh's breathing increased, becoming short groaning gasps as Lucifer gave the human's cock a final hard squeeze, and then took his hand away as Josh began to pump harder and faster, frantically pursuing his burgeoning orgasm.

Eleanor waited until Josh was on the very edge of coming, until his muscles were wire taut, his heart thundering in her ears. She waited until she heard his moan of surrender, and smelled the flood of his release as it spilled over his hand. And then as his repeated cries filled the air, she drew a final, luscious mouthful of his blood and withdrew her fangs.

Lucifer's eyes were hot, molten gold as he reached for her, gripping her hair the same way he had Josh's, pulling it tight as he yanked her closer, as their mouths met, still filled with blood, their teeth clashing, fangs ripping each other's lips as they kissed in a new kind of hunger, a desperate need not for blood, but for each other.

"Lucifer," she whispered, wanting him more in that moment than she ever had before. She ignored the groaning human between them, knowing only that she had to have Lucifer, or she'd burst from the agonizing need that was crushing her heart.

"It's okay," Lucifer said, his voice so deep that she could hardly make out the words. He licked the blood from her lips—not Josh's blood, but her own, mingled with Lucifer's from their kiss. He closed his eyes briefly, as if searching for strength. "One minute, baby."

Eleanor cried out with loss when he pulled away from her. Her mind understood a moment later when he lifted Josh from between them and carried him to the door, but her heart, her body, knew only that it *needed* Lucifer and he was leaving. She was tearing open her clothes before the door closed behind Lucifer and his unconscious burden. She ached so badly, she couldn't wait for him to come back. She needed to touch, to stroke away some of this terrible ache. She shoved her hand down her pants, her fingers finding her pussy, wet and swollen, her clit pulsing and demanding relief. Pinching her nipples with her other hand, she shoved her fingers deeper, to the hot opening of her pussy, and—

Hard fingers gripped her wrist. She moaned in protest as Lucifer pulled her hand out of her pants, his tongue wet and warm as he raised her hand to his mouth and licked, humming in lascivious pleasure at the taste of her that slicked her fingers. His eyes met hers lazily.

"*My* pussy," he drawled, and rolled her beneath him. Grabbing both of her wrists in one big hand, he stretched her arms over her head, trapping her completely. He dipped his head down to nip at her breasts, closing his teeth over first one, then the other. "Mine," he growled, and leaned over to claim a long, wet kiss, that started slow and delicious, but then suddenly became something else. Something savage.

LUCIFER GROWLED AS raw desire hit without warning, swamping all of his senses, erasing every other consideration. He was no longer worried about protecting Eleanor, about treating her gently and with care. He wanted her hard and fast. He wanted to feel her tight pussy stretched around his cock until he was so deep that she couldn't even scream, until her flesh was so hot and slick that it burned when he fucked her. Rage simmered beneath the lust, surprising him with its very presence, its intensity. He wanted to punish her for leaving him, for letting him think for so many years that she was dead. He wanted to prove to her once and for all that she belonged to him and no one else, to mark her so thoroughly that no one else could ever touch her again.

Knowing he was being too rough, but unable to stop himself, he tore the already open zipper on her jeans, making room for his much bigger hand as he shoved it down into her panties, tearing the flimsy silk as his fingers slid past her smooth mound and deep between the swollen lips of her pussy. She was soaking wet, the satiny cream of her arousal filling the space between her lips, slicking the entrance to her sex. He snarled as she gave a demanding thrust of her hips, grinding herself against his hand. He lifted his head and snapped his teeth in warning, drawing a fierce satisfaction from her wide-eyed reaction to this display of dominance. Eleanor had surrounded herself for too long with males who didn't have the guts or the power to challenge her.

No more. She was Lucifer's now. She'd always been his, even when she'd run. And she was about to learn what that meant.

"Open your eyes, Eleanor," he demanded. He could see the effort it took for her to obey, to overcome arousal enough to focus on his command. Her blue eyes finally opened, hazy with lust as they met his, silently pleading for release.

Holding her gaze with all the force of his vampire gift, he plunged two fingers into her pussy, gliding on the liquid silk of her desire, feeling the tight glove of her sheath closing around him like satin. Eleanor moaned as passion inflamed her pale cheeks, and her eyes drifted shut again.

"Look at me," he snarled, and scraped his palm over her blood-engorged clit, pressing hard on the sensitized nub. Her eyelids shot open, her gaze meeting his just as lightning shards of power shattered the brilliant blue of her eyes. She screamed as the climax rolled over her, her cunt clamping down on his fingers as inner muscles pulsed around them.

His kiss swallowed her scream, claiming even that for himself. It was a hard, possessive kiss, his lips smashing against hers, teeth clashing as he fought to go deeper into her luscious mouth. He tasted the bittersweet nectar of her blood, felt the euphoric hit his bloodstream, demanding his surrender to the sensation. But he was a vampire, and hellacious powerful. He embraced the power of the euphoric, letting it flow over and through him as he trailed his lips down Eleanor's velvety neck to the voluptuous line of her jugular. She sucked in a surprised breath at the scrape of his fangs over her skin. But before the oxygen had even hit her lungs, he bit down, slicing into her vein, reveling in the wanton spill of her blood down his throat, even as the euphoric in his bite sent her crashing into a climax that was ten times, a hundred times more powerful than the one before.

Her entire body spasmed, stiffening into immobility for a long moment, as if frozen, her mouth open in a silent scream. Visible waves of orgasm rolled over her body, leaving her trembling, whimpering helplessly, as jolting climaxes shocked her body over and over again.

A low growl filled the room, and Lucifer moved, unable to wait any longer, his cock painfully erect, his balls hot and tight. Going up on his knees, he stripped her naked, pulling her jeans and panties down her legs, and tossing them aside, tugging her sweater over her head, He reached for her bra, and he froze, staring.

His Eleanor was so beautiful. He struggled for air, the sight of her literally taking his breath away. Her nipples were dark pink and puffy beneath the lace of her bra, so hard and full that he could see them pushing against the fabric, as if straining for release. Lucifer watched her with hungry satisfaction, her legs spread around him, her pussy wide open, flushed and wet, her hips thrusting, seeking his cock. And she was moaning so softly, hungry little sounds coming in choked sobs as she reached for him.

Lucifer leaned over and sucked her nipples through her bra, then filled his mouth with a soft breast, drawing hard until half of her soft flesh was between his teeth. He bit down gently at first, teasing, dragging his fangs and tearing the lace, scraping over the delicate skin, enough to sting, but not enough to break the skin. Eleanor sighed in pleasure, her fingers twisting in his hair as if to hold him in place . . . until his teeth closed over her hardened nipple and he bit down hard. The enticing bouquet of her blood had barely coated his tongue, when she cried out again, gasping over and over as the dark thrill of his bite overwhelmed her senses. He took her right to the edge of pain, before he lifted his head and twisted the front closure of her bra open, discarding the torn garment, while his gaze never left Eleanor's.

"Mine," he said again, strumming her bloodied nipples with his thumbs.

"Take me," she pleaded, and her eyes were full of such longing that Lucifer's heart ached.

"*Bella*," he whispered. He bent over and kissed her eyes closed, tasting salty tears.

He straightened abruptly and yanked down his zipper. He was a vampire. He could have been up and stripped naked in two seconds. But he couldn't wait that long. Freeing his rigid cock, he gripped it with one hand, squeezing tightly as he positioned himself between her firm thighs and slid just the tip into her wet and waiting pussy.

She moaned, and he pushed in farther, the rough denim of his jeans scraping on the sensitive skin of her thighs, highlighting the fact that he was still mostly clothed, while his Eleanor was completely naked. That realization, the picture it created in his mind, sent a ripple of lust shuddering through his body, as he slid his cock deeper in her tight little body. She was so ready that her thighs were sticky with cream, her pussy welcoming and slick, and still he stretched her wide with his size. His cock left a trail of heat as he plunged through the sensitized tissues of her sheath, pushing until the tip of his cock slammed into her cervix. Eleanor cried out, but not in pain. A fresh wave of silky cream surrounded his hardness, as she writhed in pleasure beneath him.

Lucifer felt his power rising, saw the golden glow of his eyes lighting up Eleanor's pale skin, gleaming off the spark of power in her own eyes. His cock grew impossibly harder, his balls drawn up tight. He pulled his dick out until only the tip rested inside her, and then, in a single, forceful thrust, he plunged into her body until she was completely filled, and then he did it again, and again. Needing to get still closer, still deeper, he reached down and hooked her legs with his forearms, bending her knees and crushing her thighs against her chest, exposing her pussy, leaving it wide open and waiting for him.

Lucifer slammed in and out, his teeth bared in a snarl, his eyes two pools of golden fire. Eleanor dug her fingers into his shoulders, her own eyes shining as she looked down and watched his cock slam in and out of her body, over and over again.

"Mine," she whispered, then looked up and met his gaze. "Mine," she said more strongly, and Lucifer grinned.

"Yours," he agreed, and then he threw his head back and howled, as his release roared out of his tight balls and down his length, blasting out of his cock to fill Eleanor with his heat, leaving every inch of her, inside and out, marked with his scent.

Lucifer pumped lazily a few times, and then collapsed on top of Eleanor, quickly rolling over and taking her with him, trapping her in the circle of his arms, as she lay limply against his chest.

"You okay?" he asked quietly, kissing her eyes, her cheeks. He tasted more tears, and lowered his chin to see her face. "Eleanor?"

"I love you," she said softly, and he saw the old gold gleam of his power bathe her beloved face.

"I love you, too, *bella*. Always have. Always will."

IT WAS LATE BEFORE they stirred from the bed. Lucifer knew they should have been up and heading back to the hotel sooner, but he was reluctant to leave the deceptive safety of their private, little room. He was sure the blood club had security in place for vampires who stayed, just as he was sure he wouldn't trust them on a bet. Not with his safety, and sure as hell not with Eleanor's.

It was time to go.

"We've got to get up," he said, kissing the top of her head. She was still sprawled on top of him, her legs straddling him so that he could feel the silky plumpness of her pussy against his hip. "Time to get dressed."

"Easy for you to say," she muttered. "You've already got half of your clothes on." She lifted her head to peer at him, looking adorably grumpy. "Why is that, anyway?"

"You were simply too delicious. I couldn't wait."

She hmphed her opinion of that, and sat up, her expression going almost blank as she did the same thing he had only a minute ago. She scanned the halls and rooms outside their door, taking the emotional temperature of the club to be sure there was no threat brewing, and then gauging the pull of the sun, where it loomed not far below the horizon.

"You're right," she said, expression returning to her face as she looked at him. "We either leave now, or figure out a way to blockade that door."

"Not a chance. Get your gorgeous body moving. We're out of here in five."

Eleanor nodded her agreement, then swung her legs around and jumped off the bed. He regretted the loss of her sweet weight, but not the urgency of her response. They really would be racing the clock to get back to the hotel in the time left to them. As it was, he might end up carrying her the last little way.

"Ready." She'd been a whirlwind of vampire speed as she gathered her clothes from around the bed, and yanked them on, shoving her bra into her pocket as a lost cause. She'd pulled her long hair over her shoulder, and was twisting it into a tight braid when she looked up at him.

"The car's right outside," he reminded her. He'd paid the valet extra for the convenience. "We'll go straight through the club and out. You drive. You know the streets better."

She nodded again. "Josh?"

"His room is paid for the day, so he's safe enough, and drunk on pleasure. He already confided his willingness to, as he said, 'do it again,' if we're so inclined. I liked the boy."

"Me, too," she agreed, pulling on her hoodie. She looked up quickly. "But not like that," she clarified, her eyes laughing at his narrowed gaze.

It was Lucifer's turn to make a hmphing noise as he opened the room door and hustled her out into the hallway. They weren't the only vampires making a late exit, although there were more than a few who disappeared into private rooms with a loud click of a lock. Lucifer had been to all sorts of clubs—some with private rooms and some not—but he'd never seen so many vampires choosing to remain at the club through the day. It made him question the security at the main compound in the city, and wonder if it was a larger problem of improper facilities, or if, perhaps, there was so much turmoil among the city's vampires that no one felt safe.

"Let's go." Eleanor's voice interrupted his reverie as she pushed open the outer door, and headed for their SUV, which was parked only a few feet away. He unlocked the doors with the remote—he hadn't trusted it to the parking attendant—and opened Eleanor's door, before heading around to his own.

Eleanor started the vehicle, and pulled away from the curb with a squeal of tires, taking the first right turn so fast that he'd have sworn the big vehicle went up on two wheels. "How long?" she asked as she gunned the engine down a straightaway.

"Long enough that there's no need to kill us before we get there," he said dryly.

She grinned, but didn't slow down.

His phone rang when they were a few minutes from the hotel. He checked the caller ID, and answered, saying only, "Cal."

"Running a little late, boss," Cal said mildly.

"We had an interesting night. We'll be there in two minutes."

"I'll be waiting."

Eleanor finally slowed when they hit the narrow street where their hotel was located. She drove the two blocks, then swung into the underground parking beneath the hotel, where Cal stood next to the elevator, waiting for them.

"Cutting it close," he told Lucifer, signaling for one of his men to park the vehicle, while he rode up in the elevator with them.

"Our recon turned into a full-blown challenge fight," Lucifer told him.

Cal shot him a surprised looked. "Obviously you won."

"I did," Lucifer confirmed, grinning. "One asshole down, and who knows how many to go."

The human guard snorted. "There's an unlimited supply of those. Here we go," he said, then stepped out of the elevator and stood to one side, letting Lucifer unlock the door to their suite. "Rest well."

Lucifer pushed the door open, and scanned the empty rooms beyond, making certain they really were empty. They had too many enemies in this city, enemies that had proven themselves to be very resourceful. And while he trusted Cal and his team with his life, he didn't know how well the hotel employees had been vetted before their visit.

Finding the rooms as empty as they should be, he held the door open while Eleanor walked past him, and then turned to Cal. "See you tonight," he said, then closed and locked the door behind him, going immediately to the window controls to lower the shades.

When he turned back to the room, Eleanor was already entering her half of the suite, but Lucifer zipped over and swept her up and into his arms.

"What are you doing?" she said laughing.

"I'm taking you to my bed, where you belong."

"Maybe you belong in mine."

"We can trade off," he said agreeably, as he carried her into his bedroom and tossed her onto the bed. "Strip, woman. Time is short and I want you naked when we wake up tonight."

"You, too," she said, giving him a meaningful look.

Lucifer snorted. "Like I'm going to argue about getting naked with you."

Eleanor laughed, and it was such a lighthearted sound that it made Lucifer stop and stare. She sounded just as she used to, before so much shit had happened, and they'd been torn apart.

"What?" she asked, catching his look.

"Nothing," he said softly. "I missed you, Elle."

"Oh," she breathed, and then she was in his arms, and holding on to him as if she'd never let go. Which was exactly his plan. She swayed suddenly, and his grip tightened.

"Into bed," he said, reaching down and pulling back the covers, as she tumbled loosely onto the mattress.

"You, too," she repeated blearily, already affected by the rising sun, which was just crossing the horizon.

Lucifer stripped off the last of his clothes, and slid in next to her. Vampire sleep wasn't the same as human sleep. It was more akin to hibernation, albeit of the daily variety. Neither he nor Eleanor would move once they fell asleep, and they'd wake in exactly the same position. Which was why he pulled her into his arms, and yanked the covers over both of them.

"Sleep, baby," he whispered, kissing her forehead. And then the sun took him.

Chapter Eleven

ELEANOR BREATHED a blissful sigh and stretched luxuriously, feeling so very good . . . a blush heated her cheeks. A little too good. Her nipples were hard, her sex wet and trembling, and every nerve in her body was alive, as if . . . . She moaned out loud as two thick fingers slid into her pussy. Her hips bucked automatically, and her eyes flashed open.

"Lucifer," she gasped.

His mouth closed over her swollen clit, his tongue lashing the sensitive nub, before he lifted his head, and grinned up the length of her body. His eyes were flashing wickedly, a thick lock of dark hair hung irresistibly over his forehead. "I woke up, and there you were, all creamy pink and naked. I couldn't help myself." He bent his head and licked her again.

"Okay," she breathed.

"Excellent," he growled, and then he sucked her clit hard, until she'd have sworn she could feel the pulse of her blood, throbbing and concentrated in that hard, little pearl.

Eleanor threw her head back, panting for breath, as waves of erotic sensation coasted over her body, touching every inch of her skin, every erogenous zone. It was as if his mouth was everywhere, on her lips, her cheeks, her neck . . . and, oh God, on her breasts, her belly. How was he doing that? She was awash in glorious pleasure, convinced it couldn't get any better than this.

But she hadn't counted on Lucifer. With a soft growl, he closed his teeth over the throbbing pulse of her clit, and he bit down.

Eleanor screamed as the combination of pain and pleasure lit up her nerves like lightning. Fire burned in her veins, and she writhed helplessly as wave after wave of fierce, carnal joy flooded her senses. Her world, her universe, narrowed down to the small nexus of nerves between her thighs, and Lucifer's voracious and talented mouth.

"*Bella.*"

His warm breath brushed over her wet flesh, cool after the heat of his mouth. She opened her eyes blearily. His face was wet and slick with her juices, his fangs gleaming white where they pressed into his lips.

She had to swallow more than once before she managed to speak. "Lucifer?" she whispered.

"Are you awake?"

She nodded wordlessly. Oh, yes, she was awake. She'd never *been* so fucking wide awake.

He smiled, slow and sweet, the devil himself come to seduce her. "That's good," he murmured. And then he moved. Powerful arms flexed, and he loomed over her, his hips spreading her thighs, his fully aroused cock on gorgeous display, dragging over her drenched pussy as he crawled up her body. He paused long enough to snack on each of her nipples, leaving narrow trails of blood to drip over the curve of her breasts, as he bent low and covered her mouth with his.

She tasted her pussy and her blood on his lips, and wanted more. She drew his succulent lower lip between her teeth and bit down until the rich, dark taste of his blood joined the sensuous mélange flavoring their kiss. It tasted of sex and violence, of wanton pleasure. It tasted like Lucifer.

"I love you," she whispered into his mouth, shocked at the sob of emotion that punctuated her words.

"Baby," he murmured, touching his lips to her swollen mouth, kissing each corner, licking away the smallest hurt of her torn lips. His hips lifted as he reached between their bodies, brushing over her exquisitely sensitive clit, gliding his fingers through the creamy wetness of her pussy. And then he gripped his cock and positioned it at her entrance, holding his hips high, teasing her with the hot tip of his penis.

Her eyes met his, pleading. He grinned . . . and then he thrust into her body, going as deep as he could go, until his balls slapped her ass, and his hips crashed into hers. He held there for a long moment, groaning.

"Christ, you feel good. Your cunt is like a hot, tight glove around my dick."

Eleanor squeezed her inner muscles around the thickness of his cock, smiling smugly when he sucked in a harsh breath. He groaned. "I won't last if you do that again."

She flexed her hips against his. "Maybe I don't want you to last. Maybe I want you to come right now, to fill my pussy with your hot, thick—"

"Jesus, Elle. I'm not kidding." He covered her mouth with his, swallowing her laughter. And when he lifted his head, there was a dangerous gleam in his eyes. "Payback's a bitch, baby."

His ass tightened beneath her heels, as he flexed his hips and pulled his cock out of her pussy, and then slammed it back in again. Over and over, he drove into her, fucking her fast and hard. It was lewd and raunchy, brutal and greedy. It was the most sublime thing she'd ever experienced.

He was right with her when she climaxed, her sheath squeezing down the length of his cock, clasping and stroking until with a groan, he surrendered. And the wet heat of his release was just as overwhelming as she'd told him it would be. Their cries mingled as they bucked wildly against each other, arms and legs tangled, their panting breaths eventually the only sound in the room.

ELEANOR WASN'T sure her heart would ever return to its normal, steady beat. She remembered loving Lucifer back in New Orleans, remembered *making* love to him, *with* him. But she didn't remember anything like this. The passage of time had dulled her memories. Or maybe she'd chosen to forget how much he'd meant to her, because she'd known in her heart that she'd lost him forever.

Except she hadn't. She pressed her ear against his broad chest, hearing the regular, deep thump of his heart.

"We need a plan," Lucifer said, and his voice vibrated against her cheek. It made her smile. He caught her smile, and said, "When *you* get excited, your heart pounds so fiercely that your lovely breasts dance along with it."

She pushed herself upright and glared down at him, clutching her hands to her chest, as if to cover herself from his eyes. "They do not! And how did you know what I was—Can you hear my thoughts?"

"Clear as a bell, baby." His voice sounded in her head. *"It's the blood . . . from when we kissed."*

She gasped in outrage. "Is that why you ambushed me with sex the moment I woke? To reinforce that stupid telepathic connection?"

Lucifer's beautiful abs flexed as he sat up and shoved himself against the headboard, pulling her along with him.

"I 'ambushed' you because you're the most delicious morsel of female flesh I've ever encountered, and I can't get enough of you. And that so-called stupid connection you're talking about might save our lives tonight," he added somberly. "With any luck we'll encounter no one but guards when we go after Murphy. Between us, we should be able to take them easily. But if any of Yamanaka's co-conspirators show up—"

"You're not worried about Chase Landry, are you? Because I don't think—"

"Fuck Landry. He's a minor talent. No, I'm far more concerned about Yamanaka's mysterious European ally. We don't know anything about him."

"You think he might have some real power?"

"It's hard to say, but I don't believe for one second that Berkhard was willing to surrender all of Eastern Canada to Darren Yamanaka."

There was a thread of real concern in his voice that caught her attention. They hadn't discussed Yamanaka's death, or whatever intel Lucifer had gleaned from the dying vampire's mind.

"There's more than just Yamanaka, isn't there?" she asked. "I mean we knew he wasn't working alone, but there's someone significant. Who is it?" She braced herself for more bad news, for the revelation that she'd have to call Sophia with the name of one more trusted vampire who'd betrayed her. But Lucifer shook his head.

"It's not Sophia's people who worry me, although Yamanaka dragged more than just Chase Landry into his sordid little scheme. It's the Europeans. Berkhard didn't come to North America alone. He brought a powerful ally along with him. And while he's focused on Vancouver, he left that ally behind here in Montreal. The vampire's name is Kasimir. Yamanaka wasn't clear on the relationship, but he suspected that Kasimir was Berkhard's child, maybe even his first. They've obviously been together a very long time, because Berkhard trusts him enough to oversee the conquest of the Eastern half of Canada. Berkhard's already in Vancouver, by the way, or very close by. He wants to take out Sophia himself, in order to establish a rightful claim to all of her territory."

"She's suspected that all along. Someone's been nibbling away at her holdings, attacking small enclaves of her vampires. Almost like he's testing the waters. Christian, the new Lord of the South, warned the Council about Berkhard, and about his ambitions against Sophia specifically."

Lucifer nodded. "Before he died, Yamanaka was beginning to suspect Kasimir's motives. He'd begun making moves of his own to take Kasimir out before the end. His problem was one of power, however. I only have Yamanaka's impressions, but he was well and truly intimidated by this Kasimir fellow."

Terror rose without warning, crushing her heart and chilling her lungs. If they had to take on Kasimir, Lucifer would be the one facing him down. Again. She'd be there to help him, to keep enemies off his back, and to lend her strength when he needed it. But just as with Yamanaka, Lucifer would fight the challenge, risking severe injury, or even death. She gripped his arm, her fingers digging into the solid muscle.

"We should grab Colin tonight and fly to Vancouver. You and Sophia can join forces and—"

Lucifer smiled gently, and covered her hand with his, slowly relaxing the hold she had on him. There were dark bruises where her fingers had dug into his flesh, and five bloody crescents from her nails. He made a shushing sound at the appalled look on her face.

"It doesn't hurt." He picked up her fingers, with their nails painted with his blood, and held them to her mouth one at a time. "Blood strengthens the bond between us, *bella*. The more the better."

She sucked her fingers and found herself shuddering at the luscious taste of his powerful blood. Her nipples had already begun to swell and harden as all that power rushed through her system.

"Damn," she whispered. "How do you deal with that? Do you feel the same rush I do?"

"I sure as hell hope not," he murmured, flicking one of her eager nipples.

She gave a halfhearted laugh, too worried about the possibility of him fighting the unknown Kasimir. What if the European was too strong? Or simply older and wilier? But Lucifer clearly didn't want to discuss it.

"It is what it is," he said quietly. "It's the vampire way. If I'm challenged, I *will* fight. And I'm damn good, so don't worry so much." He gave her hair a playful tug.

Eleanor shoved down the fear that filled her throat, choking her. If Lucifer could do it, then so could she. He didn't need her doubts spilling into his thoughts. "Speaking of the vampire way," she said, forcing herself to change the subject. "Since you killed Yamanaka, does that make you Master of Toronto and Montreal? And maybe Quebec, too?"

Lucifer tilted his head, considering the question. "I suppose so. The rule is you keep what you win, right? But those cities are part of Sophia's territory, which makes it more complicated. We'll have to sort out all of that once Murphy is freed and our enemies are dead."

Eleanor nodded. "What's the plan for tonight, then?"

He shrugged. "We can't know until we get there. We've got the codes, and the basic layout. Beyond that, we'll have to play it by ear."

She felt a little sick at the idea of charging into those tunnels with so many unknowns. But he was right; there was no other way. "Okay, we should get moving then. Should we shower together in order to—"

Lucifer laughed. "Now's who ambushing whom? If we shower together, we'll never leave this room." He bent down and sucked one nipple into his mouth, and she felt the firm scrape of his fangs.

She shuddered as her pussy contracted deep between her thighs. Her body remembered the feel of his mouth, his hands, and damn it, his beautiful cock, too.

"Maybe I should shower in my room," she said breathily. "My clothes are there, and—"

"Good idea," he said, but his eyes were hot, his power limning the hazel with a gleam of old gold. He set her aside and climbed from the bed, his cock standing straight out in enticing invitation. "Eleanor."

She lifted her gaze from his erection to his grinning face.

"You can have this later," he said, gripping himself in one hand and stroking up and down.

Her eyes narrowed. "Remember what you said, Lucifer. Payback's a bitch." She stood up and stormed from the room, wishing she wasn't naked, but going with what she had. At least this way, she wouldn't be the only one getting an eyeful of what she couldn't have.

"Ten minutes," Lucifer called as she opened the bedroom door. "Make it quick, *bella*."

She snapped off a salute, and waited until she was out of his sight before breaking into a run. Ten minutes? He was insane. She couldn't even wash her hair in ten minutes, much less anything else. She'd have to leave it dirty and confine it in a tight braid, as she always did before going into a fight. Because even if the gods smiled on them, and they had no one to contend with in the tunnels but a few guards, she needed to be ready to fight. And if the worst happened, and Lucifer had to challenge Kasimir, then she'd be ready to help him with that, too.

"I REALLY HATE TUNNELS."

Lucifer glanced at Eleanor and grinned. They were creeping down the public tunnel beneath the university, heading for the utility closet with its concealed door. They had Andy's map, but Lucifer didn't need it. He remembered exactly how to get into the secret tunnel, and how to get back out again, too. That was the important part—getting safely out at the end. And tonight, with a little bit of luck, they'd be taking Colin Murphy out with them, which would make it more important than ever that they make a fast exit.

"Tunnels aren't so bad," he offered. "Especially these. They don't really go anywhere, just up and back. It's easy to figure out where you are."

"I still hate tunnels," she grumbled. "No fresh air."

He had to agree with her on that. They could use some air circulation. During the normal course of the day, there would be a lot more foot traffic down here, with people opening and closing doors almost constantly. Maybe that brought in a regular flow of fresh air during those times. But right now, the air was stale and still.

"It'll be worse once we get beyond that closet door," he warned her.

"Yeah, but I figure we'll be so busy fighting for our lives that it won't matter by then."

He chuckled softly, then held a finger to his lips, cautioning her to be quiet as he pushed open the door to the closet. Vampires had greatly enhanced hearing, compared to humans, and despite the length of tunnel and a total of three solid doors between them and the vampire guards, a stray sound could easily give them away.

Lucifer waited until Eleanor had walked past him into the closet, then quietly closed the door to the public tunnel, checking to be sure it was secure. Satisfied that they wouldn't be interrupted, he moved over to the hidden exit behind the shelves, with its keypad lock.

"Ready?" He sent the word to Eleanor telepathically, as a reminder that they had that link, and that she should use it.

She touched his shoulder briefly, and nodded. *"Be careful."*

He winked back at her and punched in the door code.

Once they were in the secret tunnel, with the closet door closed behind them, Lucifer pulled out a small flashlight with duct tape covering all but a very thin strip of lens. Vampires had remarkable sight, but even they couldn't see in perfect darkness. He flicked on the flash, and then held up a hand for Eleanor to wait a moment, while he scanned down the tunnel, using both the dim light and his vampire powers. He was risking detection by doing it; Yamanaka was dead, but Kasimir wasn't. He could easily be visiting Murphy in his cell tonight. But that was precisely why Lucifer had to scan ahead, and why it was worth taking a chance. He needed to know if his enemy was lurking behind door number two. He was fully prepared to fight Kasimir when the time came, but he'd prefer to have some warning as to when that time would be.

It wouldn't be tonight, however. There were four vampires and one human somewhere at the end of all this darkness. And none of the four vampires were powerful enough to be Kasimir.

"Four guards and one human," he 'pathed to the waiting Eleanor. *"Hopefully the human is Murphy,"* he added.

Eleanor gave him a thumb's up, and then, as if they'd been working together for years, rather than days, they eased down the dark tunnel, their footsteps perfectly silent despite the gritty floor. They didn't stop at the dead-end this time, but continued down the short hallway to the final turn, and kept walking until they were standing right outside the first, possibly guarded, door.

Eleanor examined the door, looking for a lock, and not finding one. Andy had said this first door was unlocked and unguarded, but it had been some time since his lone visit to the place, and Lucifer wanted to be sure nothing had changed. He also scanned for a guard behind the door, but didn't sense anyone in the immediate vicinity. In fact, all five of the life signs he'd picked up earlier—four vamps and one human—were remarkably stable. They all seemed to have picked a spot and stayed there. That made sense for Murphy, since Lucifer was sure the human was bound. But he would have expected the guards to maintain a shifting routine to avoid getting stale. It seemed instead that they had pulled back into the main section of their makeshift prison. Pulled back and *kicked* back by all signs of it. Maybe because they weren't expecting any visitors—something that would make Lucifer's job much easier, if it were true.

There was no handle on this side of the door, so Lucifer put one hand on it and pushed. It swung open smoothly on well-oiled, silent hinges. Once they were both inside, he started to close the door again, but decided against it. If they happened to be running for their lives on the way out, especially if they were carrying a badly injured Murphy, the few seconds it took to get the door open could make a huge difference. So he left it open, and they forged ahead.

The tunnel went straight for another twenty or so feet, and to a casual observer, that was the end of the tunnel system. But Lucifer had studied the map, and knew there was more. He led Eleanor through a darkness so deep that his shielded flashlight couldn't penetrate it, but his hands worked better than his eyes this time. Running his hand along the left wall, he located the extremely narrow passage that was the next leg of their journey. It went on for no more than five feet, which was a good thing, because it was barely wide enough for Lucifer's shoulders. He'd never been claustrophobic, but he abruptly understood what it must be like to suffer from that malady. When the passage made another right turn and opened onto a new, wider tunnel, he breathed a discreet sigh of relief.

The narrow passage had been harrowing, but it was nothing more than he'd expected. So far, everything was exactly as Andy's map had indicated. Lucifer flashed his light down the wider tunnel, and saw the second security door. This one, too, was unguarded. It should have been good news, but he frowned.

"No one there. Maybe they're on break," he 'pathed to Eleanor, smiling, though she probably couldn't see it.

Eleanor let her amusement filter through their telepathic link, and he caught the slight gleam of her smiling eyes.

"This will be their main section," he reminded her, deadly serious once more. Beyond this point they'd have to fight, and probably kill, whatever guards they met, in order to rescue Colin Murphy. He hated dragging her into this dangerous situation, but this was what she did. She was a warrior, and she belonged here just as much as he did. Maybe more. This was *her* lady's territory, after all.

She nodded solemnly.

He pushed on the door. It opened as easily and silently as the last one, but what waited for them on the other side was quite different.

Two guards stood just beyond the door, looking more like friends having a chat than vampires guarding a valuable prisoner. They spun when the door opened, their eyes going wide at the sight of Lucifer striding into their dungeon, his power revealing itself in a gold light that dripped from the walls and lit the dull, concrete floor. The two guards backed up a few steps, eyes flaring red as they reached for their blades, knowing instinctively that only hard steel was going to help them. They attacked as one, coming at him from both sides, blades cutting high and low, trying to overwhelm him before he could bring his power to bear.

Lucifer snapped out a blade of pure energy, cutting it from side to side, parrying every thrust. He could have taken them both out with raw power, could have knocked them both unconscious with a single blow. But he was reluctant to waste his power, not knowing what or who else he might be forced to deal with before the night was over.

Besides, he had a secret weapon that neither of the two vampires had noticed. Until Eleanor stepped out from behind him, and ran the lead guard through with her blade, stabbing him first in his stomach, and then pulling out her blade and running him through his heart when he bent over to clutch at his spilling entrails.

The other vamp stared at his buddy's gruesome death and shouted a warning, a call for help, as he backed farther down the hall, nearing another bend in the corridor. Two more guards raced into sight, and Lucifer stepped out to meet them, trusting Eleanor to watch his back.

These new guards were bigger than the first pair, with bright, red eyes that betrayed their minimal vampire power. They were exceedingly well trained, working together like a fine-tuned machine, their movements so coordinated that it was like facing a single, deadly opponent. Lucifer was an excellent fighter, but these two were formidable, and he was outnumbered. He could hear Eleanor at his back, cursing above the slap of flesh and the clash of blades.

A slash of unexpected pain forced his attention back to his own fight, blood dripping from his arm briefly before he used a small dash of his power to seal the wound. He snarled as anger replaced the cold determination he'd begun this fight with. His blood was far too valuable to be spilled on a filthy dungeon floor.

"Fuck this," he hissed, and let his power flow. It raced down his arm and out through his fingers, forming a golden blade of pure energy.

His opponents' faces betrayed their shock. They hadn't thought to measure his power when he'd shown up in their tunnel, and now it was too late.

Lucifer felt the sudden rush of energy that told him Eleanor had dispatched her opponent. But he couldn't turn to look, he was too busy avoiding a thrust by the vampire on his left, who'd thought to take advantage of what he'd assumed was Lucifer's distraction. Lucifer plunged the golden blade of his power into the vampire's heart, and reduced it to charred bits of flesh a moment before the vampire died in an explosion of dust.

Lucifer grimaced, baring his fangs as he twisted back to deal with the final guard. He was done with this fucking battle. It was time to grab Murphy and get the hell out of there before someone stronger showed up to try and stop them. Someone like Kasimir.

He whirled toward the last guard, golden blade shining, but Eleanor was there before him. Her bo staff was a blur of movement as she drove the guard back, jabbing him in the gut to bring him down to her level, and then snapping the staff up and striking him in the jaw, before slamming him against the wall. She could have used her blade then, could have run him through the heart and been done with it, but her teeth were bared in a grin, a low growl of pleasure humming from her throat as she spun into the air and launched a brutal sidekick.

Lucifer stood back and watched in admiration. They didn't have time for this. They didn't know if the guards had gotten off a distress call, or what other enemies might be on their way right now. But this brutal fighter was his Eleanor, and that realization had the power to stop cold every other thought in his head. She still *looked* like his pink and cream princess from New Orleans, but no one from back then would have recognized her in this fierce fighter who took such pleasure in the violence of battle.

No one but him. He'd know Eleanor anywhere. She could never hide from him. His heart sang like a tuning fork whenever she was near. He grinned as his pink princess brought the guard's head down to her knee and knocked him out cold.

"Finish it, *bella*. We have to get Murphy out of here."

She glanced over at him, and then without looking thrust her blade backward directly into the guard's heart. He died in a cloud of dust, while Eleanor gave Lucifer a wink and a smug smile.

Lucifer took her hand and kissed it. "This all seemed a little too easy. I don't like it."

She shrugged. "Maybe Yamanaka was supposed to be here tonight. You said no one would know he was dead."

"Maybe." He turned to study the door at the end of the hallway. It had a small barred window, and was secured by a thick slide bolt that looked like it weighed as much as the entire door.

Lucifer paused long enough to scan into the room behind that door. "One human," he murmured to Eleanor. But this set-up still didn't feel right. If someone had enough power, he could shield himself from detection, even from Lucifer. And, damn it, this had all seemed too easy.

"You worry too much," Eleanor said, and stepped in front of him to slide the bolt back.

Lucifer bit back a protest, but readied his power against the possibility of a booby trap on the bolt mechanism. When nothing happened, he breathed a cautious sigh of relief. But he still couldn't shake the sense that something was wrong.

Reaching out, he stopped Eleanor when she would have rushed into the room. Whatever trap their enemy might have waiting for them, he could deal with it better than Elle. She was a wicked fighter, and deadly in battle, but he was *a power*. It would take a hell of a lot to knock him out of the fight.

Lucifer stepped into the cell. Because that's what it was, no question about it. The walls were rough concrete that looked as if it had been slapped over raw dirt. The air smelled of blood and sweat, and other things that were meant to humiliate the prisoner and remind him of his helplessness. A primitive metal table was shoved to one side, and behind it . . .

"Colin Murphy, I presume," Lucifer said quietly, grinding his jaw against the rage that wanted to rise up and destroy this fucking cell, to bring down the roof so it could never be used again.

"Who the fuck are you?" Murphy demanded. His voice was scraped raw by the weeks in captivity, and he looked awful, like he'd lost a lot of weight in a very short time. His cheeks were hollowed, and the torn remains of clothing hung on his powerful frame. Dried blood streaked his face and neck, and his knuckles were torn to the bone. His ankles were shackled to each other, and the thick chain was bolted to the floor, giving him just enough room to utilize the primitive sanitary facilities that lent such a lovely bouquet to the air of the room.

Murphy's wrists were shackled as well, but despite all of that, the man stood there defiantly, his jaw clenched with determination, his gaze full of fire as he twisted the chains around his fingers, ready to fight to the death, rather than surrender.

"My name is—"

"Colin!" Eleanor shoved past him and around the table, throwing herself into the human's arms and wrapping herself around his waist.

"Eleanor?" Murphy whispered in disbelief. His head dropped down to touch hers, and for the first time since they'd stormed the room, he began to shake. "What're you doing here, babe?"

Lucifer could hear the tears in Murphy's voice, could sense the psychological toll that captivity had taken on the man, a toll he'd covered up before he'd known who they were. It was an emotional moment, a moment of life and death for Murphy. And yet . . . Lucifer eyed his Eleanor in the man's arms and wanted to rip those arms from their bloody sockets.

"Eleanor," he growled, and then warned her via telepath. *"Bella, you gotta get the fuck away from him before I shred him."*

She stiffened in surprise, then turned to give him a narrow-eyed glare. *"He's a friend, Luc. A friend who's been through hell."*

"And I'm a possessive fucking vampire with an aggression problem."

She raised her eyes to heaven, as if seeking something there, but straightened out of Murphy's embrace, careful to do it slowly, while keeping one arm around his back for support. "Sit down, Colin," she said. "Let me get rid of these fucking chains, and we'll get you out of here."

Murphy sat, but his attention was all for Lucifer, whom he eyed with suspicion. "Who's that?" he muttered half under his breath, but Lucifer could hear him.

"Lucifer," Eleanor said, identifying him absently as she worked on the locked chains. "He's one of Aden's people, on loan to Sophia to help find you. He's good at this stuff."

Murphy grunted, then shifted his gaze to Eleanor's bent head. "Where's Sophia? Is she all right? They kept feeding me someone else's blood, and I couldn't feel her anymore."

"She's fine, and once we get up to street level, you'll feel better, too. Damn it," she cursed, yanking at the chains.

"Move," Lucifer ordered, still not happy with Eleanor's proximity to a male for whom she clearly had feelings.

Her head came up at his sharp tone, but she understood his plan. She took a step to one side and braced Murphy a moment before Lucifer hit the shackles on the man's wrists with a sharp burst of power that fried the lock and snapped the heavy bracelets open.

Murphy sucked in a long breath and exhaled. And then did it again, filling his lungs with oxygen, despite the stench in the room, as if the manacles on his wrists had somehow kept him from breathing properly. Beneath the bracelets, his wrists were rubbed raw, with new abrasions on top of the old, and a glint of bone or tendon showing through.

"We can deal with that once you're out of here," Lucifer said roughly, coldly furious at what Yamanaka and his allies had done to a man who'd trusted them, who'd called them friends. A man who was mated to the now-dead Yamanaka's rightful, fucking lord. So many layers of betrayal.

"Yamanaka's dead," he growled out, figuring Murphy would want to know.

"You?" he asked.

Lucifer nodded. "Me. For what it's worth, he suffered. Not nearly enough, but I was, you know, pressed for time."

Murphy snorted a laugh, then sobered. "Yamanaka's a traitor and an asshole, but he's not the one you have to worry about. It's the German, Kasimir. Yamanaka was nothing compared to that guy."

"Shit," Lucifer muttered. "Elle, we're getting out of here. You help Murphy, and I'll lead the way."

"I should—"

"No arguments. We have to move fast, and I can't risk being distracted. You heard Murphy, this isn't all of them."

Eleanor gave a sharp nod of agreement, and as soon as Lucifer had snapped Murphy's ankle restraints, she looped an arm around the man's waist and supported him as he hobbled to the door. It might have looked ridiculous—tiny Eleanor bracing Murphy, who was well over six feet tall, and probably 250 pounds when he wasn't recovering from imprisonment and torture. But Eleanor supported him easily, her vampire-enhanced strength more than enough to keep him upright and moving.

"You ready, *bella?*"

She nodded. "You think they'll be waiting for us?"

"I think I want to be ready for whatever happens."

"Okay. You ready, Colin?"

"Shit. I'd crawl out of this place if that's what it took."

"It won't come to that," she assured him. "Let's go."

They started slowly, edging out of the dungeon cautiously, expecting danger at every turn. Nothing happened in the tunnel, but Lucifer could sense the doom hanging over their heads, and when they reached the supply closet, he took a moment to scan ahead before entering the code. He readied his shields before he opened the door, still expecting something. Or someone. He wasn't sure what.

But there was nothing there. Just the same messy shelves and a chemical smell that coated the back of his throat. He turned to check on Eleanor and Murphy once more before opening the door to the main corridor. Murphy looked exhausted. The rush of adrenaline that had boosted his initial reaction was gone, leaving him more worn than ever. Eleanor, however, was still fresh and strong, her face a study in resolve. She'd fight to the death before she'd let anything happen to her charge.

"Stay close," he reminded her, and then opened the hallway door.

The empty tunnel was almost anticlimactic. It was brightly lit, compared to the darkness behind them, its walls smooth and finished, its floor an uninspired but functional gray concrete. It seemed they'd made it. If their enemies were going to pull anything, it would have been in the isolation of the secret tunnels, not here where any passing coed could witness.

But some instinct of Lucifer's was blaring a warning that didn't agree. They weren't out of this yet. He looked up and down the tunnel. Left was the fastest route, and would take them to the exit closest to their vehicle. But it was also the most predictable, so—

"Lucifer," Eleanor said quietly. He turned, and she gave him a meaningful look that slanted upward to Murphy's wan countenance. He was giving it everything he had, but he was running on fumes, and Eleanor's support.

That decided it for Lucifer. He turned left and made straight for the stairs to their exit. They'd nearly reached their goal, and the stairs were in sight, when Lucifer suddenly stopped dead. His shields snapped up, spreading out to either side and forming a wall of protection between the three of them and whoever was coming down those stairs.

He turned to Eleanor, who was two steps behind him with Colin Murphy leaning heavily on her shoulder. "If anything happens, you and Murphy head for the other exit, you understand? I'll hold him off as long as I can."

Her gaze was fixed on him. He could read the defiance in her expression, the tension in her body, every muscle stiff, as her brain fought a war with her heart. He knew what she'd say, knew there was no way in hell she'd agree to leave him. He cut her off before she could say it.

"Sophia needs him, *bella*," he said softly, cutting a look at Murphy. "The whole territory could go."

Her expression transformed from defiance to agony. "Not fair," she whispered.

"I know."

Tears filled her big, blue eyes and spilled over, but she nodded.

"I love you," he murmured. "Now go."

She gave him a final anguished look and then turned and started in the opposite direction with Murphy. Lucifer watched their first few steps. The human was trying to carry his own weight, but his energy was visibly flagging. Lucifer only hoped they reached the SUV first. Eleanor was strong and could probably dead lift twice Murphy's weight. But Murphy had more than a foot of height on her, and that made it about more than simple weight; it was the distribution. She could drag an unconscious Murphy, but she couldn't carry him.

The soft sound of a footstep, nearly undetectable even to his sensitive ears, had him spinning back around to face his enemy.

The vampire was of modest size, no more than five feet, eight inches or so, and slender. But a vampire's power wasn't in his size. It was that indefinable something, a gift from the vampire symbiote that made one vampire ordinary and another extraordinary. Lucifer himself had been blessed by the symbiote's unpredictable selection process, but until now, he'd never truly been tested. Yamanaka had been strong, but from the first moment they'd clashed, Lucifer had known he could defeat him.

But the vampire in front of him—Kasimir, he assumed—was far

stronger than Yamanaka. Lucifer knew it, even though he couldn't get any sense from the vamp at all. Or maybe because of that. Kasimir was shielding so strongly that he was giving off nothing, and that took power. It also wasn't a complete surprise. But it did make it a lot more difficult to know if he was likely to survive the next few minutes.

Kasimir gave a slight bow and said with a heavy German accent, "Lucifer Scuderi, I presume?"

Lucifer nodded. "And you're Kasimir," he said flatly.

The vampire smiled. "The very same." He glanced around the long hallway, his gaze going beyond Lucifer, to where Eleanor and Murphy were probably still visible. "And Mr. Murphy, too. That is unfortunate." He took a step to the side, as if to gain a better sightline, but Lucifer mirrored his movement.

"Not going to happen," Lucifer growled.

Kasimir's eyes cut back to him. "I'm sorry we have to meet like this," he said conversationally, as if they weren't two enemies about to try to kill each other. "Your reputation precedes you, you know. My Sire was hoping to recruit you to our side. The offer still stands . . . if you're interested?" He brushed hair back from his forehead in an almost delicate move . . . and immediately launched a blistering volley of power against Lucifer.

Lucifer bared his teeth as the volley bounced harmlessly off his shields. He hadn't been fooled by the fingers-through-the-hair distraction. Really, who would be? No one with the strength or the guts to defeat Kasimir, that was certain.

"Does that usually work for you?" he asked, curious and taunting both.

Kasimir gave a graceful shrug. "It weeds out the competition. I meant what I said about my Sire. Berkhard would welcome you among the ranks of his supporters."

"And all I'd have to do is betray my lord, my friends, and everyone I love," Lucifer responded dryly. But privately he made a note to warn Aden. If they'd been tallying Aden's strongest people, then his Midwestern territory might well be the next target of the Europeans.

"Ah, love," Kasimir mocked. "The little blonde, I assume. Cute, but not a power. It's too bad we didn't get to you before you met her."

That would have been impossible, but they didn't know that. It was somehow encouraging to know that Berkhard and his flunkies didn't know everything, after all.

"Are we going to fight? Or is this just a midnight chat?"

The German shrugged again. "Don't say I didn't warn you." His light-colored eyes flashed nearly white as a bolt of tremendous power slammed into Lucifer's shields, and Kasimir spun to the other side of the hallway, in a blur of movement too fast for human eyes to detect.

But Lucifer wasn't human, and he wasn't a fool. He'd never relaxed his shields, not from the moment Kasimir had appeared around the corner. But they were stretched thin by the need to protect Eleanor and Murphy's retreat. Sacrificing a fraction of his attention, he sent his awareness down the hallway, their blood link speeding him unerringly to Eleanor.

"How far to safety?" he asked, using the telepathic link made possible by his unique gift and the blood they'd exchanged.

"Don't worry about us," she sent back urgently. *"We're on the stairs, out of sight."*

Something about the way she said that, combined with his knowledge of Eleanor, made him suspicious. *"Keep going, Elle. Don't stop. And don't come back."*

Silence. God damn it.

But then he didn't have the time or energy to worry about anything but surviving. Taking Eleanor at her word, he tightened his shields, collapsing them inward around his body, instead of stretched out like a curtain across the hallway. They were as unique as his telepathic talent, a swirling torrent of power that fed on its own dynamic energy, defending him while freeing up a significant amount of his power for offensive maneuvers. He used some of that power now, spinning to one side much the way Kasimir had earlier, but his motion fueled the force behind his attack, adding raw kinetic power to the grenade sized ball of magical energy he sent flying at Kasimir's chest.

It bounced off the other vampire's shields, but not before getting close enough to blacken a hole in the German's white shirt, and maybe singeing his equally white skin. Kasimir touched his chest, his eyes wide with surprise when he looked up.

Maybe they didn't know everything about Lucifer after all.

The surprise didn't last, however. It was replaced by pure, undiluted rage, as if the German vampire wasn't accustomed to being injured. As if no one had dared touch him with violence in a very long time.

His arm shot out, straight and stiff, surrounded by energy, a silver-white radiance that was so thick, it appeared solid, as if Kasimir had fashioned armor from raw energy alone. It solidified even further and then seemed to slide off, from shoulder to hand, a cylinder of energy headed straight for Lucifer. Building speed as it went, it struck his shields with the sound of clashing metal.

Lucifer had seen it coming and stiffened his shields in defense, but he didn't stop and wait for it. Taking the offensive, hoping to catch Kasimir off balance, he fashioned his own blade of power, a heavy broadsword of pure energy that even in its intangible form had weight enough to require two hands to wield it. With the sound of Kasimir's weapon still filling the air, Lucifer gripped his blade tightly and swung, slicing through Kasimir's shields and striking him in the side of his torso with an explosion of blood and bone, and a shower of magical sparks.

Kasimir howled and fired back, launching a wave of small knife-like projectiles, each one a burning point of energy that sliced a new wound into Lucifer's shields. Some of them fizzled on the surface of his power, while others penetrated but ended up snagged like bugs in amber. But a few made it all the way through, enough of them that blood began to flow, from his arms, his chest, even one high enough on his neck that he had a moment's concern. If it had been even half an inch higher it could have done serious arterial damage, and he might have lost this damn fight.

But he couldn't lose. He simply couldn't. It wasn't only his life on the line, it was Eleanor's. And in that moment, he redefined victory. Even if it cost him his life, she wouldn't die here tonight. And that was victory enough.

Pulling his shields ever tighter around himself, determined to end this fight while he still had the strength to do so, he advanced the few feet that separated him from Kasimir, until he could feel the heat of the other vampire's shield throbbing against his own, like the beating heart of a great beast. They were both injured, blood pouring from open wounds and running down their faces in sweaty trails. Kasimir's teeth were bared in a dogged grimace, his expression betraying the effort it was costing him to keep fighting. His thick hands were fisted in front of his chest, power building around them, concentrating into a single tightly-packed globe of awful vampiric energy. Lucifer could predict the force of that blow, and knew it could well take him down if he didn't strike first.

He pressed even closer to Kasimir, until the energy of their shields physically touched, each draining the other as the contact between them sparked and burned. Lucifer gritted his teeth, intentionally weakening his shield so that it merged with his enemy's. Kasimir saw what he was doing and roared furiously over this perversion of his power. But it was too late. Taking the greatest risk of his vampire life, Lucifer dropped all but his most basic, innermost shield, sacrificing defense in favor of an all-out attack. Concentrating all of his energy into the muscles of his back and shoulder, and channeling all of that power into his right fist, he drove it forward, smashing through Kasimir's compromised shield and into his chest. Ribs shattered under a cracked sternum, and Lucifer opened his fist, digging through blood and gore until he found the German vampire's beating heart. He closed his fingers around that fragile organ, watching as Kasimir's eyes grew wide with understanding and that first touch of fear. Lucifer could feel the other vampire working frantically to re-channel the power he'd been building, power he'd intended to use as a weapon, but that he now needed as a desperate defense. But even in the midst of battle, with his enemy's beating heart literally in his hand, there was something . . . off. Something about the vampire's desperation made Lucifer pause for the space of a heartbeat, and study Kasimir's thoughts in that moment. He wasn't fighting back. He was rebuilding the shields around his mind. It was as if he was accepting his inevitable death, and spending his last reserves of power to hide his thoughts instead.

Lucifer knew himself to be one of the most powerful telepaths in the world, but no matter how hard he pounded against the other vampire's mind, he was able to pick up only hints of whatever Kasimir was hiding.

He cursed viciously, but knew he had to accept what victory he could and end this battle. Time was short, and his energy was not unlimited. With an enraged snarl, he closed his fist around Kasimir's heart and crushed the life out of it, frying it to nothing but black char with an extra bolt of energy that was suddenly just *there*, filling his veins with fire and his muscles with fresh power. Power that tasted of Eleanor.

And then Kasimir, and his fucking secrets, were no more.

KASIMIR WAS DUST. It couldn't have happened to a nicer guy. Concealed in the stairwell, unwilling to abandon Lucifer no matter how much he insisted, she and Colin had observed the battle between Lucifer and the German vampire. As they watched, Colin had told her some things about Kasimir. He'd been the vampire who'd done most of the torturing, and he'd had a good time with it, too. He hadn't really cared about getting answers or information. He'd simply enjoyed hurting people, especially the ones who couldn't fight back.

Now the fucker was dead and dusted, and Eleanor was happy to have played even a small part in his demise. She'd known how close to the edge Lucifer was—yet another benefit of their blood bond, she supposed. She'd heard about such things between a vampire and his human lover, but she hadn't realized it would work just as well between two vampires. Vampire romances weren't common enough for there to be much information about them floating around.

But she'd definitely sensed Lucifer's flagging energy, and knowing him, had intuited how much he would sacrifice to destroy Kasimir. Lucifer would die before he'd let anything happen to her. The romantic idiot.

So, she'd taken matters into her own hands, and, making use of their blood-based connection, had sent him a rush of fresh energy when he could use it the most. And he had. He hadn't wasted time wondering where the power was coming from, he'd simply used what he needed, delivered the final crippling blow, and crushed the life out of that bastard Kasimir.

Exchanging a victorious grin with Colin, she stood to call out to Lucifer, only to see him crumple in on himself, falling to one knee and seeming unable to rise up. Eleanor raced down the hallway, heart pounding with fear. She'd heard of vampires winning a fight only to die of their injuries. Challenges like the one Lucifer had just survived took a terrible toll on the victor, and winning didn't give them any relief. It wasn't as if by winning, Lucifer had sucked up all of Kasimir's power. It didn't work that way.

She slid the last few feet to his side, the floor slick with blood that she realized was Lucifer's.

"Luc," she said urgently, grabbing his arm as much to stop her gruesome slide as to get his attention. "Are you all right?"

Lucifer lifted his head slowly, as if it was an effort to do so. His eyes, when he finally looked at her, were glittering with power, and with something else, too. Eleanor stared. She couldn't believe it, but he was pissed! At her!

"I told you to leave," he growled. "You said you would."

"I never said that." She flipped her hand, brushing away his comment. "And a little gratitude might be in order here."

Lucifer stared at her a moment longer, and then his anger faded, replaced by a sudden grin. "Even your power smells of peaches and cream, *bella.*"

Eleanor blushed with pleasure. She felt stupid about it, but she blushed anyway. "Yeah, okay. Let's get the hell out of here. It's starting to stink. Besides, there's no sun down here, like never ever, and people are going to wonder about this mess in the morning. We don't want to be here for that." There was no body, but there was plenty of blood and dust. Someone with knowledge of vampires might just be lucky enough to put two and two together.

Lucifer gritted his teeth with effort, but managed to stand mostly on his own. "How's Murphy?"

"About the same as you. Can you walk?"

"I can do anything I have to. "

Great, Eleanor thought. Now she had two giant, bleeding males who didn't want to accept her help. She slipped an arm around Lucifer's waist, and walked him back to where Colin was waiting, looking more exhausted than ever. It was as if now that Kasimir was dead, he could surrender to his wounds and collapse.

"You help him," Lucifer said, eyeing the semi-conscious human. "I'll stumble along."

Eleanor studied him for a moment, but then nodded. Really, what choice did she have? She was hella strong, especially for her size, but even she couldn't drag both of them down the streets of Montreal.

They made a pathetic group—limping, bleeding, creeping along at a snail's pace. The mighty vampires of North America crawling down the dark streets of McGill University, beneath a cloud cover so thick that even the nearly full moon couldn't break through to guide them.

Once they reached the SUV, Eleanor shoved both males into the backseat, where they could bleed all over the leather together, then climbed in and drove like hell to get back to the hotel before sunrise. She could already feel the warning burn against the back of her skull, and she had no desire to die because the sun rose while she was stuck at a red light.

Calling ahead for Cal to meet them, Eleanor reached the hotel with less than an hour to go. The undercarriage of the big vehicle scraped the sidewalk as she raced down the ramp to the underground garage. She screeched to a halt, then jumped down, and yanked the back door open. Colin Murphy was completely out of it, his head resting on Lucifer's broad shoulder. Lucifer didn't look much better, but being a powerful vampire had its benefits. He lifted his head and gave her a half-hearted grin. "I told you I could make it."

"Uh huh. Come on, tough guy." She reached in and unsnapped the seat belts, which she'd buckled mostly to keep them from falling over on the trip back. "If you can walk—"

"Of course, I can walk."

"Good. Then start walking. Cal can help me with Colin."

Lucifer grunted his response, but did as she asked, sliding across the seat and, more leaning than standing, stood next to the vehicle and watched while she climbed in and manhandled Colin out to the waiting Cal.

"He's completely out of it," she told the daylight guard captain.

Cal grunted as he took Colin's weight. "Looks like he's been through it."

"And then some," she agreed, and stepped up to Colin's other side. Jerking her chin in the direction of the elevator, she ordered Lucifer to go ahead of them.

"So bossy," he murmured as he walked past her. But she noticed he was leaning against the elevator wall as it raced upward.

Once they hit the penthouse level, she and Cal all but carried Colin into her half of the suite, where he collapsed onto the bed. She had hoped to give Sophia a call before he passed out. The lady was undoubtedly aware of her mate's freedom, but would want to hear his voice for herself. Eleanor had wanted to make that possible, but it wasn't going to happen. Colin was down for the count, and Eleanor was only a few minutes behind him. There was no more she could do tonight. It was very nearly morning, and her strength was starting to wane.

"He'll be hungry when he wakes up," she told Cal quickly, as she hustled out of her bedroom and across the living area to Lucifer's half of the suite. She noted in passing that Lucifer must have lowered the shutters while she was dealing with Colin. "And please leave a gun where he'll see it as soon as he wakes. He needs to feel in control again."

"Don't worry," Cal assured her. "I've taken care of plenty of wounded soldiers in my day."

"And you'll need to be extra vigilant. We got him back from the kidnappers, but there's no guarantee their human allies won't come looking to snatch him back, or to kill him. They don't strike me as gracious losers."

"My people can handle whoever comes looking for him," he said, and there was a hard edge to his voice that she found reassuring.

"Thanks, Cal," she said sincerely. And then she hurried into Lucifer's bedroom, closing and locking the door behind her.

Lucifer was already naked, lying on the big bed with his eyes closed, ignoring the blood and sweat rolling off his skin to stain the pristine sheets. Who cared about fucking sheets? He was here, and he was alive.

That was good enough for her.

Stripping off her clothes, she tossed them aside and rolled into bed next to the love of her life. She had just enough time to pull the covers over both of them, and then the sun hit and she was out.

Kelowna, British Columbia, Canada

SOPHIA LEANED OVER the downed vampire. He was stunned, not dead, not even out of the fight yet. Placing one booted foot on his chest, she gripped both sides of his head and twisted. His neck snapped with an audible crack, but she kept twisting until his head was barely attached to his shoulders, until all of the big veins and arteries in his neck were shredded and spurting blood. The gush of blood became a slow trickle as his heart stopped beating, and the vampire symbiote gave up the ghost. If the vampire had been a lot older, she'd have gone right for the heart. But this was a baby vamp, probably less than a year old, and a little variety kept her in fighting form. The symbiote hadn't dug deeply enough into his body and blood to enable him to survive near decapitation. Unfortunately, that also meant he wasn't old enough to turn to dust. He was dead for sure, but they'd have to let the direct sunlight clean him up in the morning.

The unmistakable whoosh of a blade whipping through the air had her dropping low and spinning on one leg, kicking out with the other, as an enemy sword cut through the space where her head had been only seconds earlier. Her kick connected with her attacker's knee, breaking the leg and knocking him down as he howled in pain. This one was human. She sprang back to her feet, gripped his jaw, and sliced his neck using nothing but the stainless claws on her left hand. The claws were a custom job, a weapon made just for her, fitted to her hand. Curved and wickedly sharp, it was something she only wore when she intended to kill. And today, she'd definitely intended to kill.

She was here because of Berkhard, because he'd launched a brazen attack on this remote enclave of vampires. And she was growing tired of it, tired of his petty incursions into her territory. He was picking nests with as few as ten vampires, living quietly, hurting no one. Some of them had human lovers or mates living in the compound, and some of those humans even had children living with them. These were the people that bastard Berkhard was attacking. None of the enclaves he'd hit so far had held any strategic or economic value to her or the invader, but that didn't seem to matter to him.

She understood his strategy, understood why he'd chosen such outlying vampire nests. Just as with Colin's kidnapping, his goal was to distract her. To force her to concentrate on so many different points that her entire defense collapsed. And once that happened, he'd go after his real target, the biggest prize of all . . . Vancouver. It was far more significant than Montreal or Toronto, if only because she'd made it her headquarters, her home. But there was also economic value to the city. Her private holdings alone were worth billions. Most of those had been inherited from Lucien, but she was a much better financial manager than he'd been, and her portfolio reflected that.

So, she understood why Berkhard wanted the city, and the territory, too. But that didn't mean she was going to stand by while he picked off her vampires in a bid for her attention. It was time to force the issue, to take the battle to him, instead of jumping here and there at his bidding.

She stepped over the body of the dead human, her mind scanning the building, looking for signs of life. Her vampires and their dependents—the ones who couldn't fight—had all been evacuated as soon as she and her fighters hit the ground. They'd done it enough times in the last two weeks that they had it down to a science. Clear the civilians and kill the enemy. Sometimes Berkhard's attack force included a powerful vampire or two, but more often, it was made up of baby vamps and humans. Sacrificial lambs who didn't have a hope of survival. She would have liked to question one of them, to find out what Berkhard had promised in exchange for their service, what lies he'd told to get them to take on a suicide mission like this. But so far, they'd all been so set on killing her and her people that there'd been no chance to do anything but kill them instead.

A terrified scream had her racing out of the building into the yard in time to see a huge, muscular vampire drag one of the human women out of the stone barn where she'd apparently been hiding. A slender vampire leapt on the attacker's back, and dug his fangs into the monster's neck. He was no match for the bigger vampire—not in size, but, more importantly, not in power, either. But it seemed the woman was his, or at least important enough to him that he was willing to die for her.

The big vampire tossed the woman aside, throwing her so hard that she would have died, if Sophia had not put on a burst of speed and caught her before she hit the side of the house.

"Noel," the woman sobbed, twisting to stare at the clashing vampires. Noel was apparently her vampire defender. She turned a pleading expression on Sophia. "Help him."

"Stay here," Sophia said. She stalked slowly toward the two vampires, admiring Noel's courage, but recognizing the futility of his efforts. He wasn't a trained fighter, but even if he had been, without the power to back it up, he wouldn't have had a chance. Berkhard's vampire was a true monster, a massive male with fangs as thick and long as her thumbs. There could be no subtlety with this one.

"My lady?"

Sophia glanced over to see Tambra emerge from the house, a deep laceration marring the smooth perfection of her cheek. She was smeared with dirt, and someone else's blood, but was otherwise unscathed.

"I've got this," Sophia told her. "Watch over the civilian."

Tambra nodded, her gaze returning to the uneven battle. Noel was doing far better than Sophia would have expected, but then love was a powerful motivator. Still, enough was enough.

Sophia gathered her power as she stared at the giant vampire. She formed an image in her mind of his broad chest, mentally peeling aside the skin and muscle to focus on the thick ribs guarding his heart. He screamed as a ball of concentrated energy snapped every rib on the left side of his body, as that same ball smashed into his heart. He spun, with Noel still clinging to his back like a monkey, looking for this new deadly attacker. His eyes glowed crimson when he spied her. He reached over his shoulder and yanked Noel off with one hand, tossing him aside as he headed for Sophia. His chest was a bloody mess, but it didn't stop him. The ground shook as he thundered toward her, but Sophia held her ground. Physical size was nice, but it didn't matter for shit when it came to the kind of power she wielded.

She met the monster's eyes, and smiled. She stretched out her hand, palm open and flat, and then slowly, deliberately closed her fingers into a fist.

The giant vamp grunted in shock, and then crashed to his knees, staring at her in disbelief.

"Size doesn't matter, after all," she sneered. And then she stepped back fastidiously to avoid the giant dust cloud. He'd been a very big vampire.

"Tambra," she said, turning to find her assistant. But before she could continue the thought, her senses were slammed with . . . something wonderful. She paused in mid-step, and it took every ounce of determination she had to remain upright. Because for the first time in what felt like forever, Colin was with her. He'd never left her heart, but now he was in her mind. Weak, unconscious. But there, where he belonged. Her throat thickened with emotion, with the tears she'd been holding back ever since he'd been taken. She swallowed them down one more time. She couldn't let her enemies see her reaction, good or bad. She didn't know Colin's situation. Had Eleanor and Lucifer succeeded in freeing him? Had he somehow escaped on his own? Until she knew for sure, she couldn't reveal anything that might help her enemies recover him.

"My lady?" Tambra's voice was filled with concern.

Sophia dug up a convincing smile. "Do a sweep of the building. The usual. Get rid of lingering bad guys, and help the civilians restore order. There's at least one dead baby vamp in there, and a few humans. It's bonfire time, I guess."

Tambra grinned. She appeared so normal, but she had a macabre sense of humor. "I'll handle it."

"Good." Sophia made her way over to Noel, who was alive, but in bad shape. "Noel?" she asked, going to her knees next to him.

"My lady," he whispered, which was probably all the noise he could make.

Sophia pulled up her sleeve and put a fang to her wrist, tearing a long, jagged wound. "Drink, child," she murmured. He wasn't actually her child, but she was his lord, and that made him hers. She felt the tug of those bonds, the ties that bound her to every vampire in the territory, when Noel latched on to her wrist, and began to drink.

"Noel!" The human woman he'd been defending dropped to her knees at his side, though Noel was far too busy sucking down the bounty of a vampire lord's blood to pay attention to his human lover.

"Give him a minute," Sophia murmured. "He was badly injured."

The woman had obviously been with her vampire long enough to understand, because she sat back on her heels with a nod, and watched avidly as her lover drank.

Sophia waited until his tugs on her wrist had slowed, then she stroked his cheek softly, and said, "Enough, Noel."

He lifted his head instantly, his fangs sliding out of her flesh, his tongue slipping out to lap up the last trails of blood dripping down her arm. "Thank you, my lady." His voice was slurred, reflecting the intoxicating effect of her blood.

She smiled. "You were brave. Your lady is very lucky."

He gave her a goofy grin, and then his eyes closed and between one breath and the next, he dropped into a deep, healing sleep.

Sophia transferred him to the eager arms of his mate, who held him close to her heart, and gazed up at Sophia, while tears carved paths through the soot and dirt on her cheeks. "Thank you, my lady," she whispered fervently. The gratitude Sophia welcomed, but the adoration on the woman's face was more than she could handle. She'd never wanted to be worshipped. She only wanted to be a good ruler, to keep her people safe. Maybe if she'd done a better job of that, this woman would never have come close to losing her mate. And maybe Colin would never have been taken and tortured. She'd ignored the danger for too long, hoping her fellow vampire lords would take care of the problem within their own borders, and send the Europeans packing before they ever reached her territory.

She stood and looked around. This was her fault, her failure. She could rebuild the homes that had been destroyed, replace the furniture, the cars . . . hell, the toys, too. But she couldn't replace the lives that had been lost.

What she *could* do, however, was make sure that Berkhard didn't destroy anything, or anyone, else.

"Tambra." She waited until she had her assistant's attention. "I'm returning to Vancouver. Get a team in place to fix all of this, and then join me. We have work to do."

"Yes, my lady," Tambra said, and her lips curved in an evil smile that matched Sophia's own.

They definitely had work to do, the kind that involved blood and violence. The kind that was going to end with one dead German vampire lord.

Chapter Twelve

Montreal, Quebec, Canada

BEFORE HE EVEN opened his eyes, Lucifer was unhappy. First, because he could smell himself, and it wasn't good. Second, because after
two challenge fights in two nights, he was feeling his true age. On the
other hand, he reached out and scooped the still-sleeping Eleanor into
his arms, holding her warm, curvy body against his and breathing her in.
It was her scent that finally opened his eyes, and brought back all the
events of the previous night. It also made him aware of the human in the
next room.

Right. Colin Murphy was with them. Lucifer could hear him pacing
back and forth, crossing the living room between the two bedroom
suites. The human had slept in Eleanor's room, which settled that
question, anyway. Eleanor would be sleeping in Lucifer's bed for the
duration. Although that might not be much longer. This hunt was nearly
over. They'd rescued Murphy, which had been their main assignment.
Lucifer needed to debrief the man before they left Montreal. He needed
to know if there were any vamps here who'd betrayed Sophia and
needed killing. That wasn't exactly in the purview of his assignment, but
it made no sense to kill Yamanaka and Kasimir, only to leave a rotten
core behind.

Once that was done, however, they'd be on a flight to Vancouver to
reunite Lady Sophia with her mate. And that should have been it, but
Lucifer couldn't leave.

Helping Sophia defeat Berkhard went beyond the assignment he'd
been given by Lord Aden, and possibly beyond the assistance Aden had
intended to render. But . . . there was Eleanor to consider. She was
sworn to Lady Sophia, which meant this was her home, and there was no
way in hell Lucifer was going to walk away before making damn sure her
home was safe, even if that meant helping Sophia fight off Berkhard and
whatever vampire army he'd managed to turn against their rightful lord.

For that matter, he didn't see how he could walk away even after

Berkhard was defeated and Sophia, and by extension, Eleanor, were secure. But that was a very complicated problem, so he set it aside for now. They had plenty on their plate already. Including one increasingly pissed off human in the next room.

Lucifer sighed and reluctantly set Eleanor aside, kissing her forehead and tucking the blankets around her neck without so much as a furtive glance at her naked body. Of course, he'd already felt every inch of her luscious nakedness pressed against his body when he woke up, something his cock was very happy about. But he couldn't make love to her the way he wanted with Murphy just outside the doors, and he refused to sneak in a fuck as if they had anything to be ashamed of.

Slipping out from under the covers, he headed for the shower. Murphy might be anxious, but Lucifer didn't know the man. He needed to be showered and dressed before they talked.

LUCIFER FELT ELEANOR wake as he was pulling on his boots. His awareness of her was much stronger now that they'd exchanged blood, and so he knew the moment her eyes opened. He could almost feel her gaze on him as he bent over to tie the work boots he favored whenever battle was a possibility.

He turned his head to her with a smile. "Good evening, *bella*."

She gave him a sweet smile in return, a smile that wrapped him in all the love she felt for him. His chest swelled with an emotion that he couldn't seem to get rid of. He was so damn grateful to have her back. He didn't know if he'd ever get over the realization that she wasn't dead. And that she still loved him. God knew he'd never stopped loving her.

"I'm going out to the other room, to speak to our guest," he said almost reluctantly, knowing he was shifting the mood, becoming far more serious and less romantic. He promised himself that once this was all over with, and Sophia was safe on her throne again, he and Eleanor were going to take a week—no, two weeks—and go far away. He had a spectacular house outside of Chicago, very secure, with plenty of acreage for privacy. He'd bought it mostly for the investment, and rarely stayed there. But it would be perfect for the two of them. He'd stock up on fresh blood, lock the doors, and they could fuck each other's brains out in every one of the twenty rooms.

"I need to clean up," she said, then looked at her pile of discarded clothing and made a face. "My clothes are in the other room."

"You should have moved in here sooner," he teased mildly. "Tell me what you want, and I'll go get it for you."

She snorted. "I'm not sure I trust you with my underwear drawer."

He shrugged. "Well, I'm *definitely* not letting you make a naked dash across the living room to get them for yourself. And there's no way in hell that you're showering *or* getting dressed in Murphy's room."

"It's *my* room."

"Not any longer it isn't. Tell me what you want."

"You're such a Neanderthal."

"I'm a powerful vampire, *bella*. It comes with the blood. Tell me what you want," he repeated.

"Fine. Most of my stuff is still in the suitcase, and there isn't that much anyway. Just throw everything else in there, too, and bring it over." He started for the door, and she called, "But be careful with the bathroom stuff. I don't want shampoo all over my clothes."

"I'll try."

"There is no try, just do."

He turned at the door, laughing. "You're quoting fucking Yoda at me?"

"Is that who said that? I figured it was someone old and wise."

"Yoda is old and wise, you philistine. And you got the quote wrong anyway. I'll be back."

Lucifer had erased any signs of laughter from his expression by the time he closed the door behind him. Colin Murphy spun from his place by the dark windows, and stared at Lucifer suspiciously. They'd never met before last night, and they hadn't really met then either. It was entirely possible Murphy didn't remember much about his rescue, other than that he *had* been rescued. Or at least taken out of that place.

"I'm sorry," Murphy said, looking far more defiant than sorry. "I don't remember your name."

"Lucifer Scuderi," he provided with a sideways tip of his head. "Sworn to Lord Aden, but temporarily in the service of Lady Sophia. Your mate, I believe."

"She is." His expression softened for a brief moment, then hardened again when he asked, "Where's Eleanor? She was there last night."

"She was, and she's in the shower. If you'll pardon me for one moment, I need to get her things out of your room."

"My—I need to get back to Vancouver. Sophia needs to know what's happening."

"If I may, I'll get Eleanor's things first," Lucifer said, tipping his head in the direction of Eleanor's room.

"Sure. Whatever. It's her room anyway."

Lucifer didn't bother to argue the point. There were far more important things he had to discuss with Murphy, but Eleanor would want to be in on the discussions, too. So, he made quick work of gathering her clothes and, yes, her toiletries, too. He wasn't the helpless gorilla she seemed to think. She was in the shower when he dropped everything on the bed, not bothering to take the toiletries into her. His shampoo was in the shower. She could use that for tonight—he'd enjoy smelling himself on her almost as much as he enjoyed her own unique scent.

Stepping out of the bedroom, he closed the door behind him. "Elle will be out soon. Have you eaten?" Lucifer had never seen Colin Murphy before last night, but even he could tell that the man had lost weight during the weeks of his ordeal. No surprise there. He doubted Kasimir had been overly concerned with his prisoner's wellbeing. Beyond keeping him healthy enough to torture, that is.

Murphy nodded. "Your guard, Cal. He gave me this gun—" He indicated a 9mm automatic sitting in a holster at his hip. "—and he ordered room service. I ate some, but I have to go easy. They didn't feed me much. But, fuck that, tell me what's going on out here."

"And your injuries?" Lucifer persisted.

"They'll heal," Murphy said impatiently. "Just abrasions and cuts. The shackles were too tight. And there's nothing broken . . . at least nothing they didn't heal once they were finished."

"Look," Lucifer said quietly. "You don't know me, but I *am* a friend, and I can help you heal. My blood—"

"No," Murphy said immediately. "No more fucking blood. I don't care how friendly you are. I'll wait for Sophia."

Lucifer dipped his head in acknowledgment. He absolutely understood the man's feelings. He didn't know if he agreed with it—they were at war, after all. You did what you had to do to survive in wartime. But Murphy was a warrior, too. If he said he was good to go, then who was Lucifer to question it?

The whole time he'd been talking to Murphy, he'd been exquisitely aware of everything Eleanor was doing in the next room, so he wasn't surprised when the door opened behind him.

"Colin!" She rushed around Lucifer and across the room to hug the human.

It didn't make Lucifer feel all warm and fuzzy to have his woman ignoring him and hugging another man—especially not a big, strong human capable of feeding her—but he wasn't petty enough to say anything about it. Hell, she and Murphy really were friends. And Lucifer wasn't insecure enough to feel threatened just because his lover had a male friend. But then, with vampires, it wasn't about insecurity or threat. There was no logic or reason. It was a gut-deep possessiveness that howled, "Mine!" any time his mate strayed too far.

The thought brought Lucifer up short. His mate? Well, shit. Of course, Eleanor was his mate. He'd claimed her more than twenty years ago when she'd been human, and that hadn't changed just because she was now a vampire.

Eleanor and Murphy stepped back from their embrace. She had tears in her eyes, and her presence seemed to have relaxed Murphy, too. Some of the haunted look in his eyes had eased a bit at the familiar face.

"Sophia?" Murphy asked her.

"She's great. Way tougher than those bastards expected. But she'll be a hell of a lot better once she sees you."

"Speaking of which," Lucifer said, interrupting the happy reunion. "I need to know who has to die before we leave Montreal."

"Darren?" Murphy asked, looking at Eleanor.

"Dead," she confirmed. "Kasimir, too. Do you remember the fight from last night?"

"I remember," he said bitterly. "I only wish I could have driven a stake into his heart. Sadistic asshole."

"Who cooperated with him, and who might try to continue the rebellion in Kasimir's absence?" Lucifer asked. "Not just vamps, but humans, too. I don't want to leave anyone behind who can stir up the conspiracy while Sophia's busy in Vancouver."

Murphy nodded, suddenly looking every inch the deadly warrior his reputation claimed. "The humans are all dead, guards included. Kasimir killed them two days ago."

"Ah," Lucifer said, thinking about Andy Anderson's twin brother. Though he couldn't generate much sympathy for him. "Bodies?" he asked.

Murphy gave a dismissive shrug. "Don't know, don't care."

"Fair enough. What about local vampires?"

"A few at the Montreal compound, but only a few. Not everyone betrayed Sophia, but enough stood by and said nothing that she'll need to visit the house when this is over and scour some brains. I think Darren Yamanaka stacked the deck in this city, bringing in people who were loyal to him. But Kasimir was on his own, other than Darren, whom he considered to be well beneath him. He talked a lot, though. The sick fuck liked to talk while he tortured. Mostly about his precious

Sire, Berkhard, and the big man's plans for the territory, after Sophia was dead.

"Anyway, it turns out, Berkhard didn't bring that many vamps with him from Europe. So he's creating new vamps to fill out his army. Kasimir called them 'disposable soldiers,' which made me think of something Christian said in his brief to the Council after his victory over Hubert in the South. Hubert's newly-made vamps were mindless, and somehow a function of his particular talent, but the idea was the same— to fill out his army with fresh vampires."

Lucifer nodded. "Hubert and Berkhard were allies in Europe, and both of them worked with Mathilde against Raphael, so it makes sense that they might have discussed ways to increase their manpower once they got here."

"Exactly," Murphy agreed. "When Kasimir talked about "disposable soldiers," it made me wonder if Berkhard had taken Hubert's idea and run with it somehow."

"We warned Sophia about Darren, and Berkhard's already made some moves, so she knows he's out there. But we need to warn her about these newbie vamps, too. So far, he's confined his efforts to small, remote offensives. But if you're right, and he's making an army of new vampires, he could launch a full-scale attack well before she expects it."

Murphy shifted his gaze to meet Lucifer's. "I need to get home."

"You need to call Sophia," Eleanor countered, then glanced at a clock on the table. "It's still too early on the west coast, but—"

"It's early there, but not here," Lucifer interrupted. He could absolutely understand the man's desire to talk to his mate, and, hell, to fly back to Vancouver right away, too. But there was work to be done in Montreal first. It wouldn't do any good to rush home only to leave an enemy at their backs. And, with any luck, it would only take an hour or two. "We have a few hours," he told Murphy. "I say we pay a visit to the local compound while we wait for the sun to set in the West. We need to deal with your enemies in Montreal before you fly home to Vancouver."

Murphy looked like he wanted to argue, but then his jaw clenched and he nodded. "You're right, damn it. How many people do you have?"

Lucifer laughed. "Just myself and Eleanor, and now you. I won't risk any of my daylight guards, and Sophia didn't trust Aden or Rajmund enough to let them leave vampire fighters with me. But my Eleanor's tougher than she looks—" Murphy's brows raised at Lucifer's claim on Eleanor. "—and so am I," he added.

The man barked a laugh. "Yeah, I've seen what you can do. I'm no vamp, but Sophia respected Darren Yamanaka's power. She *hated* him, but she respected his power. And *he* was terrified of Kasimir. So, I figure since you took that bastard out too, you must be a power." He paused and met Lucifer's gaze for a long moment. "I'm grateful for the rescue, Lucifer, but make no mistake, if you go against Sophia, if you try to hurt her in any way . . . I'll do my best to kill you."

Lucifer grinned in appreciation of the man's courage, if nothing else. "I mean your lady no harm. Not as long as Eleanor loves her."

Eleanor came to him then, giving him a long overdue hug. "Thank you."

"I love you, *bella*," he said simply.

She turned to face Murphy. "We know about Chase Landry. Is there anyone else?"

The human shook his head. "No one worth noting. Can you tell if they're lying?" he abruptly asked Lucifer. "I mean, I know you can detect lies in general, but if we visit this compound, will you know which vamps are loyal and which ones aren't?"

"More or less." Lucifer shrugged. "Enough to catch anyone who betrayed your lady outright. But if they're ambiguous—someone who knew about it, but who just stood by and did nothing, for example—that will take more time than we have. Berkhard already knows Kasimir is dead. Once he discovers that you're alive and free—and he will—he won't wait. He'll move on Vancouver. So we need to leave tonight."

"Then let's go," Murphy said grimly. "Might as well get this over with." He placed a hand on the 9mm automatic at his hip. "I'm going to need more guns, and better ammo."

THE MONTREAL compound was a beehive of activity when Lucifer and Eleanor showed up unannounced, with Colin Murphy beside them. There were more than a few shocked looks when they saw him alive and well and walking free. Lucifer cast a wide net with his telepathy, looking for unguarded reactions. Most were in the vein of, "Oh my God, we're so happy you've been rescued." But there were more than a few who were thinking, "Shit, how did you get loose?" Which told Lucifer all he needed to know about the locals. What the hell had happened in this city? How had Darren Yamanaka managed to turn so many against their sworn lord? Maybe Sophia hadn't been around much, spending most of her time in Vancouver, but she hadn't been cruel. She hadn't demanded unreasonable tithes, or chopped off heads at random.

"Chase Landry," Eleanor said suddenly, and Lucifer swung around to find a group of vampires blocking the main staircase, with a dark-haired vampire at their head. He was of average height, with a blocky build that gave him a vaguely square appearance. His face was set in a grim expression, his hands curled into claws at his side.

"Who the hell are you?" Landry demanded, glaring at Lucifer.

Lucifer felt Eleanor's bristling reaction, but he simply bared his teeth in a lazy grin. "In point of fact, I'm the new master of this city," he drawled, meeting Landry's gaze in clear challenge.

"Fuck that," the vampire responded. "Lady Sophia—"

"Oh, no," Lucifer interrupted. "You don't get to hide behind her skirts anymore. You lost that right when you betrayed your sworn lord and kidnapped her mate. Or have you forgotten that part?"

"I had nothing—"

"The hell you didn't," Colin Murphy growled, stepping up to loom over the much shorter vampire. Lucifer admired his courage. Landry might be shorter, but he was still a vampire. "I remember everything—every day, every fucking minute. And you were there, from the very beginning."

Lucifer felt Landry's power trying to rise, even as his supporters began inching away from him. Several of those vampires were honestly dismayed at the news of Landry's complicity in Murphy's kidnapping. Lucifer made note of their faces, as well as the others, and then turned his attention back to Landry.

"I wouldn't do that," he said, warning the vamp not to raise a challenge. He had some power, probably enough to make him a master vampire of middling strength. But he didn't have a chance in hell against Lucifer.

"Fuck you. This is my city, and—" His words choked off as Lucifer focused his power and cut off the vamp's air supply. He simply shut down his lungs. Landry coughed once. His eyes bulged and his throat began to work convulsively, desperately trying to breathe.

"Here's how this is going to work," Lucifer announced, projecting his voice to be heard throughout the compound. "My new friend Colin Murphy has a list. And we're going to find every God damned fucking vampire on it, and they're going to die, along with anyone who tries to stop us. And after that, I would suggest the rest of you contemplate the perils of betraying your lady. Murphy?"

As if they'd rehearsed it, Murphy stepped up to Landry, raised the Glock already in his hand, and shot the vampire in the heart at very close range, using what he called, "Cyn's vampire killer rounds." It was a very specific type of ammo, apparently recommended by Raphael's mate, that blew the hell out of Landry's heart, killing him in minutes and leaving nothing but a pile of dust on the floor.

"Next?" Lucifer asked mildly.

TWO HOURS LATER they were piling into the SUV outside the Montreal compound, which now contained eleven fewer vampires. Some of those had been identified by Murphy as having participated in his kidnapping and imprisonment, but others had been discreetly pointed out by their fellow vampires. Not everyone at the compound had approved of Darren Yamanaka's betrayal of Sophia. Some hadn't even known about it. And they were more than happy to help the conspirators on their way to justice. In the world of Vampire, the only "justice" for betraying one's lord was death. Usually, the sentence would be carried out by the betrayed lord herself, but in this case, Lucifer was more than happy to act as Sophia's inquisitor, with Murphy as her executioner.

That didn't mean Lucifer trusted everyone left at the compound, not even the vampires who'd snitched. Even knowing that they'd helped his investigation, and helped achieve vengeance for Murphy, Lucifer couldn't bring himself to trust the rest of the Montreal compound. Could you really trust a vampire who ratted out a nestmate?

If this was going to be Lucifer's city—and the more time he spent with Eleanor, the more he realized the decision he was going to have to make—he'd have to do some serious vetting of the Montreal vampires. He'd pried into their tiny little brains enough to assure himself that they were telling the truth about the vampires they'd given up to him, but that wouldn't be nearly enough if he was going to be in charge.

But those concerns were for a future that might never come to pass. Right now, he needed to get Colin Murphy—and Eleanor—home to Vancouver. Sophia's war with Berkhard was quickly coming to a head, and she was going to need all the help she could get. But more than that, she needed to know that her mate was alive and free. Or rather she needed to hear the news from his own voice. She surely knew by now that Murphy had been rescued. Even with their bond weakened by weeks of forced blood feedings from Kasimir and others, and compounded by his imprisonment deep underground, she'd have sensed the moment he rose to the surface and walked free again.

Lucifer knew too well how desperate she'd be to hear his voice, to have the proof with her own ears that he was alive. He'd have given anything in the first weeks after Eleanor disappeared to have picked up the phone and heard her voice on the other end of the call. Even if only to tell him that she wasn't coming back. Just knowing she was alive and well would have meant the world to him.

He glanced over to where she was sitting behind the wheel of the SUV. The lights of the dashboard cast her delicate features in stark relief, making her seem far grimmer that she was. Or maybe not. It had been a fairly grim evening so far. He didn't know how much experience she had with vampire executions. From his perspective, it couldn't be much. Sophia had been far too kind to her vampires up 'til now. Though he had a feeling that her ruling philosophy would never be the same.

"I need to call Sophia," Murphy said urgently. "It's past sunset in the West."

Eleanor fished her cell phone out of the center console, and held it over her shoulder in his general direction. "You can use my phone. She's on speed dial."

But Murphy didn't take it. "No. Thanks, but . . . I think I'll wait until we get back to the hotel."

For privacy, Lucifer surmised. He didn't blame the man. It would be an emotional conversation on both ends.

Vancouver, British Columbia, Canada

SOPHIA'S FIRST THOUGHT, even before she opened her eyes, was that Colin was free. The knowledge was a warm glow in her thoughts, a whisper in her ear, a lightness in her heart. Her eyes were already filled with tears when she opened them to the soft light of their bedroom, tears she didn't bother to wipe away. There was no one to see them, and she welcomed the emotional release. She hadn't realized the full weight of the strain she'd been under until it was gone.

Feeling lighter than air, she jumped from bed, wanting to shower and dress before Colin called, and laughing at herself in the next minute. He wouldn't be skyping her, for God's sake. He'd probably use a cell phone. His own was almost certainly long gone, but Eleanor had hers, and that damn Lucifer probably had one, too. There were a few vamps who clung to the old ways, but Lucifer hadn't struck her as one of them.

Thoughts of Lucifer made her frown, despite the joy that had her skipping around the room, as if happiness was making her too light for her feet to touch the floor. Lucifer was a big unknown. A big, giant, *powerful*, fucking unknown. At a minimum, he was going to steal Eleanor away from her. And try as she might, she couldn't begrudge her bodyguard's obvious happiness. After all, she'd been the one advising her to grab this second chance.

But Lucifer had the potential to steal a lot more than Eleanor. That fucking Aden. He'd known what he was doing when he'd sent his cuckoo in her Montreal nest. If she hadn't been so desperate for help to find Colin, she'd never have tolerated it. But Lucifer had come through for her. He'd gotten Colin out, hadn't he? With Eleanor's help, of course. And Eleanor was hers, so he didn't get all the credit. But still. She had to give Lucifer his due.

She was standing in front of her mirror, weaving her hair into a tight French braid, when her cell phone rang. It was sitting on the counter, and she knew, even though the caller ID said "Eleanor" that it was Colin calling. After a quick panicked glance in the mirror—totally irrational—she hit "Accept" and sank to the floor, her legs unable to hold her.

"Colin?" she practically whispered.

"It's me, Sophie."

"Colin," she repeated, her throat thick with tears that she was desperate to conceal from him. He didn't need to worry about *her.* Not with what he'd been through.

"I'm okay, darlin'. Honest."

"Are you coming home?" she asked, and her voice sounded choked, even to her.

"I'll be there when you wake up tomorrow night. We're leaving as soon as we can get to the airport and get in the air."

"It's late, you'll need—"

"A human pilot, I know. We've got that covered. Lucifer's daylight security team will be coming with us, and they include a couple of pilots. Plus there's, you know, *me.*"

She laughed, and it felt like a thousand years since she'd done so. "Is Lucifer's jet the same as ours? And how long's it been since you piloted the Lear, anyway?"

"Some things you never forget, don't you worry."

She made a dismissive noise. "That's all I do any more is worry. I need you."

"The feeling is mutual," he teased, pronouncing "mutual" as "moo-tual," in reference to one of their favorite movies.

"It's so good to hear your voice, *meu querido,* but you must get to the airport if you're to arrive before sunrise. Human pilot or not, I don't want you flying through sunlight."

"You remember that I'm human, right, Soph? It's only Eleanor and her friend that you need to worry about."

"Speaking of that . . . where are you?" she asked in sudden realization. "Can they overhear?"

"Honestly, Soph, it's like you've forgotten how long I've lived with you. I know what vampire hearing is like, you know. And, no, they can't. We're at the hotel, and I'm in the bathroom off the bedroom in my half of the suite, with the door closed, and with both Eleanor and Lucifer all the way across the common area and in their own bedroom."

She smiled at both the exasperation in his voice and the precautions he'd taken to avoid being overheard. But that was her Colin. He'd been a boy scout long before the U.S. Navy got a hold of him and made him a SEAL.

"I've forgotten nothing about you," she murmured. "Nothing."

Colin's breathing became uneven, and her smile became a grin. By this time tomorrow night, they'd be enjoying a fine reunion. But right now, she needed information.

"There was some housecleaning tonight in Montreal. I'm assuming that was you."

"The three of us, yeah."

"Did you learn anything?"

"Nothing that won't wait, but there is something you need to know. Berkhard might be patterning his attack on Hubert's down South. Remember what Christian said, about the zombie vamps?"

"Of course," Sophia said, calmly enough. But privately, she was thinking, *"Oh, fuck."*

"Berkhard can't do exactly that, but he *is* creating an army of newbie vamps for himself. We don't know where, or if he's even started yet. But—"

"But he knows by now that Kasimir has failed in Montreal. Which means he might fast-track his plans for Vancouver, before he loses whatever advantage he has. Or thinks he has."

"Exactly."

Sophia's mind was racing, filled with the million and one details that would need to be dealt with. She had a good core of fighters now, people she could trust. Colin's kidnapping had done that at least, which, certainly hadn't been Berkhard's intention. But what she could really use was a strong ally, a lieutenant like what Aden had with Bastien, or Raphael with Jared. That's what Darren should have been, but he'd chosen to side with her enemies instead. She frowned.

"Tell me about Lucifer," she said suddenly. "Do you trust him?"

"What can I say, babe? He saved my life. He's the one who took out Darren, you know, but that's not half of it. He faced down Berkhard's lieutenant, Kasimir, to protect me and Eleanor, and Kasimir was one powerful, fucking vampire. I was there for the whole fight. I saw what they did to each other, and I saw how beat up Lucifer was at the end. But he did it. He took out that sick motherfucker, and I'm pretty sure he enjoyed every minute of it."

"That's what worries me."

"That he liked it? Nah. Because there's one more thing you need to know about Lucifer. That vamp *loves* Eleanor. I'm talking deep down, kill you if you look at her, give his life in an instant kind of love. He'd never risk her life, and he won't trust it to anyone else, either. You haven't acquired an enemy, Soph, but you may have picked up a damn powerful ally."

Sophia listened to Colin's analysis with interest. He was far more intuitive about such things than she was, despite the advantage her vampiric power gave her. She could read a man's thoughts most of the time, but Colin could read his face and the subtleties in his words, and come up with the emotional nuances that she sometimes missed. People's thoughts weren't always the same as their feelings.

"Okay," she said thoughtfully. "Let me talk to Eleanor for a moment."

"Give me a minute."

She heard movement and footsteps, and then a door opening, more footsteps, and then Eleanor's familiar voice in the distance, before Colin said, "Sophia wants to talk to you."

"Good evening, my lady," Eleanor said warmly.

"Eleanor. Thank you," Sophia said, and tears filled her eyes once more. She'd have to put a stop to all of this emotion before she faced any of her people. No one wanted to follow a weepy vampire lord.

"It was Lucifer, my lady," Eleanor assured her. "All I did was help."

"Hmm, so Colin tells me. He also tells me the handsome brute loves you."

"Oh," Eleanor said faintly, obviously surprised by either Colin's assessment or Sophia's frank mention of it. "Well. I told you. We have a history."

"And I'm happy for you, Eleanor. As long as it doesn't mean I'm losing you."

"We haven't—" Eleanor cleared her throat nervously. "—that is, we haven't discussed it yet."

Sophia decided to give the young woman a break. After all, Lucifer *had* saved Colin's life, so, she supposed she owed him the benefit of the doubt. Maybe. And there were far more serious matters afoot than Eleanor's love life.

"Colin tells me you're flying home tonight."

"Yes. Lucifer has already contacted the pilots, and they're prepping now. And his daylight security team will be coming with us."

"Who are these people?"

"If you want specifics, I'll have to ask Lucifer. But I know they're part of Aden's daylight guard contingent, and Lucifer knows them well. He does quite a bit of traveling on his own, and this particular team always goes with him."

Sophia scrunched her face up, glad that no one could see her. She could hear it in Eleanor's voice. The woman was besotted. Had she ever sounded like that? Well, okay, maybe a little bit when she'd heard Colin's voice a few minutes ago, but that was different. Wasn't it? Damn it.

"Well, either way, it will be good to have you back here where you belong. And if your handsome devil wants to come along, I can certainly use the fire power," she said casually. "Now that Berkhard knows he's failed in the East, he may accelerate his plans for Vancouver. We've managed to forestall him at every turn, but not without casualties."

"Colin told you," Eleanor concluded grimly. "Well, he can't attack before tomorrow night. And we'll be there by then."

"I'm counting on it. Let me say good-bye to Colin now." She heard a shuffle as Eleanor handed over the phone, and then Colin was back, his smooth voice bringing to mind the brush of warm lips against naked skin on a hot, moonlit night.

"Sophie," he said, and she shivered, so full of wanting that she wanted to scream.

"Come home, *meu querido.*"

"I'm coming, darlin', fast as I can get there."

"Take care until then. Berkhard knows you're free by now, and he's a dangerous enemy."

"Yeah? Well, so am I. And I have powerful friends."

Montreal, Quebec, Canada

LUCIFER HAD SAT quietly on the living room sofa, and pretended not to listen to every word being said. First, between Sophia and Murphy, and then Eleanor. He'd heard Eleanor's reassurances, her utter confidence in him, and guessed at what Sophia had asked her. But oddly enough, it was Murphy who'd had the right of it. The human had done what he could to avoid being overheard, but vampire hearing was extraordinary, and Lucifer's hearing was augmented by his powerful telepathic gift. Murphy was the one who'd understood that Lucifer would never betray Sophia as long as Eleanor would be hurt by it.

He glanced up when she joined him on the couch, her thigh sliding next to his, as his arm came around her. He leaned over and kissed the top of her head, while Murphy finished his phone conversation with Sophia.

Murphy had just disconnected, and was about to join them, when Lucifer's cell phone buzzed in his pocket. Frowning, he dug the phone out and checked the incoming ID.

"I have to take this," he told Eleanor, showing her the screen. "I'll do it in the other room, so the two of you can make any final arrangements." He kissed Eleanor's raised mouth, then stood and walked into his bedroom suite and closed the door. Eleanor might be able to hear, if she was inclined to listen, but Murphy wouldn't.

He brushed the cell screen to accept the call just before it would have gone to voicemail. "Bastien," he said.

"Took you long enough. I thought maybe you were off killing more vampires."

"Who'd you talk to?"

"It's who talked to *me*. I have a friend in the Montreal compound who'd rather not have his name bandied about. Sophia doesn't know he's ours."

A spy, in other words. Not exactly a shock. All of the vampire lords had spies in each other's territories. Or maybe not all. Raphael's relationships with both Lucas and Duncan were incestuous enough that it probably wasn't necessary. Those two would never do anything that went against Raphael's interests, and that loyalty probably ran both ways. But that Aden had a spy in Montreal? Lucifer would have been more shocked to discover he *didn't* have one. He probably had one or two in other cities, too. Including Vancouver.

"My friend's holding on to his head tonight," Bastien said, laughing. "I think he was worried about losing it earlier. You cleaned house, *mon ami*."

"I was careful," Lucifer said casually. "Your friend was never in danger, as long as he hadn't befriended anyone else," he added darkly.

"So I told him. Ah . . . Lord Aden wants details."

Lucifer took a moment to prepare a report in his head, gathering and organizing his thoughts, and was just about to deliver his report to Bastien, when a frisson of power shivered through him, and Aden's deep voice rolled over the line.

"I sent you to find Sophia's mate, not to clean out the fucking territory for her."

"My lord," Lucifer said immediately. "My intent was only to free Colin Murphy, but there were those who stood in the way. Darren Yamanaka was—"

"Don't worry about Yamanaka. He was dead the moment he betrayed his sworn lord. What about the others? I'm assuming one of them was Berkhard's agent in the city. He wouldn't have trusted Yamanaka that much."

"Kasimir. Berkhard's lieutenant, but more than *just* a lieutenant, I think," he said, remembering the thoughts he'd picked up from the other vampire. "He was Berkhard's child, and a favorite. They'd been together a very long time."

"He was the real power in Montreal?"

"Definitely. Yamanaka believed all of Eastern Canada was going to be his, but that was never the plan. Berkhard and Kasimir were going to split Canada between them, just cut it in half somewhere in the middle."

"And the Montreal compound? Bastien says we're lucky our man wasn't among the bodies you dusted there."

"An exaggeration, my lord. There were several traitors in the house, vampires who'd actively conspired to betray Sophia, and who'd participated in Murphy's capture and imprisonment. He wanted them dead, and I agreed. We're departing for Vancouver, and I had no desire to leave our enemies alive."

"What the fuck's in Vancouver?"

Lucifer grimaced. He was going to have to man up and tell Aden about Eleanor. He respected his lord too much to deceive him, and, in any case, he was too proud to lie. But he didn't have to lead with that. There were plenty of other reasons to go to Vancouver. Beginning with what else he'd read in Kasimir's thoughts. Or rather, what he hadn't.

"I don't know exactly what's in Vancouver. And that's the problem, my lord. I was inside Kasimir's head while he was dying. I could read everything, Berkhard's strategy, their duplicity with Yamanaka, their history together. But he was hiding something. Something important enough that he spent the last of his power to keep it from me."

"Has that ever happened before? That you couldn't read some-one?"

"Never. Especially not when a vamp's dying, and I'm in his fucking head. Kasimir gave up his own defense at the end to protect his secret."

"Did you get any hints at all about what it might be?"

"Something to do with the fighters Berkhard has with him in Vancouver. I know he's turning new vampires to create an army, but there's something more, and I don't know what it is."

"All right, you convinced me. If Berkhard springs a surprise, and you save Sophia's ass, she'll owe me. Now what aren't you telling me?"

Lucifer stifled a groan. Dealing with powerful vampires was a pain in the ass sometimes. "Well . . . there's Eleanor."

"Who the fuck is . . . ah, shit. That little blonde?"

"We have a history, my lord. I knew her long ago, before she was made vampire."

"Damn it. Tell me I'm not losing you over a woman."

Lucifer thought privately that Aden didn't have a leg to stand on when it came to a woman disrupting a vampire's life. He was one of the toughest, most humorless men Lucifer had ever met, except when his mate, Sidonie, was around. She softened Aden up like cheese left too long in the Sicilian sun.

"My loyalty is yours, my lord, but Eleanor . . ." He didn't know exactly what to say. He and Eleanor hadn't made any decisions yet. He only knew he couldn't lose her now that he'd found her again.

"Well, shit," Aden cursed. "What're you planning? And don't tell me you don't know. You're always three steps ahead."

Lucifer cast a glance in the direction of the sitting room, then stepped into the bathroom and turned on the water. "Darren Yamanaka was the master of three cities, and I killed him. It could be argued that his cities are now my cities."

"Except they're in Sophia's territory."

"Right, but Sophia needs a new lieutenant."

"Damn it. I *am* losing you over a woman."

"My lord," Lucifer insisted. "You will always have my respect and my gratitude. You showed me that I could be something more than I was, and I will never forget that."

Aden grunted wordlessly, so Lucifer continued. "And nothing is certain. None of this has even been broached with Sophia, but *if* it worked out, you would have a solid ally on your northern border, and my services would always be available to you."

"For a price."

"With a substantial discount."

Aden laughed. "All right, I'll deal with it if it happens. In the meantime, you go ahead and help Sophia stop those fucking Europeans. A plague on all of them."

Lucifer smiled. Aden was tough as nails when he needed to be, but he respected those vampires with whom he worked closely. And while Lucifer had never been in the innermost circle of Aden's advisors, he'd consulted one-on-one with the vampire lord enough times to be convinced that Aden valued him for more than just his abilities.

"We're leaving for Vancouver within the hour, my lord. Eleanor and I will be daylighting on the plane, but Cal Christensen and his team are traveling with us, so he'll be providing security at the airport."

"Keep me informed," Aden snapped, and hung up, leaving nothing but dead air.

"Well," Lucifer said out loud. "I think that went well."

"What did?" Eleanor asked, as she opened the bathroom door.

Lucifer turned off the water. "Lord Aden. I briefed him on the operation so far."

She gave him a sober look. "Is that why you had the water running? Does he want you to come back?"

He shrugged. "The water was so that he would know I could speak freely. And, no, he agrees I should go on to Vancouver, and offer my assistance to Sophia. We all want the Europeans gone."

"And then?" she asked tightly. "Will you have to go home?"

Lucifer reached out and drew her into his embrace, leaning over to nuzzle her soft cheek. "You *are* my home, *bella*."

She pulled back far enough to look up at him, her big eyes wide with worry. "But—"

"We'll work it out, Elle," he told her. "But right now I need you focused on the situation in Vancouver. Mark my words, Vancouver will soon be a war zone, and we're going to be right in the thick of it."

Chapter Thirteen

Vancouver, British Columbia, Canada

ELEANOR LIFTED THE jet's window shade one last time. The sky was still black, but that inner sense that all vampires possessed told her the sun would soon be burning up the horizon. She was already feeling slow and tired, and definitely ready to retire to the special sleeping chamber at the back of the jet. Portions of the main cabin could also be made vampire-safe for daylight sleeping, but that wasn't necessary on this flight. She and Lucifer were the only vampires on board.

Lucifer was at the small table across the aisle, conferring with Colin Murphy.

"Sophia and I have plans for our reunion tonight, so there's no need for you all to rush to the estate." Colin leaned back with a smugly masculine smile, and Lucifer laughed.

"We'll take our time getting there," Lucifer agreed. "But we can get started without you. We'll need a briefing on the military situation. We've been totally focused on Montreal these last few days."

Colin nodded in Eleanor's direction. "Eleanor knows where to get that. She has full access."

Lucifer glanced over and must have noticed how close to sleep she was, because he stood, then reached over in front of her, and closed the window shade. "Time for bed, *bella*."

He extended both hands, and she could tell he was ready to scoop her up like a child, so she let him pull her to feet, but then held his hands tightly. He gave her a knowing smile, and turned her in the direction of the sleeping compartment.

"We'll see you tonight, Murphy," he called over his shoulder. "Give my regards to Lady Sophia."

Colin's loud snort of derision followed them down the aisle, with Lucifer's laughter right behind it.

The sleeping chamber was large for a private jet, with the bed filling the space wall-to-wall in the back two-thirds of the room, but it was still small by her usual standards. And Lucifer was a very big guy. On the other hand, once a vampire was asleep, comfort didn't really come into it. He might wake with a crick in his neck, but it wouldn't affect his rest.

She pulled off her shoes and pants, and her bra, but left on her top and panties. As much as she trusted Cal Christensen and the other daylight guards, Eleanor wasn't inclined to get naked with so few and flimsy walls between her and them. She knew it wasn't logical. After all, if they really wanted, they could break into the bedroom and strip her naked, and she'd never know it. She thought Lucifer might know what was going on, though. Even in his sleep. And she knew he'd take revenge on anyone who dared to so much as enter the room during daylight, except in an emergency. But she didn't find much reassurance in that either. So she crawled onto the bed, still half-clothed, and pulled back the covers.

Being a guy, of course, Lucifer didn't care who saw him naked. He stripped down like he was in the most private accommodations on the planet, then slid beneath the sheets, and pulled her into his arms.

"Sleep, baby," he whispered. "I'll be here."

She smiled as she cuddled close to his warmth, finding comfort in his assurances, no matter how illogical they were.

"I love you," she whispered, and then the sun rose, and she slept.

VAMPIRES WEREN'T supposed to be aware of anything while they slept. But vampire lords weren't your typical vampire.

Sophia knew the moment Colin's plane touched down on the tarmac. She felt him getting closer and closer as he left the plane and drove home, and when he finally slid into bed next to her, she was calmer and stronger than she'd been since his capture. With her mate by her side she was unstoppable. Berkhard thought he could steal her territory? Could torture her mate and kill her people? Thought she was weak because she was a woman? That European bastard was about to see just how wrong he was.

But first . . . the sun sank, and her eyes opened. And she was wrapped in warmth, soaked in the masculine scent of her lover, surrounded by his powerful arms.

"Colin," she said on a broken whisper, and he held her tighter.

"I'm here, darlin'. And I'm sorry."

She pulled back to look at him, raising a hand to cup his stubbled cheek. "Sorry for what, *meu amor?*"

"I should have suspected Yamanaka. Hell, I *did* suspect him, but I never thought he'd go that far. I thought I could handle him."

"I've seen Eleanor's reports," she said softly, stroking her hands all over his big body, reveling in the knowledge that he was here, that he was hers. She knew him so well, and yet they'd been separated for so long, and by more than simple distance. His captors had tried to break their mate bond. They hadn't succeeded, but she felt as if she needed to reclaim every inch of him. He was so beautifully made, with his broad shoulders and narrow waist, the smooth definition of toned muscles. And his face . . . she cast her gaze over every beloved inch of it, noting each new scrape and scar. Anger built at the knowledge of where those injuries had come from, of who was responsible.

"Sophie," he murmured, stroking her in return.

She tried to cast away her anger, knowing he was picking up on it, and trying to soothe her. But every time she thought about what he'd endured. . . . Tears threatened, so she went with outrage instead.

"You're still injured. Didn't Lucifer offer to—?"

"He offered," Colin interrupted, brushing a kiss over her lips. "I refused. I've had enough strange blood for one lifetime, even if my life's a long one. Yours is the only blood I want."

She gasped when his fingers closed over her nipple, pinching hard enough to send a sharp zing of arousal storming through her body. Colin took advantage of her gasp, pressing his lips over hers in a kiss and sliding his tongue between her teeth to explore every inch of her mouth. It was as if he needed to reclaim *her* body, just as she had his. He kissed her deeply, longingly. And she kissed him back, her hunger rising, and not only for his blood. She wanted his body. She *needed* him.

Gripping him tightly, she used her vampire strength to roll them both over until she straddled him. She smoothed her hands all over his torso, molding the lines of muscles, the flat planes of his belly, and . . . his cock. Long, thick, and so very hard.

She licked her lips, her tongue sliding over her fangs as they emerged from her gums. With her gaze locked on his, she crushed her breasts together between her arms, then reached down to wrap her fingers around his cock. Squeezing the thick shaft, she began stroking him, feeling the answering surge of heat between her thighs, the rush of arousal leaving her wet and aching to be filled.

Colin groaned. His strong hands gripped her thighs hard enough to bruise as his hips lifted against her, driving his cock between her fingers, and scraping against her swollen pussy with every thrust. His eyes were blue flame as he stared at her breasts, until finally, he lifted up with a flex of his gorgeous abs and captured her breast in his mouth, his teeth closing on her nipple as his arms banded behind her back and he pulled her down over his chest until he could suck on her breasts at his leisure. And he did, his cheeks hollowing out as he filled his mouth with her tender flesh, sucking hard until her nipples were stiff peaks begging for his bite.

With a growl, he closed his teeth over one nipple. Sophia choked on a breath as he bit down just hard enough draw blood, and a shot of insatiable lust shot from her breast to her clit, his strong throat moving as he swallowed her blood. He groaned again as the euphoric in her blood hit his nerves, and his cock stirred against her belly, growing impossibly harder, seeming to lengthen as his fingers dug into her ass.

"Sophie," he hissed, thrusting against her hungrily, demanding entrance to her soaking wet sex.

Sophia closed her eyes, drinking in the waves of arousal rolling between them, her body undulating against his in sensual pleasure. Her breasts ached, crushed against his chest, and her pussy seemed to pulse with the need to have him inside her.

"Fuck me," she whispered, then moaned when he first lifted her, and then lowered her body down, sliding his wonderful, thick cock between her swollen pussy lips, burying himself inside her, as her sheath tightened around him. They both groaned as the profound joy of being *together* nearly overwhelmed the sexual ecstasy of their joining. And, for just a moment, they froze, holding on to the moment, savoring it, as his cock flexed deep inside her triggering a responding contraction of her uterus that rippled up through her torso to her breasts, as if to caress her from within.

His eyes flashed open, and he bared his teeth in a snarl as he began fucking her. Powerful arms held her above him as he thrust upward, slamming his cock into her, holding her as effortlessly as if she weighed nothing. Sophia closed her hands over her breasts and squeezed, pinching her nipples, relishing the sparks of pain left from his bite. Her pussy heated as his fucking grew more intense, his hips thrusting faster and faster until she thought they'd both burn up.

Hunger struck without warning, a low growl searing her throat, as her gaze fixed on the pounding of his blood, the swell of the big vein in his neck. She leaned forward without warning, gripping his hair and wrenching his head to one side, straining his neck and tightening the skin until she could see the blood pulsing just below the surface, could smell the deep, rich fragrance.

Her fangs grew longer, scraping against her lower lip as she opened her mouth and sank her fangs into his neck. Colin bucked wildly, as the full effect of her bite hit him. His cock seemed to swell and then he was coming, hot jets of release filling her as he gripped the back of her head, and held on, almost demanding that she drink.

And drink she did, deep drafts of his blood, the blood of a powerful man, the man she loved, her mate. They were bound blood to blood, soul to soul, and in that moment, it was as if something clicked between them. It was love and lust, it was heat and desire. It was coming home at last.

Tears rolled down her cheeks as she drank. All the emotion that she'd been forced to suppress, to hide lest others think her weak—it all came tumbling out when Colin's blood ran down her throat, when his climax shot hot and thick against the walls of her womb.

She barely remembered lifting her head, or retracting her fangs and licking the puncture wounds to stop the bleeding. She lost time for a moment, coming back to the sound of Colin crooning her name, to the warm stroke of his hands up and down her back, fingers digging in, soothing her muscles as the sound of his deep voice soothed her heart and soul.

"Sophie, come back to me, darlin'."

She smiled against his neck, then surrendered to desire and licked his neck. "I never left, *meu querido.*"

She heard the grin in his response. "Hmm, you want to stay here all night and fuck? Or do we have to be all responsible and shit?"

She laughed, but let regret color her response. "I doubt our enemies will wait. And I suppose I must deal with Aden's Lucifer."

"He seems like a decent guy, Soph."

"And Eleanor loves him."

"She surely does that, but no more than he loves her. They go back a ways, you know."

"Yes, and *you* know," she said, finger-combing his dark hair away from his face, before kissing the now smooth skin where cuts had bled earlier, "that I'm a sucker for a long lost love story."

He cupped the back of her head, bringing her down for a long, wet kiss. "I love you."

Sophia nodded, her throat too tight with emotion to speak, as Colin sat up suddenly, taking her with him. He kissed her forehead. "You want to shower together?" he asked, with a suggestive wiggle of his eyebrows that made her laugh.

Her fangs pressed into her lower lip, and she growled hungrily. She'd been starved for him when he'd been gone, and now she couldn't get enough of his rich blood . . . or his delicious cock. "Definitely," she said, taking his hand and pulling him toward the shower. "I'm going to need all of my strength to deal with Aden's wonder boy."

PLEASURE ZINGED through Eleanor's body like a lightning bolt, and she found herself on the edge of an orgasm. She bit back a scream, mindful of the humans only a few feet away, but couldn't stop herself from moaning as sexual hunger jolted her wide awake. She blinked her eyes open, trying to figure out where she was and what . . . . She caught the flash of a dark head between her thighs, muscled shoulders holding her legs wide.

"Lucifer," she whispered, and his head came up. He grinned at her, his mouth slick with her juices, his fangs gleaming in the low light.

"Good evening, *bella*."

"What are you—?" A gasp of shock cut off her words as he slid two thick fingers into her wet pussy. She tried to breathe, but then he scraped the rough pad of his thumb over her clit and pressed down hard. The climax hit with a rush, her body already as aroused as if he'd been priming her long before she'd been awake to enjoy it. On the one hand, she was pissed that she'd missed all that warm up. On the other . . . her nails dug into his arms as carnal pleasure rolled through her. Her skin shivered, her muscles contracted, and her sex pulsed with a frenzied bliss that rolled in waves up to her breasts, arousing her nipples to hard, little peaks that she simply had to pluck.

"That's a pretty picture," Lucifer growled, his eyes glowing darkly gold as he stared at her hands on her breasts, her fingers pinching her nipples until they were bright red and engorged with blood. Lucifer was so fast that she was barely aware he'd moved, before his mouth closed over her nipple, biting her fingers, and pushing them away with his tongue, until he had her breasts all to himself. He sucked each nipple firmly, until they were swollen like ruby, ripe cherries, just waiting to be . . .

Eleanor bit her lip again to keep from screaming as Lucifer's teeth closed over her nipple. Blood filled his mouth and ran over her breasts, like bright, red juice, and he lapped it up. When he was done with the first nipple, he moved on to the second, his gaze locked on hers as he sucked the nipple into readiness and bit her. Knowing what was coming, knowing the shocking pain and the incredible pleasure, made it worse, not better. Worse being a euphemism for the fire of arousal burning its way through her veins as he sucked and licked her second breast clean, and then trailed his tongue up to her mouth, where he sucked on the lip she'd made bloody with her own teeth.

"You're delicious, *bella*. My pretty pink princess."

Eleanor knew she should reject the idea that she was anyone's princess. She was a strong, capable woman. A vampire who could toss grown men aside like toys, and who was bodyguard to a vampire lord. And yet, some part of the old Eleanor remained. The human Eleanor who still wanted to be Lucifer's treasure, his princess. And that part of her flushed with happiness at his words. But the other part of her wanted to be dirty tonight.

So using some of her vampire strength, she shoved him to his back and ran her hands over his chest, stroking him, admiring the smooth stretch of muscle over bone. He hissed as she dug her fingernails into his skin, leaving raw-looking stripes of color as her fingers moved down over his ripped abdomen, his flat belly, to his hard, thick cock. Gripping the rigid shaft in one hand, she bent over and took him into her mouth, her eyes wide open and meeting his as her mouth slicked up and down, her tongue sliding around and grazing his length.

Lucifer fisted her long hair, holding it away from her face so he could watch her suck his cock, tightening his hold almost painfully when she swallowed the full length of his cock into her throat. She held it there, her throat working around his thickness, caressing him as she fought against the urge to breathe. Finally, a moment before she would have lifted her head, Lucifer tugged her head up and she drew in a long breath, but then she sucked him deep again, reveling in the harsh groan that rolled from his throat as his hips began thrusting against her mouth, almost as if he couldn't hold still any longer.

Eleanor withdrew almost to the tip of his cock, her tongue swirling round and round as she looked up and met Lucifer's hungry gaze. Gripping his cock at the base, she began pumping and sucking in unison, her head bobbing up and down, his cock hitting the back of her throat every time his hips thrust against her. She moaned with pleasure at the feel of his cock, the thick velvety skin over a steel-hard shaft, and the salty taste of his cum when her tongue dipped into the slit at its head.

"Shit," Lucifer hissed, and both of his hands fisted in her hair. "Baby . . ."

It was all the warning she got before his cock grew impossibly harder, his balls tightened, and his release filled her mouth. Lucifer held her head down as she swallowed jet after jet, licking up every drop until he was dry and wrung out.

"You have no idea how hot that is," he groaned. "My pink princess sucking my dick, swallowing it all. Fuck me."

Eleanor sat up, licking her lips deliberately, as his eyes followed her tongue. "I'm not sure we have time for me to fuck you," she whispered, suddenly wondering just how much of a show they'd been putting on for the guards. She blushed hotly, and Lucifer gave a low, masculine chuckle.

"This chamber is reasonably soundproofed, *bella*." He pulled her up his body, wrapping her in his arms. "But you've drained me dry. And we'll need blood before we head to Sophia's, just in case."

"There's blood available on the estate," she told him, but he shook his head.

"That's not the first impression I want to make. We have blood here on board the jet. We'll feed, and then shower. Time to face the night."

"*And Sophia,*" he thought privately.

ELEANOR FLICKED ON the TV, leaving it on mute, while she waited for Lucifer to shower. Normally, she'd have been in that shower with him. There was something very sensuous about lots of hot water and steam on smooth, wet skin. Especially when the wet skin covered a body as gorgeous as Lucifer's. All those muscles made a vampire feel almost like a girl again.

She smiled at the thought. The truth was that she didn't miss being human, and wouldn't choose to go back even if she could. She liked what she was now a hell of a lot more. And the virtual immortality didn't hurt either. She'd never have to worry about wrinkles or hip replacements, or any of the other frailties of the human body.

An image on the TV screen suddenly drew her notice, enough that she picked up the remote and clicked on the sound. It was one of those 24-hour news channels, with two separate ribbon scrolls running below the live feed of the current news anchor. Eleanor frowned, trying to figure out what had drawn her attention and why. It was a filler kind of story about a Canadian Army training camp, and a company of soldiers who'd been involved in a training exercise that had taken them away from camp for two weeks, and who were now a week overdue on their return. Eleanor didn't know why that was even a story. They were soldiers, after all. They were the ones usually called to search for missing civilians, so who better to survive in the wild, right? Besides, the report was out of the Chilcotin, which was a wild area not exactly known for its cell phone reception. It wasn't as if the troop could call home every night. She'd never been there herself, but several of her fellow body-guards liked to spend their free time facing off with nature to see who was stronger. This wasn't Eleanor's idea of a good time, but she'd heard their stories. And that was all fine and good, but why—Shit! Shit, shit, shit! Was it possible?

She rushed for the bathroom as the water turned off, shoving open the door and whacking Lucifer who was just stepping out of the shower, his head buried in a towel as he dried off.

"Fuck!" He dropped the towel, all ready to demand an explanation, when he caught the look on her face. "What is it?" he asked sharply.

"You're not going to believe this," she muttered, and grabbed his arm, dragging him out of the small, steamy room and into the passenger cabin. They had the plane to themselves for now. Cal and his team had all deployed outside to the hangar where the jet had parked for the day.

"What's going on, Elle?"

"Listen." She pushed buttons on the remote, rolling back the news story. She listened with half an ear, her attention focused on Lucifer's reaction, wanting to know if she was making connections that didn't exist, or if—

"Fuck." Lucifer's soft curse answered *that* question.

"So you think it's something?"

"You mean do I think Berkhard has caught himself a trained military unit and made some vampires? Fuck, yeah, I do. We need more information. How many newbie vamps could Berkhard handle at once?" he asked, mostly muttering to himself. "He's had a couple weeks to turn them, and let's suppose he's managed to turn one or two fledgling masters who could help out a little. So, we're probably looking two or three platoons, maybe a small company."

All of that went in one ear and out the other for Eleanor. She wouldn't know a platoon from a company if they camped in her living room. If she had a living room, which she really didn't. But what she did catch was the real likelihood that Berkhard would be attacking Sophia with an army of trained soldiers.

"Soldier or not, they'll still be new vamps, which will limit their effectiveness, right?" She followed Lucifer as he went back to the bedroom to dress.

He didn't answer her question, asking one of his own instead. "How many guards does Sophia have in Vancouver? How many can she trust?"

"She has a solid core of around fifty. Like everything else, she's had to build from scratch after Lucien's death. He barely had a doorman at his headquarters. Colin's been pushing her to recruit, but—"

"How many are loyal?" he asked again, sitting down to pull on his boots.

"Most of them," she insisted. "I've worked with these guys night after night for more than a year. They're good people."

"Uh huh. Like Yamanaka?"

"No, not like him. Darren was always an asshole. He never got over the fact that Sophia won the territory."

"And he wasn't alone. Montreal proved that. Get Colin on the phone," he asked, as he rushed to finish dressing.

Eleanor stared at him, startled by his abrupt manner. "You think they're already here," she whispered.

"I think there's someone inside your lady's camp, someone she trusts, who's betrayed her. And what better time to launch a surprise attack than Colin's first night back? There's not a vampire alive who doesn't know what those two are doing right now, and it's not getting ready for war."

Eleanor reached for her cell phone, her heart tripping with fear. Not for herself, but for her lady, and for Colin. If Lucifer was right, if Berkhard was planning an attack tonight, then Sophia needed to be warned. Her guards were good, but they couldn't stand up to a vampire as powerful as Berkhard without Sophia to back them up. What if she and Colin had locked themselves away, turned off their phones? Someone would be able to reach them, someone Sophia trusted. But what if Lucifer was right, and that person couldn't be trusted at all?

Colin's phone rang and rang, not even going to voicemail. She tried Sophia next. As the lady's bodyguard, she was one of the few who had her private cell number. But it, too, went unanswered. And with every trilling ring, Eleanor's fear grew.

"Nothing," she said, when Lucifer looked up and met her eyes. "No answer, no voicemail on either of their phones. Should I call—?"

"No," he said, cutting her off. "We don't know who the traitor is. Better to keep our presence a secret until we can get to Sophia. Let's go."

SOPHIA STOOD BACK while Colin entered the code that would open their private sleeping vault. No one had the code but the two of them, which was unusual. More typically, a lord's lieutenant would have the code in the event of an emergency, but in Sophia's case, she would never have trusted Darren Yamanaka that far. And besides, Colin was her lieutenant in all but name.

Feeling more relaxed than she had in weeks, she strolled through into their private quarters, and then on to her formal office. She knew the feel-good buzz couldn't last, but she clung to it with both hands, wanting to prolong the joy of Colin's return as long as possible.

"Anything from Eleanor?" she asked Colin, as she sat at her desk and pulled up the daily transition reports from her daylight and nighttime security teams.

"Call log shows she called, but she didn't leave a message. And I told them not to rush, that we'd be busy," he said, absently. "Is this everything we have on Calgary?"

She looked up. "I haven't read any of the reports, since I was there. Why, is something missing?"

"It's probably nothing. I'll let you know." He dropped whatever he'd been reading, and crossed to the big gun safe, entered the code, and started pulling out weapons.

Sophia watched him with a frown. If it was nothing, then why was he gearing up as if the gates of hell were about to open and spill forth its horde?

"Colin?" She asked, coming to her feet. "Is there something—?"

A huge explosion cut her off, rocking the compound and rattling walls, cracking the big window on the far side of her desk.

"What the hell?"

Colin's phone rang, and she listened, furious and frustrated, to his terse replies.

"Talk," she demanded, the minute he disconnected.

"An explosion at the back wall," he said, as he finished arming himself, checking magazines, and stowing both ammo and a variety of offensive explosive devices in the various pockets of his black combat pants. "There's a team checking it out now. They should be reporting in—" His cell rang again. "—right now. Sit-rep," he said, answering the call.

Sophia listened with half an ear as the caller provided what Colin called a "situation report," or "sit-rep." The rest of her attention was on the security screens she'd pulled up on her computer, showing the various video feeds scattered throughout the estate. She ignored the interior cameras, focusing instead on the perimeter. The camera closest to the back wall had been taken out by the explosion. The feed up to that point showed a huge flash, and then nothing but gray screen and static. Moving out from that camera, she picked a direction and checked each vid feed, noting the disciplined response of her people to the explosion, and not seeing anything that led her to believe any of them had been involved. They were all rushing to their crisis positions, beefing up the perimeter all around on the off-chance that the explosion itself was naught but a diversion.

Colin's phone rang again. He disconnected the first call and answered this one instead. He listened intently for several minutes, then swore viciously, "Fuck! All right, we're on our way."

Sophia was already on her feet, having seen something on the main gate monitor that gave her a good idea of what Colin had just discovered. "Colin." She said it softly enough, but something in her tone, or maybe it was the link they shared as mates that had him striding across the room to stare at the monitor with her.

"What is it, babe?"

"That one," she said, pressing a finger to the monitor over the face of a dark-haired vampire who stood surrounded by an army just beyond her front gate. "That's Berkhard."

Colin was bent over, staring at the image. "Are those . . . are those vampires wearing uniforms?"

Sophia gripped Colin's arm. "The something extra that Kasimir was hiding," she whispered.

"What?"

"We have to get out there *now*."

THE FRONT GATE was down by the time Sophia reached it. It had never been meant to withstand a military attack. They'd always assumed the estate house itself would be their final stand, as it might end up being tonight. It could be hardened into a fortress in a matter of minutes, if necessary.

Unfortunately, their enemy didn't seem likely to give them those minutes. Berkhard had made himself a vampire army, a literal army of vampires. She didn't know where he'd gotten them, but she could tell they were all newly turned. That disadvantage seemed to be nullified by their discipline and skill, however. They were used to working in concert, used to taking orders. And they were armed with rifles—Colin could have told her what kind, but it didn't matter. You might not kill a vampire with a gun, but you could put him down long enough to chop off his head. Or, hell, the right kind of ammo, the kind Colin used, could kill a vampire by blowing his heart to shreds. Not even the symbiote could recover from that.

And that's what she saw happening all around her. Vampires were dying. Some were hers. A lot more were Berkhard's newbies, but he had plenty.

Wanting a better view of the battlefield, she climbed a stable section of the wall and surveyed the scene. Small skirmishes were happening everywhere, with Berkhard's people trying to overwhelm her smaller numbers. As she watched, ten soldier vamps swarmed one of her people, burying him under bodies as they clubbed him with their weapons. Were they so disoriented that they couldn't even use their weapons to their best advantage? Good for her, bad for them. Focusing her power, she blew the newbie soldiers away, knocking them unconscious as they flew backward. At the same time, she fed her own vampire a concentrated dose of power, healing his injuries, and lending him strength. He sent her a mental thanks, rose to his feet, and rejoined the fray.

She took a moment to let her power flow over the battlefield, bolstering all of her vamps just as she had the one who'd been down earlier. She was a good enough fighter, as focused as a bulldog, and vicious when she had to be. But the biggest weapon she had was her ability to bolster her vampires' courage and strength.

"Why didn't they shoot him?" she asked Colin, who'd appeared on the wall at her side.

"They're out of ammo," he said, drawing his own weapon and spraying the battlefield over the heads of her people, taking out some of Berkhard's reserve troops. "Berkhard took the soldiers, but forgot the supplies."

A heavy truck rolled down the road and slid to a stop. Sophia groaned as twenty fresh troops jumped onto the road and raced into the battle.

"How many could he have?" she asked.

"Depends on where he got them, and how many he can handle. Could be an entire company of fighters. Let's hope it's a not a battalion."

"Numbers, Colin," she said tightly, sending a fresh blast of power at the new group of soldiers who were indiscriminately aiming their weapons at the combatants, apparently willing to kill their own in order to get rid of hers.

"A small company's around a hundred, but could go higher. And a battalion starts around four or five hundred. Could he do that?"

She swung her head around to stare at him. "Five hundred," she whispered. Then gritted her jaw, and stared down at the battle. Her greatest weapon might be the ability to lend strength to her vampires, but what they needed right now was another fighter. "I'm going down there," she decided.

"I'm with you."

"No. I need you at the back wall. That explosion was more than a diversion, and I want someone there who can think straight in the middle of a battle."

"Fuck that, babe. I'm your shield. You're the only person in this battle who *has* to survive. You die, they all die. And I already sent Tambra to the back wall with several fighters."

Sophia wanted to punch him. She'd known he wasn't needed back there. She just wanted him safe. But she should have known better. He was a warrior down to the very marrow of his bones.

"All right," she agreed. "But if you get killed—"

Colin laughed as he wrapped an arm around her, and then jumped off the wall with her held close to his side. "Better men than these have tried to kill me, darlin'. Let's kick some ass."

LUCIFER BRACED A hand on the dash as Eleanor raced down the dark streets. It reminded him of their race through the streets of Montreal just two nights ago, when they'd been bringing Colin back to the hotel. The tires on the big SUV squealed as she made a sharp right turn onto a private road that ran along what looked like a river. Lucifer wasn't all that familiar with the geography of this area. He knew the ocean was out there somewhere, but other than that . . .

"There," he murmured suddenly, as the battlefield came into view. The estate was lit up like a beacon, and there were fires burning on both sides of the big house, with fighters milling back and forth in waves, and no one side seeming to gain permanent advantage. It was clear that Sophia's people were holding the line for now. They had the better position, behind the high wall of the estate, while Berkhard's people were concentrated around the blown gate, seeming not to have the initiative to climb the wall instead. It supported his supposition that the European vamp couldn't control so many newbie vamps at once.

"You were right," Eleanor said, her gaze fixed ahead. "They're wearing uniforms."

"*You* were the one who made the connection. *I* was almost too late in figuring it out. Stop here."

Eleanor hit the brakes, skidding to a stop a good hundred yards away from the estate. She looked at him in question. "I need to get over there, Lucifer. I need to back up Sophia."

"And you will, but we need to go where we'll do the most damage." Closing his eyes, he let his awareness drift to the battlefield. He could smell the blood and guts from here, could hear the howls and the gunfire. Not so different from a human war. Until he opened his eyes into the realm of magic. He wasn't seeing soldiers and vampires anymore, but waves of pure power, like the light show at a concert. Sophia was marked by the enormous swell of power that surrounded her like a cloud, with flashes of amber lightning streaking out over the battlefield from her position. Duller spots of color indicated her stronger vampires. But the dullest ones of all were Berkhard's baby vamps who were gathered around the gate, and dying like flies. It didn't look like Berkhard had given them any direction at all. He'd simply pointed at the gate and said, "go." And they'd all gone.

Lucifer tightened his jaw in anger at the waste of life. These men hadn't been given a choice, either in their deaths or in becoming vampires. Berkhard had plucked them from the shelf like poorly honed blades, and thrown them at his enemy to die.

Lifting his gaze, he scanned the battlefield. He'd found Sophia, but where was Berkhard?

"Fuck," he swore softly. There *was* a pattern to the fight, and he knew where Berkhard was, but did Sophia? "Let's go," he snapped. "We're moving fast, Elle. We have to get to Sophia."

She didn't argue, but simply took off at his side, two blurs in the dark night, moving far too fast for their enemies to hit with their rifles even if they'd seen them.

As they got closer to the battlefield, they were still outside the wall, and they had to fight. Standing back to back, Lucifer wielded raw energy like sharp steel, and Eleanor slashed left and right, wielding her bo staff with deadly accuracy. As they fought, they maneuvered closer to the wall, aiming for a section that was still standing, and therefore less congested. Making a final dash to their target, they leapt to the top, lingering just long enough to get a mental picture of the scene, before jumping to the ground and racing along its perimeter to the spot where Sophia stood, shining like the sun itself, while her fighters battled around her.

The main conflict was taking place in a huge muddle of fighters where the gates used to be, the enemy forces surging forward and back, like a monster trying to force its way through the blasted opening. Lucifer's biggest danger at this point was being "fired on" by his own allies. He was a significant power, but mostly unknown to Sophia, and completely unknown to her people. She could easily lash out reflexively if she sensed him coming in without warning. So maybe they should warn her.

"Elle," he said urgently. "Let Sophia know we're here."

She gave him a startled look, clearly not understanding what he meant. He forgot sometimes that not everyone had his enhanced telepathic ability.

"Just blast your presence into the ether. She'll feel it."

Eleanor frowned, but he knew the moment she did what he'd asked, because he felt it, too. Eleanor's presence was a warm embrace, familiar and loved, and he'd have pulled her down right there, and kissed the hell out of her if they'd been anywhere else. But for now he had to be satisfied knowing that Sophia would have felt it, too—differently than he did, to be sure, but just as strongly. Eleanor was sworn to the Canadian lord, and she'd been at her side for a long time.

"Let's go," Lucifer said, and raced toward the battle once more, confident that he wouldn't find himself the target of Sophia's wrath.

SOPHIA FOUGHT. IT felt like hours had passed, but the truth was far grimmer. It was barely a single hour since they'd been attacked. Berkhard's vampires had given nearly as good as they got at first, but then they'd seemed to simply run down and wear out. Berkhard had miscalculated, or maybe he'd been forced to bring the battle to her earlier than he'd planned. But his fighters, for all their human military skill and discipline, were just too young as vampires. They needed more blood than he could possibly provide in his tight timeframe, and their early bursts of energy had depleted too quickly. They were so young, and innocent of Berkhard's crimes. She hated the necessity of killing them, and spared them when she could, but her own people had to come first.

An unexpected swell of power had her spinning to the right just in time to meet a phalanx of soldiers charging through the fray. Sophia braced, and gathered her power, prepared to knock back this attack as she had the others, when a concussion of vampiric power slammed through the crowded battlefield, crushing friend and foe alike, and leaving only one vampire standing to oppose her. One very powerful vampire. Berkhard had finally shown his face.

Sophia glared at him over the field of fallen soldiers. Some of hers had died, but more were wounded, lying twisted among Berkhard's dead who couldn't even dust yet.

"Colin," she said quietly. She felt him there at her back, as he always was. Her fierce and loyal mate, whom they'd tried to take from her.

"Don't get between us, *meu querido*. No matter what happens."

"Fuck that, darlin'."

His response made her smile, despite the blood and gore all around her, despite the desperate seriousness of their situation.

"I love you, Colin Murphy."

"Show me later, babe. Now let's kill this motherfucker."

Sophia was still laughing when she launched a fireball of pure power, not at Berkhard's head—which he instinctively hid behind a hardened shield, but at his gut, which he'd left vulnerable behind only a thin layer of power. It was a trick Colin had taught her. Hell, every trick she had was one she'd learned from him. He was the one who'd taught her to fight.

Berkhard stumbled back several steps, his gut dripping blood, and the smell of ruptured intestine wafted over the battlefield. He forced himself upright, weaving a solid shield around himself with every curse he uttered in his native German. His hatred scorched the air between them, and he grunted in pain as the vampire symbiote worked to heal his injury.

Sophia bared her teeth at him, mocking and smug, even as she constructed her own shields, layer by layer. It had been a lucky strike that hit him so hard, one he hadn't anticipated, and she'd hurt him, forcing him to use a good chunk of his energy to heal himself early in the battle. But she didn't delude herself into believing this fight was over.

Drawing on the core of her power, feeling Colin solid and sure at her back, she let her energy flow, trailing it down her arms to her fingertips and letting it fly. It hit Berkhard like a hundred grenades of power, pounding his shields, creating divots of energy that were more an irritant than a threat to him. The danger lay in his distraction, in the anger that fractured his discipline.

He roared furiously, and raised both arms, hands fisted as he crafted a response. Not grenades of energy, but bombs that crashed into her shields, shattering her outermost layer and bowing her entire construct inward.

Sophia forced herself to stand strong, ignoring the pain in her chest that felt as if he'd punched her heart. She ground her teeth. Berkhard might be the toughest bastard she'd ever fought, but he wouldn't be the last. Because she intended to smoke his ass.

Re-forming her damaged shields, she eyed Berkhard's still-gruesome gut as she twisted her energy into a lance of power. She could feel him gearing up for a fresh attack, could see his hands working behind his strengthened shields. She worked faster, wanting to hit first, to strike while he was wounded and still vulnerable.

But Berkhard recovered faster than she'd thought possible. He was old and powerful, and far more brutal than she was, as evidenced when he reached out and, without so much as a whisper of regret, simply sucked dry all of the baby vampires who'd made the mistake of standing too close to their Sire. Uniformed vampires fell as Berkhard laughed, reveling in the surge of power. When he finally lowered his gaze, it was to attack, standing there like an old bull, shoving both hands away from his body as he hurled a volley of crushing force that plowed into Sophia, cracking her shields and throwing her off her feet. She flew backwards, cursing herself for being too slow, for underestimating her opponent. Colin was there, yanking her to her feet, leaving himself wide open if she needed to draw energy from their bond. But for all his willingness, he was human, his power limited. She reached out. Her strongest people were still fighting—some few on the field before her, but most in the rear, where Berkhard's allies had launched a sneak attack through the blown back gate. She couldn't drain power away from any of them. If anything, it was her duty to lend them strength when they needed it to protect her fighters.

She felt a moment's despair. There could be no victory if it meant sacrificing her own people the way Berkhard had done. She would rather die fighting to save them. She reached out . . . and suddenly there was Eleanor, strong and loyal, and wide open, her strength at Sophia's disposal. And with her . . . *meu Deus*, with her was Lucifer. And no wonder Eleanor loved him. He glowed with power, a golden star come to earth. With all that power, he could have seized the territory for himself, could have simply waited until she was sufficiently weakened to attack her, and then destroyed an exhausted Berkhard in turn.

Instead he was offering that power to her, taking on the burden of her fighters and freeing her to concentrate on Berkhard.

With a whispered thanks, she stood, her legs braced wide, her eyes lighting the battlefield in an amber glow. "This is not your land," she growled. "These are not your people."

Berkhard's eyes widened in shock. He'd been so certain that victory was his.

It was Sophia's turn to laugh as renewed power filled every inch of her body, heating her veins, electrifying her nerves. It was delicious, addictive. She stretched her arms out, as if gathering in all the energy of universe. And then she lowered her gaze to Berkhard and grinned.

"Time to die, asshole."

LUCIFER HAD RACED onto the battlefield with Eleanor a moment before Berkhard rose up like a monster of old and sucked his people dry to feed his own power. He scanned the destruction around him, noting too many bodies of vampires waiting for sunlight to turn them to dust. There was something uniquely cruel about creating baby vamps just so that you could kill them. And Berkhard had been a busy vampire. Piles of dead vamps formed a gruesome stage for the showdown between Sophia and Berkhard, but all around them the battle still raged. The numbers were dwindling, but Sophia's vampire defenders still fought. Berkhard's newbie vamps outnumbered them, but military discipline alone wasn't enough to defeat Sophia's well-trained and much older vampire guard force. For all their experience and skill, however, they were still leaning on Sophia for support—both psychological and physical—and that was preventing her from concentrating her power against Berkhard.

He and Eleanor maneuvered closer, focused solely on protecting Sophia's back. But Lucifer was almost distracted by his awareness of a second battle that was raging behind the house. If their enemy managed to break through there, it would force Sophia to fight on two fronts, fracturing her power, and greatly diminishing her ability to engage Berkhard one on one, which was the only way this battle could end. One of the vampire lords had to die tonight, there was no other way. And Lucifer was determined that it wouldn't be Sophia.

He knew the moment Sophia became aware of Eleanor's presence, because she almost immediately began drawing on her for support. Berkhard was pressing his attack, killing off his people as necessary, while Sophia was trying to fight him, and support everyone else at the same time. What she needed was the powerful lieutenant she'd never had. Someone like Lucifer.

"*Bella,*" he whispered into Eleanor's mind, not wanting to distract her. "*I'm moving to the rear gate. You stay safe.*"

She turned enough to flash him a confident smile. "*You, too, baby.*" And then she was back in the fight, her bo staff a black blur as she waded into the battle throng between Sophia and Berkhard.

Lucifer lingered long enough to satisfy himself that she was safe and strong, and then he raced for the back gate, circling around the big house until he could see with his eyes the battlefield he'd been sensing ever since they'd arrived. He stood for a moment, scanning the fighters, gauging the ebb and flow of the battle. And then, with an exultant roar, he unleashed the bonds that locked his power down, and let it flow.

SOPHIA RALLIED, flush with power as she formed a gleaming lance of energy and sent it slicing through the air like hot lightning. It slowed when it struck Berkhard's shield, but it didn't stop. Like a diamond-hard drill, it kept digging, ignoring Berkhard's attempts to repel it, attempts that only weakened his defenses as he took energy away from his shields to attack the lance. It penetrated finally, breaching the German lord's shields with a crack of sound, like ice breaking in the sunlight. And like sunlight for a vampire, it destroyed everything it touched, churning into Berkhard's already-wounded gut, boring a hole that he fought frantically to repair, even as Sophia dispersed the lance's energy, letting it expand into his torso, until his entire chest was bloody and torn, as if her power was eating him from the inside.

Berkhard howled and reached out to his remaining vamps, but he was too weak to draw on them, and they were too weak to offer. He fell to his knees, his power a mangled swirl of energy that struggled to form something coherent and useful.

Sophia stalked closer, wanting the European vampire to know exactly who it was who'd bested him. She stared down at her enemy, meeting his furious glare, seeing his eyes grow dull with hatred as his power drained into the earth. She raised one hand in an intentionally negligent gesture, wanting this bastard to know just how little his death mattered to her, or to the world. And then she summoned all of the fear and rage she'd felt for Colin's torment, the desolation at the possibility of his death. She shaped all of that into a hot ball that gleamed with the brilliant amber of her power, then she lifted her hand and blew on the sphere of energy. It shot from her hand as if driven by a hard wind, covering the short distance and driving itself into Berkhard's gruesome chest like a bullet. It hung there for a long moment, as flesh melted and blood sizzled, and then it exploded, scattering the vampire lord into a million tiny pieces that hung suspended in the air for the beat of a heart before disintegrating into dust.

Sophia's triumphant cry of victory soared over the battlefield, finding an echo in the cries of her people. Strong arms circled her from behind, and she turned into Colin's embrace, holding him tightly, letting his broad chest hide her tears of joy and relief. She didn't give a fuck what the surrounding vampires thought, didn't care if they judged her weak for shedding tears of relief that her enemy was dead, and her mate was alive.

She was the God damned Lord of the Canadian Territories, tested and proven on the bloody fucking field of battle, and they could all go fuck themselves.

LUCIFER FOUGHT HARDER than he ever had before, using his power to shield the small force defending the hole in the wall that used to be the back gate. The gates themselves lay in a twisted pile of metal, where they'd been blown using ordinary human explosives. And beyond that was a group of about fifty newborn vampires, fighting for all they were worth. These soldiers were on their own, commanded by an officer who'd been human no more than two weeks ago. Lucifer could taste the newly-made vampire's desperation and confusion, but there was also hatred and a burning rage that drove the young officer forward, ordering his vampire force against the defenders time and time again. And every time they rushed forward, they left a few of their own lying dead behind among Sophia's injured fighters.

Lucifer strode back and forth on the combat line, shielding Sophia's defenders from the common gunfire, boosting their energy for the hand-to-hand battles that occurred whenever Berkhard's people launched another desperate assault. The newly-made vampires fought with a fierce desperation, as if Berkhard had planted an order in their minds that they were to keep fighting at any cost. Setting aside their use-less weapons, they ripped at their opponents with gleaming fangs and curved fingers, gouging eyes and shredding flesh. It was brutal and primitive, and just plain, fucking sad. For all their urgency and courage, they had no chance against Sophia's much smaller force, and especially not with Lucifer's power bolstering their organized defense.

The battle was nearly over, the ground littered with dead vampires too young to dust, when suddenly a blast of unfettered energy blasted through the ether, and hard on that came a howl of agonized defeat. Lucifer sensed Eleanor's triumphant rush of victory a moment before the remaining newbie vampires at the gate fell to their knees and then collapsed completely, too weak to continue without the goad of Berkhard's command.

Lucifer grinned as all around him Sophia's guards shouted their own victory to the night skies, some of them leaning on each other in exhaustion, but all of them laughing or smiling, exulting in the knowledge that they had survived, while their enemies had not.

Lucifer's grin died as his telepathy blared to sudden life, filled with images of vengeance and death. Not for Berkhard, he realized, but for

Sophia. He spun, searching for the source, and his gaze settled on a female vamp racing across the empty ground behind the estate, rushing around the house, fangs bared in a determined grimace.

Lucifer lashed out with his power, wrapping it around her and freezing her in place as he strode closer.

"Eleanor," he telepathed his lover, framing her name with just enough urgency to grab her attention.

"Lucifer?" Eleanor's response was hesitant and worried.

"Bring Sophia, bella. *I've found your traitor."*

Eleanor's response was wordless alarm, as he sensed her racing toward him. He was waiting when she rounded the house, her eyes wide with concern, blond braid flying behind her. She was the very picture of a vengeful warrior princess, and his heart swelled at the knowledge that she was his.

Sophia and Colin came into sight behind her, moving quickly. Sophia's power reached out to her people, the vampire guards who'd successfully defended this position. There was love and pride in the ephemeral embrace she wrapped around them, and her vampires straightened with pride and renewed energy.

Eleanor reached Lucifer first, her eyes wide in disbelief, when she saw his prisoner.

"Do you know her?" he asked unnecessarily. It was obvious that she did. Just as it was obvious his would-be assassin knew Eleanor. She struggled abruptly against the hold he had on her, her thoughts loud to his telepathic sense, her hatred burning for Sophia.

"Tambra?" Eleanor faced the captured vampire, her face a mask of hurt and confusion.

"She was going to assassinate Sophia," he explained. "She was bound to Berkhard, emotionally at least."

"But that's impossible. She's one of Sophia's closest—"

"Not impossible, *bella.* Truth."

"So that's my traitor." The slow, lazy tone of Sophia's observation was belied by the fire in her gaze as she regarded the frozen Tambra. "She was the only one of my inner circle that I never had a chance to interrogate. She was in Calgary. I considered her a fucking hero in that battle."

"What better way to secure your confidence in her?" Lucifer suggested. His head was filled with Tambra's images of revenge, of vampires sacrificed to secure her position with Sophia, to prove her false loyalty.

"Was it *all* staged then? For my benefit? People *died* in Calgary, damn you."

"I can dig through her brain for you, if you'd like," Lucifer offered, "discover her co-conspirators."

"No. I'll handle that," Sophia said grimly. And with a wrench of power that Lucifer felt like a tug on his own heart, Sophia rammed her awareness into Tambra's mind.

Lucifer released the female vamp with a growl, pissed that Sophia hadn't given him any warning of her intent. But he stood back and watched in vicious admiration as Sophia literally scoured the female vamp's brain clean, until Tambra's eyes were vacant holes and drool dripped from her open mouth, with her fangs a grotesque exclamation over a drooping lower lip.

When Sophia finally withdrew, Tambra slouched like a puppet whose strings had been cut, her hands practically dragging on the ground. But not for long, as Sophia lashed out with a blast of focused power and dusted the traitor where she stood.

"Well," Sophia said, brushing her hands together in an efficient motion, "*that's* done with."

"Are all of those newbies dead?" Colin asked, shifting everyone's attention to the Canadian soldiers, who'd done nothing to deserve their fate.

Lucifer surveyed the battlefield, looking for signs of life. "Most of them," he admitted. "Those who survived the fighting couldn't handle the shock of Berkhard's death. There might be one or two still alive, though."

"Danika," Sophia said, gesturing to a sturdy-looking blond vamp who was just rounding the house. "We need to set up search teams. Anyone who's still alive goes inside before sunrise. I don't care which side they fought on. Those boys didn't sign up to support Berkhard. They were forced."

"My lady," Danika said, and rushed off to gather a search party.

"You two," Sophia said, smiling at Eleanor, and then giving Lucifer a grim look. "I'll see you tomorrow night."

"My lady," Eleanor said immediately, bowing her head. Lucifer tipped his chin down slightly, but no more than that. He'd saved Sophia's ass tonight, and he wasn't going to let her forget it.

ELEANOR LED LUCIFER into her quarters in the barracks' section of Sophia's estate house. Though calling it a "barracks" was misleading.

One entire wing of the huge house was dedicated to private quarters for Sophia's guard contingent, and her other vampire staffers.

She glanced around when she walked into the room, trying to see it through his eyes. It had always seemed spacious enough for her, but when she turned, the room shrank around the physical presence that was Lucifer. His muscular six foot, three inch frame took up so much of the available space that she was embarrassed at her suddenly modest digs. She was certain he had better living arrangements back in Chicago, probably a big house all to himself, while all she had was this single, small room. And a private bathroom. Yippee.

"It's not very big," she said ruefully.

He'd been studying the place, but his gaze settled on her, and he smiled. "But then, neither are you, princess."

"Shut up," she said in mock irritation.

He chuckled knowingly. "We're definitely going to need something much bigger than this, though. And far more private."

"We?" she repeated. She told herself to be cool, and not to make assumptions. But he'd said, "we." That had to mean something, right?

Lucifer stepped closer and cupped her face with both hands. "I love you, Eleanor. I always have. And if you'll have me, I want to be with you forever. Here, Chicago, or somewhere else. I don't care where, as long as we're together."

Eleanor fought not to cry. She'd given up on love a long time ago, because deep in her heart she'd known there could never be anyone but Lucifer. But she'd never once considered the possibility of finding him again, or of him finding her. This was like a dream come true. Her best. Dream. Ever.

The tears came anyway.

"*Bella*," he whispered, kissing away the tears as they rolled down her cheeks. "Don't cry. If you don't want—"

"No!" she protested, wrapping her fingers around his wrists. "I *do* want. I'm happy. These are *happy* tears."

"Okay, then," he said, smiling. "Cry away. But you know what happens to your face when you cry. You'll get all blotchy, and your eyes will puff up, and—"

"Shut up!" she said again, slugging his arm.

"Don't worry. I'll still love you, blotchy face and all."

"You're so romantic," she murmured, going up on tiptoes to kiss him. "I love that about you."

"So, you *do* love me."

She smiled against his lips. "I do love you, Lucifer Scuderi."

He kissed her, but ended the kiss with a quick nip to her lower lip, mindful of the looming sunrise. "We need to sleep on the plane, Elle. Or, at least, I do. I know Sophia's your lady, but she's not mine, and she'll see me as a threat."

"Oh, I don't think so. You just don't know her very well. You saved her life. She won't forget that."

"I'm sure she's grateful, but that won't trump her vampire instincts. I'm too powerful, and, on top of that, I'm sworn to another lord. She'll want to be rid of me."

"But . . ." Eleanor looked up at him unhappily. "Does that mean you can't stay in Canada? What does that mean for—?"

"It doesn't mean anything. Not yet. But we need to have a conversation with Sophia, or rather, *I* need to have a conversation. I'm the problem, not you. And I have a solution. I'm just not sure she'll listen to it."

"Sunrise is still more than an hour away. We can find her tonight, and—"

"Not tonight. Sophia has other business to take care of, and I'm tired. I've spent a lot of energy on your lady's interests over the past few nights. Besides, I don't know how our meeting's going to go, and I need to be at full strength."

"Should I ask for a private meeting tomorrow night? I can call her directly."

Lucifer thought about it, and said, "Sure. Go ahead. But make it late enough that we don't have to rush. I want time to feed and fuck."

She gasped in feigned shock at his crudeness, but there was nothing feigned about the blush that heated her face.

He stroked a finger over her hot cheek, and grinned. "The two activities often go together, *bella.*"

"Well, I know that," she said primly. "How about midnight, then? Will that be enough time for you, you big stud?"

Lucifer barked a surprised laugh. "There's *never* enough time when it comes to fucking *you*. But I can make do for one night."

"You're incorrigible," she muttered, and pulled out her cell phone.

"Why on earth would you want to *corrige* my perfection?"

She just rolled her eyes and listened as Sophia's direct line rang, before someone picked up, and a deep voice said, "Yep?"

"Hey, Colin," she said, recognizing his voice. "Lucifer wants to meet with Lady Sophia at midnight tomorrow. We'll both be there. Does that work?"

She heard the rumble of his voice, but he'd covered the phone and she couldn't make out the words. He was obviously checking with Sophia, though.

"Midnight tomorrow it is, babe. Anything else? Sophia needs to rest."

Eleanor looked up at Lucifer in question, knowing he'd have heard every word of the conversation. When he shook his head, she said, "That's it. Enjoy your . . . um, *rest*."

Colin gave a smug laugh. "You, too." And he hung up.

"You heard," she said to Lucifer, disconnecting and pocketing her phone.

He nodded. "Gather whatever you need. I don't want to cut it too close, just in case we hit delays on our way back to the airport."

"Delays?"

"Enemies. Erstwhile allies. The usual."

"You're paranoid," she observed, but set about gathering some fresh clothes. After too many battles in too few days, everything she'd brought with her to Montreal was now in desperate need of cleaning. She pondered the difficulties of getting out bloodstains. And other stains, too. Ick.

Chapter Fourteen

LUCIFER'S FIRST thought on waking the next night was that he was tired of sleeping on planes. He rolled over and studied Eleanor in her sleep. She was on her belly, which was the same position she'd favored as a human. He'd worried back then that she couldn't breathe, but she'd just laughed and said that it suited her. And it did. It also suited him because her tight, little ass was on full, pert display. Once he'd pulled the sheet down, that was. Something he did without any qualms. He was a greedy male, and Eleanor was his.

She stirred, and for a moment her pretty ass lifted up even higher. But then her eyes opened, and she smiled. "Are you staring at my ass?"

"Yep."

"I thought you wanted to hit up a blood club."

His eyelids drooped as he contemplated the sexual temptation that was Eleanor. "I don't feel like sharing you tonight," he murmured, and pulled her across the bed until he could feel every inch of her soft curves against his body.

Bending his head, he nuzzled her ear, smiling when she shivered against his lips. Kissing and licking his way to her mouth, he touched his lips to hers in a soft and sensual kiss, barely touching the tip of his tongue to hers, before continuing his assault. Eleanor moaned softly, arching her back in invitation when he licked along the curve of her clavicle. His hand closed over her breasts, one at a time, weighing the heavy mounds, pinching her tender nipples until they thrummed between his fingers.

He pulled back to admire the beauty that was Eleanor's breasts. They were full and round, with pale pink areolae and large nipples that darkened to a bloody rose when she was aroused, as she was now. Those nipples were part of what had earned his nickname for her, his pink princess, and he lowered his head to suck on their loveliness, to feel them harden like precious pearls against his tongue.

But there was more to his princess—more pink, more lusciousness. His slid his hand between her thighs, feeling the heat of her pussy . . . her pretty, very *pink*, pussy. He smiled against the delicate skin of her breast as he stroked her gently, listening to the rapid beat of her heart, her quick indrawn breath.

The soft folds of her sex were puffy and swollen when his fingers slid between them, when he delved even deeper and felt the liquid heat of her arousal.

"So very wet and *hot,*" he murmured, his tongue rasping over her nipple. "Such a slick, pink pussy you have for me."

He sensed more than heard the sudden hitch in her breath as he dipped two fingers just barely inside her, teasing her, before filling his mouth with her breast, pulling the entire tip between his lips, and his teeth. He bit down carefully, wanting the taste of her blood, but unwilling to mar his Eleanor's tender flesh.

But Eleanor had no such reluctance. She groaned loudly, and scraped her fingers against his scalp, twisting to rip at his hair as she tugged him closer, thrusting out her breasts in silent demand. She wrapped one leg around his hips and crushed her hot cunt against him hungrily.

"Shall I fuck you?" he whispered, before closing his teeth over one engorged nipple, and biting hard enough to draw blood. He hummed deep in his throat at the delicious taste. He couldn't feed from her, couldn't draw nutrition, but her blood was still delectable. Hot and sweet, and spiced with power. Just like his Eleanor. "What do you want, *bella?*" he murmured.

Eleanor bit back a moan, covering her mouth with one hand and sinking her teeth into it, before whimpering, "Don't tease." She was panting, her breath coming out in short puffs as she tried not to cry out loud.

Fuck that. Lucifer knew she worried about the guards, but they were all outside in the hangar, and wouldn't hear her cries of pleasure. He didn't tell *her* that, however. He wanted her to lose control, to scream his name, no matter who might hear her.

"Tell me what you want," he insisted, lifting his head to blow on her wet and bloody nipple, the perfect color of a red rose.

"Lucifer," she pleaded softly, but he had no pity.

He bent his head and his tongue swept out to curl around her other nipple, sucking that breast into his mouth and sinking his teeth into the satin flesh. The pulse of her blood was loud in his ears, a seductive counterpoint to the pleas she was whispering over and over again.

He soothed her abused flesh with another swipe of his tongue, then lifted his head to stare at her, his eyes narrow slits as he demanded, "Tell me what you want."

Eleanor growled and lifted her hips to smash against his, holding their bodies together as her strong legs wrapped around his hips and she began thrusting against him. She was so close that her pussy slid along the length of his rigid cock, hot and slick and delicious. Lucifer swallowed a groan of his own. He was going to fuck her so hard, ram his cock so deep in her sweet cunt, but first he was going to hear her say the words.

"I can feel your pussy, baby. It's dripping wet, like silk against my cock, and so fucking hot. I love your cunt when it's like this."

Elle whimpered softly, but just kept writhing against his shaft, rubbing her pussy along the hard length as if seeking her own release. But that wasn't going to happen.

"Tell me what you want," he repeated, demanding. "I need to hear it."

"I want," she whispered, and then hiccupped a sobbing breath. "I want you to fuck me. I want—" A low, shuddering moan escaped her lips, making his already stiff cock swell until it ached. "I want your cock," she cried at last. "Fuck me, damn you!"

Lucifer didn't wait any longer. Before the last syllable had left her lips, he'd slid his hands down to her thighs, easily prying her loose, before gripping her hips and flipping her over onto her belly. Lifting her ass into the air, he rammed his cock into her slippery sex, shoving her thighs apart so he could go even deeper.

Eleanor cried out, arching her back, shoving her ass into his thrusts. She climaxed instantly, coming around his dick almost before he'd plunged his full length into her sweet body. Her pussy clamped down on him, her inner muscles rippling up and down his shaft. But he didn't stop fucking her. He kept slamming in and out, determined to make this last, loving the feel of her around him, the way he had to drive his thick cock into her tight, tight pussy, loving the heat of her flesh, the creamy wetness of her arousal as it lubricated his passage until he hit the firm cone of her cervix. Loving Elle's soft cry of pleasure every time he plunged into her again and again.

Wanting to hear her scream, to feel the tight glove of her body as she came around him one more time, Lucifer splayed his fingers wide over her hips, and reached his thumbs down to spread the round globes of her ass until he could see the darkest rose of her anus. Using the slick liquid of her arousal, he eased one thumb into her ass, and then reached around with his other hand, and found the firm nub of her clit. Pressing hard, he trapped her between the searing pleasure of his fingers on her clit, his thumb stroking against the sensitive nerves of her ass, and his cock slamming in her pussy.

Eleanor gave a full-body shudder as the orgasm rolled through her body with such force that he could see ripples beneath her skin, as her muscles contracted. Her pussy clamped down on his cock, squeezing hard enough to hurt before her body started to pulse, squeezing and releasing, the climax rolling in waves of sensation that was keeping time with her heart as she thrashed beneath him. Her arm was bloody, her fangs sinking into her own flesh as she sought to muffle her cries, until finally, she surrendered. She lifted her head, and screamed.

Lucifer grinned, relishing her utter loss of control, the sweep of her orgasm as it crashed its way over her. He felt his own release growing, the heat building in his balls, his muscles flexing uncontrollably as excitement coursed through him, growing higher and higher, until . . . Fuck! His fingers dug into her hips hard enough to bruise, his eyes closed and his head thrown back as the climax claimed him, raging down his cock to spill deep in Eleanor's luscious body as they convulsed together, their souls linked, their hearts pounding the same rhythm.

When it was finally over, and his body was his own again, they collapsed together, struggling for breath, sweat cooling on their hot skin. Lucifer reached down and pulled the sheet over both of them, holding Eleanor close, soothing her still-trembling form.

"You're mean," she muttered at last, her breath cool against his still-hot flesh.

He smiled. "How's that?"

"You know how."

"I know how hard you came. Is that what you mean?"

She pinched his chest, and he laughed.

"I can't move," she moaned. "I don't *want* to."

"I know," he said soothingly, matching the stroke of his hands to his words. "But we have a meeting, *bella*. And I'll need to feed before then. You've drained me utterly."

"Oh, you poor baby," she said in a flat monotone.

He laughed again. "Blood house or bag?"

Eleanor groaned. "If we stick with a bag, I won't have to move yet."

"Bag it is then," he agreed, kissing her temple. "Cal brought in a fresh supply. He has connections."

"Oh, good," she murmured lazily, and snuggled closer, leaving Lucifer with a contentment greater than any he'd ever known before.

SOPHIA HAD ORIGINALLY planned to sit behind her desk for this meeting. It was the position of power in the room, especially with her mate standing guard just over her left shoulder. Only a short time ago they'd been fucking each other senseless, not worrying about rival vampires or anything else, but now they were here, taking care of another kind of business.

Colin gave her a reassuring hug, and kissed the top of her head. She was so fortunate to have him by her side. He was strong and powerful, and loyal to the death. He was also smart enough to understand the nuances of her current predicament, and a good enough tactician to leave his ego in the drawer when it came to doing what was necessary to defend her territory.

And it was that necessity which had made her decide on the conversation group near the fireplace for her meeting with Lucifer and Eleanor, who hadn't left his side since they'd arrived in Vancouver.

Whether Sophia liked Lucifer or not, whether she approved of him for Eleanor or not, he'd more than proven his strength and his reliability in a fight. That fact was even more impressive considering that the fight had been one in which he had no obligation to help her. Of course, he'd also rescued Colin, and killed not only the traitorous Darren, but the European invader, Kasimir, as well. He'd certainly exceeded the parameters of the job assigned to him, and he would have been within his rights to fly directly home to Chicago from Montreal, skipping the Vancouver battle altogether.

But instead, he'd arrived in time to back her up against Berkhard, and had proven his usefulness not only in that fight, but in stopping that faithless bitch Tambra, too.

The big question, then, the one that needed to be answered tonight, was what happened next? Sophia didn't believe for one minute that Lucifer was prepared to board his private jet, and disappear from her life and territory forever. But what exactly did he want?

She and Colin had gone over the events of the last few weeks, dissecting not only *what* had happened, but why. And they had both agreed that changes were necessary. Her first mistake had been leaving Darren Yamanaka alive, a mistake compounded when she'd sought to ease the tension between them by appointing him as her lieutenant. Especially since Darren and everyone else knew that the appointment had been a formality only. Colin had been her true lieutenant, the only one she trusted enough to rely on.

And maybe as a result of that, Darren had never accepted his fate, had never for one minute been loyal to her. A part of her had recognized the truth even back then, but there had been so *much* that was wrong with the territory that Lucien had bequeathed to her. And Darren had, at least, dealt efficiently with any problems that arose in the cities under his control. His loyalty, or its absence, had taken a back seat to far more pressing matters, like securing the Vancouver region and bringing in a whole new security apparatus. Or looking after the welfare of her many vampire subjects in the less populated parts of the territory, where too many of them had been ignored for decades, and were languishing under the neglect.

She hadn't counted on the Europeans and their greed for expansion. Even after Mathilde had gone after Raphael, Sophia had never imagined the invaders would be interested in her sparsely populated territory with its large swaths of empty land.

That had been the second mistake on her part, and it was Colin who'd paid the price. She reached out blindly for his hand, needing the reassurance of his presence. His healthy, secure presence.

"I'm fine, darlin'," he murmured, understanding without the need for words. He kissed her upturned mouth, and she squeezed his fingers before letting go. It wouldn't do for anyone, friend or enemy, to see how much it had wounded her to know what Colin had been through. He'd glossed over the worst of it for her benefit, but she knew the truth. She'd read it in his uncensored thoughts. She was a woman in love, but she was also a damn powerful vampire lord.

Something Lucifer would do well to remember.

But just as she knew that changes were necessary, she also knew why Lucifer was coming here tonight. Oh, certainly, Eleanor had stressed that the meeting was for both of them, but Sophia understood power, specifically the kind bestowed by the vampire symbiote. She knew how it drove the strongest vampires, goading them to levels of rivalry and ambition that they might not have pursued otherwise. Tonight's meeting was all about that kind of power, and Lucifer had it in spades. He was young, and still refining his skills, but he had all of the greed and avarice, all of the aggression, of a vampire lord.

There was no doubt in her mind that Lucifer wanted power. But, apparently, he wanted Eleanor even more. And that was the real reason for tonight's meeting. Because Lucifer wanted Eleanor to be happy.

Sophia knew the moment her guests stepped into the hallway outside her office. Eleanor's power signature was familiar and welcome, a friend as well as a protector, her loyalties unaffected by recent events.

Lucifer, on the other hand, was like a simmering cauldron of energy, sparking with the magic of Vampire. He might be young, but he'd spent years under the tutelage of Aden and his lieutenant, Bastien. Those two knew power, and they knew how to use it.

Sophia nodded at Colin, who crossed the room and opened the door before anyone could knock. A petty display of power on her part, but one any visitor would expect.

"My lady." Eleanor was the first one through the door. Wearing a broad smile as she strode across the room, she stopped herself at the last minute from hugging Sophia, settling instead for a more dignified greeting, taking Sophia's proffered hand and dipping low in a move that was half bow and half curtsey.

Sophia squeezed Eleanor's hand in return, putting as much affection as she could into that fragile connection. If they'd been alone, or with only Colin present, the two women would have hugged. But Lucifer changed the equation. "Eleanor," she said affectionately. "A job well done, child. I can never thank you enough."

"It was an honor, my lady." She looked up at Colin then, and gave him a grin. "You're looking better," she told him.

"Feeling better, too, babe. But then, so are you, I'm guessing."

Sophia bit her lip to keep from laughing, when Eleanor blushed a bright pink at the sexual innuendo. She'd been aware of her bodyguard's sexual celibacy over the years, and, while she had her doubts about Lucifer, she had to admit that Eleanor seemed much happier now that she'd been reunited with her long lost lover.

That reluctant admission made Sophia lift her gaze to the cause of both Eleanor's blush and Sophia's problem. "Lucifer," she said, her voice considerably cooler than when she'd greeted Eleanor. "Welcome to Vancouver."

He dipped his head slightly, a knowing little smile playing around his lips.

"Arrogant bastard," Sophia thought sourly.

"Thank you, Lady Sophia. I was pleased to be of service," he said. It was a greeting calculated to remind her of just how much of a service he'd been.

"Right," she said sharply, suddenly tired of all the vampire bullshit. "Let's get to it, shall we? What do you want?"

He tipped his head sideways, acknowledging the point, as he took a seat on the short sofa opposite hers, without waiting for an invitation.

Probably because he was smart enough to know she wasn't going to offer one.

"What I want, my lady—" He reached up and lent Eleanor a hand as she stepped over his legs and sat next to him, and then lifted her hand and kissed her fingers where they were twined with his. "—is Eleanor."

"Lucifer," Eleanor whispered, scandalized by his statement. As she should have been. Eleanor wasn't a pawn to be bartered.

"But does she want *you?*" Sophia snapped, and saw the first flash of anger in Lucifer's odd-colored eyes.

"Why don't you ask *her?*" he responded silkily, throwing the query back in her face.

Eleanor looked between them, and made a loud tsking noise. But when she spoke it was to Lucifer, not Sophia. "Play nice," she scolded, but then leaned her weight against his arm, and touched her cheek to his broad shoulder. Which told Sophia everything she needed to know. She could tell Lucifer to take a hike, to leave her territory and never come back. And he'd probably go, but when he left, he'd take Eleanor with him. Because just as much as Lucifer wanted *her*, Eleanor wanted *him*, too. She might not *want* to choose, but if forced into it, she would choose Lucifer.

Lucifer's eyes never left Sophia, as she contemplated the full ramifications of the choices before her, and there was nothing but smug assurance on his handsome face.

"It would seem you have her already," Sophia said, and it was an effort to keep her tone neutral. She was pissed as hell that this arrogant ass had stolen Eleanor away from her. And, yes, she realized what a foolish thought that was. She'd encouraged Eleanor to follow her heart. But she couldn't help how she felt. Eleanor was the closest thing Sophia had to a friend, other than Colin.

"I have her heart, my lady," Lucifer said. "Just as she has mine, and always will. But *I* need more than that to make her happy. And *you* need what I can give you," he added, spearing her with a sharp look. He kissed the side of Eleanor's head, but drew his hand away from hers as he sat forward on the sofa. It was almost as if he was putting some distance between them, protecting her from whatever attack Sophia might launch his way, whether verbal or something far more dangerous. "You need a lieutenant, Sophia. Not to replace Yamanaka, who was never truly yours, but to replace Murphy," he said bluntly, with a nod in Colin's direction.

Sophia raised her power enough to be felt, but kept it banked. For now. "I'd think very carefully about my next words, Lucifer Scuderi," she said mildly. "I am lord here, not you, and I will say who serves—"

"You are lord," he agreed, daring to interrupt her. "But not even Raphael has undertaken to rule a territory as large as Canada all by himself. Perhaps it made sense when the territorial lines were drawn more than a century ago, but it doesn't any longer."

"So I should just hand a chunk of it over to *you*?" she growled.

He shrugged. "You could do worse. But, no, I have no desire to rule a territory . . . yet." He leaned back, and stretched his arm out behind Eleanor, the very picture of a vampire at ease. It was almost insulting, except that Sophia could feel the power hovering just below his outward calm. "What I'm offering is what *you* need, my lady. A *vampire* lieutenant."

"I had one of those, and look how that turned out."

Lucifer shrugged. "Yamanaka was *never* committed to your rule. I was in his head when he died, when *I killed* him. He's been planning this revolt from almost the moment you took control of the territory. But I suspect you know that already."

"Darren and I were always rivals, so, no, his betrayal wasn't a surprise. But what does that have to do with you selecting yourself as my next lieutenant?"

"Because you need a loyal *vampire* lieutenant. Murphy's one hell of a warrior, and he has my utmost respect," he said, tipping his head Colin's way. "But he doesn't bring you any real power. Yesterday's battle with Berkhard proved that, if nothing else."

"Perhaps. But of all the vampires in North America, why would I choose you?"

Lucifer gave her a flat stare. "Darren Yamanaka called himself master over three cities—Toronto, Montreal, and Quebec City. By vampire law, those cities are now mine. We keep what we win, Sophia. That's the only law we recognize. And, like it or not, winning usually means killing."

"What Darren *claimed* is irrelevant. Those three cities, and everything else in this territory, belong to *me*, not Darren. And not you either."

Lucifer glanced at Eleanor, and shrugged slightly, as if to say, "I tried." Then he took her hand and started to rise.

But Colin's voice stopped him. "He's right, Sophie."

Sophia looked up at him in surprise.

Colin came around to sit on the sofa arm closest to her, and took her hand. "I will support and defend you to my last breath," he said gently. "But I'm no vampire, and yesterday's battle proved what Lucifer is saying. I can't sense the ebb and flow of power, but I know tactics, and I know *you*. You were pushed to your limits out there, trying to support your fighters on two fronts and defeat Berkhard at the same time. You needed a good lieutenant yesterday. Someone who could free you to concentrate on the greatest danger, while providing a reservoir of power for you to draw upon, far *more* power than I could ever give you. And, most importantly, someone to cover your back, to recognize and negate traitors like Tambra before they could act."

"I'm not asking for anything more than what you freely gave to Yamanaka, my lady," Lucifer interjected softly. "But with far greater return to *you* in terms of power and stability."

"You want to be the new Darren?" she mocked, and regretted it almost immediately.

Lucifer's handsome face tightened with anger. "Darren Yamanaka was *nothing* compared to me, and you know it. For *Eleanor's* sake, I will take oath to you. My power, my loyalty will be yours to rely on. But understand, my lady, that while the entire territory is yours, the province of Ontario and everything east of it will be mine to rule as I see fit, within the bounds of your sovereignty."

Sophia stared at him. Then she glanced at Eleanor, who was looking very worried and a little sick. But her emotions told the whole story. She was still loyal to Sophia, but her love for Lucifer burned as bright as a full moon in summertime.

Still, as reluctant as Sophia was to admit it, the most convincing reason to accept Lucifer's service was Lucifer himself. Because he and Colin were both right. She needed a strong lieutenant to help her rule the territory, and Lucifer was one of the strongest around. Damn it.

"Is Aden aware of your defection?" she asked Lucifer, unable to stop herself from pricking his feelings.

"There is no *defection*, my lady," he said slowly, eyeing her with dislike. "Lord Aden has always recognized the strength of my power, and encouraged its growth. He is sorry to lose me, but he understands my reasons."

It was impressive, actually, the way he managed to keep his temper, despite all of her prodding and poking.

She drew a deep breath. She knew what had to be done. And, *meu Deus*, how she hated to admit it, even to herself. But she was a realist.

Dragging it out further wasn't going to make it any more palatable, so she shoved up the long sleeve of her cashmere sweater, and held out a hand to Colin. He'd been with her long enough to understand what she

wanted. He reached down and handed her the short combat knife he
kept in his boot.

With her eyes meeting Lucifer's gaze in clear challenge, she sliced
open her vein. It was time for him to make good on his big words.

Lucifer's pupils flared slightly. He glanced at Eleanor, cupped her
cheek on one hand, and leaned over to touch his lips to hers. And then
he slid to his knees, and with surprising gentleness took Sophia's bloody
arm in both of his big hands.

"Lucifer Scuderi," she began, launching the formal words, "do you
come to me of your own free will and desire?"

Lucifer's eyes met hers, and she read a brief reluctance there, before
his gaze cleared, and he said, "I do."

"And is this what you truly desire?"

"It is my truest desire."

"Then drink, Lucifer, and be mine."

He held her eyes a moment longer before lowering his lips to her
arm and drawing a single mouthful of blood. His head lifted and his
throat worked as he swallowed it, and then he released her arm. He sat
back on his heels briefly, and then stood and gave her a formal bow from
the waist.

"My lady," he said. "We'll be leaving for Toronto tomorrow night,
but I would like an hour of your time to discuss the territory before our
plane departs. If that's convenient?"

Sophia studied him silently. She hadn't considered what it would
cost him to break his connection to Aden in order to swear loyalty to
her. She'd never had to make that choice. Lucifer's extraordinary telepathic ability apparently included the ability to lock up his own thoughts
tight as a drum. But his body language was that of a man trying to conceal some heavy emotion, like grief.

She nodded. "Check with my assistant. I'll accommodate my schedule to your flight."

He nodded his thanks, gave Colin one of those male chin lifts that
could mean almost anything, and then glanced at Eleanor.

"Go ahead," she said, reaching out to stroke his arm. "I want a moment with Lady Sophia. I'll catch up before you leave the house."

He gave a short, sharp nod, and strode from the room without a word.

Eleanor watched him go, worry written on her deceptively delicate
face, before she turned back to Sophia. "He really does love me, you
know. He always has."

Sophia nodded. "I believe that. I can only hope it's enough to secure his loyalty."

Eleanor shook her head. "No, my lady. What will secure his loyalty is his oath to *you*. Lucifer is an honorable man. Whatever else you think of him, never doubt that."

"He's a dangerous vampire, Eleanor. And he *will* want a territory of his own someday."

She grinned. "You're right. But when that day comes, he won't waste time sneaking behind your back. He'll tell you to your face."

Sophia laughed. "Oddly enough, I find that reassuring. Be happy, Eleanor."

"I am. And I'll see you tomorrow night. Someone has to stop you two from killing each other."

LUCIFER HEARD ELEANOR'S thoughts before her footsteps tapped up behind him on the hardwood floor. He stopped and waited for her, turning just enough that he could watch her walking toward him, enough that he could see the love for him in her eyes. If he lived another thousand years, he'd never tire of that.

"Sorry," she said, taking his hand.

"She's important to you. I understand."

Eleanor pulled him to a stop. "She *is*, but no one is more important to me than you. I need you to believe that."

He cupped her face with his free hand, and kissed her. Soft and gentle, and full of love. A romantic kiss that spoke of devotion and promises that lasted forever. "I love you, Eleanor. Now tell me something . . . is there a decent hotel for vampires in this city? I'm sick to death of sleeping on an airplane."

She grinned against his mouth, and said, "I think we can work something out."

"Forever and ever, *bella*," he murmured. "Forever and ever."

Epilogue

Chicago, Illinois, USA—two months later

ADEN WELCOMED EACH of his fellow lords as they arrived in the big conference room, exchanging careful greetings with most of them. They were all allies, but they were still vampire lords, with egos the size of Willis Tower. It was always best to assume the worst, and be polite.

On the other hand, his exchange with Lucas was downright friendly, since the two of them had shut down more than a few bars and whorehouses together in their day. Their "day" being before they both settled down and took mates. Lucas slapped Aden's shoulder, then walked over to torment Raphael. He was the only one who could get away with that shit.

Sophia was the last to arrive, and it was an effort to keep up that polite thing. He was still pissed about Lucifer leaving him to become her lieutenant, although he understood the younger vampire's reasons. He'd have done far worse than switching liege lords for his mate. Sidonie had him wrapped about her delicate little finger, and he loved it.

But this meeting was for Council members and their lieutenants only, so Sidonie and all of the other mates were out having fun somewhere, while he was stuck playing the dutiful host.

Lucifer had arrived with Sophia, of course, so he and Aden shook hands, then turned it into a friendly shoulder bump, and that in turn became a test of strength. It was idiotic, but they couldn't help it. They were vampires, damn it. Competition was in their blood. They both laughed.

"How's fucking Canada?" Aden asked him.

"Nearly as cold as Chicago," Lucifer said, grinning. "How the hell this nice Sicilian boy ended up in a place where snow is measured in God damned meters, I don't know."

"Maybe because you were never nice," Bastien chimed in, stepping up and going through the whole shoulder bump ritual himself. "How's Eleanor?"

"Beautiful and happy, just the way I like her."

Bastien grinned, then turned to Aden. "Everyone's arrived, my lord. We can start."

Aden had his back to the room, so no one but Lucifer and Bastien saw the Lord of the Midwest roll his eyes in disgust.

Lucifer snorted a laugh, and moved on into the room to sit next to Sophia, with Rajmund's lieutenant, Emelie, on his other side. Two women in the whole damn room, and Lucifer managed to sit next to both of them. He might be settled down with Eleanor, but some things never changed.

Aden walked over and sat at the head of the table, while Bastien closed the conference room door. Once Bastien took his seat, Aden nodded at Raphael, who was sitting at the opposite end. One could argue that Raphael was at the head, and Aden at the opposite end, but it was a fine point, and not worth arguing over. Aden didn't give a fuck who sat where. This was Raphael's party. Aden just happened to draw the short straw as host.

"Gentlemen," Raphael said. "And ladies," he amended, and then looked around the room, drawing the attention of every lord and lieutenant, before continuing. "Fuck this," he said sharply. "No more waiting for the next invader from Europe. It's time for us to take the war to them."

To be continued …

About the Author

D. B. Reynolds arrived in sunny Southern California at an early age, having made the trek across the country from the Midwest in a station wagon with her parents, her many siblings and the family dog. And while she has many (okay, some) fond memories of Midwestern farm life, she quickly discovered that L.A. was her kind of town and grew up happily sunning on the beaches of the South Bay.

D. B. holds graduate degrees in international relations and history from UCLA (go Bruins!) and was headed for a career in academia, but in a moment of clarity she left behind the politics of the hallowed halls for the better paying politics of Hollywood, where she worked as a sound editor for several years, receiving two Emmy nominations, an MPSE Golden Reel, and multiple MPSE nominations for her work in television sound.

Book One of her Vampires in America series, RAPHAEL, launched her career as a writer in 2009, while JABRIL, Vampires in America Book Two, was awarded the RT Reviewers Choice Award for Best Paranormal Romance (Small Press) in 2010. ADEN, Vampires in America Book Seven, was her first release under the new ImaJinn imprint at BelleBooks, Inc., and won EPIC's 2015 e-book award for Paranormal Romance.

D. B. currently lives in a flammable canyon near the Malibu coast with her husband of many years, and when she's not writing her own books, she can usually be found reading someone else's. You can visit D. B. at her website www.dbreynolds.com for information on her latest books, contests and giveaways.

Made in the USA
San Bernardino, CA
12 November 2016